THE INHERITANCE

Also by Simon Tolkien

Final Witness

THE INHERITANCE

Simon Tolkien

MINOTAUR BOOKS

A Thomas Dunne Book
New York

A THOMAS DUNNE BOOK FOR MINOTAUR BOOKS.
An imprint of St. Martin's Publishing Group.

THE INHERITANCE. Copyright © 2010 by Simon Tolkien. All rights reserved. Printed in the United States of America. For information, address St. Martin's Press, 175 Fifth Avenue, New York, N.Y. 10010.

www.thomasdunnebooks.com
www.minotaurbooks.com

Library of Congress Cataloging-in-Publication Data

Tolkien, Simon, 1959–
    The inheritance / Simon Tolkien. — 1st ed.
        p. cm.
    ISBN 978-0-312-53907-8
    1. Historical—Crimes against—Fiction.   2. Fathers and sons—Fiction.   3. Inheritance and suc-cessional—Fiction.   4. Lost works of art—Fiction.   5. Oxford (England)—Fiction.   6. France, Northern—Fiction.   I. Title.
    PR6120.O44I65 2010
    823'.92—dc22

                                                                    2009041517

First Edition: April 2010

10 9 8 7 6 5 4 3 2 1

For my mother,
Faith Tolkien

ACKNOWLEDGMENTS

I am indebted to the following people, who have all helped me in different ways with the writing of this book: Tracy Tolkien, Priscilla Tolkien, Fiona Taylor, Christine Groom, Gini Scott, Michael Radulescu, Anna Lvovsky, Elizabeth Byrne, Kevin Sweeney, Angela Gibson, Thomas Dunne, and last but not least, my wonderful agent, Marly Rusoff, and my insightful editor, Peter Wolverton.

INTRODUCTORY NOTE

The controversial executions of Derek Bentley and Ruth Ellis in the 1950s increased public pressure in the United Kingdom for the abolition of hanging, and this was answered in part by the passing of the Homicide Act in 1957, which limited the imposition of the death penalty to five specific categories of murder. Henceforward only those convicted of killing police officers or prison guards and those who had committed a murder by shooting or in the furtherance of theft or when resisting arrest could suffer the ultimate punishment. The effect of this unsatisfactory legislation was that a poisoner or strangler acting with premeditation would escape the rope, whereas a man who shot another in a fit of rage might not. This anomaly no doubt helped the campaign for outright abolition, which finally reached fruition with the passage of the Murder (Abolition of Death Penalty) Act in 1965.

Death sentences were carried out far more quickly in England in the 1950s than they are in the United States today. A single appeal against the conviction but not the sentence was allowed, and, if it failed, the home secretary made a final decision on whether to exercise the royal prerogative of mercy on behalf of the Queen, marking the file "the law must take its course" if there were to be no reprieve. There was often no more than a month's interval between conviction and execution. Ruth Ellis, for example, spent just three weeks and three days in the condemned cell at Holloway Prison in 1955 before she was hung by Albert Pierrepoint for the crime of shooting her boyfriend.

There was thus very little time available for lawyers or other interested parties trying desperately to uncover new evidence that might exonerate a client sentenced to die. They were quite literally working against the clock.

PROLOGUE

Normandy
1944

They were safe in the trees, waiting for the Germans to come. Carson had driven the Jeep off the drive, and the silver-grey branches had crackled and broke as he'd wedged it into its hiding place. And now they waited on either side of the road with their fingers on the triggers of their American-made machine guns. Nothing. No wind in the trees, no movement in the air, until just after eight o'clock, when the dust came up in a yellow cloud and the two trucks came round the corner.

And then Ritter felt the bullets feeding through the magazine, the quick vibrations in his arms from the gun, and saw the men in the trucks jumping up and down like puppets. There was one young soldier at the end who ran away down the road, but Colonel Cade walked out of the trees with his rifle and shot him in the back of the head just before he reached the corner. It was a good ambush.

Afterward, Carson and Ritter pushed the trucks into the woods, while the colonel selected rifles and pistols from the bodies of their dead owners. Three of each. He made them leave their own guns behind.

And so they walked on up to the house with the dead soldiers' rifles slung over their shoulders and the snub-nosed German Mauser pistols in their pockets. They were a strange, ill-assorted group. Walking in the middle, the tall, thin colonel towered over his two companions. His pale blue eyes were almost opaque, revealing nothing of the man inside, and his long aquiline nose gave him an ascetic look that seemed oddly at variance with his uniform. And yet he carried himself with an air of natural authority that made it obvious that he was the man in charge.

On the colonel's right, Sergeant Ritter was far more clearly a military man with his clipped black moustache and polished shoes and buttons. He was a big man and he had begun to sweat in the evening heat. But he didn't complain. He knew that they had work to do. Looking past the colonel, Ritter glared over at Corporal Carson, who was walking with a deliberate swagger, swaying his narrow hips and shoulders as he expertly flicked a piece of chewing gum from one side of his mouth to the other in time with each step he took. The young man's disrespect disgusted Ritter. But he kept his peace. Carson had been the only soldier he could find to do the job. He'd have to do.

They walked past green stony fields and rows of overgrown vines until they came to a fork in the drive and passed an old sign on which someone had once upon a time painted the words "Proprieté Priveé." It was nailed to the trunk of a plane tree, and Carson read it out loud in his cockney accent and laughed like it was some kind of joke. But the colonel ignored him. He had other things on his mind.

One more turning and the trees stopped suddenly on both sides, and there was the house. It was much smaller than Ritter had expected—not his idea of a château at all. The glass was broken in several of the small windows that appeared at regular intervals in the stone façade, and the guttering was hanging loose from one corner of the roof. Over to the left, a solitary black-and-white cow stood in the shade of a primitive lean-to. Her great red tongue was lolling out of her mouth, and she had clearly been suffering in the afternoon heat. It was unusual for the time of year, and Ritter wondered inconsequentially whether she was aware of the lake that stretched out like a sheet of black glass several hundred yards beyond the house. On the far shore, the town of Marjean shimmered in the distance.

The church stood on a ridge above the château, and it was clearly the more impressive of the two buildings. Even Ritter could sense its antiquity. The bell tower glowed silver in the translucent evening light, and the gargoyles—devils and apes with deformed backs and monstrous faces—gaped down at the world below.

There had been devils here already—German devils—but they seemed to have left the church well alone. A swastika flag hung limply from a pole standing near the corner of the house, and a litter of papers on the dried-up lawn bore witness to the suddenness of the Germans' departure. But their hosts had remained behind, and Henri Rocard and his wife were already standing in the doorway of their house when the three British soldiers came out of the trees and walked across the grass toward them.

It was the colonel who did the talking, and Ritter understood almost none of it, but then again he didn't need to. He knew already that the colonel wanted something from these people, and he was here to help the colonel get it, if the colonel needed help. Back at the camp outside Moirtier, Cade had already explained that he was prepared to pay good money for what he wanted. More than the thing was worth. It was Rocard who was being unreasonable.

Ritter didn't like the look of the Frenchman. He was thick and short, built like one of those middleweights that Ritter had gone to watch in Nottingham when he was a boy. And his dark eyes were small, staring out suspiciously from his wrinkled face. He had probably not yet turned fifty, but the sun had burnt his skin to a pale leather, aging him beyond his years.

Madame Rocard seemed to be a little older than her husband, but she remained an attractive woman. She stood up straight, and her black hair was pulled back severely from her well-shaped face. She was full-breasted and defiant, and Ritter would have liked to have pushed her back into the cool interior of her house, down onto the red flagstones in the hall, and fucked her until he'd had his fill. They were collaborators, and they deserved everything that was coming to them—unless they were reasonable. And the anger in the squat little Frenchman's voice, his evident hostility toward the colonel, didn't make a peaceful solution seem likely.

Suddenly the colonel went forward and took hold of the Frenchwoman's arm, pulling her toward him. And in the same movement, he took the German pistol out of his pocket and pushed it hard against the side of her handsome head. But still Rocard refused to give way, even when Cade let go of the woman's arm and used his free hand to pull back the hammer of the gun.

Quick movement and sudden stillness. This was how Ritter remembered it all afterward. The silence in the trees shattered by the sudden rat-a-tat-tat of the machine guns. And now the angry foreign words, followed by the colonel's seizure of the woman, seemed to leave them all immobilised, frozen in a tableau of fear.

It was the dog that broke the standoff. It must have been barking for some time, tied up somewhere inside the house, and Ritter was surprised that he hadn't heard it before. All his attention must have been focused on the scene in the doorway. It was a black mongrel dog almost as big as a Labrador, and it came at them suddenly, its lip curled back over its yellow teeth. But it never got to bite anyone. The colonel had wonderfully quick reactions back then, and he pulled the gun down from the Frenchwoman's ear and killed the animal with a single bullet.

It was funny that it was the dead dog, and not the threat to his wife, that cracked the Frenchman's resolve. Or perhaps it was the killing of the dog that made him believe that the colonel would really kill his wife. Whatever the truth, they did not need to do any more. Rocard agreed to give the colonel what he wanted.

"He's going to get something for me, from inside the house," said the colonel to Ritter. "You go with him, Reg, and watch what he does. Check he hasn't got a gun, and make sure he doesn't get one while he's in there."

The Frenchman didn't react when Ritter patted him down. He just kept his eyes fixed on his wife and on the gun that the colonel had brought back up to the side of her head straight after he'd killed the dog. Rocard had nothing in his pockets. Not even a penknife. But Ritter didn't trust him, and he kept close behind when the Frenchman went back into the house, pressing the muzzle of his gun into Rocard's back, feeling out the concave hollow between his shoulder blades.

It was cool inside. Crossing the hall, Rocard started up a narrow staircase in the corner and Ritter, following behind, found himself stepping from light into semidarkness and back, again and again, as they crossed pools of evening sunlight let in by the small rectangular windows set high in the walls of the house. In the rooms on either side Ritter could see evidence of the Germans' recent occupation—a photograph of the Führer hanging slightly askew on a whitewashed wall, a trestle bed lying overturned on its side, and papers, both handwritten and typed, strewn about everywhere. On one of the desks Ritter noticed the remains of someone's supper—a crust of black bread and a half-eaten German sausage. The man who'd been eating it only an hour before was now lying in a pool of blood halfway down the drive, baking in the last of the sun. The thought made Ritter smile. Life was a funny thing sometimes.

They carried on up the stairs to a room at the very top. It was almost an attic, and Ritter had to half stoop to get through the door. This was evidently where Rocard and his wife slept—the only place left to them after the house was occupied, and the bed was the main piece of furniture. It was old and ornate, with elaborate carving on its four posters, but it had lost its canopy and the coarse army-issue blankets covering it were out of keeping with its grand design. It took all Rocard's strength to move it away from the wall, but he didn't ask for any help, and he didn't try to hide what he was doing when he pulled up one of the rough floorboards that he had exposed. Underneath, Ritter saw over the Frenchman's shoulder that the hollow space contained an old thin book in a heavy leather binding. Wasting no time, he seized the book out of Rocard's hands.

On the way back down, the Frenchman remained compliant until they turned a corner of the stairs and started down the final flight into the hall. Then, suddenly, there was an outbreak of shouting from beyond the entrance to the living room, and a second later Ritter caught sight of Carson framed in the doorway, and below and to the side of him an old man half shouting, half kneeling on the floor. He looked to be in his seventies, but he could have been older. Time seemed to have been kind to him up until now. He'd kept his teeth, and his hair hadn't fallen out but had instead turned bright white with age. Now, however, Carson was using it to half drag, half pull him toward the front door. Halfway across the flagstones, Carson noticed Ritter on the stairs and laughed.

"Here's the old sod that let the dog out," he shouted to make himself heard above the old man's cries of pain. "The colonel saw him peeping out the window and sent me in to bring him out. On all fours was my idea. Just like his fucking dog."

Carson's antics enraged the Frenchman. Seeing his old servant reduced to a howling animal, he started forward down the stairs, and Ritter had to drop the book and seize Rocard by the collar of his shirt to pull him back. At the same time he thrust the barrel of the gun hard into the small of Rocard's back, and now the Frenchman stood almost doubled up with pain at the foot of the stairs, powerless to help his old servant as Carson dragged him out of the house, administering several kicks to the old man's back and ribcage before he dumped him on the ground at the colonel's feet, beside the dead dog.

"He was hiding behind one of the big heavy curtains in there," said Carson, pointing back at the house. "And it was him that let the dog out. I found him with this bit of rope in his hands. Why don't we use it to string him up? What do you say, Colonel? Let's teach these Frenchies a lesson."

"That won't be necessary, Corporal," said the colonel acidly. Carson was joking, but he had no time now for the man's petty sadism. All his attention was focused on Ritter and the Frenchman. "Did you get it, Reg?" he asked. "Show me what you got."

"Just this old book. He had it under the floorboards," said Ritter, handing over the thin leather-bound volume that he had seized from the Frenchman up in the attic. "Is that what you wanted?"

The colonel didn't reply. His hands were shaking as he took the book from Ritter and let go of the Frenchman's wife. She immediately went over to the old servant and raised him unsteadily to his feet. He couldn't stand unsupported, but Carson did nothing to help her. He was still trying to control his laughter.

The colonel turned the pages quickly but carefully, ignoring the dust that flew up into his eyes.

"It's the codex, all right," he said as if to himself. "From the moment I read that letter in Rome, I knew it was here. Here all the time."

"Colonel," interrupted Ritter. They needed to decide what they were going to do with these people before someone from the regiment came looking for them.

"Colonel, it's getting late," he tried again a moment later.

This time Cade looked up from the book. "Where did you say it was, Reg?" he asked, as if he hadn't heard Ritter's question.

"In a hollow space under one of the floorboards in their bedroom," said Ritter.

"Was there anything else in there? In the space?"

"No. I checked."

Still, the colonel seemed dissatisfied. He closed the book and began speaking to the Frenchman in his own language again. Quickly. Question after question. Ritter could understand almost nothing of what was being said, but it was obvious that the colonel was getting angry. He kept repeating a word that sounded like *roi* or *croix* in a voice that demanded a response, but it was a one-way conversation. The Frenchman raised his hands several times in a gesture that seemed to imply that he didn't understand what the colonel was talking about, and then after a while he just looked away.

Suddenly the colonel took hold of the woman again, squeezing her wrist and saying that same word over and over again. *Croix* or *roi*. *Roi* was a king, and Ritter didn't know what a king had to do with it, but perhaps that wasn't the word. The woman struggled, and Ritter was about to go over to help restrain her, when she threw her head back and spat at the colonel full in his face. It made him drop the book, and he used his freed hand to slap her hard across both cheeks. They were hard blows and she fell to the ground, weeping.

"We've got to decide what to do, Colonel," said Ritter. He felt worried now. The sun had almost set and they needed to stay in radio contact with the camp. The colonel seemed to be getting nowhere with the Frenchies.

"All right, Reg, I know that," said the colonel. "It's just that they know more than they're saying. A little bit longer and I can get it out of them. I can feel it. Help me take them over to the church. We can work on them in there. And you, Carson, come up there with us and keep a lookout. We won't be long."

PART ONE

1959

ONE

Detective Inspector William Trave of the Oxfordshire CID felt the pain as soon as he'd passed through the revolving entrance doors of the Old Bailey and had shaken the rain out from his coat onto the dirty wet floor of the courthouse. It hurt him in the same place as before—on the left side of his chest, just above his heart. But it was worse this time. It felt important. Like it might never go away.

There was a white plastic chair in the corner, placed there perhaps by some kind janitor to accommodate visitors made faint by their first experience of the Old Bailey. Now Trave fell into it, bending down over his knees to gather the pain into himself. He was fighting for breath while prickly sweat poured down in rivulets over his face, mixing with the raindrops. And all the time his brain raced from one thought to another, as if it wanted in the space of a minute or two to catch up on all the years he had wasted not talking to his wife, not coming to terms with his son's death, not living. He thought of the lonely North Oxford house he had left behind at seven o'clock that morning, with the room at the back that he never went into, and he thought of his ex-wife, whom he had seen just the other day shopping in the covered market. He had run back into the High Street, frightened that his successor might come into view carrying a shared shopping bag, and had ducked into the Mitre in search of whisky.

Trave wanted whisky now, but the Old Bailey wasn't the place to find it. For a moment he considered the possibility of the pub across the road. It was called The Witness Box, or some fatuous name like that, but it wouldn't be open yet. Trave felt his breath beginning to come easier. The pain was better, and he got out a crumpled handkerchief and wiped away some of the sweat and rain. It was funny that he'd felt for a moment that he was actually going to die, and yet no one seemed to have noticed. The security guards were still patting down the pockets of the public just like they had been doing all morning. One of them was even humming a discordant version of that American song, "Heartbreak Hotel." A rain-soaked middle-aged policeman sitting on a chair in the corner, gathering his breath for the day ahead, was hardly a cause for distraction.

A sudden weariness came over Trave. Once again he felt weighed down by the meaninglessness of the world around him. Trave always tried to keep his natural nihilism at bay as best he could. He did his job to the best of his ability, went to church on Sundays, and nurtured the plants that grew in the carefully arranged borders of his garden—and sometimes it all worked. Things seemed important precisely because they didn't last. But underneath, the despair was always there, ready to spring out and take him unawares. Like that morning, halfway down his own street, when a young man in blue overalls working on a dismembered motorcycle had brought back the memory of Joe as if he had gone only yesterday. And fallen apples in the garden at the weekend had resurrected Vanessa stooping to gather them into a straw basket three autumns before. It was funny that he always remembered his wife with her back turned.

Trave gathered himself together and made for the stairs. When he got time, he'd go and see his doctor. Perhaps the GP could give him something. In the meantime he had to carry on. Today was important. *Regina v. Stephen Cade*, said the list on the wall outside the courthouse. Before His Honour Judge Murdoch at twelve o'clock. Charged with murder. Father murder—patricide, it was called. And the father was an important man—a colonel in the army during the war and a university professor in civilian life. If convicted, the boy would certainly hang. The powers that be would see to that. The boy. But Stephen wasn't a boy. He was twenty-two. He just felt like a boy to Trave. The policeman fought to keep back the thought that Stephen was so much like Joe. It wasn't just a physical resemblance. Joe had had the same passion, the same need to rebel that had driven him to ride his brand new 600cc silver motorcycle too fast after dark down a narrow road on the other side of Oxford. A wet January night more than two years ago. If he'd lived, Joe would be twenty-two. Just like Stephen. Trave shook his head. He didn't need the police training manual to know that empathising with the main suspect in a murder investigation was no way to do his job. Trave had trained himself to be fair and decent and unemotional. That way he brought order to a disordered world, and most of the time he believed there was some value in that. He would do his duty, give his evidence, and move on. The fate of Stephen Cade was not his responsibility.

Up in the police room, Trave poured himself a cup of black coffee, straightened his tie, and waited in a corner for the court usher to come and get him to give his evidence. He was the officer in the case, and, when the opening statements were over, he would be the first witness called by the prosecution.

The courtroom was one of the oldest in the Old Bailey. It was tall, lit by glass chandeliers that the maintenance staff needed long ladders to reach when the bulbs blew out. On the wood-paneled walls, pictures of long-gone nineteenth-century lawyers stared out on their twentieth-century successors. The judge sat robed in black in a leather-backed armchair placed on a high dais. Only the dock containing the defendant and two uniformed prison officers was at the same level. Between them, in the well of the court, were the lawyers' tables; the witness box; and, to right and left, the benches for the press and the jury. The jurors were now in place, and Trave felt them slowly relaxing into their new surroundings. Their moment in the limelight, when they stumbled over their oath to render a true verdict in accordance with the evidence, had come and gone. Now they could sit in safe anonymity while the drama of the murder trial played out in front of them. Everyone—members of the press, the jurors, and the spectators packed together in the public gallery above the defendant's head—was focused on the prosecutor, Gerald Thompson, as he gathered his long black gown around his shoulders and prepared to begin.

"What time did you arrive at Moreton Manor, Inspector?" he asked, "on the night of the murder?"

"Eleven forty-five." Trave spoke loudly, forgetting for a moment the acoustic qualities of the Old Bailey.

"Were you the first policeman on the scene?"

"No. Officers Clayton and Watts were already there. They'd got everyone in the drawing room. It's across from the front hall."

"And the victim, Professor Cade—he was in his study. On the ground floor of the east wing."

"Yes. That's right," said Trave.

There was a measured coldness and determination in the way the prosecutor put his questions, which contrasted sharply with his remarkable lack of stature. Gerald Thompson couldn't have been more than five feet tall. Now he took a deep breath and drew himself up to his full short height as if to underline to the jury the importance of his next question.

"Now, tell us, Inspector. What did you find?"

"In the study?"

"Yes. In the study."

Trave could hear the impatience in the prosecutor's voice, but he still hesitated before beginning his reply. It was the question he'd asked himself a thousand times or more during the four months that had passed since he'd first seen the dead man, sitting bolt upright in his high-backed armchair, gazing out over a game of chess into nothing at all. Shot in the head. Detective Inspector Trave knew what he'd found, all right. He just didn't know what it meant. Not in his bones, not where it mattered. Pieces of the jigsaw fit too well, and others didn't fit at all. Everything pointed to Stephen Cade as the murderer, but why had he called out for help after killing his father? Why had he waited to open the door to his accusers? Why had he not tried to escape? Trave remembered how Stephen had gripped the table at the end of their last interview in Oxford Police Station, shouting over and over again until he was hoarse: "I didn't do it I tell you. I didn't kill him. I hated my father, but that doesn't make me a murderer."

Trave had got up and left the room, told the sergeant at the desk to charge the boy with murder, and walked out into the night. And he hadn't slept properly ever since.

Thompson, of course, had no such doubts. Trave remembered the first thing the prosecution counsel had told him when the case was being prepared for trial: "There's something you should know about me, Inspector," he'd said in that nasal bullying tone with which Trave had now become so familiar. "I don't suffer fools gladly. I never have and I never will."

And Trave was a fool. Thompson hadn't taken long to form that opinion. The art of prosecution was about following the straight and narrow, keeping to the path through the woods until you got to the hanging tree on the other side. Defence lawyers spent their time trying to sidetrack witnesses and throw smoke in the jurors' eyes to keep them from the truth. Trave was the officer in the case. It was his duty not to be sidetracked, to keep his language plain and simple, to help the jury do its job. And here he was: hesitant and uncertain before he'd even begun.

Thompson cleared his throat and glowered at his witness.

"Tell us about the deceased, Inspector Trave," he demanded. "Tell us what you found."

"He'd been shot in the head."

"How many times?"

"Once."

"Where in the head?"

"In the forehead."

"Did you find the gun?"

"Yes, it was on a side table, with a silencer attached. The defendant said he'd put it there after picking it up from the floor near the french windows, when he came back into the study from the courtyard."

"That was the story he told you?"

"Yes, I interviewed him the next day at the police station.

"His fingerprints were on the gun. That's right, isn't it?"

"Yes."

"And on the key that he admitted he turned in order to unlock the door into the corridor. The defendant told you that as well in his interview, didn't he, Inspector?"

"Yes. He said the door was locked and so he opened it to let Mr. Ritter into the study."

"Tell us who Mr. Ritter is."

"He was a friend of Professor Cade's. They fought together in the war. He and his wife had been living at the manor house for about seven years, as I understand it. Mrs. Ritter acted as the housekeeper. They had the bedroom above the professor's study, overlooking the main courtyard."

"Thank you, Inspector. All the fingerprint evidence is agreed, my lord."

"I'm glad to hear it," said the judge, in a tone that suggested he'd have had a great deal to say if it hadn't been. His Honour Judge Murdoch looked furious already, Thompson noted with approval. Strands of grey hair stuck out at different angles from under his old horsehair wig, and his wrinkled cheeks shone even redder than usual. They were the legacy of a lifetime of excessive drinking, which had done nothing to improve the judge's temper. Defendants, as he saw it, were guilty and needed to be punished. Especially this one. People like Stephen Cade's father had fought in two world wars to defend their country. And for what? To see their sons rebel, take drugs, behave indecently in public places. Stephen Cade had made a mistake not cutting his hair for the trial. Judge Murdoch stared at him across the well of the court and decided that he'd never seen a criminal more deserving of the ultimate punishment. The little bastard had killed his father for money. There was no worse crime than that. He'd hang. But first he'd have his trial. A fair trial. Judge Murdoch would see to that.

"Let's stay with the interview for a little bit longer," said Gerald Thompson, taking up a file from the table in front of him. "You have it in front of you, if you need to refer to it, Inspector. It's an agreed version. The defendant told you, did he not, that he'd been arguing with his father shortly before he found Professor Cade murdered?"

"Yes. He said that he went to the study at ten o'clock and that he and his father played chess and argued."

"Argued about his father's will? about his father's intention to change that will and disinherit the defendant?"

"Yes. The defendant told me they talked about the will but that their main argument was over the defendant's need for money."

"Which his father was reluctant to give him."

"Yes . . ."

Trave seemed to want to answer more fully, but Thompson gave him no opportunity. "The defendant told you in interview that he became very angry with his father. Isn't that right, Inspector?" asked the prosecutor.

"Yes."

"The defendant admitted to shouting at Professor Cade that he deserved to die." The pace of Thompson's questioning continued to pick up speed.

"Yes."

"And then he told you that he left the study and went for a walk. That's what he said, wasn't it, Inspector?"

Thompson asked the question in a rhetorical tone that made it quite clear what he, at least, thought of Stephen Cade's alibi.

"He said he walked up to the main gate and came back to the study about five minutes later, when he found his father murdered."

"Yes. Now, Inspector, did you find any footprints to support Stephen Cade's account?"

"No. But I wouldn't have expected to. The courtyard is stone and the drive is Tarmac."

"All right. Let me ask you this, then. Did you find any witnesses to back up his story?"

"No. No, I didn't."

"Thank you. Now one last question," said Thompson, smiling as if he felt he'd saved his best for last. "Did you find any of the defendant's belongings in the study?"

"We found his hat and coat."

"Ah, yes. Where were they?"

"On a chair beside Professor Cade's desk."

"And the professor himself. Where was his body in relation to this chair and in relation to the entrance doors to the room? Can you help us with that, Inspector?"

"Why don't you give the jury a chance to look at all this on the floor plan, Mr. Thompson?" said the judge, interrupting. "It might make it clearer."

"Yes, my lord, I should have thought of that. Members of the jury, if you look at the plan, you can see the courtyard is enclosed on three sides by the main part of the house and its two wings. Professor Cade's study is the last room on the ground floor of the east wing. It faces into the courtyard, and you can see the french windows marked. The internal door in the corner of the room opens out into a corridor which runs the length of the east wing.

You can take it up from there, Inspector," said Thompson, turning back to his witness.

"Yes. The deceased was seated in one of the two armchairs positioned in the centre of the study, about midway between the two entrances," said Trave, holding up the plan. "The desk and the chair with the defendant's hat and coat were further into the room."

"So the professor was between the doors and the defendant's hat and coat?"

"Yes. That's right."

"Thank you, Inspector. That's what I wanted to know. No more questions."

Thompson sat down with a self-satisfied expression on his face and stole a glance at the jury. He knew what the jurors must be asking themselves: Why would Stephen Cade have gone for a walk at half past ten at night? And if he did, why didn't he take his hat and coat? It was obvious he hadn't been wearing them, because not even he could pretend that he put them back on the other side of his dead father's body on his return.

No, the truth was inescapable. Stephen Cade never went for any walk at all. He was in the study the whole time, arguing with his father about his will, threatening him, and finally killing him with a pistol that he had brought along for that precise purpose.

Then, the next day, he'd told the police a ridiculous story in order to try to save himself. But it wouldn't wash. With a little help from the prosecution, the jury would see right through it. It'd find him guilty, and then Judge Murdoch would make him pay for what he'd done. With his neck.

TWO

That same evening, after court, Stephen Cade's girlfriend, Mary Martin, came to visit him in Wandsworth Prison.

Sitting in the car in the early October twilight, she blocked out her companion and his anger and focused instead on the prison walls, which reared up high, black, and imposing at the end of the side street of terraced Victorian houses on which they'd parked a few minutes before.

Beside her, Paul kept his eyes half closed and his breath came slowly, as if he was visibly trying to calm himself after his outburst moments earlier. But the grip of his hands on the steering wheel hadn't relaxed and the whites of his knuckles showed through. Yet Mary remained impervious, her mind concentrated on preparing for the ordeal ahead. The first day of the trial was always going to be stressful, and the prison intimidated her for some reason—more each time she came. But that only increased her resolve to go through with the visit. She'd promised, and she wasn't one to break her word, however much Paul pressed her to stay away.

Pulling down the mirror in the sun visor above the dashboard, she inspected herself closely. She was wearing no jewellery or cosmetics, but she didn't need to. She had good, regular features, yet there was more to her face than just that. The fullness of her lips and the curves of her figure spoke of a sensuality that was half belied by something watchful, almost withdrawn in her eyes. It made her mysterious and somehow challenging, and at times it almost made her beautiful.

Mary knew this, but the knowledge gave her no particular pleasure. She was a person entirely without vanity. Her pretty face was an asset to be exploited in her career. Nothing more. It got her better parts than plainer girls could hope for. And for that she was grateful. She certainly had no wish to be a poor actress. The life was difficult enough without being unsuccessful.

Satisfied with her appearance, Mary ran her hand through her thick chestnut-brown hair one last time, took a deep breath, and opened the door of the car. It was cold outside and she walked away quickly without a word to Paul or even a backward glance.

Inside the prison Mary waited with the other visitors in a whitewashed room dimly lit by a dusty tube of fluorescent lighting that flickered overhead as if it was just about to give up the ghost. All the walls were decorated with poorly typed notices about what could not be brought into the prison and what could not be taken out, and the biggest sign over on the far wall listed the penalties for assisting a prisoner to escape. Underneath it a young mother with an old face was trying to calm a screaming undernourished baby, while a warder sat behind a metal desk near the door reading a tabloid newspaper with his blue cap tipped down over his wide forehead.

Time passed slowly, and Mary counted out the minutes on the old black institutional clock hanging above the warder's head. One, two, three, four, five, until exactly half past six when an invisible bell rang and everyone got to their feet, shuffling out into the main courtyard of the prison. It was almost dark now and Mary stayed at the back, following behind two local South London women who seemed to know each other well.

"That's where it happens. That's where they do it. Florrie told me when I was last here," said one, adopting a theatrical stage whisper as she pointed excitedly over toward a two-storey red-brick building close to the west side of the perimeter wall. Its ordinariness was what made it noticeable. That and the lack of windows. There was only one, high up near the roof.

The unit, as it was known, was approached through a door in a wire fence, to which had been affixed a prominent "No Entry" notice. The instruction did not seem necessary. Everyone in the courtyard, prisoners and warders alike, seemed to instinctively avoid going anywhere near the death house.

"I know all about it. I've been here a lot more times than you, you know," said the other woman irritably. "I've seen them putting up the notices on the prison door in the early morning, and I've watched the families waiting outside, which is more than you have, Ethel. Huddled up in their cars in the cold. Some days they don't let us in when there's been a hanging. The prisoners get restless and the screws can't control them properly. My Johnny's told me what happens."

"Is that when they do it then? At dawn?" asked Ethel, who was obviously used to accepting her friend's sharp words without complaint.

"No. It's usually seven or eight o'clock in the morning, after the poor sod's been nicely softened up by a night in the death cell, vomiting up his last meal if he was stupid enough to eat it in the first place. And stop bloody talking about it, Ethel. People don't do that in here. You should know that."

Ethel was silenced, and the two women covered the rest of the walk to the visitors' block in silence, leaving Mary alone with her thoughts. She had known, of course, that they carried out executions here, but she had successfully managed to avoid identifying the actual place where it happened during her previous visits. She'd somehow assumed that it would be out of sight, but now she knew better. Ethel and her friend had seen to that, and Mary accepted the knowledge like an obligation.

At the door to the visits hall she paused, blinking in the sudden bright artificial glare of the overhead lights. There were no dark corners here where contraband could be passed across, under, or around the wooden tables, which were ranged in long rows from one end of the hall to the other. And along each wall warders in blue serge uniforms stood watching, occasionally stepping forward to enforce the rules forbidding any form of physical contact between inmates and outsiders.

Waiting in line for her pass to be checked at the front desk, Mary thought that the ceaseless unified drone of all the voices in the hall made the place seem like a vast beehive, but then she realized the comparison was far from apt. There was nothing productive happening here, and for most of the people in the room the short time together only made the subsequent separation from their loved ones even harder to bear. In the grip of a sudden claustrophobia, Mary half wished she hadn't come.

Directed to a table at the far end of the hall, Mary caught sight of Stephen before he saw her. His bright blue eyes were wide open but clearly unfocused on his present surroundings. Always the dreamer, she thought as she walked toward him down the aisle.

He had changed out of the suit he'd worn for court into the standard-issue prison uniform of blue-and-white-striped shirt and jeans, and he was now sitting in a characteristic pose: his elbows resting on the table, his head resting on his hands, and his long, tapering fingers interlaced as if in prayer, while his thumbs rhythmically caressed his Adam's apple and the stubble on the underside of his chin. The top of his shirt was open, exposing the whiteness of his throat, and Mary suddenly stopped in her tracks, fighting to hold back images of the executioner fitting a noose around her lover's neck, of the snap as the trapdoor opened beneath his feet, of Stephen hanging in the air, twisting and turning this way and that. All trussed up and dead. Everything around her suddenly seemed too real, too brightly lit, and she steadied herself for a moment against an empty chair.

I shouldn't have listened to those bloody women, she thought as she caught Stephen's eye and drew the outline of a smile across her suddenly pale face.

But for Stephen there was no effort. His face lit up as soon as he saw her. And the sudden glow transformed his features. The stubborn line that sometimes seemed fixed around his mouth disappeared in the radiance of his smile as he got up to pull out the chair on the other side of his table and instinctively brushed it down with a prison-issue handkerchief extracted from the pocket of his trousers.

"Quite the gentleman," said Mary.

"It's the training," said Stephen. "English public schools, dinner parties at home, you know."

"Not exactly the ideal preparation for life inside this place," she said, looking around her at the lines of broken-down men in their ill-fitting prison uniforms. Stephen's, surprisingly, fitted him quite well. He seemed to have the knack of making any clothes he wore seem like they were tailor-made.

"Well, that's where you're wrong," he said, smiling. "My school had a lot in common with prison as a matter of fact. Lousy food, endless rules and regulations, an all-male population thinking about what they can't have. And a whole lot of men in uniforms making sure they don't get it."

"Don't be ridiculous," said Mary, laughing. "This is Wandsworth Prison, for God's sake."

"True. And I'm sorry. I'm not thinking as usual. I hate you having to come here. It's a horrible place. I wish they'd let me see you at court."

Instinctively Stephen stretched out his fingers and touched the top of Mary's hand for a moment. She looked up into his eyes for the first time since her arrival and thought how strange it was that he should be so concerned for her welfare when he was the one shut up inside this God-forsaken place, on trial for his life. He'd changed since Oxford, she realized. He wasn't a boy anymore; prison had made him a man.

"Kissing's not allowed, I'm afraid," he said, holding her gaze. "Strictly against the rules."

Mary could understand why. She could hardly fail to have noticed the lust in many of the prisoners' eyes when she'd walked past them. Sexual frustration hung in the air like a cloud of atmospheric pressure.

"You looked good in court today," she said. "I liked the suit."

"I'm glad. Can't say I did much. Made me feel like I was going to my own funeral."

They were silent for a moment, both back in the courtroom with the dwarflike prosecutor relentlessly outlining the evidence against the accused.

"You mustn't worry, you know," he said, as if reading her thoughts. "I'll be all right. Truth will out, you'll see. Old Murder can do his damnedest, but it's not his decision at the end of the day."

"Old Murder?"

"Oh, sorry—that's what they call our judge in here. They say he's the worst of the lot. But the nickname's pretty good, don't you think? He looked at me today like he'd got half a mind to come down off his bench and throttle me himself. God knows why. It's not like he even knows me."

Stephen fell silent, as if frightened at how doubt had so quickly replaced his earlier optimism. But then his lips tightened in defiance. "I didn't do it, you know," he said suddenly. "I couldn't have killed him even if I'd wanted to. He was my father, for Christ's sake. It'd be like murdering part of myself."

"You said you hated him," she said.

"Yes. And I loved him too. Love and hate aren't so far apart, you know."

Stephen was silent again for a moment, and there was a faraway look in his eyes when he went on: "There's not a day goes by that I don't feel guilty about leaving him alone that night. Opening the door for whoever it was to walk straight in there and put a bullet through his head."

"How were you to know?"

"I wasn't. I just wish I hadn't left him, that's all. No one deserves to die like that."

"What about that family in France?" asked Mary, leaning forward across the table. "He herded them into a church like cattle. That's what you told me. Did they deserve what happened to them?"

"No, I know. You're right. There are just too many ghosts. That's the trouble. Too many unanswered questions," said Stephen, returning to the present with a half-forced smile. "Like who killed my father. My defence team doesn't seem to be getting too far with that one unfortunately. And there's not much I can do to help them while I'm sitting here."

"You've got to trust them," said Mary. "You've got a good barrister. Everyone says so."

"I know, I know. You're right as usual. But enough about me. Tell me about yourself. Are you working?"

"No, of course not. How could I come to court if I was acting as well? The stress is bad enough as it is."

"You're right. It's not easy."

Mary bit her lip, unable to understand her irritation. What was she doing complaining about stress when Stephen was on trial for his life?

"How's your mother?" asked Stephen, trying to keep up the conversation. "Is she any better?"

"A little, maybe."

"I'm sorry. Have you been to see her again?"

"Yes."

"And your brother. Did he go too?"

"No. Yes. What do you want me to say? Why do you always keep asking me about Paul?" asked Mary, irritated again.

"Sorry," said Stephen defensively. "I guess it just felt a bit strange that you never wanted to introduce him to me. That's all. It doesn't matter now. Let's talk about something else."

But there was no time. A speaker on the wall crackled into life giving a two-minute warning. And it had the same effect as on Mary's previous visits, pressurizing them both into an awkward silence.

"I love you, Mary," said Stephen.

"And I love you too," she replied.

But it was too pat. The place robbed their words of meaning. And there was no time left to explain, to connect, to try to work out where everything had gone wrong.

Mary got up to go. And afterward, left on his own at the table, Stephen followed her with his eyes until she disappeared into the throng of other visitors leaving through the door at the back of the hall. And involuntarily he wondered whether she would be driving away from the prison alone or whether there would be someone waiting to meet her on the other side of the high wall surmounted with barbed wire that separated him so entirely from the life he'd left behind.

THREE

In court the next morning, Gerald Thompson watched his opposite number get slowly to his feet. John Swift was a tall, willowy, good-looking man in his late forties. He'd been a pilot in the war, one of those who'd led a charmed life, guiding his Spitfire through everything the Germans and later the Japanese had been able to throw at him without once being shot down. Things came easily to him. As a barrister, he had an instinctive ability to see what mattered, to find what was persuasive in a case and get it across to a jury in a way that they could understand. Except in this case. Here, everything seemed to point toward the defendant's guilt, and on top of that Stephen Cade was his own worst enemy. He was headstrong and unmalleable. And his interview with the police was a disaster.

Swift was the son of the second to last lord chancellor, born with a solid silver spoon in his mouth. He'd been educated at Eton and Oxford. He was rich and well liked. A true war hero. He was, in short, everything that Thompson was not, and Thompson hated him for it, hated him secretly and with a passion. This high-profile case was exactly what Thompson had been praying for. He'd get his conviction, and he'd make a fool of John Swift in the process. No one would call him Tiny Thompson after this or poke fun at his working-class origins behind his back. Swift sensed the prosecutor's malevolence, but there were other more-pressing things on his mind as he began his cross-examination of Inspector Trave. He couldn't get a handle on the case. He needed a way in and he couldn't find one, though it wasn't for want of trying.

"My client was arrested on the same night that his father's body was discovered. Is that right, Inspector?" asked Swift.

"Yes. On the fifth of June. He was arrested on the basis of what we were told by Mr. Ritter at the scene. That the defendant had unlocked the door of the study from the inside to let him in."

"And Mr. Ritter was the first to respond to my client shouting in the study?"

"I don't think I can answer that, I'm afraid. I can only tell you the reason why we arrested Stephen Cade. I can't give direct evidence about what happened in the house before I arrived."

"Of course he can't. You shouldn't need a policeman to tell you that, Mr. Swift," said Judge Murdoch irritably. "How can the inspector know who shouted, or if *anyone* shouted for that matter?"

"He can't, my lord. I'm sorry. Let me ask you about the cause of death, Inspector. Only one bullet had been fired from the pistol that you found on the side table. Is that right?"

"Yes."

"And it had entered the professor's forehead?"

"Yes. And lodged in his brain."

"To use a popular expression, he'd been shot between the eyes."

"Just above a point between the eyes."

"Thank you. It was an execution-type shooting. That's my point. Would you agree with that description?"

"Yes, I suppose so."

"To achieve that kind of precision with a bullet, wouldn't you need considerable skill as a marksman?"

"I don't know. I'm not an expert."

"No. Quite right, Inspector. You're not," said the judge. "Is there evidence of the distance from which the shot was fired, Mr. Thompson?"

"About twelve feet according to the report, my lord," said the prosecutor, reading from a report in one of his many files.

"I see. Not exactly a great distance, Mr. Swift."

"No, my lord. I've made my point. I'll move on. You've told us about Mr. and Mrs. Ritter, Inspector. Who else was in the house on the night of the murder?"

"The defendant's girlfriend, Mary Martin; his elder brother, Silas Cade; and Sasha Vigne."

"Who's she?"

"She was Professor Cade's personal assistant. The professor had a large collection of valuable manuscripts, which were housed in a gallery on the second floor of the main body of the house. It's my understanding that she helped the professor with cataloguing them and with research for a book that he was writing on medieval art history."

"I see. Now where were these other people located in the house?"

"Everyone was in the drawing room when I arrived. Awaiting questioning."

"No, that's not what I meant, Inspector. Where were their bedrooms?"

"All on the second floor of the west wing. Only the Ritters and Professor Cade himself slept on the east side."

"And what about the grounds? They're quite extensive, aren't they?"

"Yes. There are stone terraces around the house with lawns beyond."

"And quite a lot of trees as well?"

"Yes."

"The drive is tree lined, is it not?"

"Yes, it is."

"We don't need a National Trust tour of the Moreton Manor gardens, Mr. Swift," interrupted the judge. "What's the point you're trying to make?"

"That an intruder could hide in the trees, my lord."

"If there was an intruder. You'd better ask the inspector about the security system. It looks fairly state-of-the-art in the photographs."

"I was just about to," said Swift, keeping a smile stretched across his features by an extraordinary effort of will. "Please do as his lordship asked, Inspector. Tell us about the security system."

"The main gate is the only exit from the grounds," said Trave. "A Tarmac drive leads up to it from the courtyard. Otherwise there's a high brick wall surmounted by broken glass and electric wiring surrounding the estate. The wiring is connected to an alarm system operated from inside the house."

"I see. The professor must have been very worried about the possibility of a break-in. Would you agree that the system would have cost a lot of money?"

"Yes. I'd say so."

"And what about the main gate? How is that opened?"

"It's also operated electronically either from a unit beside the gate or by remote control from inside the house."

"Was the gate open or closed when police arrived?"

"Officers Clayton and Watts were the first to attend. It's my understanding that they found the gate closed."

"And what about the doors of the house itself?"

"I entered through the main front door, which was half open when I arrived. All the other exit doors of the property were locked except for the french windows in the professor's study, which were also partially open, and the door at the front of the west wing, which was closed but not locked."

"These french windows to the study. There are thick, floor-length curtains in front of them. Isn't that right, Inspector?"

"Yes. They were half drawn."

"And there would be space between the curtains and the doors for a person to hide if he wanted to?"

"I suppose so."

"Making him invisible to a person inside the room."

"Yes."

"Thank you. Now Mr. Thompson asked you some questions about my client's interview . . ."

"One moment, Mr. Swift," interrupted the judge. "I'm sure you want the members of the jury to have a full picture of this security system. Isn't that right?"

"Yes, my lord."

"Well, perhaps the inspector can help us with whether there is any record of the alarm going off on the night of the murder."

"No record, my lord," said Trave.

"And is there any forensic evidence of anyone breaking into the house or the grounds? Any disturbance to the broken glass on top of the perimeter wall that you were telling us about? Any cut wires?"

"No, there was nothing like that."

"Thank you, Inspector. I just wanted to clear that up, Mr. Swift."

"Of course, my lord," said the defence counsel, trying not to allow his irritation to creep into his voice. "Now, Inspector, you will recall that my client told you that he walked up to the main gate twice that evening."

"Yes. Once before his interview with his father and once afterward."

"And on the first occasion he told you that he found the main gate open."

"Yes. He said that he closed it. And that it was still closed when he went back there after seeing his father."

"Thank you. Now, what else did my client tell you about his first visit to the main gate?"

"He said that he saw a black Mercedes parked on the verge a little further down the road on the opposite side from the gate. It was parked beside a public telephone box, and the door of the kiosk seemed to be wedged open. He said that he saw the same thing when he went back there an hour later."

"Did he say that he saw the driver of the car on either occasion?"

"He said he could see the figure of the driver but nothing more than that."

"Why are we hearing about all this now, Mr. Swift?" asked the judge. "Your client's interview can be read to the jury at the appropriate time, and he himself can give evidence about what happened if he chooses to."

The judge's tone of voice made it clear that he thought the defendant might have very good reasons for not going into the witness box and exposing himself to cross-examination. But Swift was ready for the judge this time.

"It's a matter of timing, my lord."

"I know that. That's what I just said."

"No, I don't mean that. I believe that the inspector will have something else to say about the Mercedes car on the night of the murder, and it's important that my client told the police about it before the further information became available to them."

"All right. Well, get on with it then."

"Thank you, my lord. Inspector, were there any other relevant reports of a black Mercedes in the vicinity of Moreton Manor on that night?"

"Yes. There was a car of that type stopped for speeding on the road from Moreton to Oxford. It was stopped at eleven fifteen p.m. The driver gave his name as Noirtier and provided an address in Oxford, which subsequently turned out to be false. He did not respond to a summons to attend court, and there has been no trace of him since. The record of the stop says that he was aged about thirty and spoke with a thick foreign accent."

"Did you notice the black Mercedes when you arrived at the manor house, Inspector?"

"No. But I wasn't the first to arrive."

"Yes. Officer Clayton may be able to help us. Returning to my client's account of events in interview, Inspector, he told you that he wore his hat and coat on his first visit to the main gate. Isn't that right?"

"Yes."

"But he then left them in the study after his interview with Professor Cade."

"Yes, that's what he said."

"The weather conditions on that night are going to be relevant here, Inspector. Would you agree that there was some light rain in the early part of the evening?"

"Yes, it died out about eight, and it was dry after that."

"And the temperature was in fact quite warm."

"I'd say it was average for the time of year. There was some wind, as I said earlier."

"Thank you. Now, there's just one other area that I want to cover with you, Inspector. My client, Stephen Cade, told you in interview about somebody else with a motive and desire to kill his father. That's right, isn't it?"

"He talked about certain events involving his father that occurred in northern France in the summer of 1944." Trave spoke slowly, as if he were choosing his words carefully.

"Basically, Stephen told you that he and his brother Silas discovered about two years ago that their father and Sergeant Ritter, as he then was, had killed a French family and their servants at a place called Marjean, in order to obtain a valuable medieval manuscript known as the Marjean codex."

"Yes. That's what he said."

"And that the professor was subsequently shot and wounded in his left lung during a visit to France in 1956, which was the cause of the serious ill health that he suffered from during the last three years of his life."

"I believe so."

"And finally that the professor received a blackmail letter the following year, threatening to expose him if he did not go to London and hand over the codex."

"Yes."

"Is that a fair summary of what the defendant told you in interview about this aspect of the case, Inspector?"

"Yes, I suppose so." Trave looked uncomfortable.

"Well, then, I'm sure you know what my next question is going to be. Why didn't you go to Marjean to investigate for yourself who shot Professor Cade in 1956 and sent him the blackmail letter the following year?"

Trave gave Swift a look of quick penetration, and then closed his eyes hard, as if he wanted to blot something out of his consciousness. When he opened them again he was looking at Gerald Thompson, and he was still looking at the prosecutor when he gave his reply.

"It was a prosecution decision," he said quietly.

"But was it your decision?"

Gerald Thompson gave Trave no chance to answer Swift's question. "With respect, Mr. Swift's question is an improper one, my lord," he said, getting to his feet. "The decision to charge the defendant was based on very strong evidence of motive, opportunity, and fingerprint connection to the gun and the locked door of the study. The defendant's interview did not change any of this, and it is not for the prosecution to build a defence."

"No, you're quite right. It isn't," said the judge nodding emphatically in agreement. "If you have an alternative explanation for the victim's murder, then advance it in the proper way, Mr. Swift. Don't attack the prosecution for not doing your own work."

Swift turned his head away from the judge's glare and made a series of mental calculations. He itched to take on Murdoch, who seemed intent on conducting the trial on just the legal side of bias. But the unanswered question might play best on the jury's mind if it remained unanswered, and he could make more mileage out of Marjean when it came to cross-examining Ritter. He had one good question left to ask the officer. He'd ask it and leave the French business hanging in the air for the present.

"It's right, isn't it, Inspector, that my client, Stephen Cade, is a young man without any previous convictions? He had never been arrested before the night of his father's murder and it was the first time he had been interviewed by the police."

"Yes, that's true," said Trave. "He is a man of good character."

Swift felt a note of resignation or even sadness in the policeman's voice and half wished that he had persisted with his questions about the investigation, but it was too late now. The policeman's evidence was over.

It was the mid-morning recess and Trave waited for Thompson to come out of court. He knew he was wasting his time, but he still had to try.

"What do you want, Inspector?" asked the prosecutor. He didn't make any attempt to conceal his irritation.

"A moment of your time."

"Very well."

The two men walked over to a corner of the great hall outside the court. Trave was at least a foot higher than the barrister, and his attempt to walk with a stoop so as to bring their heads closer together only accentuated Thompson's consciousness of his shortness. The barrister's irritation grew into outright anger.

"What's wrong with you, Trave?" he said. "Are you trying to prosecute that young hooligan or are you trying to defend him?"

"What are you talking about, Mr. Thompson?" Trave was unprepared for the prosecutor's sudden verbal assault.

"I'm talking about your evidence. About the doubt and uncertainty that you've been helping friend Swift throw around in there."

"I told the truth, Mr. Thompson," said Trave, becoming annoyed himself. "And yes, I do have doubts. Frankly, I don't understand why you don't too. The truth is I didn't investigate this case properly. I see that now and I feel bad about it. It's not too late for me to go to France."

"Yes, it is." Thompson almost spat out the words. "Stephen Cade is guilty. I've got his fingerprints on the weapon and the key. Ritter heard him unlock the door. And in a few minutes the jury is going to hear from the victim's solicitor about his motive. A powerful motive, Mr. Trave. Now I'm not going to allow you or friend Swift in there to muddy the water. Do you hear me, Inspector? Stay out of it. Your work on this case is over."

Thompson pushed past Trave, and the artificially heightened heels of his shiny black patent-leather shoes rang on the marble floor as he crossed to the door of the courtroom. After a moment Trave followed him. His work might be over, but he felt an obligation to see out its results. He sat down, waiting for Thompson to call his next witness.

Several minutes later a small balding man in a tight-fitting pinstripe suit came into court, fidgeting with his bowler hat.

"Charles Blackburn's my name. I'm a solicitor by profession," he announced in a slightly pompous voice after taking the oath.

"Is it correct that one of your clients was the late Professor John Cade?" asked Thompson, getting straight to the point.

"That's right."

"What work did you do for him?"

"I looked after some of his business affairs. I drew up his will . . ."

"When?" asked Thompson, interrupting. "When did you do that?"

"About seven years ago. The will had to be changed after Mrs. Cade died. But it was still fairly simple. The residual beneficiaries were the professor's sons, Stephen and Silas."

"And did you then have any further discussions about the will with the professor?"

"Not until earlier this year. It would have been about a month or so before his death that we first discussed new arrangements."

"Tell us about those arrangements, Mr. Blackburn," asked Thompson encouragingly.

"Well, basically he was talking about setting up a trust to run Moreton Manor House as a museum, housing his collection of manuscripts."

"Who were the trustees going to be?"

"The professor hadn't finally decided. Sergeant Ritter was going to be one of them."

"What about the sons?"

"Probably not. The effect of the change of will would have been to disinherit them."

"I see," said Thompson, pausing to allow the jury to absorb the full implications of the solicitor's last answer. "Now I'd like to show you exhibit fourteen. It's the professor's engagement diary, which was found on the desk in his study. It was open at the entry for June eighth. Read us the entry please, Mr. Blackburn."

"Blackburn. Will. Three o'clock."

"That's right. Can you tell us anything about that?" asked Thompson.

"Yes. I had an appointment with Professor Cade at that time for him to give me final instructions, so that I could draw up the new will and trust documents."

"But his death prevented him from keeping the appointment."

"Yes."

"Thank you, Mr. Blackburn. You've been most helpful. No more questions."

Deep in the bowels of the Old Bailey, the gaolers allowed Swift a short interview with his client.

The barrister took off his horsehair wig and laid it down beside his file of papers on the iron table that separated him from Stephen. The headgear was useful sometimes for intimidating witnesses, keeping lines of division intact. But now Swift wanted to connect. He needed to get through to his client, make him understand that a change of direction was necessary.

"The will gives them the motive, Stephen. That's the problem."

"I wouldn't have killed my father for money. Or anybody else for that matter. It's so stupid. Can't you see that?" Stephen's sudden anger took the barrister aback, even though it was not the first time that Swift had seen it. The trial was clearly beginning to take a toll on the young man.

"Listen, Stephen," he said. "You've got to calm down. Take a few steps back. Get a little less passionate."

"Less passionate! You'd be passionate if you had to sit up there all day watching that old bastard twist everything round against me. I thought he was supposed to be impartial."

"He is. But there's not much we can do about it at the moment, and your anger just plays into the prosecution's hands," said Swift, putting sufficient urgency into his voice to make Stephen look him in the eye. "The jurors are watching you, Stephen. They can see you boiling over, and it makes them think you're capable of doing what the prosecution says you did. Capable of killing."

"Whoever killed my father didn't lose his temper. You made that point yourself when you were cross-examining that policeman. You called it an execution-type killing. Not the same as a crime of passion."

"No, it isn't. But don't bank on the jury being as clever as you, Stephen. The case against you is too strong for you to stay out of the witness box . . ."

"I want to give evidence," said Stephen, interrupting. "I'd insist on it, even if you tried to stop me. They're going to hear the truth from someone before all this is over."

"But the truth isn't always enough in this place, Stephen. Can't you see that? It's what the jury decides is true that matters."

"No, I don't see it. I'm not a cynic like you. I believe in something, even if you don't."

"I believe in trying to keep you alive." Swift stopped suddenly. He'd have given a great deal to take back his words, but it was too late now. His need to get through to Stephen had got the better of his own judgement and had led him to break one of his most important rules: Never talk about execution to a client on a capital charge; keep him focused on the past and the present, but never the future. He'll fall apart otherwise.

"I'm sorry, Stephen," he said, breaking the awkward silence. "I shouldn't have said that. Please forgive me."

"Okay," Stephen agreed softly. There was a tremor in his voice.

"Let me start again," said Swift. "My point is that you have to keep your emotions in check, particularly when you come to give evidence. Thompson will try to provoke you into anger, and if he succeeds, he'll turn it against you. He's clever at what he does. I've seen him do it before. Many times."

"You saw it, members of the jury, didn't you?" Swift said in sudden imitation of Thompson's voice, and Stephen was struck by the accuracy of the impression. "You saw the way his fists clenched in rage when I asked him just a few simple questions. Imagine those hands on a pistol, members of the jury. Imagine the fingers clenching around the trigger."

"All right," said Stephen, holding up his hands. "I get the point. I'll watch myself."

"Thank you. Now there's one other thing. I need you to let me widen the net."

"What net?"

"The net of possible suspects. This foreigner in the Mercedes just isn't enough."

"But I'm not the only one who saw him. That police officer, the one who first came to the house, says in his statement that there was a car parked on the other side of the road. By the phone box."

"Officer Clayton?"

"That's right. He says that it drove off while he was buzzing to be let in at the gate."

"I know he does," said Swift patiently. "But the man could just have been making a phone call."

"Not all evening he wasn't. I saw him twice earlier, remember."

"There's only your word for that."

"Then what about the Frenchman in the Mercedes that was stopped for speeding? At eleven fifteen. The time fits. You said that yourself."

Swift could hear the anxiety creeping back into his client's voice. He didn't want to press Stephen any further, but he felt he had no choice.

"Don't worry," he said. "Clayton will give evidence, and I'll make all the points about the Mercedes—the one at the gate *and* the one that was stopped for speeding. But the driver's still never going to be anything more than a sideshow, whatever I say."

"Why?"

"Well, for a start, we can't explain how he could've entered the house. He can't have come through the gate because you closed it on him when you went up there before seeing your father, and any other route of entry is scotched by this damn security system. I'm sorry to have to tell you all this, Stephen, but it's no use denying facts. I know you think everything's related to the black-mail letter and what happened in France fifteen years ago. But it's all just too tenuous. We did what you asked us to. I sent an investigator over to Rouen, and the records office told him there were no close living relatives of the mur-dered family or their servants."

"Maybe he didn't look hard enough?"

"No, he did. I promise you he did. He went to Marjean as well, but the place is a ruin and everyone in the village said the same thing: no survivors. Same with the local police."

"Why couldn't you go yourself?"

"Because that's not what I do," said Swift, trying to keep the exasperation out of his voice. "I'm in court almost every day, and I can't do two different jobs even if I wanted to. The man we sent is one of the best. You can take my word for it."

"But didn't you tell me before that some of the records got destroyed when the Germans invaded?" asked Stephen, unwilling to leave the subject.

"Only for the two years up to 1940, which aren't relevant. The rest were in secure archives. Monsieur Rocard was an only child. His wife was from Marseilles and had a couple of brothers, but they were killed in the war. They married late and didn't have any children. End of story. We did what you asked us to do, and it's not really taken us anywhere, Stephen. We need something more than that your father had a murky past."

"Like what?"

"Like an alternative suspect to you. Somebody real. Somebody the jury can believe in. Not some phantom foreigner who's run away from a speeding ticket."

"Well, there isn't anybody else," said Stephen.

"Yes, there is. Your brother Silas had just as much of a motive to kill your father as you did. You heard what the solicitor said. He was going to be disinherited too."

"No," insisted Stephen, suddenly angry again. "My brother wouldn't kill anyone. He always got on better with our father than I did, for God's sake."

"Perhaps he was better at concealing his true feelings than you were."

"No. I know him."

"Do you, Stephen? How can you be so sure? He's not your blood brother, is he?"

Stephen's brow was creased with thought but he didn't respond, and after a moment Swift got up, noticing the gaoler waiting impatiently outside the glass door of the interview room. Then, as Stephen was being handcuffed, Swift made one last effort to get through to his client. "Silas will be in the witness box the day after tomorrow, Stephen. If I'm to help you, I need you to help me."

But Stephen didn't reply. Instead he turned away from his barrister and allowed himself to be led away down the whitewashed corridor and out of sight.

Swift climbed up the stairs from the cells and found Stephen's girlfriend, Mary, waiting for him in the foyer of the courthouse. She was clearly agitated, and her cheeks were flushed. It made her seem even prettier than he remembered.

"Have you seen him?" she asked.

"Yes. Just now. Down in the cells."

"How is he?"

"All right. I'd say he's bearing up pretty well, all things considered. There's a long way to go yet."

"He's going to get off, isn't he?" she asked. "He's going to be all right."

"I certainly hope so," said Swift, inserting a note of optimism into his voice that he was far from feeling. His interview with Stephen in the cells had left him more downcast about the case than ever before. He smiled and turned to go, but Mary put her hand on his arm to detain him.

"You don't understand," she said. "I need to know. What are his chances?"

Swift paused, uncertain how to answer the girl. Was she looking for reassurance or an assessment of the evidence? Catching her eye, he decided the latter was more likely.

"It's an uphill struggle," he said. "It would help if there was somebody else in the frame."

Mary nodded, pursing her lips.

"Thank you, Mr. Swift," she said. "That's what I thought."

FOUR

Moreton Manor in the morning was a pleasing sight. The dappled early autumn sunlight glistened on the dew covering the newly mown lawns and sparkled in the tall white-framed sash windows that ran in lines around the manor's classical grey stone façade, which rose in elegant symmetry above the ebony-black front door to a slanting, tiled roof surmounted by tall brick chimneys. A single plume of white smoke was rising into a blue, cloudless sky, but otherwise there was no sign of life apart from a stray squirrel running in unexplained alarm across the Tarmac drive, which cut the lawns in half on its way down to the front gate. An ornamental fountain in the shape of an acanthus plant stood in the centre of the courtyard, but it was a long time since water had flowed down through its basin. The professor had found the sound of the fountain an unwanted distraction from his studies, and without it the silence in the courtyard seemed somehow solemn, almost oppressive.

Trave stood lost in thought, gazing up at the house. He'd been awake since before the dawn, restless and unable to sleep. He kept on turning over the events of the previous day in his mind: Stephen in his black suit looking half-ready for the undertakers; old Murdoch, angry and clever up on his dais; and the barristers in their wigs and gowns reducing a murder, the end of a man's life, to a series of questions and answers, making the events fit a pattern neatly

packaged for the waiting jury. But it was all too abstract: a postmortem without a body. There was something missing. There had to be. Trave knew it in his
bones.

And so he'd driven out to Moreton in the early light and now stood on
the step outside the front door, hat in hand, waiting. It was Silas who answered, and once again Trave was struck by the contrast between Stephen
and his brother. Silas was just too tall, just too thin. His sandy hair was too
sparse and his long nose spoilt his pale face. But it wasn't his physical appearance that predisposed Trave against the elder brother; it was the lack of
expression in the young man's face and his obvious aversion to eye contact
that struck Trave as all wrong. Silas was concealing something. Trave was sure
of it. God knows, he had as much motive for the murder as his brother. They
were both going to be disinherited. But then Silas wasn't the one in his father's
room with the gun. That was Stephen, the one who reminded Trave so forcibly
of his own dead son.

"Hullo, Inspector. It's a bit early, isn't it?" There was no note of welcome
in the young man's flat, expressionless voice.

"Yes, I'm sorry, Mr. Cade. I was just passing. On my way to London for
the trial."

Silas's eyebrows went up, and Trave cursed himself for not thinking of a
better excuse.

"I just wanted to check a couple of things if it's not inconvenient," he finished lamely.

"Where?" asked Silas.

"Where what?"

"Where do you want to check them?"

"Oh, I'm sorry. In the study, the room where your father died."

"I know where my father died," said Silas, opening the door just enough
to allow the policeman to pass by him and come inside.

The room was just the same as Trave had described it in court the day
before. And yet there was something else, something he was missing. His
eyes swept over the familiar objects: the ornate chess pieces on the table, the
armchairs and the desk, the thick floor-length curtains. And now Silas, standing and watching him by the door, the door his brother had unlocked on the
night of the murder.

"Did you like your father?" Trave asked, catching the young man's eye for the first time.

"No, not particularly. I loved him. It's not the same thing."

"And what about your brother? How do you feel about him?"

"I feel sorry for him. I wish he hadn't killed my father."

"Your father?"

"Our father. What difference does it make? What's done is done."

"And now someone has to pay for it."

"Yes, Inspector. Someone does. Look, is there anything else I can help you with? I have things to do. This isn't a good time."

Silas made no effort to keep the impatience out of his voice, but Trave wouldn't allow himself to be put off so easily.

"Is there something you're not telling me, Mr. Cade? Is there something you know that I don't?"

Again Trave caught Silas's eye, but it was only for a moment before the young man looked away.

"No, Inspector," he said quietly. "I believe I made a very full statement to the police back in June. I've nothing to add."

As Silas led him back along the corridor, Trave wondered to himself what it was he had seen in Silas's face. Guilt or fear, anger or remorse? He couldn't put his finger on it; the glance had been too fleeting. Outside, Trave tried one last time.

"You know where I am, if you think of anything else?"

"Yes, Inspector. I know where you are," said Silas, closing the door.

Back in his bedroom, Silas stood at the window and bit his lip as he watched the policeman drive away. He already felt nervous about having to give evidence, and Trave's visit had broken the fragile calm that he'd worked so hard to achieve in recent weeks. Once again he felt the familiar sense of half-controlled panic that had engulfed him so often since the night of his father's murder. It was the house that was the problem. It was his inheritance and his curse. He felt it weighing on him even when he took refuge outside. In fact, out there it was just as bad. The house seemed to be watching him. In defiance he had started taking pictures of it, concentrating particularly on the shadowy times of day—just before dusk and after the dawn—and had then found himself examining his prints for apparitions. He remembered a story he'd once heard about a haunted castle in Scotland where one after-noon the guests at a huge house party had gone to every room and waved coloured handkerchiefs out of every window all at the same time. The people watching down below had seen one empty window, but afterward no one could ever find out which one it was. Silas didn't believe in ghosts, but part of him knew that he couldn't come to terms with the death of his father.

Not that John Cade had been his real father. Silas had never been left in any doubt about that. He was adopted because Clara Cade couldn't have children of her own, or thought she couldn't—until Silas was three and his adoptive mother was forty-one, at which point Stephen appeared, kicking and screaming his way into the world. Silas had been forgotten in the draw-ing room downstairs, and he had sat undetected in an armchair three times his size while his father walked the length of the room and back. Up and down, again and again. His father loved his mother but he didn't love Silas, and so Silas was quiet. Children were to be seen very little and to be heard not at all, except that the rules didn't seem to apply to the new arrival. It was as if the experience of carrying a baby and giving birth had made Clara re-alise the lack of a bond between herself and her first son. Nothing was the same for Silas after Stephen was born.

And now they were all dead. All except Stephen, and he was going to die too, once the lawyers had finished with him. Silas was the one who had sur-vived, and the house would soon be his. His alone. Strange then that he could not enjoy it but was instead haunted through sleepless nights and long, restless days. Perhaps this was the lot of survivors the world over. Silas didn't know.

He crossed to the window and looked down into the empty courtyard. He closed his eyes and saw his parents waving to him from the front door on the day he went away to boarding school. Stephen was between them, and his mother had her hand in his unruly blond hair. His brother had supposedly been sick that day, or at least that was the reason his mother gave for the change of plan. She had to stay home. Silas would understand. Clarkson, the driver, was completely reliable, and the housemaster would take care of Silas when he got to school. Silas had never forgiven her. For sending him away. For keeping Stephen at home when he reached the same age. For never visiting him, except once when she and his father were passing that way anyway, en route to some country-house weekend. They went to a fancy restaurant and talked about people that Silas had never heard of.

Silas didn't resent his father in the same way. He was selfish with everyone, not just Silas. Looking after his own creature comforts. Blinking in the sunlight like an overfed cat. Silas had watched him, listened to him, observing the perfect egoism of the man. The key to Professor John Cade was quite simple. He wanted to own. He had exquisite taste and knew the value of things, and he wanted to possess the best. Like his wife. John Cade had owned Clara Bennett from the date of their marriage. He had bought her, and he had put her on display with the rest of his possessions through the long summer evenings after the war, to show the world what he had and they didn't. The dust was gathering now on the heavy Victorian furniture in the dining room, but ten years earlier the silver had glittered on the polished mahogany surfaces, when Silas had gone outside into the night and stared in through the window, watching his father watching his mother. Professor Cade wore evening dress, and his wife sparkled with white jewels clipped in her beautiful fair hair and hanging round her perfectly shaped neck.

Silas pictured the elaborate dresses that his mother wore so effortlessly as she moved among her guests, the cream of university society, unaware of her adopted son only a few yards away on the other side of the window. And Stephen would be upstairs, sleeping in his nursery, surrounded by a hundred furry animals. John Cade's brow always creased with momentary irritation when his wife left to check on her little soldier, as she insisted on calling her younger son. But the professor swallowed his annoyance. The boy made his wife happy, and her happiness increased her beauty. John Cade never seemed to get tired of looking at his wife, and in Silas's memory she never changed. She was always young and lovely, right up until the day she died.

It was Christmas Eve, and 1951 was almost at an end. Soon the country would have a new queen, and Clara Cade had promised her fourteen-year-old younger son a new five-speed bicycle for Christmas. When it didn't arrive, she took her husband's car and drove into Oxford to collect it herself. Silas had watched her departure from the same bedroom window where he was standing now. She was wearing a heavy black fur coat and a hat with a veil, and she'd come down the front steps almost at a run, half tripping at the bottom on her high heels. The snow had been falling for most of the night, and after she drove away, Silas had gone down into the courtyard and stood in her footprints.

She never came back. Clara's own car was in the garage being serviced, and she was unused to the heavy Rolls-Royce. On the way back from Oxford, she lost control halfway down a steep hill, and the car swerved off the road at high speed, hitting a telegraph pole. Clara Cade flew through the windscreen and died instantly, or at least that's what the police told her husband. Silas wasn't so sure. He pictured his mother revisiting the scenes of her life, her blood seeping away into the snow. Perhaps Silas needed the consolation that she had regretted her treatment of him for a moment or two at the last.

He had visited the scene of the crash with his father the following day. It was still snowing, and the fields were white and silent. It was as if his mother had never been there at all. She seemed to leave no mark on the world.

Silas remembered when the police came. He didn't know why, but he had known what had happened as soon as the black cars had drawn up in front of the house and the men in uniform started getting out. The car doors had shut one after the other like reports from a gun, and Silas had watched as his father came out through the french windows of his study, bareheaded into the snow. Moments later he had sagged at the legs, held up between two policemen, and it was then that Silas had noticed the bicycle in the back of the police van, just before his father did. Stephen's present had survived its purchaser's death intact, and there it was, bright and gleaming, ready for Christmas.

The sight had enraged John Cade. He had pulled himself free of the policemen's hands, crossed to the van, and seized the bicycle. Then, holding it half above his head, Cade had gone almost at a run up the steps of his house, into the drawing room where Stephen was lying on the floor by the fire reading a book. The Christmas tree was big and full of lights behind him. Clara and her younger son had spent the day before decorating it with coloured globes and swans and silver trumpets until it was perfect, and now Stephen wanted to be near it all the time. His childhood was almost over, and the tree's magic kept its end suspended for a little while longer.

Cade stood in the doorway watching his son for a moment, and then, using all his strength, he threw the bicycle at the tree. Silas, standing behind his father in the hall, watched the Christmas decorations crash to the floor all around his brother, shattering into thousands of tiny pieces, meaningless shards of brightly coloured glass.

Two weeks after the funeral, Stephen was sent away to join Silas at his boarding school in the west of England, and Sergeant Ritter and his silent wife came to live at the manor house. There was no turning back the clock.

Silas never saw his father display such energy again after the day he threw the bicycle. He became watchful and reclusive, spending his days analysing complex chess problems in his study or gazing at the old hand-painted manuscripts that he kept catalogued and ordered in the long gallery at the top of the stairs. Watching him, Silas often thought of the silent, solitary monks who had copied and painted the sacred texts a thousand years before. Such a contrast to his father, with his love of sweet food and wine and his constant preoccupation with his failing health. Much good that it did him. Silas looked across to the east wing and remembered his father dead in his leather armchair. Silas had taken photographs. Of the dead man. Of the room. In the evenings he took them out and ran his index finger along the outlines of the body. He didn't know why. Perhaps he was seeking a closeness with his father that had eluded him in life.

Now the front door of the house opened, and Sasha came out. Silas stiffened as he stepped back, almost involuntarily, from the window of his room. It was second nature to him to seek concealment, to watch without being seen.

Sasha was wearing a sun hat that Silas had never seen before. Its wide brim concealed her face from Silas as he looked down on her from above and felt the usual agitation that she aroused in him. Sasha's movements were erratic. She would spend days poring over manuscripts in the long gallery or in the professor's study, and then would disappear without warning into Oxford. Silas had watched her, focusing his telephoto lens through the different windows, and it hadn't taken him long to see that she was searching for something specific, something that she hadn't yet found. Silas guessed at what it might be, but he hadn't so far had the courage to talk to her about it. She was supposedly staying at the manor house to finish cataloguing the manuscripts, but that task must now be long done. Silas feared that any discussion of her reasons for remaining would force Sasha into an early departure, and that was something that he could not bear to contemplate.

Acting on impulse, he pushed up the lower part of the sash window and called down.

"Where are you going, Sasha?"

Sasha jumped at the sudden noise breaking the stillness of the morning and put her hand on the crown of her head, as if to prevent her hat from falling off. It was the old preoccupation: Her elaborately structured brown hair and high collars were there to hide the livid red burn that disfigured her neck and shoulders. But the burn was too high, and she could never fully conceal it. Men were drawn to her brown eyes and full lips and the clear soft complexion of her face, but the contrast with the ravaged flesh below only increased their repulsion when they got closer to her. All except Silas, who seemed to follow her all the time. With his eyes. In person. Recently he'd seemed almost omnipresent. It was as if he was attracted by her disfigurement. She dreaded that one day he might ask her about it.

"I'm going into Oxford. I need to do some things," she said, filling her voice with all the discouragement that she could muster.

But Silas was undeterred. Sasha's upturned face and his position in the window above her gave him a sense of power.

"Let me give you a lift. I can have the car out in a moment."

It was his father's car. The Rolls-Royce was the first concrete proof of his inheritance. He wanted Sasha inside it, the sense of her body resting against the soft grey leather of the seat beside him, so that he could take his hand off the steering wheel and caress that place at the nape of her neck where her perfect skin met its burnt counterpart.

Silas turned away from the window without waiting for Sasha to protest any further and ran down the stairs. Five minutes later he had his wish, and they were passing through the sleepy village of Moreton. In the valley below, the city of Oxford was spread out before them: rivers and parks and old stone buildings surrounded by high walls. The sun glinted on the silver and gold domes of the city's churches, and Silas pressed his foot down on the accelerator and allowed the car to gather speed as it went down the hill and up again, past the scene of his mother's death.

"That policeman was here today," he said, making conversation.

"Which policeman?"

"Trave. The one in charge of the case."

"What did he want?"

"I don't know. Just poking around, asking stupid questions."

"About what?"

"What I felt about my father. Things like that."

"What did you feel about him?"

"I don't know. He was selfish—I mean really selfish. But you know that. It was like he didn't feel anything. And yet he was clever. He knew a lot, more than I'll ever know."

"You admired him?"

"In a way. He was my father."

"I know that." It sounded like an accusation.

They lapsed into an uneasy silence and Silas found it almost painful not to reach out and touch Sasha, who sat with her head turned away, willing herself toward her destination.

"Have you seen the Ritters today?" Silas asked, not because he was interested, but in order to get some reaction out of his companion.

"Him, but not her. He said she was sick again."

"He probably hit her. Didn't you hear the shouting two nights ago?"

"Yes, he's disgusting. Like an animal." Sasha spoke with sudden passion, and at the same time, two bright red patches appeared in the centre of her normally pale cheeks.

"I'll ask him to leave if you like." The idea had often crossed Silas's mind since his father's death, but he had never quite had the courage to go through with it.

"That's up to you. It's your house. Perhaps you don't want me there anymore either."

"No, I do. Really I do."

Silas cursed himself for raising the possibility of Sasha's departure, and he turned round toward her to add emphasis to his words, taking his eye off the road as he did so.

"Look out," Sasha shouted, and Silas was only just in time to slam his foot down on the brake and bring the car to a shuddering halt, inches away from an old woman crossing the road in front of them. His arm shot out across Sasha to prevent her being thrown forward, and he felt her breast against his hand for a moment, before she pushed him away.

"You're an idiot, Silas," she said angrily. "You could have killed that old woman, and us too."

Silas said nothing. Instead he bent down to help Sasha, who was busy picking up the papers and books that had fallen out of her bag onto the floor. There was one yellowed document that caught his attention. It was covered with a spidery handwriting that Silas didn't recognize. He noticed the date 1936 in the top corner and a name, John of Rome. It seemed to be a translation of some kind, but Silas had no chance to read any more before Sasha snatched the paper out of his hand.

"Its part of our work on the catalogue," she said, even though Silas had not asked for any explanation. "Your father would have wanted me to finish it."

They drove on into Oxford in silence, passing Silas's little photographic shop and studio on Cowley Road. He had spent hardly any time there since the murder, and he made a mental note to give the landlord notice at the end of the month. His inheritance at least meant that he wouldn't need to earn his living as a humble portrait photographer any longer.

Sasha got out of the car almost without warning at a traffic light in Holly-well and hurried away down a side street, clutching her shoulder bag tight to her side. Silas pulled over, half onto the pavement, and left the car unlocked as he ran after her. But she was already out of sight by the time he got to the first corner, and after a minute or two he gave up looking for her and went home.

FIVE

Sasha stepped out from behind the back gate of New College and looked around. Silas was nowhere in sight. She'd known instinctively that he'd try to follow her, although she still couldn't understand his apparent infatuation. It repelled her, and she wished she could leave the manor house and never see its new owner again. Perhaps she should. In truth she was close to giving up on finding the codex. In the last five months, she'd turned the leaves of every manuscript that John Cade owned, but nothing had fallen out. She'd stared into every recess, tapped every wall, and found nothing—only the diary secreted in the hollow base of the study bookcase that she'd discovered two days ago.

Sasha held the book close to her as she hurried through a network of narrow cobbled lanes, turning left and right, apparently at random. She remembered her excitement when she first found it. The study had been dark apart from her flashlight, and for a moment she felt as if Cade was there, watching her from the armchair where he used to sit, slowly rotating his thick tongue around his thin lips as he turned vellum pages one by one. Sasha had never been a superstitious person, but still she'd shivered and hurried away with the book to study it in the privacy of her room. Pausing for a moment to take a key out of her pocket, Sasha remembered the disappointment she'd felt as the first grey light had filtered through her window and she'd realised that the diary had taken her no nearer to the object of her search. She felt certain now that the old bastard had had the codex, but she still had no idea where it was. It was a secret that he'd taken with him to the grave. Unless her father could help. He was her last chance.

Sasha had stopped outside a tall old house that had clearly seen better days. The paint was cracked and dirty, and a row of bells by the door pointed to multiple occupation. But she didn't press any of them. Instead she used her key to unlock the door, and then climbed four flights of a steep, uncarpeted staircase to the very top of the house, knocked lightly, and went in.

A white-haired man in a threadbare cardigan sat in the very middle of a battered leather sofa in the centre of the room. He looked at least ten years older than his real age of sixty-seven. His whole body was painfully thin, his face was deeply lined, and he sat very still except for the hands that trembled constantly in his lap. In the corner, a violin concerto that Sasha didn't recognise was playing on a gramophone balanced precariously on two towers of books. Everywhere in the room were similar piles, and Sasha had to navigate a careful path between them to reach her father. She arrived just in time to stop his getting to his feet. Instead, she kissed him awkwardly on the crown of his head and then went over to a rudimentary kitchen area beside the single dirty window and began making tea.

"How have you been?" she asked.

"Not bad," said the old man just like he always did, speaking in the hoarse whisper that represented all that was left of his voice after the throat cancer he had fought off three years before. Now it was Parkinson's disease that he was up against, and Sasha wondered how long his ravaged frame would hold out. She loved her father and constantly wished that he would allow her to do more, but he was obstinate, holding on fiercely to what was left of his independence.

"You've brought something," he said, looking down at the bag that Sasha had left on the sofa.

"Yes, it's Cade's diary. I found it hidden in his study. It's only for five years though. From 1935 through to 1940. Nothing after that. I don't know whether he stopped writing it or whether the next one's hidden somewhere else."

"It was the war," said the old man. "Professor Cade became Colonel Cade, remember? No more time for autobiography."

"You're probably right. The book's pretty interesting, though. Except that there's nothing in it about what he did to you. Look, here." Sasha opened the book and pointed to a series of entries dating from late 1937. "Anyone reading this would think that he won that professorship on merit. It's vile. He called himself a historian, and yet he spent his whole life falsifying history. He knew you were going to win, and so he fabricated that story about you and that student."

"Higgins. He wasn't very attractive." Andrew Blayne smiled, trying to defuse his daughter's anger.

"I thought I could get you back your good name."

"I know you did. But it doesn't matter now. It's all ancient history."

"It matters to me." Sasha's voice rose as her old sense of outrage took over. She felt her father's humiliation like it had happened only yesterday. Cade had persuaded one of his rival's pupils to allege a homosexual relationship and the mud had stuck. Andrew Blayne had lost the contest for the chair in medieval art history and had then been forced by his college to resign his fellowship. Since then he had supported himself through poorly paid private tutoring and temporary lecturing jobs at provincial universities, until ill health had put a stop even to that.

His wife, Sasha's mother, was a strict Roman Catholic and had chosen to believe every one of the scurrilous allegations against her husband. She'd left him in his hour of need, taking their five-year-old daughter with her and had then stopped the girl from seeing her father for most of her childhood. Sasha had always found this cruelty harder to forgive than all her mother's neglect, and Andrew Blayne had remained the most important man in his daughter's life.

"Clearing my name wasn't the main reason why you ignored all my objections and went to work for that man, was it, Sasha?" said Andrew reflectively, as he stirred the tea in his chipped mug. He noticed how Sasha had filled it only halfway to the top to avoid the risk of his spilling hot tea on his trousers. It suddenly made him feel like an old man.

"You wanted to find the Marjean codex. Just like I did years ago. Because you thought it would lead you to St. Peter's cross," he went on when she did not answer. "You should be careful, my dear. You're not the first to have followed that trail. Look what happened to John Cade."

"That's got nothing to do with the codex," said Sasha, sounding almost annoyed. "Cade's son killed him. He's on trial at the Old Bailey right now, and I've got to give evidence next week. Don't you ever read the newspapers?"

"Not if I can avoid it. And plenty of innocent people get put on trial for crimes they didn't commit, Sasha. They get convicted too."

"Not this one. The evidence is overwhelming. But look, I didn't come here to talk about Stephen Cade's trial."

"You came here to talk about the codex."

"Yes." Sasha's voice was suddenly flat, full of her disappointment over all her fruitless searches of the last few weeks.

"I'll tell you again. I think you should leave it alone."

"I can't."

"Why not?"

"Because the codex, the cross—they should be yours. He stole everything from you."

"No, he didn't, Sasha. I could have looked for the cross if I'd wanted to, but I didn't. I chose not to."

"With no money?" said Sasha passionately. "What could you do after he'd taken your livelihood away?"

The old man didn't answer. He looked up at his daughter and smiled, before using both hands to contrive a sip of tea from his mug. But Sasha wouldn't let it go.

"I want to make it all up to you, Dad. Can't you see that?"

"I know you do, Sasha. But can't *you* see that I don't need objects? They mean nothing to me any more."

"I don't believe you. Not this object."

Not for the first time her father's quiet stoicism grated on Sasha. It was beyond her comprehension that he could be so indifferent to what had been taken from him. Did he know more than he was saying? about Cade's death? about the codex? and the cross? Suspicion creased her brow.

"Look, I can't even hold a cup of tea properly in my hand," said Blayne, gesturing with his shaking hand.

"I know," she said. "I know." She felt foolish for a moment, ashamed of herself, looking down at her father's ravaged body. She felt as if her long, fruitless search for codex and cross had started to make her see shadows in even the brightest corners.

"I just want to have you and for you to be happy. That's all," said Blayne.

It was hard to resist the appeal in his quavering voice or the tears glistening in his eyes, but Sasha's face hardened, and she turned away from her father. Her jaw was set, and her lips folded in on themselves. She looked almost ugly.

"I have to find it," she said quietly. "I've gone too far to stop now."

Father and daughter looked deep into each other's eyes for a moment before Andrew Blayne let go of Sasha's sleeve and allowed his head to fall back against the sofa. He seemed to concentrate all his attention on a stain on the corner of the ceiling, and he kept his gaze fixed there even when he started speaking again.

"Perhaps you're wasting your time," he said. "Perhaps Cade never even had the codex."

"But I know he did," said Sasha passionately. "That's why this diary is so important. Look, let me show it to you. You remember that he supposedly hired me to help him with research for his book on illuminated manuscripts?"

"The magnum opus."

"Exactly. But he didn't really care about that at all. He was obsessed with St. Peter's cross. He kept sending me to this library and that, looking for clues. But it was a wild-goose chase, and I think he half knew that deep down. He was like a man who's followed a trail to its logical end and found nothing there. He goes back, taking every side turn that he passed before but without any faith that they'll lead anywhere."

"And he needed you because he couldn't do his own research. Because he wouldn't go out."

"Yes, he was always frightened," said Sasha. "But the interesting part was that he was always looking for the cross in any place except the one where it ought to be."

"In Marjean?"

"Yes. It was like he already knew it wasn't there. I tested him once. I showed him the John of Rome letter. It was a risk that he'd connect me with you, but I don't think he did. I said that I'd found a copy in the Bodleian

Library. But he wasn't interested. He said it was a false trail. A waste of time."

"I remember you telling me that," said the old man, becoming increasingly interested in spite of himself. "I was the one who showed him the letter back in 1936 when I thought we were friends. He pretended not to be interested then too."

"Except that he was," said Sasha excitedly, pointing to an entry in the diary. "Here it is. May thirteenth, 1936. He's copied out the whole of your translation, word for word." Sasha held up the yellowed document covered with spidery blue handwriting that she'd snatched from Silas in the car. "Here's your copy and that's his. They're the same."

Blayne took the manuscript in his trembling hand and began to read it aloud. The hoarseness seemed to go out of his voice, and Sasha felt herself transported back five hundred years, out of her father's disordered attic room in Oxford to a wood-panelled library in the Vatican.

Another old man in a black monk's habit was writing a letter, dipping his quill in the inkwell at the top of his sloping mahogany desk. The sunshine sparkled on the Tiber and illuminated the parchment across which his old bony hand was moving steadily from side to side.

> *My dear brother in Christ,*
>
> *Let me tell you then what I know of the cross of Saint Peter. It has long been lost, but is perhaps not destroyed. Perhaps you will one day see what I have never found.*
>
> *Certain it is that the cross was made from a fragment of the true cross on which Our Lord suffered. Blessed Saint Peter, our first Holy Father, wore it when he took ship and crossed the great sea to spread the word of God. And he gave it to Tiberius Maximus, a citizen of this town and a good Christian before he, Peter, suffered death at the hands of the unbelievers. The people of God kept the holy relic safe through centuries of war and persecution, until it passed out of recorded history at the time of the invasions from the North, when this holy city was sacked by the barbarians.*
>
> *Yet I have long believed that the cross survived and that it is the same as the famous jewelled cross that the great king Charlemagne*

kept in his royal chapel at Aachen in the eighth century. Many years ago I was working in the French king's library in the city of Paris when I came upon an inventory of Charlemagne's treasury made by a Frankish scribe. I attach a copy, and you will see that he speaks of the cross of Charlemagne as being the holy rood of Saint Peter made from the wood of the true cross.

It was adorned with gems, the like of which the world has never seen before or since. The great diamond at the centre of the cross was said to be the same white stone that Caesar once gave to Cleopatra, Queen of Egypt, to seal their illicit union, and the four red rubies were taken from the iron crown of Alexander the Great. The Franks believed that the cross had magical powers. Charlemagne used it on feast days to heal his sick subjects. It was truly one of the wonders of the world.

My brother, I have traveled in many lands during my long life, and I have never found any other written record of the cross of Saint Peter. I had thought that perhaps it was lost when the pagans came into France four hundred years ago, but I do not now believe this to be true. There are men that I have spoken to in the city of Rouen who say that the monks of Marjean kept the cross of Charlemagne in a reliquary behind the high altar of the abbey church for generations, until an unsuccessful attempt was made to steal it and the cross was hidden.

The fate of the community at Marjean was no different than that of so many of the other monasteries of France. The great plague that many called The Black Death came there out of the east in the year of our Lord 1352, and there appear to have been no survivors. Marjean is indeed a desolate place, and I have taken no pleasure from my visits there. Some of the monastic library was preserved in a château nearby, but I found no record of the cross there or anywhere else. Only this. I passed through the town once more last year and found an old man living in the ruins of the monastery. He said that his father's uncle was one of those monks killed by the great plague and that his father had told him when he was a child that the hiding place of the cross had been recorded in a book made by the monks. I asked the old man many questions about the book, and I formed the opinion that he was speaking of the holy Gospel of Saint Luke. I now feel sure that he was referring to the famous Mar-

jean codex of which you will have doubtless heard yourself. But it too is missing, and I am no nearer to finding the cross of Saint Peter, if it does indeed still exist.

I am old in years, and I must turn away from the love of this world and make myself ready for the next. I leave to you this account, which is all that I know of Saint Peter's cross.

May God be with you.

Andrew finished reading and handed the paper back to his daughter.

"I remember when I first read that," he said. "In Rome before the war. I had gone there with Cade for a conference, but he wasn't in the library when I found it. There was this little room at the back, and I don't even know why I went in there. It was more like a cupboard, really. Shelves of old dusty religious commentaries and John's letter neatly folded between the leaves of one of them. God knows how it got there. All I know is that it had been there for a long, long time. I remember it was early evening and I sat at a table in the summer twilight and made this copy, and then I showed it to Cade back at the hotel. I was excited. The city was ablaze with fires. Mussolini had just conquered Abyssinia, and I had found John of Rome. But Cade made me lose belief. The cross was an old wives' tale, he said. An invention of jewel-crazy adventurers. It was a waste of time to even think of it."

"But he was lying. You knew that already, Dad. After all, it was you who told me that he was in Marjean at the end of the war. You thought he'd gone after the cross."

"I said it was possible."

"Well, it was more than possible. That *was* what he was doing. This diary proves it."

"I thought you said that it stopped in 1940."

"It does. But by then he'd visited Marjean twice and was planning a third visit. The war stopped him, but then the end of it gave him the opportunity to take what he wanted by force. That was when he stole the codex."

"Who from?"

"From a Frenchman called Henri Rocard, who was the owner of the château at Marjean up until 1944, when he and his family were all murdered. Allegedly by the Germans."

"But you say it was Cade who did it?"

"Yes, I'm sure of it. Him and that man Ritter. Look, go back to John of Rome's letter. See near the end, where he talks about visiting Marjean? He says that some of the monastic library was preserved in a château nearby."

"But he also says that he found no record of the cross there or anywhere else," countered Blayne, reading from the letter.

"Perhaps he didn't look in the right places," said Sasha. "Cade realised early on that that was the most important sentence in the whole document. He says so in his diary. The year after you found the letter he went to Marjean and visited the château there. Henri Rocard was away from home, but Cade spoke to the wife. He describes her as proud and rude."

"Is that all?" asked Blayne, laughing.

"Pretty much. She didn't invite him in. Said she knew nothing about the codex. Cade didn't believe her, of course."

"So what did he do?"

"He went to the records office in Rouen and settled down to do some research."

"On the Rocard family."

"Yes. And he got lucky. Not to begin with, but he was persistent."

"Always one of the professor's qualities."

"He had no qualities. Look, let me tell you what's in the diary, Dad," said Sasha impatiently. "There was no reference to the codex in the first place he looked. Land deeds and wills and the like from before John of Rome's time right up until the Revolution. But then in 1793 there was something. Robespierre and the Jacobins were in power in Paris, and it was the time of the Terror, soon after the king was guillotined. Government agents sent out from Paris arrested a Georges Rocard as a counterrevolutionary, and a record was made of a search of his château at Marjean. Cade copied part of the record into his diary. It says that the government agents found no trace of the valuable document known as the Marjean codex."

"Just like John of Rome, when he searched for it four centuries earlier," said Blayne, sounding unimpressed.

"But that's not the point," said Sasha. "What's important is that there were people at the end of the eighteenth century who believed that the codex was in the château at Marjean. There must have been some basis for that."

"Maybe," said her father, still unconvinced. "What happened to Georges Rocard?"

"He didn't escape, I'm afraid. Almost no one did. He was guillotined in Rouen a few weeks after his arrest. But his family got away to England, and Georges's eldest son returned to Marjean and the château when the monarchy was restored in 1815. After the Battle of Waterloo."

"And this Henri Rocard was a descendant of his?"

"Yes. Cade went back to the château, and this time Henri Rocard was there in person."

"Proud and rude like his wife?"

"Worse, apparently. Rocard told Cade that he knew nothing about the codex, and when Cade persisted, Rocard and his old manservant set the dogs on him."

"Did they bite?"

"I don't know. The point is that the reception he got from Madame Rocard and then from her husband convinced Cade that they had the codex."

"So what did he do?"

"He wrote to Henri Rocard offering to buy it. There's a copy of his letter in the diary. He pointed out that the château was in a state of serious dilapidation and that the money could be used to carry out all the necessary repairs. But he got no reply. He wrote again but still heard nothing, and he was just about to go to Marjean again when the war broke out."

"So he was cut off from the object of his desire for more than four years," said Blayne musingly. "The professor must have been a very frustrated man by the time D-day came around."

"Exactly," said Sasha. "We know he went to that area in 1944 and the whole Rocard family died. I believe Cade killed them, and that he stole the codex at the same time. He'd already been there and done that, and that's why he always acted like he was so uninterested in Marjean and the codex."

"So where is the codex, if you're so certain he had it?" asked Blayne.

"I don't know. I thought you could help me. I've looked everywhere." The frustration was back in Sasha's voice.

Blayne looked hard at his daughter and shook his head.

"Leave it, Sasha. It's dangerous. I can feel it. The man spent almost half his life searching for something, and now he's dead. It's not the first time he was shot, either. Somebody tried to kill him in France three years ago. You tell me it's got nothing to do with the cross, but I'm not so sure. Let it die with him. Let it go."

"That's easy for you to say," she blurted out and then immediately turned away from her father, trying to clear her mind. Again she had that same fleeting sense that he knew more than he was saying. Why hadn't he been more surprised by her revelations—more excited? No one had suffered more at the hands of John Cade than her father. No one except Cade knew more about the codex. The codex and the cross.

"I don't understand why you're so calm about all this, so accepting," she said, challenging him.

"Because I'm old," he said. "Old before my time. Can't you see that, Sasha?"

Blayne put his hand out toward his daughter, but she turned away and walked over to the window. She looked down into the stony courtyard, and her resolve hardened. "I'll leave the diary here," she said. "You can call me if you think of anything. I'll find the codex. And after that I'll find the cross."

"And then?" asked Blayne, looking up sadly at his daughter. "What happens then, Sasha?"

She didn't answer. Just lay her hand for a moment over her father's shaking hand and then walked out the door.

SIX

"Widen the net . . . somebody the jury can believe in . . . not some phantom foreigner . . . your brother Silas . . ."

Stephen couldn't sleep. His mind kept turning over Swift's words, twisting them this way and that, seeking a way out. However hard he tried, Stephen couldn't believe it of Silas. Couldn't or wouldn't. Stephen didn't know. What he did know was that somebody who was not his brother had tried to kill their father. It was no phantom who had come to their house threatening John Cade with a pistol, no ghost who had put a bullet in his lung. That man was real. He had a name: Carson, Corporal James Carson, once of the British army in France. The only problem was that he was dead.

Stephen remembered the first time he'd met Carson. How could he forget? He'd just turned thirteen and had been out running, practicing for the cross-country season at his school. The man had been standing in the trees across the road from the front gate, looking up toward the house, and he had called to Stephen as he went past.

"Cold weather to be out running, young man," he had said, stepping out into the road. He was wearing a heavy black army greatcoat with its collar pulled up around his ears, and yet he still seemed cold. There was a shiver in his voice, and when Stephen looked down, uncertain of what to say, he noticed a hole in the stranger's boot.

Stephen muttered something indistinct and would have turned away if the man had not spoken again.

"Are you the colonel's son?" he'd asked.

"The colonel," Stephen had repeated, not following the stranger's meaning.

"Colonel John Cade. He used to be a military man like me. But perhaps he's too proud to remember old comrades."

"Oh, yes. I'm sorry. Yes, I'm one of his sons." Stephen had stumbled over his words. The man had made him nervous, as if Stephen realised even then that this stranger's coming would cause trouble.

The man hadn't stayed long after Stephen had walked with him up the drive and knocked on the door of his father's study. The professor had not been pleased to see his visitor. That much was obvious. Carson had raised his hand to his forehead in a mock salute, but Cade had not returned the gesture. He'd just stared angrily at Carson for a moment or two, and when he eventually spoke, it was his son he addressed, not his visitor.

"Go to your room, Stephen," he'd said. There was a harsh edge to his father's voice that had frightened Stephen, and he had backed away into the corridor. A moment later his father crossed to the door and shut it with a bang that reverberated right round the east wing of the house.

Stephen had done what his father told him to. He had gone to his room and stood by the open window, looking down into the courtyard where the rain had started to fall. And it was no more than ten minutes later that the french windows of his father's study opened and Carson came out. Cade had stood on the threshold behind him, and Stephen had heard his father say quite clearly:

"That's all, Corporal. Don't you come back here, because there'll be no more. Do you understand me?"

"Right you are, Colonel," the man had said, giving the same mocking salute that Stephen had seen earlier. Then he had walked away up the drive, making no effort to protect his head from the falling rain. Stephen had stood watching him until he disappeared from view.

Nearly a year passed before Stephen saw the man again. It was May, but he was wearing the same old greatcoat, and he had come into the courtyard shouting and waving a pistol in the air. He'd obviously been drinking. His sunken cheeks were bright red, and there was an alcoholic slur to his voice.

"Come on out, Colonel," he'd shouted. "And bring your pretty wife too. I've got something to tell her about France. About being a war hero."

Stephen had watched the pistol, wondering if it was loaded, but he never got to find out. His father came out of the front door holding a rifle and fired it twice, aiming just above Carson's head.

The shock caused Carson to drop his pistol, and Cade walked over quite calmly and picked it up.

"You could have killed me," said Carson, and Stephen, standing in the corner of the courtyard, could hear the fear and the anger equally present in the man's voice.

"I will. Next time I will," said Cade, and in one fluid movement he turned the rifle in his hands and hit Carson with the butt, full on the side of the head.

Carson fell to his knees, but amazingly the blow did not knock him out.

"You'll have no more from me. I won't tell you that again," said Cade. "Now get off my property."

Carson got up, holding his head, and began to stagger away down the drive. But after no more than a hundred yards, he turned around again.

"Watch your fucking back, Colonel," he shouted. "I'll find you when you aren't looking. You'll see."

Stephen knew better than to ask his father about what had happened. Instead he had told his mother when she came back from the hairdressers in Oxford later that afternoon. Silas was away at school.

She had wanted to go to the police, but Cade wouldn't hear of it.

"He needed to be taught a lesson. I've done that, and now he won't come here again. You can trust me, my dear."

And Clara had left it at that. She had always trusted her husband, and there was no reason to stop now. Except that Stephen felt sure that his father did not believe his own optimism. It was only two weeks later that electronic gates were installed at the manor house and Sergeant Ritter began work on a new security system. Not that that saved Stephen's mother.

Stephen did not want to think about that black Christmas. He did what he always did when he started to remember it. He began to count quickly, thinking about anything except that. The day the lights went out.

After the funeral he'd been sent away to school. Stephen knew what his father was thinking. He looked too much like his dead mother, and if it hadn't been for Stephen's Christmas present, she'd still be alive. Cade had stayed in his room when the car had come to take his sons away, and when they came back at the beginning of the holidays, Sergeant Ritter was installed in the east wing with his silent, frightened wife.

Stephen thought that Ritter would have come to live at the manor house earlier if it hadn't been for his mother. Clara had always had an aversion to the sergeant, and it was an aversion her sons shared. Particularly Silas. Ritter was an expert at identifying a person's weaknesses and then probing them relentlessly until his victim could stand it no more. Except that Silas never allowed his obvious anger to get the better of him. Ritter called him Silent Silas, or sometimes just Silence, and the name became increasingly appropriate.

Stephen could never forget those long horrible evenings around the dinner table at the manor house in the years after his mother died. Ritter, with his short curly black hair and his huge double chin, dominated the conversation, asking Silas when he was going to get a girlfriend, wondering why he didn't have one. Stephen felt desperately sorry for his brother but powerless to protect him. The sergeant was too clever, too frightening.

Cade, meanwhile, would sit at the top of the table with a half smile playing across his features, and Ritter would watch him out of the corner of his eye until the professor gave an imperceptible nod, and Ritter ended his performance for another night. Stephen wondered if Silas had noticed their father's control over the obnoxious sergeant. He must have. Perhaps Silas did hate his father. Perhaps Swift was right.

No. Stephen was not Cain, about to spill his brother's blood. It wasn't Silas who'd accused him of murder, and he had no right to accuse Silas, however convenient it might be for his barrister. Stephen wished he could speak to his brother, but Swift had explained that the law said prosecution witnesses must not talk to the defendant.

Stephen remembered how his brother never wanted to cross their father. Silas always wanted the old man's approval. Like with the letter. Silas had refused to go with him to confront his father about what it said. It was Stephen who had broken with the old man and left the manor house estranged. Silas had remained behind, even though he knew what their father had done. To those poor defenceless people. They had survived the war, but they didn't survive Colonel John Cade. Stephen shut his eyes, trying to hold back the anger and disillusionment that he always felt when he thought of his father's crime. And shame too. A terrible shame that he was the son of the man who had killed the Rocards. Shame that he had remained silent for so long about what he knew. It felt too much like collusion.

It was nearly two and a half years ago now that the letter had come. June 1957. It was a year after Ritter had brought Stephen's father back from France with a bullet wound in his lung, and Cade had been an invalid ever since, often sleeping in his study because he couldn't make it up the stairs to his bedroom or the manuscript gallery on the second floor. He'd retired from the university and he had no visitors. He had had the respect of his academic colleagues but not their liking and, looking back, Stephen suspected that they must have been glad to see the back of him.

Moreton Manor had become a fortress that Cade never left. Ritter ran the house, patrolled its boundaries. More than once he'd cross-examined Stephen about the man in the greatcoat, but no one had seen the man since his last visit six years before.

Ritter seemed to be everywhere: At a turn in the staircase or at the end of a corridor, Stephen would suddenly come upon him. The brothers called him the tree frog because of his double chins, and he was truly an ugly man—big black glasses over his small mean eyes and his great stomach bulging inside huge trousers held up by wide, garishly coloured suspenders. But then he could move so quickly and quietly when he wanted to, turning up when you least expected him. Although he refused to admit it to himself, Stephen was secretly frightened of the sergeant, and perhaps he would not have had the courage to confront his father about the letter if Ritter had been home. But Ritter was away on business the day the letter arrived, and it was Stephen and the housemaid who had to help Cade to his bed when he suddenly felt sick and faint.

Returning to the dining room, Stephen found Silas sitting in their father's place at the head of the table, reading the letter. Stephen had always disapproved of his brother's interest in the private affairs of his fellow human beings. Spying and eavesdropping were not honourable activities in Stephen's book, and at first he refused to read the letter that Silas held out to him.

"All right, I'll read it to you then," Silas had said impatiently, closing the door of the dining room.

It wasn't a long letter, and Stephen could still remember its awkward wording, as if it had been written by a foreigner or someone trying to disguise his identity.

"Colonel," the letter had begun. Not "Dear Colonel" or "Colonel Cade." Just "Colonel"—the same name that the visitor in the greatcoat had used for Stephen's father six years earlier when he had emerged from the trees and stopped Stephen at the gate.

> *Colonel,*
>
> *I saw what you did at Marjean. You thought no one saw and lived but I did. I saw the bodies and the fire, and I saw what you took. I want what you took. Bring the book to Paddington Station in London and put it in the locker that is marked 17. Bring it yourself and use the key that is in this letter. Do it on Friday. In the morning. If you do this, I will be silent. If you do not, I will go to the police. In France and in England. You know what will happen.*

There had been no signature on the letter, and the message and the address on the envelope had been typed. It had been posted in London the day before, Monday. The envelope contained nothing else except a tiny silver key that Silas had already shaken out onto the tablecloth.

There was no time for the brothers to talk about the letter before Cade reappeared to reclaim it. And Stephen was astonished at the speed with which his brother replaced paper and key in the envelope as the door opened. Their father's face was very pale, and he went to the drinks tray in the corner and poured himself a generous measure of whisky before he left with the letter in his hand. It was the only time that Stephen ever saw his father drink alcohol at that time of the morning.

Afterward, Stephen spent the best part of an hour arguing with his brother about what to do, but Silas was adamant. He would not talk to their father about the letter. It was as if Silas knew more than he was saying about what the writer meant. Or perhaps it had just been Silas's dislike of direct confrontation. He was certainly frightened of his father.

Ritter was due back on the following day, so Stephen decided not to delay. He needed to know what his father had done. The man was cold and distant, but he was also a genius and a war hero. Stephen had spent hours with his mother as a child, examining his father's medals. In the young Stephen's imagination, Colonel Cade had marched through France with Eisenhower and Montgomery, liberating the country from the Nazis. But what if it wasn't true? What if his father was instead nothing more than a murderer and a common thief? What did that make Stephen? He had to know the truth.

He felt his heart pounding in his chest when he knocked at the door of his father's study. He longed to run away but forced himself to stand still waiting for the door to open.

"Stephen, I've been expecting you."

Cade was smiling, and he put an arm around his son's shoulder as he ushered Stephen to one of the leather armchairs in the centre of the room and sat down opposite him in the other. Stephen had never sat with his father like this, like they were equals, and it made his spirits soar. He had never wanted to believe in another human being as much as he did then.

"You're worried about that letter, aren't you, Stephen?"

Stephen nodded, wondering how his father knew that he'd read it. Perhaps he'd overheard him talking to Silas.

"Well, I can understand that," his father went on, without a word of reproof to Stephen for reading it. "But it's not true, you know. Not one word of it. You remember that man, Carson, who came here? The one with the gun?"

"Yes."

"Well, he wrote it. He hates me."

"Why?"

"I don't know exactly. He was passed over for promotion. Fell on bad times. Blames me for some reason. It doesn't really matter. The main point is that he tried to kill me last year. Damn near succeeded. And now he's written this letter to try to lure me somewhere where he can have another go. But he won't succeed, Stephen. Your old man's not going anywhere."

Cade smiled encouragingly at his son, and Stephen smiled back. He felt better already but he knew he couldn't leave without asking about what the man had written in the letter. He needed to know that his father had done nothing wrong.

"What's Marjean, Dad?" he asked, swallowing hard so that his question came out almost as a whisper.

Cade didn't answer immediately but instead looked at his son meditatively as if deciding how far he could trust him.

"I feel I owe you an apology," he said finally. "You're a grown man now and I should have more confidence in you. I've tried to shelter you too much since your mother died. I see that now."

"Thanks, Dad."

"Marjean's a little town in Normandy. No more than a village really. There's a château and a church. I went there in the war with Carson and the sergeant. Carson was a corporal then."

"After D-day?"

"That's right. It was a bad time. The Germans were a cruel lot at the best of times, but by that time they were losing and that made them vicious. They'd been using the house as a headquarters, and we ambushed them when they were leaving, but we were too late to save the family. It wasn't the first time that happened or the last. War's an ugly thing, Stephen."

Cade got up and went over to a filing cabinet in the corner of his and took out two documents fastened together with an old paper clip.

"Here, read this," he said, giving them to Stephen. "Then you'll understand."

It was a British military report on the events at Marjean château on August 28, 1944, and everything was set out in black and white. Before they left, the Germans had taken the owner of the château and his wife into the church that was no more than two hundred yards from the house. There was an old family servant there too, and the Germans had shot all three of them. Then they had set the house on fire and an old woman, perhaps the wife of the servant, had died in the flames. The Germans had even shot the dog. This was how they had repaid their hosts' hospitality. They'd been thorough as always.

The report had been written by Cade and cosigned by another officer whose signature Stephen couldn't read. Attached to it was a shorter handwritten document bearing the signature of a Charles Mason, Army Medical Officer. He stated simply that he'd been called to the church at Marjean by Colonel John Cade on August 28, 1944, and been asked to examine three dead bodies dressed in civilian clothing and located in the crypt. He had extracted bullets from each of the deceased and was able to say that they were of German origin, fired from Mauser pistols of the type then in use by the German army.

The documents seemed entirely authentic, and they were enough for Stephen. He wanted to believe his father, and so he did believe him. He had stayed on at school for an extra year and had got a place at New College to study history, and his father seemed proud of his achievement. The start of term was only two months away, and Stephen was busy planning how to decorate his rooms. Outside it was summer and everything seemed full of hope and possibility.

But Stephen's mood didn't last. One night less than a week later, he had just got into bed and turned out the light when Silas knocked on his door.

Perhaps if Stephen had known where they were going, he would have refused to follow his brother down the west-wing stairs, out through the door into the night, and round the back of the house. But Silas's air of mystery drew Stephen forward, and when they got close to the study window, Silas's hand on his arm meant that Stephen would have had to struggle to get himself free. The window was open, and Stephen was not prepared to risk discovery. And he needed to hear what Ritter and his father were saying. They were talking about the letter.

One time only Stephen raised his head above the windowsill to look in, before Silas pulled him back. There was no light in the room except from the green reading lamp on his father's desk. Ritter and Cade sat in the leather-backed armchairs in the centre of the room with their heads close together. They were talking about what to do, and it didn't take Stephen long to realise that he had been lied to. The men inside the room were cold-blooded killers, and they were about to kill again.

"There wasn't anyone else, Colonel. You know that as well as I do." It was Ritter talking. His voice was soft but pressing, with the usual tone of false jocularity entirely absent. It made Stephen feel cold inside, even though the night was warm.

"I hope you're right." Cade sounded anxious, petulant almost, like a man who craves reassurance but can't accept it when it's offered to him.

"It's the house that worries me, Reg," he went on after a moment. "You should have searched it before, when you got the book."

"Maybe I should've done. But you wanted to get them in the church straight away. It was your call."

"I wasn't going to stand there asking them questions out in the open."

"And the church was safe. You knew that because you'd been there before." Stephen sensed a slight impatience in the sergeant's voice as if he'd been over this ground many times before. "The point is that it didn't make any difference," he went on after a moment. "No one left the house while we were in the church or Carson would've seen them. It wasn't that dark, and he had a view of all the exits. I asked him about it afterward, and he had no reason to lie."

"He had no reason to shoot me."

"That was twelve years later," said Ritter. "No one got away. I'm sure of it. You found everyone you expected to. You told me that yourself."

"I didn't know about the old woman."

"Fine. And she burnt up like a stick of old firewood."

Ritter laughed harshly, but Cade didn't join in.

"That was Carson too," he said, sounding even more agitated than before. "He caused that fire. He didn't need to shoot back like that. He must have seen the lamp in the window. He knew the risk. Maybe what I really wanted was in that house. It hurts not knowing whether it was there or not. It'd be easier to know it was destroyed than not to know one way or the other. Part of me wishes there *had* been a survivor."

"Well, there wasn't. Just you and me and Carson."

"I don't know how he even made corporal," said Cade quickly. "I should have killed him when he came here before."

"You couldn't. Not with the boy watching."

"No. Maybe not. But I didn't realise then how persistent he would be," said Cade. "The best thing would have been not to have got the bastard involved in the first place."

"There's no point in going over all that again, John. You thought we needed him at the time, and I agreed with you. We didn't know how many Germans there would be, and we had to have a lookout. For afterward."

"Afterward," repeated Cade bitterly. "That's when I talked about the book. And the cross. Babbling about them like some idiot schoolboy. Making out as if they were the most valuable things in the world. I wouldn't have said anything if it hadn't been for the fire."

"How valuable *is* the book?" Ritter's voice was suddenly much softer than Cade's. It made Stephen shiver.

"It's worth money. But no more than some of the other manuscripts here. And that's not why I wanted it. I needed it because of where I thought it would lead me. But it hasn't. All it's done is get me a bullet in the lung and this bastard Carson stalking me. I don't think he even wants the codex. It's double Dutch to him, and he couldn't fence it even if he wanted to. He just wants to hurt me, because he's got it in his head that I'm the reason he's poor and unsuccessful. And shabby. God, you should have seen him when he came here the second time, Reg. He looked like a tramp."

"I wish I had," said Ritter. There was no mistaking his meaning.

There was silence for a moment before Cade spoke again, and then the fretful note was back in his voice.

"You're sure it's him, Reg. Nobody else?"

"I know it's him. There were no witnesses and no survivors. Nobody except him. Look, give me that again." There was a sound of paper rustling. Ritter was obviously reading the blackmail letter. "Here. Paddington Station's where you're supposed to meet him. And he lives just round the corner from there. Or at least he used to. In some dive up above a paper shop. I visited him there once. And seventeen's probably his lucky number."

"Was his lucky number." Cade laughed. "What are you going to do to him, Reg?"

The sadistic curiosity in his father's voice was too much for Stephen. Swallowing the bile that had suddenly come up into his throat, he took an involuntary step back from the window. Several twigs had blown down with the leaves from the nearby grove of elm trees earlier in the day, and one broke now with a snap under Stephen's foot. Inside the room Ritter reacted instantly, pushing back his chair and crossing to the window. But Silas was quicker, pulling his brother down and round the corner of the house into the darkness.

Less than six feet away from where they were standing, the brothers could sense Ritter at the window peering out into the night.

"What is it?" asked Cade from inside the room.

"Nothing. Some animal," said Ritter. "Nobody's going to get into these grounds anymore. We'd hear the alarm if anyone tried."

"I hope you're right. So what *are* you going to do to him?" Cade repeated his question, once Ritter had come back from the window.

"I'll deal with him."

Just four words, but so full of meaning. Ritter would murder Carson when he found him. Stephen was sure of that. After a hearty breakfast at some local café, he'd go upstairs to Carson's flat and shoot him full of holes.

"When?" Cade's voice was soft now too.

"Soon," said Ritter. "I'll leave tomorrow. If there's anything I need to know, you can send a message to the usual place. But leave it to me. I'll take care of him. It'll be a pleasure."

The next day, true to his word, Ritter was gone. Stephen didn't see him leave. He'd been up most of the night, tossing and turning in his bed until he had fallen into an uneasy sleep just as the grey light of the early dawn had started to seep into his room.

In the far corner, Stephen's collection of children's books was carefully arranged on wall-length shelves. Most of them were about heroes. Stephen had known for a fact that his father was a hero for as long as he could remember. It explained why he could not get close to his father, however hard he tried. Heroes lived in their own world, an English version of Mount Olympus, and they couldn't be expected to worry too much about mundane things like children. People like Stephen's father had their hands full making discoveries and saving the world. Cade's coldness had just made his younger son love him even more, and his wholesale rejection of the boy following his wife's tragic death had done nothing to change Stephen's inmost feelings.

Stephen never really knew what he was going to do when he grew up, but it would be something that would change the world. He would follow in his father's footsteps. Except that now he knew where those footsteps led.

Stephen felt as if he had lost his hold on everything. His father's shame was his shame. And yet he could not stand aside and do nothing. He had to make a stand. And for that he needed Silas.

Dressing quickly, he went in search of his brother and found him eventually, crouched over a tray of developing fluid in a makeshift darkroom that

Silas had created in one of the unused cellars under the west wing. And Stephen had to practically force his brother out into the sunlight. He had no intention of discussing inside the confines of the house what they had overheard.

The brightness of the day did not accord with either brother's mood. Stephen had torn a piece of green wood from the branch of an oak tree and was using it to behead the stalks of nettle and cow parsley growing in the hedgerows beside the road, while Silas walked with his head hunched over between his shoulders, as if hiding from the sun overhead.

"I can't believe it," said Stephen, angrily swishing his stick from side to side through the still air. "He lied to me about everything."

"What did you expect him to do?"

"I expected him not to have killed those people. In a bloody church too."

"Well, I'm sorry you couldn't keep your illusions. That's part of growing up, I guess."

"What? Finding out our father's a mass murderer?"

"He's not my father."

"Well, he's the nearest you'll ever get to one." Stephen paused, regretting his words. "Sorry, Silas," he went on after a moment. "I know it's not easy being adopted, but it doesn't mean you haven't got a responsibility."

"For what?"

"For saving this man Carson for a start. The sergeant's already left. But perhaps you didn't know that."

"Just because Ritter's gone doesn't mean he's going to kill Carson," said Silas doggedly. "I don't recall Ritter saying he was going to do that."

"Not in so many words. But that's what he meant. It was clear as a pikestaff. Don't be so bloody naïve."

Silas glanced up, and it seemed like there was a ghost of a smile playing around his thin lips.

"We've got to do something," said Stephen insistently.

"What?"

"I don't know. Warn the man. Go to the police. Do something."

"We don't know where he is to warn him. And you better think carefully before you go to the police."

"Why?"

"Because of what'll happen to Dad if you do. That's why. Maybe you can get him to stop the sergeant."

"You! Why not we?"

"Because I don't want to," said Silas, raising his voice for the first time. "It's all so easy for you, isn't it Stephen? Running around like a knight in shining armour dealing out justice right, left, and centre. But you don't know what it's like to have as little as I have. Maybe, if you did, you wouldn't be so happy to throw it all away."

"What's that supposed to mean?"

"I won't get involved. That's what."

"You weren't so reluctant when it came to dragging me round to Dad's window last night, were you?"

But Silas would say nothing more. It was as if a wall had gone up between them, and they walked back to the house in an angry silence.

Outside the front door Stephen put his hand on his brother's arm, determined to make one last effort to get him to change his mind.

"This is about more than you and me, can't you see that, Silas? This is about right and wrong. You've got to draw the line somewhere. You've got to stand up and be counted."

Stephen could feel Silas's arm tighten under his hand. Silas hated to be touched. But Stephen didn't let go. He needed an answer.

Finally Silas looked up into his brother's eyes, and Stephen felt the distance between them open like a chasm.

"Count me out," said Silas. He almost spat out the words.

And Stephen lost his temper. Letting go of Silas's arm, he raised his open hand in one fluid movement and smacked his brother across the face. Immediately he regretted what he had done, but it was too late. Silas gave him one last look of pure hatred and ran into the house.

Sitting in his prison cell, Stephen remembered that look in Silas's eye. Did his brother hate him still? Stephen didn't know. The truth was that Stephen could not read Silas. He had always been the opposite of Stephen. He held everything back, while Stephen wore his heart on his sleeve. Stephen was always the favourite, and yet Silas never complained, never protested, not even about Stephen's staying at home all the time he was away at school. There was something unknowable about Silas, and Stephen had always felt the distance between them as a reproach. He couldn't help it that he was the natural son, the favoured child, but it still made him feel guilty. Stephen wanted to be a good person, and Silas made him feel that he wasn't.

As he grew older, Silas had seemed to cultivate a studied politeness. He spoke slowly and carefully, as if he had thought out exactly what he was going to say before he said it, and sometimes he seemed just like a puppet master, watching events that he had set in motion but refusing to participate in any of them. It was Silas who had engineered Stephen's estrangement from their father and had then reunited them less than a month before the old man's murder. Why? John Swift wanted Stephen to point the gun at his brother, but Stephen wouldn't—or couldn't. To accuse Silas would be to betray himself. It wasn't Silas who had shot their father in France or sent the blackmail letter. That was Carson. But Carson was dead. And if it wasn't Carson who had shot John Cade, then who had? Who had?

Stephen had never forgotten that day when he broke with his father. For the first and last time in his life, he rushed into the study without knocking. And looking up from a manuscript, Cade had needed no more than a moment to know that the time for pretending was over. He sat back in his chair and sighed, waiting for what was to come.

"You lied to me," Stephen shouted with tears in his eyes. "Everything you've ever said was lies."

"Who told you?" asked Cade, ignoring his son's accusation.

"You did," said Stephen with a bitter laugh. "I heard you talking last night. In here. You're guilty, Dad. Guilty of everything."

But Cade did not react to Stephen's anger. He sat silently, looking up at his son as if he was measuring him, and this only served to enrage Stephen further.

"Why?" he asked, half shouting, half crying. "Just tell me why!"

"It was an accident," the old man said. "Things got out of hand."

"An accident! Killing all those innocent people. It was a massacre. That's what it was."

But Cade shrugged his shoulders and opened his hands, neither agreeing nor disagreeing. "It was a long time ago," he said.

Stephen was dumbstruck, horrified by his father's apparent indifference to the enormity of his crime.

"So what are you going to do, Stephen?" the old man asked after a while, breaking the silence.

"Do? I don't know. I haven't thought about it."

"Well, before you do anything, think what a trial will do to me. It'll kill me, you know. I'm not a well man, Stephen."

Stephen looked at his father, disgusted by the pleading tone in his voice.

"This isn't about you," he said. "It's about what's right and wrong."

"All right. Well, think of your mother then, if you don't care about me. Is this what she would have wanted? To have her family disgraced?"

"It's you who did that. Not me."

"Please, Stephen. I haven't much longer to live. You know that. Going to the police won't solve anything."

Suddenly Stephen felt deflated. The fight went out of him as he realised that there was nothing he could do to change the past. His father was right. A trial would achieve nothing.

"What about Carson?" he asked in a flat voice, keeping his eyes on the floor.

"What about him?"

"If I keep quiet, Carson goes free. You'll call that psycho off. Yes?"

"Yes, I swear it. On Clara's grave I swear it," said Cade, suddenly animated as he sensed the chance of escape for the first time.

Stephen didn't know whether to believe his father or not. All he knew was that he had gone as far as he could go. He felt torn up inside. He couldn't stand to spend another minute in the man's presence.

"You're not my father," he said flatly. "Not anymore. I'm going, and I'm not coming back."

But it hadn't been that easy. The shame had followed Stephen wherever he went, growing inside him like a tumour, until he had finally gone home and ended up sitting in this prison cell, fighting for his life, paying for his father's crimes.

SEVEN

Trave arrived late, anxious to avoid if possible another encounter with Thompson, and earned himself a malevolent glance from the judge as the swing door banged closed behind him and he took a seat at the side of the court.

Silas was already in the witness box, and he kept his eyes fixed firmly on the floor as he answered the prosecutor's questions, studiously avoiding the eager stare of his brother, who was gazing at him expectantly across the well of the courtroom. Trave realised that it must be four months or more since the two had last met.

Unsurprisingly, Silas looked more ill at ease than when Trave had seen him at the manor house the day before, but there was the same lack of expression in his voice as he answered the prosecutor's questions, and the way in which he always seemed to think before he spoke made Trave more sure than ever that the young man was hiding something. Not for the first time Trave wished that he'd had the chance to interrogate Silas in that same windowless interview room at the back of Oxford Police Station, where he had questioned Stephen on the day after the murder. The trouble was that the evidence against the younger brother was just too strong. Trave had had no option but to charge the boy, and that had put an end to further investigation. Trave stirred in his seat, trying unsuccessfully to shake off his frustration and concentrate on the evidence.

"How would you describe the relationship between your brother, Stephen, and your father?" asked Thompson, getting straight to the point.

"When?"

"Let's say, in the last two years of your father's life. I don't think there's any need to go back further than that."

"They were estranged."

"They didn't speak to each other at all?"

"Not as far as I know. My brother was at the university, and my father lived at home. He never went out," Silas added, as if it was an afterthought.

"Why was that?" asked Thompson.

"He couldn't because of his health, but he was also concerned about security. Although less so toward the end. I don't know why. In the last couple of months he would sit outside in the garden sometimes, which he never used to do before. But he still didn't leave the grounds."

"What was wrong with your father's health?"

"He was shot in the lung while on a trip abroad about three years ago. He never really recovered."

"Was he working? During his last two years?"

"Yes. He'd retired from the university, but he was writing a book on illuminated manuscripts. That was his real field of expertise. Sasha helped him with the research, and I did the photography."

"What did that involve?"

"My father had his own collection, and I was mainly documenting that. He wanted to use as many of his own manuscripts as possible in the book."

"I see. This collection must be very valuable."

"Yes."

"And what did you believe would happen to the manuscripts after your father died?"

"I hadn't really thought about it. I suppose I assumed that Stephen and I would inherit from my father. That is until I heard him talking about his will with Sergeant Ritter."

"This is admissible hearsay, my lord. It will go to the defendant's state of mind," said Thompson, anticipating a defence objection.

"Very well, Mr. Thompson. Carry on," said the judge. He looked almost benign this morning. The trial was going well. The prosecution seemed to have everything: motive, fingerprints, and now a history of ill will between victim and defendant. Getting a conviction should be child's play.

Thompson turned back to his witness and asked Silas to tell the court about the conversation he'd overheard.

"They were in my father's study."

"And where were you?"

"I was in the corridor outside. I heard them talking about the will, and so I stopped to listen. They didn't see me."

"What did they say?"

"It was my father who was speaking. He was telling Sergeant Ritter that he didn't have long to live. I don't know how he knew that, but I assume his doctor had told him. And it was then that he told Ritter that he was intending to change his will. The house, my home, was going to become a museum for the manuscripts, and Ritter was to be one of the trustees." A note of emotion had crept into Silas's voice when he was speaking about the house, but it was immediately suppressed. "I don't know who the other ones were going to be," he added. "My father's solicitor, perhaps."

"How did you feel about what you heard?" asked Thompson.

"I was shocked. Obviously. I hadn't expected it. I suppose I felt betrayed."

"So what did you do?"

"I tried to talk to my father, but he wouldn't listen. It's hard to explain. We didn't have the sort of relationship where I could talk to him about things like money."

"Did you do anything else about the situation?"

"Yes. I went to talk to my brother, so that we could decide what to do. He was in his rooms at New College. Mary was there too, but I waited until she left."

"How did your brother react to what you told him about the will?"

"He was very upset."

"Just that. Upset?"

"He was angry too. You need to understand—Stephen was in a very confused state those first two years he was up at Oxford. Our father had always been very important to him, and when they quarreled, it was like . . ." Silas hesitated looking for the right word, "it was like a light went out somewhere inside him. He didn't seem to believe in anything anymore. I didn't see him very often but I know that he drank a lot. He tried to cover it up, but I think he was very unhappy."

"Please stop the witness from speculating, Mr. Thompson," said the judge, stirring in his seat.

"Yes, my lord," said Thompson. "Tell us, Mr. Cade, what you and your brother decided to do about your father's will."

"We agreed that Stephen should try to end his quarrel with our father. He is the natural son, whereas I was adopted. He always got on better with our parents when we were younger, and I—we—felt that my father might listen to him. Stephen's always been better at speaking his mind than I have."

"So what did you do?" asked Thompson.

"Do?" Silas seemed momentarily lost, remembering a childhood that he always tried to forget.

"Yes," said Thompson, failing to keep the impatience out of his voice. "What did you both decide to do in order to end your brother's quarrel with your father?"

"Stephen wrote a letter, and I took it back with me to Moreton and gave it to our father. He agreed to allow Stephen to visit, and my brother came out for lunch on the following weekend. He brought Mary with him."

"Was your father enthusiastic about the meeting?" asked the judge, holding up a hand to stop Thompson's next question. "How did he respond to the olive branch?"

Silas didn't answer for a moment, and when he did, he seemed almost surprised at what he was saying.

"I don't know. It was like he was indifferent. He didn't seem to care much what Stephen did. Whether he came or whether he stayed away."

"Why?" The single word escaped from Stephen in the dock as if it was a sudden exhalation of breath, and it brought an immediate response from the judge.

"You will be silent, young man. Do you understand me?" Murdoch's voice was harsh, meant to make Stephen realise the power arrayed against him. "If you are not silent, you will be removed."

Murdoch stared at Stephen Cade a moment longer and then nodded to Thompson to continue.

"How did the lunch go?" asked the prosecutor.

"It was okay," said Silas. He had looked up at his brother for a moment when Stephen had shouted, but now he had reverted to his former posture with his eyes fixed on the dark wood of the witness stand in front of him. "I mean, it was fairly awkward," he went on, "but that was only to be expected. Stephen hadn't seen my father for two years."

"Was the will discussed on that day?" asked Thompson.

"No. I don't think Stephen saw my father alone, and there was obviously nothing said about it at the lunch. Anyway, Stephen wasn't going to talk to my father about the will straightaway. That only changed because of what I saw in his diary."

"What was that?"

"An appointment for my father to see his solicitor at three o'clock on Monday, June eighth, about the will."

There was something too precise about Silas's recollection of time and date, thought Swift, leaning back in his chair. It was frustrating. He wanted the chance to rattle Silas Cade and see what came out, but his client wouldn't let him. Swift was convinced that Silas knew more than he was letting on.

"Is this the entry you're talking about?" asked Thompson handing up the same engagement diary that he had shown to the solicitor the previous day.

"Yes, I saw it on the Wednesday. I was in my father's study getting something, and the diary was open on the desk."

"What did you do about what you'd seen, Mr. Cade?" asked Thompson, eager to move the story on.

"I told my brother. He arranged to come out to Moreton on the Friday evening with Mary, and he told me that he was going to talk to my father in his study at ten o'clock. That was the night my father was murdered."

"All right, let's deal with that night. Who was there at dinner?"

"Stephen and Mary. My father. Jeanne, that's Mrs. Ritter, and the sergeant. And me, obviously."

"What was the atmosphere like?"

"Strained. Like I said before, Stephen and my father hadn't been together for a long time."

"What time did the dinner end?"

"Nine o'clock, maybe. I can't be sure."

"And where did you go then?"

"I went to my room. I had some work to do. I was in there for a couple of hours before I heard shouting coming from the east wing, and so I went downstairs. My father was dead in his study."

"Where is your room, Mr. Cade?"

"It's in the west wing, but it faces east looking down on the courtyard."

"And were you alone during the two hours that you were in your room after dinner?"

"Yes. Completely alone."

"Thank you, Mr. Cade," said Thompson. "That's all I have to ask you. If you wait there, there'll be some more questions."

"May I speak to my client a moment?" Swift asked the judge.

"Very well. But don't be too long about it. The jury is waiting," said Murdoch.

Swift leant over Stephen in the dock, enveloping him in an intimacy that excluded the prison officers on either side.

"It's not too late to change your mind," he whispered. "Why don't you at least let me put it to him?"

"No."

"Are you sure?" he pressed. "Silas had a motive, and there's something he's holding back. I can feel it."

"I'm sure he didn't kill my father," said Stephen. His voice was soft but firm. "And I won't have you accuse him of it."

Swift turned away. There was no time for further argument. He'd already spent an hour with Stephen in the cells before court, trying to persuade his client to change his instructions, but he'd got nowhere. The die was cast.

"You have told us, Mr. Cade," Swift began, "that your brother and your father had been estranged for two years prior to your father's death."

"Yes."

"Tell us, please, what was the cause of that estrangement?"

The question seemed to agitate Silas. He looked over at his brother for a moment and swallowed deeply.

"I'd prefer not to answer that," he said.

"I'm sorry, Mr. Cade, but I must insist," said Swift. "It's important that the jury has the full picture."

When Silas still did not answer, the judge intervened. "Answer the question, Mr. Cade," he ordered. "You're a witness in a murder trial. This isn't some tea party."

"My brother believed that my father had killed a number of French civilians at the end of the war in order to steal a manuscript." Silas spoke slowly and with visible reluctance.

"And did you believe it?"

"Yes. I had to. Stephen and I overheard my father and Sergeant Ritter talking about what they'd done. My father couldn't deny it after that."

"And that made Stephen angry?"

"Yes. Angry and ashamed."

"And what did it make you feel?"

"I don't know. I felt bad, but I lived with it. Perhaps I don't expect as much from people as my brother does."

"I see," said Swift. "Now, I want to ask you about a blackmail letter that your father received two years before his death. You and Stephen read this letter, did you not?"

"Yes. That was when the trouble between them started."

"What did the letter say?"

"That the person had seen what my father did at this place called Marjean. He wanted the manuscript if he was going to stay quiet. My father was supposed to take it to him in London."

"Did he?"

"No. My father never left the house. Sergeant Ritter went. He said he was going to deal with the man. There were no more letters after that, or at least none that I knew of," said Silas, correcting himself.

"So Professor Cade and the sergeant seemed to know who had written the letter," said the judge.

"Yes. They were certain it was someone called Carson, who'd been with them at this place—Marjean. My father said he was the one who shot him in France."

"Carson," said the judge repeating the name.

"Yes," said Silas.

The judge made a note on a piece of paper and nodded to Swift to continue.

"You told the court earlier that your brother decided to seek a reconciliation with your father about a week before his death," said Swift.

"Yes."

"And that this decision was because of what you'd told your brother about your father's intention to change his will."

"Yes."

"But that wasn't Stephen's only reason for going to Moreton, was it, Mr. Cade?"

Silas didn't respond, and so Swift answered his own question.

"You said to your brother when you visited him that you'd overheard your father telling Sergeant Ritter that he didn't have long to live. Isn't that right, Mr. Cade?"

"I told Stephen a lot of things. That was just one of them."

"But it upset him, didn't it, to hear that his father was going to die?"

"He was upset by everything I told him," said Silas. "Angry too."

"Angry," repeated Swift. "But that doesn't mean that he said that he was going to harm your father."

"No. We wanted to get our father to change his mind. About his will."

"Did you ever see your brother with a gun?" asked Swift, changing tack.

"No. Not that I remember."

"Are you sure? Didn't Sergeant Ritter make you and Stephen fire his pistol in the garden once?"

"Yes," said Silas after a moment. "I'm sorry, I forgot about that. We didn't want to, but he made us."

"He nailed a target to one of the oak trees, and you and Stephen took turns shooting at it."

"Yes."

"How did your brother do?"

"I don't remember."

"He missed every time, didn't he, Mr. Cade? He didn't even hit the target."

"I told you. I don't remember. I was concentrating on what I was doing."

"And how did you do?"

"I was better than my brother, but that doesn't make me a marksman," said Silas, suddenly defensive.

"Thank you. No more questions," said Swift, resuming his seat.

EIGHT

There was a table in the corner of Stephen's unbelievably small cell deep inside Wandsworth Prison. It had no legs but instead opened out directly from the wall. Table legs could be used as a weapon, and the authorities were taking no chances. Stephen had arranged the few personal possessions that he had brought with him on the surface of this table, and in the centre was a framed photograph of Mary. It had been taken a few weeks after they first met, when the world had been an entirely different place and he'd been as happy as he'd ever been in all his life. She was standing on a bridge and the wind had blown up her brown hair into a whirl around her face. She was wearing a white cotton shirt and a linen skirt and she was laughing. Stephen remembered the moment. They had been walking across Port Meadow, and Mary's straw hat suddenly blew away on the wind. Stephen had pursued it, jumping uselessly from tussock to tussock until it had sailed down into the water and been borne away on the current. And Mary had laughed almost until she cried, making her look impossibly pretty, with her lips parted to reveal her perfect white teeth, her dark eyes full of life. Stephen had got out his camera and taken a photograph. Then they had continued on past the boats and the swans and the swaying poplar trees to a high stile, and when he had put out his hand to help her over, she had kept hold of it as they walked up the

path to the Perch. Stephen remembered that day so clearly. They had sat outside in the pub's garden drinking low-quality white wine and he had told her
all about his family: his dead mother and his soon-to-be-dead father and the
terrible crime that Colonel John Cade had committed fourteen years earlier
in a small French village called Marjean.

He had to tell someone, because the truth was that Stephen had never been
able to get the place out of his head since that night when he and his brother
had crouched below his father's study window and heard the truth for the first
time. God knows, he'd tried. From his first day at New College he'd thrown
himself into student life. Politics was his passion—changing the world; and
the river winding under the willow trees, the quiet quadrangles, and the college chapel with Epstein's statue of Lazarus, who turned in white burial
clothes while rising from the dead, were all invisible to him as he hurried
through the medieval streets to some meeting of bearded socialists in the back
of a crowded pub or rushed off to London to march against the bomb. Then,
suddenly, he was at the end of the first year and the exams were upon him. He
stayed up all night for a week and just scraped through. And in the summer he
worked picking fruit for a month before he took off and traveled through Eu-
rope, eating almost nothing so that he'd have enough money for the train
fares. He went through France and northern Italy and even a bit of Switzerland before he realised where he was really going and wound up outside the
ruins of Marjean Château on a hot afternoon in late August. The sunlight
glistened on the glassy dark blue surface of the lake, and blackbirds flew in and
out of the empty paneless windows of the gutted house, and at the top of the
hill the church was locked with a rusty padlock. Stephen had never experi-
enced such emptiness. The people who had lived here and loved this place were
all dead, and there was nothing he could do to redeem what had happened to
them. He had nothing to offer, no solution to the terrible silence, and so, after
only a few minutes, he turned tail and walked quickly back up the overgrown
drive, ignoring the thorny branches that snapped back on him as he passed,
cutting his bare arms and face. On the main road he thumbed down a passing
truck and hitched a ride all the way to Rouen.

Afterward he couldn't get the place out of his head. He cursed his own
curiosity, wished he hadn't gone to Marjean. He was drinking more than a

bottle of wine every day when he went to the Playhouse one afternoon early in the new year at the suggestion of his friend, Harry Brooks, and met a young actress called Mary Martin for the first time.

Except that it wasn't the first time. He was sure of that now. She'd been sitting on one of the stone seats in the college's medieval cloister about a week before when he came round the corner one evening, burdened with two heavy bags of pamphlets that his action group had had printed at the University Press.

Half the cloister was dark even on sunny days, since two of its four sides were in the shadow of a great oak tree growing in one of the corners, and it was long past sunset when he saw her. In fact, the only light came from the moon hanging overhead, and Stephen could hardly make out the woman's features, although he stopped when he came upon her and dropped his bags on the ground, arrested by her unexpected presence, almost jumping to the conclusion that she was a ghost, the spurned wife or mistress of some long-dead professor. But then he'd remembered that he didn't believe in ghosts and been about to apologise when the woman got up and walked away. They hadn't exchanged a word, but still, looking back now, almost a year later, he was certain it was Mary whom he'd seen in the cloister.

The strange part was that, all the time they were together, neither of them had ever referred to that first encounter. At the beginning he couldn't be sure it was her, and later he'd forgotten all about it, but now he couldn't get the memory of that January evening out of his mind.

And then the following Saturday after that first meeting, Harry came to his rooms with two tickets for a play. It was some forgettable melodrama, and Stephen never went to the theatre. He had more important things to do. But Harry insisted. He'd met this pretty actress at a party and she'd given him the tickets for the matinée, with an invitation to come backstage afterward. Stephen went reluctantly, complaining all the way, but then, when the curtain went up, he sat transfixed by the girl with the beautiful chestnut hair and the liquid eyes, whom Harry pointed out was the actress from the party, the one who'd given him the tickets. Stephen felt sure he'd seen her before, but he couldn't remember when. She was so alive, it was as if he could feel the red lifeblood pumping through the myriad of blue veins under her unblemished skin.

Afterward, Harry took him backstage, and there she was, looking back at him from a mirror hung on the wall of the dressing room, with her blouse half unbuttoned so that he could see the beginnings of her breasts. She smiled at him, and he sensed her understanding of his confusion. He stammered out some compliment about her performance and she laughed. It was infectious and it came from deep inside, and he laughed too, forgetting his awkwardness in the doorway.

"And so you must be Stephen," she'd said, and he had never asked her then or later how she knew his name before they'd been introduced. He just assumed that Harry must have told her at the party. The way she said his name had made him feel that she had singled him out, selected him for whatever was going to happen next. Harry stood forgotten in the corner. He felt ill treated, but there was nothing he could do, and his friendship with Stephen didn't survive that afternoon.

But Stephen didn't care. He was in love, and the next day, in the early morning, Mary met him outside the front gates of New College and they went cycling away into the countryside. Mary had brought wine and sandwiches, and once or twice they stopped to drink, sitting on the roadside grass, which was still wet with the morning dew. But Mary wouldn't tell him where they were going, until she suddenly turned off the main road just outside the village of Burford and freewheeled down a grassy path to the ruins of a medieval manor house, standing on the bank of a fast-flowing river called the Windrush. She said the name of the house was Minster Lovell, and it reminded Stephen irresistibly of Marjean, although he didn't mention that to Mary. The present was good: an escape from his father and the past.

They sat in the shadow of a silver-grey tower with curving, well-worn steps that led up into thin air, and Mary told him the story of Francis, the last of the Lovells, who'd shut himself up in a secret room beneath the manor house after joining in a failed rebellion against King Henry VII at the end of the fifteenth century. An old servant had brought him food and all was well for a while, but then the servant died and Sir Francis Lovell, unable to get out of his hiding place from the inside, slowly starved to death. Two hundred years passed and no one knew his fate, until a party of workmen broke into the underground chamber by accident and found a skeleton sitting at a table with its hand resting on a pile of papers, which crumbled into dust with the sudden ingress of outside air.

Mary delighted in stories like this. Another time she took Stephen to a little nondescript cottage down by the canal and told him about an Oxford bargeman who had once lived there with his young wife. One day he had come back home unexpectedly from work and found his wife in bed with his neighbour, and so he picked up a hammer and killed the man. He was restrained before he had time to start on his wife.

"What happened to him?" Stephen asked.

"They didn't hang him because it was a crime of passion," said Mary. "They locked him up for twenty-five years instead. But the wife was already pregnant with the other man's child, and she gave birth just a few days after the trial."

"And then?" asked Stephen, realising that there was more to come.

"The bargeman did his time and got released early for good behaviour, and the same day he got out he killed his wife and her son, even though twenty years had gone by and the young man had nothing to do with what had gone before."

"What a bastard," said Stephen. "Did they hang him then?"

"They didn't need to. He killed himself. He'd done what he'd been waiting to do, you see? His revenge was complete. There was no more reason to stay alive."

"How do you know all this?" he asked.

"Books. Chapters in guidebooks. They come with being a tourist."

"You're not a tourist. You work here," said Stephen, seeking reassurance that she wouldn't be going away.

"The play won't go on forever," she said. "I'll have to find other work when it's over."

But the season was extended and they didn't return to the subject of separation for a while.

They were terrible stories that Mary told him, the stuff of nightmares, but she never explained why she felt the need to tell them. Stephen just accepted the stories with everything else that came with his new girlfriend. She made the rules and he was only too happy to play by them, if it meant that he could be with her. He could think of nothing else. It was as if she had him under a spell. And in truth Stephen was happy to submit himself to Mary. She gave him back the love he'd lost when his mother died. She put the magic back into his life. And telling her about Marjean seemed to have exorcised his ghosts, at least for a while.

But then sometimes she would disappear for days without a word. Stephen hated her absence, but he knew better than to complain, and anyway he wouldn't have known where to look even if he had tried to track her down. She'd told him she was sharing a flat somewhere in North Oxford with another actress, but Mary never invited Stephen there, and he never met any of her friends or relations—except Paul, and that was only in passing.

Paul was Mary's brother. And the first Stephen knew of him was one morning soon after he and Mary had become lovers. He'd slept late into the morning, and not for the first time. Being with Mary seemed to have this effect, turning him from a virtual insomniac into a deep sleeper who sometimes slept ten hours a night.

There were voices in the room next door. One of them was Mary's; the other Stephen did not recognise. Pulling a dressing gown around him, Stephen opened the door. Mary was standing over by the window talking to a tall, well-dressed man with a bony face and short cropped hair. They both seemed startled by his sudden entrance. Mary was the first to recover her composure.

"I'm sorry, Stephen. I didn't want to wake you," she said, coming toward him with a smile. "This is my brother, Paul. He had some news to tell me that couldn't wait."

"Hullo," said Stephen awkwardly. He had a strange sense of being an intruder in his own rooms, and being half dressed put him at a disadvantage.

And there was something off-putting about the man. There seemed to be no warmth in his narrow eyes, and he didn't look like Mary at all. He nodded a response to Stephen's greeting and turned away, picking up a briefcase that he'd left on the floor by the door. And it was as he turned the handle of the door to leave that Stephen noticed he was wearing gloves.

"I didn't know you had a brother," said Stephen, after Paul had left. "You never mentioned him to me before."

"There was no reason to. He's quite a bit older than me and I don't see him very often. He wouldn't have come here unless it was urgent."

"What's wrong?"

"Our mother's sick again. I must go and see her for a couple of days."

Stephen *did* know about Mary's mother. One evening soon after they first met Mary had told Stephen all about her. She was a Frenchwoman who had come to England in the 1930s to marry Mary's father, an Englishman who hadn't survived the war, dying like so many others on the shores of Normandy in 1944. And Mary had grown up in Bournemouth of all places—Mary's mother had been told by her doctors that the sea air would be good for her delicate health. They spoke French at home after Mary's father died, and Mary's slightly accented English stood her in good stead when she started out acting in repertory theatres along the south coast after she left school. It gave her a touch of glamour and won her roles that she might not have got otherwise.

Stephen was impressed by Mary's success at earning her own living, but he could never quite come to terms with her acting. Her transformation on stage into another person excited and frightened him all at the same time. In the week after they first met he went to see her perform almost every night, but afterward he preferred to wait for her at the stage door. It was easier that way.

The truth was that Stephen was jealous of this other world that Mary inhabited. It increased her attractiveness but also made him uneasy. And he had the same feeling when he thought about her brother, although in fact he only saw Paul once more before the end. It was one evening about a month later, and Stephen was returning from a lecture. It started raining suddenly, and he stepped into a coffee shop for shelter, and there they were, Mary and her brother, sitting at the back, deep in conversation. He thought of going up to them but something held him back, and, with a start, he realised that he was feeling something very close to jealousy, which was of course absurd. Conquering his hesitation, he called out Mary's name and waved to get her attention. She seemed flustered when she caught sight of him and spoke quickly to her brother before she smiled, beckoning him over. And, by the time he got to the table, Paul had got up to go. He nodded to Stephen without speaking, and there was the same blank expression in his eyes that Stephen had noticed at the time of their first encounter. And then he was gone.

"Your brother doesn't seem to like me much," said Stephen, sitting down in the chair that Paul had just vacated.

"It's not that," said Mary. "He was in a hurry."

"Obviously."

"All right," she said, smiling. "You're right. He was rude. And I'm sorry he was. It's because he's shy. He's not academic, literary, like you. He doesn't feel at home here."

"So where does he feel at home?"

"London," said Mary briefly.

"Then why does he come here?"

"To see me. He is my brother, you know. It's your choice that you hardly ever see yours."

And they began talking about Silas and Stephen's father and all the reasons why Stephen had left his past behind, until it was time to go home and Stephen didn't even remember that Mary had changed the subject.

Summer had almost arrived and the play's run had long since finished, but Mary had stayed on in Oxford, and Stephen had no idea how she was supporting herself. They'd never talked about money, until she told him one afternoon that her mother's health had become much worse to the point that she urgently needed an operation that could only be performed in Switzerland. It was an unusual illness that had something to do with her heart, although Stephen never understood the details. Just that it would cost a lot of money. Mary said she'd have to go away and get a part in Manchester or London unless she could raise what she needed here in Oxford. It was his fear of losing Mary just as much as pressure from Silas that made Stephen write to his father, asking to come home, and the old man's last act before he died was to refuse to give his son the money he needed for Mary, even though he had more than enough money to fund a hundred operations. If Stephen had won the game of chess, he could have had the money, but he had lost, and so he'd got nothing.

Stephen remembered like it was yesterday the mean, tight-lipped way in which his father had refused him. Enraged, he'd practically run out into the courtyard, gasping for air, because God knows what he would've done if he'd stayed in there with the old bastard. Instead, as it turned out, he'd left his father behind for the last time, because, in the few minutes that it took him to walk to the gate and back, someone calmly went into the study and shot John Cade in the head—put an end to him once and for all and left

Stephen to pay for something he'd never done. Who had it been? Who had it been?

Stephen banged his head against his hands in frustration, but there was no relief from the incessant pounding of the thoughts inside his brain. His life hung on the answer to a question, and he was no nearer to solving it than he had been on the night of his arrest.

NINE

Ritter had woken up as he always did at half past five. He didn't need an alarm clock. His sleeping and eating were set to an internal timer that ticked away somewhere deep inside his big frame, measuring out the days of his life.

He got out of bed almost immediately, crossed to the window, and pulled back the curtains, allowing the early morning light to fill the room. He stretched for a moment and then walked into the bathroom. Stripping himself naked, he looked at his big bulk in the mirror, and an expression of self-satisfaction settled over his features. He washed noisily and shaved before settling to the detailed task of clipping back the tiny rogue hairs that had grown out of his military moustache during the night. Finally content, and clothed only in a towel, Ritter went back into the bedroom and sat on the edge of the bed nearest to his sleeping wife.

His. Mine. The possessive pronoun was always uppermost in Ritter's mind when he thought of Jeanne. She was pretty and foreign and desirable, and she belonged to him and nobody else. When he used violence against her, he took care never to leave any mark on her face or her hands or her calves. She was living proof that Reginald Ritter counted for something in the world. He owned her, and she was worth owning. Ritter wasn't blind. He'd seen men looking at his wife, knowing they couldn't have her because she belonged to him. As always the thought acted on Ritter's psyche like an aphrodisiac. He laid his hand on his wife's shoulder and turned her over to face him. The force of the movement woke her, and he was in time to see the fear in her eyes before the usual unreadable mask descended over her face.

Roughly, Ritter used his right hand to pull open his wife's nightdress while his left hand retained its grip on her shoulder.

"No, Reg. No. Not today."

Ritter loved his wife's voice. He loved the Frenchness in it. The way she rolled the *R* when she called him by his name. It inflamed him, and he climbed onto the bed and forced himself into her, even though he had previously intended to do nothing of the kind. Today was an important day. He and Jeanne were going to London to give evidence. Ritter relished the thought of it: all the lawyers and the newspapermen listening to him and Stevie in the dock waiting for the noose to be fitted round his neck.

Beneath him his wife lapsed into French. "Non, non." The words came out in small cries, and Ritter ignored them just like he always did. Instead he gathered her white breasts in his big hands and thrust himself deep inside her one last time, before he subsided down onto her body, half crushing her with his weight.

Ritter had already chosen his wife's dress for the day. Conservative black with a high collar. Ritter would have liked a veil too, but this was a court of law, not a church. Now he lay back on the bed, spent, and watched Jeanne move about the room, allowing his mind to wander back through their mutual past.

Fifteen years before, he'd found her standing in the remains of a kitchen in a burnt-out house in Caen. Incongruously, she'd been holding an umbrella, as if it might protect her from the catastrophe that had overtaken her family. Her mother was dead on the other side of the room, lying in a mess of apron and blood and broken china, and there was no trace of any other members of her family, even though she told Ritter afterward that her father and a lodger had also been living in the house. That was when she got her voice back. At first she could not speak at all. Ritter visited her every day in the hospital until the army moved east. She had looked at him and said nothing, but he felt that she belonged to him. After all, she had nowhere else to go.

All the time he was away, Ritter couldn't stop thinking about her pale blue eyes set in the small oval of her face and the way she kept entwining her fingers in her lap. She was waiting for him in Caen when he came back from Germany nine months later, and she looked just the same, except that the nuns at the hospital had cut off most of her long auburn hair. It made her look even more vulnerable than before, and Ritter wasted no time marrying her. The colonel had been their only witness.

Jeanne had become part of Ritter's identity. But that did not mean that there was any real communication between them. Her English was far from perfect, and Ritter spoke almost no French. And in truth he had never had any idea how to talk to women. Perhaps it was that even more than his physical ugliness that explained his complete lack of success with the opposite sex until he found Jeanne. And she of course had had no choice.

Ritter missed the army. Its vertical ranking of men made sense to him. On civvy street after the war he'd drifted from one job to another, living in London bed-sits with Jeanne, eking out a living. The colonel had sent him money, and Ritter knew he'd have done more if it hadn't been for his wife. She'd never liked Ritter. He was bad with children, and she was always obsessed with her younger son. Stevie this and Stevie that. Ritter didn't know how the colonel had put up with it, although at least the younger boy had some spirit. The elder one just snuck about, taking photographs of people, listening at their keyholes. Ritter had enjoyed tormenting him on those long evenings after he and Jeanne had come to live at the manor—in the good days after the colonel's wife died, smashed to bits in a car wreck. Silas had taken photographs of that too. Little bastard. And now he owned the place. One day he'd gather up enough courage to tell Ritter to leave, and there would be nothing that Ritter could do about it. He half wished that it was Silas, and not Stevie, who was on trial for murdering the colonel. Except that Silas would never have had the guts to kill anyone, let alone his father. And all the evidence pointed to Stevie. Ritter had caught him red-handed.

Ritter missed the colonel. He missed him terribly. He missed those long evenings in the study, sitting in the tall leather armchairs smoking cigars and remembering the war. The colonel had given him a home and an income and a place in the world. He'd made Ritter think well of himself. But now the sergeant was cut adrift, at the mercy of Silas Cade.

Downstairs in the kitchen, Ritter fried sausages and bacon on the stove.

He stood in his shirtsleeves, methodically turning the cooking food, enjoying the smell of the sizzling fat in his nostrils. He had the place to himself, and he basked in the solitude. The kitchen in the morning made him think of his own father. As a child in Nottingham, he'd sat on a stool in the corner watching his father eating, making big doorstep sandwiches, filling his flask for the mine, until one day when he didn't come back and Ritter ran away to join the army. Anything was better than going underground.

Sasha came in when he was finishing his breakfast, sitting at the deal table under the window, and he looked up annoyed. Silas had stayed the night in London to be closer to the court, and Sasha was never usually around this early in the day. He hadn't expected to be disturbed.

"You're up early," he said, wiping egg yolk from the corners of his mouth with an already-soiled napkin.

"Yes." Sasha remained in the doorway, looking down at Ritter, making no effort to conceal her disgust.

"Do you want something?" he asked. He'd expected her to leave once she saw him, avoiding him as she usually did around the house, but today was different for some reason.

"Yes, I want you to leave your wife alone. That's what I want," she said defiantly. "She's crying again upstairs in case you didn't know. I heard her as I came down."

"What did you say?" asked Ritter, unable for a moment to believe his ears. Sasha's audacity astonished him, and he sat rooted to his chair with his mouth half open, gaping up at her.

"I said you better leave Jeanne alone. Because if you don't, I'll make sure you don't."

Sasha's voice shook but she stood her ground and the threat jolted Ritter into life. A wave of anger swept over him. What he did with his wife was his business. Not bloody Sasha's. He got to his feet, violently pushing his plate away so that some of the uneaten food spilt over onto the table.

"You'll make sure I don't, will you?" he shouted, advancing on Sasha across the room. "And who the hell are you to give me orders if you don't mind me asking?"

"I'm a private citizen protecting another private citizen. That's all. And if you hit me, you'll just make it worse for yourself."

Ritter paused. His arm had been raised, but now he lowered it to his side. Sasha was right. He didn't need trouble. Not today of all days, when he and Jeanne were going to London to give their evidence. He breathed deeply, working to control his temper. It was something he was good at, and it didn't take him long.

"It wouldn't be the first time someone's hit you, I suppose, would it, Miss Vigne?" Ritter's voice was quiet now, almost casual sounding.

"What are you talking about?"

"That burn you're so worried about. Always wearing high collars, changing your hair style, hoping we won't notice. But we do notice, you know. We notice all the time. Everybody does."

It was Sasha's turn to become angry. Her cheeks flushed a deep red and she had to fight down the impulse to put her hand up to her neck in that same self-protective gesture that had become second nature to her over the years. Ritter smiled and his eyes glinted as he sensed her vulnerability.

"Funny to be so pretty and so ugly all at the same time," he went on musingly.

"Damn you!" Sasha spat out the words. It was as if they had been physically expelled from deep inside her body.

"And fuck you too, Miss Vigne," Ritter said evenly. "Not that that's something very likely to happen anytime soon, I imagine."

They stood staring at each other for a moment, their roles reversed. Ritter was now fully in control of the situation, and it was Sasha who was on the defensive. Enjoying his advantage, he picked up his napkin from the table and dabbed it around his moustache, watching Sasha's hands clenching into fists at her sides.

"My advice to you, Miss Sasha Vigne, is to stay with your books. Much safer than poking your nose into other people's business."

There wasn't room for the two of them in the doorway and Sasha instinctively backed out of the way, avoiding contact with Ritter's big bulk as he went past her. It felt just like a defeat.

Upstairs, Jeanne cried a little as she washed away the traces of her husband from her body. Sometimes the marks he left couldn't be removed so easily, and inside she always ached with a dull pain that never quite went away. But over the years she had learnt to live with Ritter's petty cruelties. She knew that showing fear or anxiety enraged him, and so she had grown a mask for her emotions that she rarely let slip. She had worked out how to survive, and she would no doubt have passively grown old that way if Silas Cade hadn't made her realise there was an alternative.

At first she had only felt a dull sense of kinship toward the colonel's elder son. He was her husband's public victim; she suffered in private. At dinner she always said very little, keeping her head modestly bent down over her plate while her husband made bad jokes about Silas's sexuality. In truth, she herself suspected that Silas was homosexual. He never seemed to look at her, and anyway it was none of her business. Life was something to be survived. She wasn't looking for friends.

Then one day she was in the laundry washing her husband's clothes. It was hot and steamy, and Jeanne pulled up the white sleeves of her blouse almost to her shoulders. The laundry was a place she could be alone, and she felt no risk that anyone might come in and see the red marks on the inside of her forearms that her husband had left the night before. The work was hard, and she didn't hear Silas walking in the corridor outside or see him as he stood in the doorway watching her.

Afterward, Silas was amazed that he had spoken to Ritter's wife. It was so unlike him. Women scared him. He thought about them all the time, but he never had the courage to approach them. He was almost painfully aware of his own physical shortcomings, and his rejection by his mother after Stephen's birth had wreaked havoc on his inner sexuality. Her death had sealed him up complete with his damaged personality, and Ritter's jibes in the years that followed had found their mark partly because Silas half believed them himself. His sexual experience was limited to a single night two years earlier, when he had got very drunk and visited a prostitute in Oxford. The result had been disastrous, and Silas had concentrated all his mental energy for weeks afterward on expunging the memory of his failure in that dingy third-floor bedroom overlooking the canal. He was still frightened that he would come face-to-face with the woman somewhere in the city, although it hadn't happened yet.

The marks on Jeanne's arms were what gave Silas the courage to cross the threshold of the laundry and speak to her. He'd asked her what they were, even though he already knew the answer. If Ritter was a sadist at the dinner table, there was no reason why he should change his spots when he took his wife upstairs to bed.

Jeanne flushed and did not answer. Instead she pulled her blouse down to her wrists and turned away, and perhaps that would have been an end of it if her husband had not come calling. He'd lost a cufflink and wanted his wife to find it for him. Silas was still close enough to Jeanne to feel her aversion, the way she physically shrank away from her husband's voice, and instinctively he reached out and pulled her back against the wall. A moment later Ritter was in the room, blinking against the steam. Silas sensed the sergeant on the other side of the open door. He felt the weight of the man, and he strengthened his hold on the sergeant's wife. Silas had never before been so frightened or felt so alive. Jeanne's heart was beating hard against his chest as she leant into him. It was as if their bodies had made a decision for them, and now they were powerless to stop the ongoing course of events.

After Ritter left, Jeanne emptied the clothes from the laundry baskets onto the stone floor and then pulled off her own to add to the heap. Her nakedness inflamed Silas, not only because he thought her beautiful but also because of her defiance. Then and afterward, the thought of Ritter was never far from either of their minds when they made love. They were settling scores with passion.

At first they were happy. Ritter was often away on business, and the Professor never left the manor house. His health had deteriorated since he had broken with his younger son, and there was a grove of trees near the west wall of the grounds where Silas and Jeanne felt safe from detection. It was invisible both from the professor's study and from the manuscript gallery on the second floor.

Jeanne lay on the floor of pine needles and unwound the mane of her rich auburn hair so that it fell across her lover's knees. Looking dreamily up through the treetops toward the sun, she told him the story of her past. She'd kept her family dead and buried deep inside herself all the years she'd been married to Ritter, but now they came to life again. Her father had been the local postman, and in the years before the war she and her younger brother would walk out with him into the countryside beyond Caen after his rounds were over for the day. They took straw baskets and picked blackberries in the hedgerows, and Jeanne looked for the wild woodland flowers to take home to her mother, who wouldn't be separated from her kitchen. She always kept one back for her father to wear in the buttonhole of his green tweed jacket.

Philippe, her brother, was ten years old and still he couldn't read or write. But he made up for it by his innate kindliness. If you asked him to fetch the coal, he would do it again and again until you had to order him to stop. He had curly black hair and was a little overweight. Everyone loved him and wanted to protect him. Except that when it mattered, they didn't. After the Germans came, they built a house for backward children on the coast, and one morning, when Jeanne's father was out at work, the nurses came and took Philippe away. There were other children in the truck, and there was no real time to say good-bye. Jeanne never saw her brother again, and after that day her father stopped taking her out into the countryside. Instead he began to drink too much red wine in the evenings and took to singing patriotic songs out of key. He swore to Jeanne and her mother almost every day that he would protect them from the Nazi bastards, but in the end, when the British came, he hadn't been able to save himself, let alone anyone else. He'd been caught in the cross fire just like so many others.

Jeanne wept when she thought of her father and her mother and Philippe and everything she had lost. All the emotions that she had kept battened down since she left France thirteen years before rose to the surface and burst through the floodgates of her self-control. She emptied herself onto Silas, and it wasn't long before he began to feel suffocated by her. All his life he had learnt the virtues of self-restraint. To show your heart only meant more hurt from adopted parents or bastards like Ritter. And the truth was that Silas couldn't have exposed himself to another human being even if he had wanted to. He had long since locked himself up and thrown away the key. He couldn't provide Jeanne with the emotional response she craved, and so she began to make him angry. But he took care not to show her what he felt. He wanted her, and besides, he was frightened of Ritter. Silas tried not to think of what the fat man would do to him if he ever discovered the truth.

But sometimes he didn't succeed. There was one day that Silas would never forget as long as he lived. It was the summer after his mother died, and he had gone into his father's study, as he sometimes did, early in the morning when he was sure that no one was around. The professor never got up before ten, and Silas thought that Ritter was away on business. He sat at his father's desk and idly opened the drawers one by one. Ritter found him with several letters in his hand. Silas didn't have time to replace them in the drawer from which he'd taken them. The sergeant had done that, keeping hold of Silas's wrist as he did so. And then he'd squeezed. Lightly at first, and then harder and harder still. Silas hadn't tried to struggle. It was as if the pressure of Ritter's thumb had paralysed him. It felt like the sergeant was exploring him in some horribly intimate way. Silas remembered how Ritter had looked down at him from above. There was a look of rapt concentration on his face, and then, just before the end, the tip of Ritter's tongue had come out, flicking round the corners of his big mouth.

The physical pain had been bad, but the shame afterward was worse, far worse. Silas felt as if Ritter had looked deep down inside him—at his guts, his intestines, his liver and kidneys. And after he let go, Ritter only said one thing: "No more sneaking about, Silence, you hear me. You know what I'll do if I catch you again, don't you? You know what'll happen next time."

And Silas had known. He didn't need to be told. He could imagine exactly what it would feel like when the sergeant's big hand reached between his legs and took hold of him down there.

Silas was frightened, and so he was forever urging caution on Jeanne. It made her think that he didn't really love her, and part of her didn't want to be careful. It was almost as if she wanted her husband to know what she was doing to him. But now her meetings with Silas became less frequent, and when they met, they argued. Silas wanted to finish the affair, but he didn't have the courage to tell her how he felt. He couldn't let her reach the point where she had nothing left to lose.

In truth, he grew tired of Jeanne. It wasn't in Silas's nature to want what he already had. Instead he lay awake at night and thought of Sasha, who seemed so entirely indifferent to him. Now when he met Jeanne in the trees out near the west wall of the manor grounds, he would close his eyes and pretend that she was Sasha. And afterward, in the evening or the early morning, he would return to the same place with his camera and focus his telephoto lens on Sasha's windows. Sometimes he'd get lucky. The curtains would remain undrawn, and he could take photographs. He kept them under lock and key in his room and gazed at them at night when everyone was asleep. There were several of Sasha in her robe, leaning over with her breasts partially exposed, and one where she was naked with her back to the camera. It was extraordinary, the contrast between her perfect neck and her burnt, ravaged shoulders.

Jeanne guessed nothing of all this. She knew that Silas often avoided her, but she put this down to his almost irrational fear of her husband. For her it was different. Now that she had begun to live a little bit, Ritter seemed less significant. Once or twice she even caught herself laughing at his situation. He guessed nothing of her infidelity. He carried on abusing her without once imagining that she was cuckolding him with the colonel's son.

Jeanne stepped out into the corridor but then paused before going downstairs, looking out through a tall narrow window at the grey, overcast sky. A big wind was blowing the elm trees from side to side, and Jeanne felt glad of the coat that she carried over her arm. In the kitchen she could hear her husband washing the plates from his breakfast, but it wasn't fear of him that made her hesitate in the hallway. She was too busy remembering the past. Closing her eyes, she could hear the running and the shouting all around her once again. She had stood exactly here, a few paces back from the thick front door, waiting for the right moment to pick up an overcoat and hat that had fallen on the floor. When everyone had gone, she'd hung them back on the rack and then stood waiting behind the locked door for the police cars to arrive.

"Wake up, Jeanne. You look like Lot's wife. Not mine."

Jeanne turned, startled out of her reverie. Ritter was inches behind her, his fat face creased with laughter. She hadn't heard him coming. He must have crept up on her. It was a favourite trick of his. For a big man, he had an uncanny ability to move almost soundlessly, and he always enjoyed the moment of shock induced in his victim when he suddenly announced his presence behind them. It was juvenile, but Jeanne had long ago realised that her husband was at bottom extraordinarily immature. He pursued his own pleasure, usually at the expense of other people, and was able to do so with such single-mindedness because he had no capacity to imagine what they were feeling. He was entirely without empathy. It was what made him capable of first raping his wife before she had even had time to wake up, and then playing a practical joke on her half an hour later.

Ritter had never really grown up. That was the key to understanding him. It made him both strong and weak. He had considerable native cunning, and he was almost entirely unrestrained by conscience. But he wanted to be led—to be led and to be loved, and the colonel had given him what he needed. In the army and afterward. Now, with the colonel gone, Ritter felt lost. He ate even more than ever—big breakfasts like today—but it did nothing to fill the emptiness that he felt inside.

Ritter had understood nothing of the colonel's manuscripts, but John Cade's desire to own things and people had made perfect sense to him. The colonel's ruthlessness and singularity of purpose had been the qualities that Ritter most admired in his leader. John Cade had made him feel special, and later, in the last years when the older man had become frail and frightened, Ritter had found fulfillment in protecting him. Except that he had failed. He could protect Cade from the outside world but not from his sons. The younger one had put a bullet in his father's head, and the older one had probably put the younger one up to it. Ritter hated them both. He felt that *he* was Cade's true son, and today was his day to honour the dead.

Ritter put his hands on his wife's shoulders and turned her round as if she was on a pivot. By and large, he was satisfied with what he saw.

"You'll give your evidence standing up," he told her. "Don't sit down even if they ask you if you want to. It puts you at a disadvantage. Every lawyer has his bag of tricks, so you be ready for them."

"Yes, Reg," said Jeanne, keeping her voice flat and compliant.

"And don't pull at your hands and your sleeves like you do at home all the time."

"No."

"I'll be watching you to see that you don't. You're to be a credit to me and to the colonel. Without us, you'd be nothing. You know that, don't you, Jeanne?"

"Yes, Reg."

"Turning tricks in some seedy French town. That's what you'd be doing to make ends meet."

This time Jeanne didn't reply, but she didn't need to. Ritter, amused by the image that he had summoned up from the depths of his imagination, had burst out laughing. And he was still laughing as he eased the car into second gear and turned out of the manor gates onto the road to London.

TEN

Detective Constable Clayton wouldn't have admitted it for the world, but the truth was he felt intimidated by the Old Bailey. He was only five years out of police training college, and he'd never given evidence at a murder trial before. It was just luck that had got him involved in the case in the first place. He and Watts had started the nighttime roster less than two hours before the call came in to attend at Moreton Manor. Clayton remembered his first sight of the victim. There was very little blood. Just a small hole in the middle of his forehead. The study looked like it was a theatre set down at the Oxford Playhouse, with the professor in his armchair at the centre of the stage.

They'd waited for Trave to arrive and then gone to work: asking questions of the people in the house, looking through their rooms, searching for evidence. Not that they'd found anything to move the finger of suspicion away from the main suspect. Clayton had felt sorry for him at the time. Stephen Cade seemed so young, even though he was in fact less than five years younger than Clayton. He and Watts had taken turns guarding him in the kitchen. He'd been noisy at first, shouting out his innocence and demanding to see a lawyer, but by the time it was Clayton's turn, Stephen had subsided into a quiet misery, sitting slumped at the long deal table with his head in his hands.

It was funny, his lack of bravado. He had to have planned the murder. The gun wouldn't have just been sitting in the study waiting for him to use it. He would have had to buy it from some black marketeer, weigh it in his hand, practice with it a few times, setting up a target in some deserted place, and then wait for his opportunity. Strange, then, that he should be so distraught after the event.

But that wasn't evidence. You had to concentrate on the facts and follow them where they led, and this was a fairly simple case: Stephen Cade had been caught red-handed. Most of the work had seemed to involve filling in endless forms, tapping away on the old Remington typewriter that had seen better days even before it became the property of the Oxfordshire Police. Still, it had been a privilege to work with Trave, and Adam Clayton hoped he'd have the chance to do so again. Trave was something of a legend in the local force. He was very good at his job. Everyone agreed about that. He got results, but he did not inspire affection. He had no nickname, and no one seemed to have ever visited his house. Trave's fellow officers knew where his lines were, and they took care not to cross them. He was a loner, and perhaps this was why he had not achieved promotion above the rank he'd held for the last fifteen years.

But Clayton had seen another side of Trave. It was standard practice for two policemen to attend autopsies, and Clayton had been picked to accompany Trave to the Cade postmortem. He'd thought he was prepared for the experience but had found to his shame that he wasn't. He'd felt violently sick even before the first incision and had been unable to conceal his distress. Trave hadn't wasted time asking him if he was all right. He'd just told the pathologist to wait, taken Clayton by the arm, and walked him out into the air. They'd crossed the road to a pub where Trave had ordered two whiskies and then waited for the younger man to regain his composure. And after that it had been all right. Not great, but all right. With Trave's help, he'd got through it.

Clayton half wished that Trave was with him now, but Trave had already given his evidence at the start of the trial, and so there was no reason for him to be in the witness waiting room. It was an airless place on the fourth floor of the courthouse with a row of small grimy windows above head height, which let in precious little light. Clayton sat at a Formica table with his back to the door, trying to distract himself with a copy of yesterday's *Daily Mail.*

"Mind if I join you?" Bert Blake, the police photographer, sat down opposite Clayton without waiting for an answer to his question. Some of the coffee from his Styrofoam cup spilled onto the table as he settled his large bulk into the chair, but he made no move to clear it up even when it began to drip down onto the floor between them.

Clayton groaned inwardly. Blake was a gossip. Always ferreting out information and then passing it on to people he hardly knew. He was a lonely man and gossip made him feel important, even though his indiscretions had already got Blake into serious trouble on several occasions. He was kept on because he was one of the best at what he did. His photographs left nothing to the imagination.

"When are you on?" asked Blake. His coffee was hot, and he spoke in between noisy sips.

"I don't know. They said it wasn't likely before this afternoon."

"Which means tomorrow," said Blake, with the knowledgeable air of someone who spent a good part of his working life lazing around in courthouse cafeterias waiting to give evidence.

"Do you think so?" Clayton was unable to keep the anxiety out of his voice, and Blake was quick to pick up on it.

"Is this your first time here?" he asked.

"No."

Surprisingly, Blake seemed to accept the lie and transferred his attention to a bar of half-melted chocolate that he had extracted from the pocket of his crumpled suit jacket. Clayton watched mesmerised as Blake slowly separated the runny brown chocolate from its purple wrapping, and he didn't notice Ritter and his wife come through the door behind him and sit at a table in the corner.

"Why do you say tomorrow?" Clayton repeated.

"Well, they've got the brother in there now—you know, the one with the funny name." Blake stopped and scratched his head as he made a vain search through the junkyard of his memory.

"Silas. Silas Cade," said Clayton.

"That's right. Silas. Well, I wouldn't mind betting that he's going to take some time."

"Why?" asked Clayton, curious in spite of himself.

"You know what I'm talking about. Your lot found some pictures in his room, which I'd be proud of. Naughty pictures. Taken with a telephoto lens."

"Who told you that?"

"A friend of a friend," said Blake mysteriously. He swallowed the piece of chocolate that he had just fitted into the corner of his mouth, and then leant forward conspiratorially toward Clayton.

"Did you see them?" he asked.

"No, I didn't search the rooms on that side of the house."

"But you heard about them, didn't you?" asked Blake with a leer.

"I heard that there were some photographs found but that they were returned to Mr. Cade because they weren't relevant."

The photographer's sudden proximity repelled Clayton. He pulled his chair away from the table and raised his voice instead of lowering it as he answered Blake's question. He wanted to keep Blake from coming any closer, but instead he succeeded in drawing everybody in the room into their conversation.

In the corner Ritter noticed the sudden alertness in his wife. She had been listening with a bowed head as he gave her a few last-minute reminders on how she was to give her evidence, and he had begun to be irritated as usual by the way in which she continually entwined her arms and hands. But now she became motionless, listening intently to the conversation between the big man in the dirty suit and the young policeman whom Ritter recognised from the night of the murder.

Blake was aware of the interest he'd aroused, and he seemed to enjoy the attention almost as much as he did Clayton's discomfort.

"They may not have been relevant," he said. "But they were certainly revealing. I can tell you that much. Slippery Silas must have had a tripod set up in the woods with the camera fixed on that girl's bathroom, trying to catch her getting out of the shower before she drew the curtains. That was his game."

In the corner, Jeanne Ritter blushed crimson. She was no longer a girl, but still she had no doubt that the fat man was talking about her. It all made sense. Silas avoided her because he was frightened of Ritter, but that didn't mean he didn't love her. He was watching her through his camera the entire time. She glanced up and met her husband's gaze for a moment, and then turned away. She could see his brain working, and it scared her. She didn't know what he would do if he ever found out about Silas.

Clayton saw none of this. He was fully occupied by his own embarrassment and remained completely unaware that two of the most important witnesses in the case were sitting only a few feet behind him. Hoping that his obvious lack of interest would stem the flood of Blake's revelations, Clayton picked up his newspaper and turned a page, but his clumsy attempt at a rebuff had the opposite effect of what he intended. Blake became even more voluble than before.

"He's obviously a pervert. Most of these amateur photographers are," said Blake, who obviously thought of himself as a model professional.

"I thought he had a shop," said Clayton, returning to the conversation reluctantly.

"Oh, yes. In some street off Cowley Road. It's probably just a front for him to sell dirty pictures under the counter."

"You've got no evidence for that." Clayton couldn't contain his irritation at Blake's air of self-satisfied certainty.

"I don't need any. There's a big market for that sort of thing, you know, particularly in a place like Oxford, with all those weird university types. Apparently this girl over at the manor had some tropical skin disease or something like that. A lot of people like that. Adds to the price."

Blake smirked, amused by the look of disgust written across Clayton's face. There was nothing he liked more than getting a rise out of police officers who were a bit green behind the ears. It was a small revenge for being stuck in a dead-end job. Police photographers remained just that. There was no promotion ladder for them to climb.

Clayton was still trying to think of some clever one-liner that would shut Bert Blake up once and for all, when Jeanne Ritter finally lost her self-control. Her husband had watched the colour drain from her face as she took in the impact of what the fat man was saying. Perhaps she would have been able to absorb the shock if she hadn't thought that he had been talking about her before. But now her eyes were opened, and she realised what a fool she had been. Silas had been avoiding her for months. Love struck, she had put it down to his fear of Ritter, when it should have been obvious even to her that he'd just lost interest.

Except that it was worse than that. Silas had got bored of her because he wanted Sasha Vigne. Jeanne felt wave upon wave of angry jealousy grip her body like electricity. She needed to get out into the open, and she pushed her chair violently back against the wall and ran out of the room.

Ritter got up as if to follow her but then resumed his seat. His wife was highly strung, and he knew she was worried about giving evidence, but that didn't seem enough to explain her strange behaviour. Still, there'd be time to ask questions later. For now, he had to stay put in the waiting room. The usher had told him on the way up that he was the next witness due in court.

Clayton followed Jeanne out. He'd turned around in time to see her sudden departure, and he felt he needed to talk to Trave about what had happened. The photographer watched Clayton leave with a grin and then turned his attention to the policeman's newspaper.

ELEVEN

Standing in the witness box, Reginald Ritter looked exactly like what he was: a sergeant without his uniform. His black suit, white shirt, and tie were pressed to military standards. His shoes shone and his thick moustache had been waxed at each end. He'd used more than half a bottle of expensive hair oil back at the manor in order to flatten his curly hair onto his scalp, and he had the overall appearance of a man eager to serve his Queen and country by giving evidence for the prosecution. It cheered Gerald Thompson up just to look at Reg Ritter. Here was the kind of witness he wanted. A military man. And that was where he'd start. With the sergeant's credentials.

"What do you do for a living, Mr. Ritter?" he asked.

"I'm between jobs at present. I used to work for Colonel John Cade. Up until he was murdered." Ritter shot a glance at Stephen in the dock. He hadn't seen the boy in months, and he liked what he saw now. Long hair, disheveled, slumped in his seat. This was getting to Stevie, and there was worse to come. Ritter had seen hangings. In France at the end of the war. They weren't a pretty sight.

"How would you describe your relationship with your late employer?" asked Thompson.

"Very good. He always treated me well, and I looked up to him. He was a brave and generous man, and the world's a worse place without him."

Ritter felt pleased. He'd practiced this little speech in front of the mirror at home, and now he'd got to say it in full, right at the start of his evidence.

"When did you first meet Professor Cade?"

"The colonel, you mean. I always called him that because we were in the war together. He was my commanding officer all the way from France in thirty-nine through North Africa in forty-two and back to France at D-day. We went all the way after that: Battle of the Bulge and into Germany. He was a war hero. Simple as that."

"And more recently you worked for the colonel at Moreton Manor in Oxfordshire?"

"Yes. My wife, Jeanne, and I went to live there in 1953, and we've been there ever since."

"Tell us about the relationship between the colonel and his youngest son, Stephen, during that period," asked Thompson, ready to focus in on the accused now that his victim's good character had been established.

"He was away at boarding school for the first few years that I was there, and then he had some time on his hands before going to university. It was the summer of 1957, and he was at the manor house almost all the time, causing trouble."

"What kind of trouble?"

"He had it in for his father. Wouldn't leave him alone, even though the colonel was a very sick man by then. Eventually Stephen left home, and then he had nothing to do with his father until a couple of weeks before the murder. Acted like he didn't exist."

"What happened then?"

"He wrote to the colonel asking to come out to Moreton, and the colonel agreed. He was generous like that. He didn't hold grudges. So Stephen came to lunch. Brought his girlfriend. And then they came again the following Friday to stay the night. I don't know what his game was, but that was the night the colonel was murdered."

"We'll come to that in a moment, Mr. Ritter, but I just want to ask you first about what you knew at the time about the colonel's testamentary intentions."

"His what?"

"His will."

"Well, I always knew he was going to leave me a legacy, if that's what you mean. I'd been with him a long time."

"Yes, I understand that, Mr. Ritter. But do you know what he was intending to do with the rest of his estate?"

"Well, in the last months before he died, he did talk about changing his will. He wanted the house to be a museum for his manuscripts. And he'd decided that I was going to be one of the trustees. Not because I knew anything about the manuscripts, but because he knew he could trust me."

"Who else knew about this?"

"I don't know. He was going to see his solicitor, but he obviously didn't get round to it, because he hadn't changed his will by the time he was shot."

Thompson paused before asking his next question. He'd like to have added that somebody must have got to the colonel first, but he wasn't entitled to comment, and besides, the implication was clear. The jurors weren't fools.

"I'd like to focus now on the murder itself," he said. "Tell us what happened on that night, Mr. Ritter."

"Well, Stephen and his girlfriend were staying the night, but otherwise I'd say it was a fairly normal evening. I don't really remember what we talked about at dinner. Afterward, the colonel went to his study like he usually did. He wasn't a good sleeper, and he did a lot of his work at night. Jeanne and I went to bed quite early. I don't know what anyone else did."

"Where is your bedroom? Use the plan if it helps you, Mr. Ritter."

"It's on the second floor of the east wing, with windows looking down on the main courtyard. It's next to the colonel's bedroom, and his study is directly below."

"Did you go to sleep?"

"Yes. With my wife. I was woken up because someone was shouting down below."

"Who?"

"I don't know. I'd just woken up. It sounded like a man, not a woman. I can't really say more than that."

"What was he shouting?"

"I don't know. It sounded like he was shouting for help, but it could have been something else."

"What did you do?"

"I got out of bed and ran downstairs."

"What about your wife?"

Ritter didn't answer at once. He closed his eyes, and the look of strained concentration on his face showed how hard he was trying to remember.

"I think she was already out of bed and over by the window when I got up. She probably left the room about the same time that I did. There was no time for me to say anything to her. I don't remember her being in the corridor outside the colonel's study. In fact, I don't think I saw her until quite a bit later," Ritter added.

"Tell us about what happened in the corridor."

"The shouting had stopped by the time I got downstairs, but I could hear someone moving about inside the room. I tried the door but it was locked. I know it was, because I kept trying to turn the handle. And that really alarmed me, because the colonel never locked the internal door, the one leading out into the corridor. So I started banging on the door, shouting that I wanted to be let in. I was hammering on it for at least thirty seconds, before I heard a key turn in the lock and Stephen opened the door."

"You heard the key turn. Are you sure about that? This is very important, Mr. Ritter."

"I'm one hundred percent sure. And when I got into the study, the key was in the lock on the other side of the door."

"What else did you find when you got inside?"

"The colonel was dead. I could see that right away. He was looking straight at me. Sitting in his armchair with a game of chess on the table in front of him. And I could see what had killed him too. There was a bullet hole in his forehead, right between his eyes, and the gun was on a table by the door. I didn't pick it up because I knew it would be evidence. And I didn't let Stevie get near it either. He'd done enough for one night."

"What was the defendant doing?"

"Walking round the room. Running his hands through his hair. Muttering things. I think it was Silas who got him out into the corridor. Or it might have been Sasha. I stayed in the room and called the police. I didn't bother with an ambulance. There was no point."

"Did the defendant say anything?"

"When?"

"When you got into the study. After he opened the door."

"He said that his father was dead."

"What was his tone of voice?"

"Quite matter of fact. Just like, he's dead, call the funeral director. I slapped him across the face with the back of my hand. I don't know what he was saying after that. He was muttering, like I said before."

"Why did you hit the defendant?"

"Because of what he'd done. It was obvious. You didn't need to be a mathematical genius to see what had happened in there."

"Thank you, Mr. Ritter. I've no more questions," said Thompson. He allowed himself one glance across at the jury as he sat down, and then had to hold himself back from rubbing his hands with glee. Almost all of the jurors were sitting forward in their chairs, looking alert. Ritter's evidence had obviously had a powerful effect on them. If he didn't have any doubt about what had happened in the study, then why should they?

"You assaulted my client, Stephen Cade, because you believed he'd killed his father. That's your evidence. Yes?" Swift asked his first question as if it was a challenge, and Ritter responded in kind.

"I didn't just believe it. I knew it," he said.

"No, you didn't. You weren't there when it happened. You came in afterward and jumped to a conclusion."

"The right conclusion."

"Well, let's examine that, shall we? You said that there was a bullet hole in the colonel's forehead, right between his eyes."

"Yes."

"And that didn't give you pause for thought?"

"Why should it?"

"Because you knew that Stephen was a terrible shot, that's why. You set up a target in the garden, and he missed every time. And yet he's capable, according to you, of dispatching his father like some gangland executioner."

"It was four years ago that I took him and Silas out in the garden. Anything could have happened since then. He could have learned to shoot like a marksman."

"I see. Well, let me ask you this, then. Did Stephen Cade try to escape?"

"No. He probably didn't think there was much point. He wouldn't have got far. I'd have seen to that."

"What he *did* do was cry out for help, and then open the door and let you in."

"I don't know whether it was his shouting that woke me up. It could just as well have been the colonel. And he didn't let me in straightaway. He waited and then he unlocked the door. I'd been hammering on the outside for at least thirty seconds."

"Why didn't you go round into the courtyard when you found the door was locked? You could have cut off his escape route that way."

"I didn't think of it. I wanted to get in the study. I was worried about the colonel."

"But when you got inside, the french windows were open, weren't they?"

"I believe so."

"Stephen Cade could have escaped?"

"I suppose so. He was probably just too shocked by what he'd done. He was behaving pretty strangely after he let me in. Like I said before."

Swift changed tack, realising that he'd gone as far as he could with the night of the murder. Ritter was proving to be a stronger witness than he had anticipated.

"I want to take you back in time, Mr. Ritter," he said. "Back to the summer of 1944. To a day when you and Colonel Cade went to a small country house outside the town of Marjean in northern France."

"We went there with Corporal Carson. There were three of us," interrupted Ritter. He spoke quickly and confidently. He'd been expecting this line of attack.

"Why did you go there?" he asked.

"The Germans were falling back all across the front. There were reports that they'd been using the house as their local headquarters. The colonel wanted to stop them from getting away and to ensure the safety of the French family living there. But we were too late. The Germans set the house on fire before we got there, and there were no survivors."

"What about the Germans?" asked Swift. "What happened to them?"

"We ambushed two trucks on the drive. I don't know if any others had already left."

"Why wait to ambush them? Why not go straight to the house, if it was on fire?"

"It wouldn't have been safe. There were only three of us."

"And why was that? Surely it would've been most unusual for a colonel to go on a dangerous mission like that, taking just two soldiers with him?"

"I don't know about that. I was just a sergeant. I was following orders."

"Your orders were, in fact, to kill the French family, not to save them, and to take something that was theirs. A valuable book. Isn't that right, Mr. Ritter?"

"No, it's a lie."

"You set the house on fire after you murdered them. To hide what you had done."

"No." Ritter half spat out the word. It was almost as if he was back on the parade ground issuing commands. "There was an investigation by the army," he went on after a moment, having regained his composure. "We were fully exonerated. They found German bullets in the bodies."

"But why would there have been an investigation? It was wartime, and you say you'd done nothing wrong."

"I don't know. The colonel wanted one."

"You're lying, Mr. Ritter," said Swift. "Both the colonel's sons heard you and him in his study, talking about what you'd done."

"No."

"Silas Cade has told this court what you said. And his brother will do the same."

"They're lying."

"Why should they be? Stephen had nothing to gain by quarreling with his father."

"I don't know about that. He had plenty to gain by killing him."

"And why should someone send the colonel a blackmail letter about what happened at Marjean if nothing did? Answer me that, Mr. Ritter."

"It must've been Carson who sent the letter. He was a born liar, and he always wanted money. He kept asking the colonel after the war, and the colonel was foolish enough to give him some. He gambled that away in no time, and then he wanted more. When the colonel said no, he developed a grudge against him. It became like an obsession."

"Why would the colonel have given him money?"

"Because he was generous that way. He shouldn't have done it. I told him not to."

"He gave him the money because he wanted to keep Carson quiet. About what he'd seen at Marjean. That's the truth, isn't it?"

"No."

Swift pulled his gown up around his shoulders, locking eyes with Ritter, before he asked his next question.

"Somebody had tried to kill Colonel Cade before, hadn't they, Mr. Ritter? Back in 1956?"

"Yes."

"Was that at Marjean?"

"Yes. We went there together. The colonel wanted to go back and see some of the places where we'd been in the war."

"And he came back in a wheelchair and became a recluse. Wasn't that when you helped him install the best security system his money could buy?" asked Swift.

"That's right. No burglar was going to get through that."

"And then came the blackmail letter asking the colonel to go to London. Someone couldn't get in and so they were trying to lure him out. Yes?"

"If you say so."

"What's your point, Mr. Swift?" asked the judge, who had been stirring impatiently in his seat for some time. "This history lesson is all very interesting, but perhaps you wouldn't mind telling us what it's got to do with the charge against your client."

"Certainly, my lord. I am trying to show that someone else, who was not my client, had been trying to kill Professor Cade for a long time before he was finally murdered."

"And my understanding is that Mr. Ritter is saying that it was this man, Carson."

"Yes, my lord."

"Well, you may well be right, Mr. Swift. But I don't see how it helps you. Mr. Carson was already dead when Professor Cade was murdered. He'd fallen from a moving train near Leicester after drinking too much alcohol. Inspector Trave found a newspaper article about what happened on the floor beside the professor's body. It's in his witness statement. Do you want me to read it to you?"

"No, my lord. I'm aware of the article. But, with respect, that's not the end of the matter. The defence suggests that the person who wanted to kill Professor Cade because of what happened in France was still alive on the night of his murder."

"What's the basis for that?"

"The Mercedes car outside the gate, my lord. And the foreigner who was stopped for speeding in it shortly afterward."

"The one who can't be traced?"

"Yes, my lord."

"Well, if that's your client's defence, I'm not going to stop you advancing it. The jury will be free to form its own conclusion. Do you have any other questions for this witness, Mr. Swift?"

"No. Nothing else," said the defence barrister, realising that there was nothing to be gained by carrying on with Ritter. He sat down heavily, trying to keep the sense of defeat that he felt inside from showing too clearly on his face. Judge Murdoch had done no more than demonstrate the weakness in the defence that he had been telling Stephen about for months. There wasn't enough evidence that the massacre at Marjean ever happened. And even if it did, there seemed to have been no survivors. And no witnesses except Carson, who was dead too. The man in the Mercedes was interesting, but he wasn't enough. There was no evidence that he'd got inside the grounds, let alone the house. There had to be someone else. An insider. But who? All the evidence pointed to Stephen. Perhaps he did kill his father, just like the Crown said. And this trial was just a waste of time.

Swift glanced back at the dock. Stephen was leaning forward in his chair, cradling his head in his hands. The barrister felt the case weighing him down like a stone around his neck. He wanted it to be over.

TWELVE

Ritter couldn't find his wife anywhere. He didn't search too hard, since he had better things to do. She was probably crying somewhere. At the back of the women's toilets with a wad of tissues in her hand, maybe. Ritter didn't suspect her of any wrongdoing with Silas. That would have been an enormity beyond his wildest imaginings. But he had understood enough of the policeman's conversation with the man in the dirty suit to realise that Silence had been taking long-distance photographs of Sasha. Perhaps he'd taken some of Jeanne too, when Sasha's curtains were drawn. Nasty little sneak. Ritter made a mental note that he needed to see the photographs, and then he'd have a few words to say to Silence. Ritter smiled. He thought about taking hold of Silas's delicate white hands again—women's hands, they were—and squeezing them, gently at first, and then harder and harder, watching the surprise and then the pain registering on Silas's thin sallow face.

That's what had happened with Carson. Sitting in an empty second-class compartment of the intercity express with dirty Midland towns rushing past the grimy window. Cigarette butts overflowing out of the metal ashtrays and a few tears in the cushion covers of the seats. They'd sat side by side just like old pals, and Ritter had poured Bell's whisky into the yellow plastic toothbrush mug that he'd brought along for the purpose. Glug, glug, glug. The whisky had loosened Carson's tongue, got him talking about the old times.

Arab women in North Africa, French women in Rouen. Carson and his whores and all the money he'd frittered away in second-rate casinos. It made Ritter want to puke. But he'd kept his hands off the little shit long enough to move the conversation round to the blackmail letter and the shooting at Marjean. Carson had pretended not to know anything about them, and the funny thing was he'd carried on saying that right up to the end. Ritter had put a gag in Carson's mouth while he'd broken his fingers one by one, but that was a punishment. Ritter had given up on trying to get any worthwhile information out of the chubby corporal by then. And when he'd taken the gag out and held him at the open door near Leicester, ready to throw him out, Carson had been saying the same thing: "I didn't do it, Reg. I had no reason to. I swear I didn't, Reg."

That was the last thing that Jimmy Carson said before Ritter pushed him down to his death: "I didn't do it, Reg." But he did. It had to be him. And the colonel didn't have any doubts either. Those last few months, the old man had slept better than he had in years. He was frail obviously, and he was always going to be an invalid—Carson's rifle bullet had seen to that. But he was more like his old self again. He'd go out on the lawn, sit on the bench under the honeysuckle, talk about the future, and not worry so much about the past. Ritter had wished at the time that he'd found Carson sooner. It had taken him nearly two years. The bastard had changed his name and disappeared, gone west maybe. He only reemerged when his mother died. Like some pathetic old East End gangster, Carson had always loved his mother. Ritter knew that, and he'd had her watched. Funny, though, that Carson had waited to visit her until after she was dead, when there was no point anymore. He'd got word that Ritter was after him, and so he'd gone to ground. And that was a sure sign of his guilt. You didn't need a confession for a conviction. Look at Stevie. Still protesting his innocence back in Court number 1, trying to cheat the hangman.

Ritter smiled. Giving evidence had been easier than he thought. He'd known that he'd be asked about Marjean. Stevie was fixated on it. That was the reason he'd quarreled with his father. Couldn't stand the thought of a couple of Frenchies getting potted. He'd probably have even objected to the dog. So Marjean was going to come up, and Ritter had been prepared for it. He'd remembered what the colonel had told him fifteen years before. If you've got to lie, lie well. And Ritter had lied well. Solemnly and on oath, and the jurors had believed him. He'd watched them and he knew. And then the judge had weighed in and told them that it was all irrelevant anyway. Carson was the only other witness, and he was dead. He couldn't have killed the colonel.

Only Ritter was left. He was the only one left alive of all the people who had been there that day. The Germans had been first. Ritter had told the truth about that. There had been two trucks, and they had ambushed them on the drive. But the house had not been on fire. Not yet. That had come later.

Sitting on the municipal bench in High Holborn, Ritter lost touch with the present. The passing traffic and the men in city suits pounding the pavements through their lunch hours were all outside his consciousness. He was back in France in the late summer of 1944 and the hot hard sun was hanging low over the western horizon as Rocard and his wife and the old man staggered up the sloping path to the church with their British captors following close behind. The old man was still suffering the effects of the beating that he had received from Carson and leaned heavily on the Frenchwoman's shoulder for support, so that they made fairly slow progress.

There was time therefore for Ritter to really take in the façade of Marjean Church, and he didn't like what he saw. It gave him the creeps. Perhaps it was the hour of the day or the proximity of the black empty lake, but he couldn't escape the sense that he was being watched. It made him nervous and angry with himself all at the same time. If there was one thing that Ritter was sure of, it was that superstition was stupid.

A grey stone statue of some French saint missing half his head stood above the entrance, and when Rocard pushed open the heavy wooden door of the church at Cade's direction, Ritter had to fight down an impulse to run back down the slope, in headlong retreat to the safety of the house. But instead he swallowed his anxiety and followed the others into the airless twilight interior, wishing that the colonel had picked somewhere else to continue the interrogation. Still, at least they were out of sight, and Carson would be able to see everything from where he was standing outside. It was a grandstand position. The lake and the sky and the house and the drive were all in view. There would be plenty of time for Jimmy Carson to shout out a warning if he saw someone coming.

The church was simply furnished. There were ten pews on either side of the uncarpeted nave, with a few chairs at the back and an old organ that looked the worse for wear. Up beyond the chancel, the altar was covered with a thin white sheet and adorned with nothing except a small brass cross, and the walls too were bare of decoration. The last of the evening light came in through high leaded windows.

Cade didn't stop when they got inside. He seemed to know exactly where he was going. He was now ahead of Madame Rocard and the servant, walking almost parallel with her husband toward a half-open door at the back of the church.

"Where are we going?" asked Ritter, but he never got an answer to his question.

Perhaps they were going too fast and she lost her footing on the uneven stone floor, or perhaps she could no longer bear the weight of supporting the old man. Whatever the reason, Madame Rocard suddenly stopped and put her hands up to her head, and the old man fell to the ground, taking his mistress with him. Ritter had been following close behind them with the safety catch on his German pistol released. He didn't trust any of these people and was taking no chances. Now he too lost his balance, and fell almost on top of the woman. Ritter had always been a heavy man, and Madame Rocard screamed with renewed pain as she felt his full weight land on her body.

Her husband turned round instantly, and the sight of the fat British sergeant on top of his wife enraged him. It broke his self-control and he started raining blows down on Ritter's head. Everything went black, and it was just instinct and not any kind of conscious decision that made Ritter squeeze his finger down on the trigger of the gun in his hand. Not once, but again and again.

There was a huge explosion in Ritter's ears, and then complete silence for a moment before everyone seemed to start shouting all at once. Ritter felt the taut wiry body above him go suddenly limp, and then the Frenchman's warm blood began seeping down over his arm. It brought Ritter to his senses, and he pushed Rocard's dead weight away and got to his feet.

What happened next he never forgot. It was the only time that the colonel ever lost his temper with him, and it hurt Ritter deep down inside with a pain that he never wanted to feel again.

"Fuck you, Sergeant." The colonel was white with anger, but he didn't raise his voice. "Do you know what you are?"

Ritter shook his head.

"You're a fat, trigger-happy idiot who's probably just cost me my life's work. But you wouldn't understand that, would you, you dolt?"

Cade would have gone on and on, heaping abuse on the one person he could really rely on in the world, if Rocard's wife hadn't suddenly started screaming. She was bent over the body of her husband, plucking at his face, trying to get him to come back to life, and now, in despair, she began beating his chest and crying out his name over and over again while the old servant tried ineffectually to pull her away.

Cade reacted instantly. He pulled her roughly to her feet, and then slapped her across the face again and again until she stopped screaming and fell silent.

"She may know something," he said. "Get the old man and follow me. We'll take them downstairs."

The old servant didn't seem to have much life left in his legs, but Ritter had just got him moving when Carson appeared in the doorway behind them.

"What the fuck happened?" he shouted at Cade. "You told me there wasn't going to be any killing."

"I told you to follow orders, and you'd get rewarded for it. If you still want the money, shut up and get outside. Do you hear me, Corporal? Do your fucking job."

Ritter had never seen the colonel so angry or so powerful. It was certainly too much for Carson, who turned away without further protest and went back to his post, half closing the heavy church door behind him.

"Now, let's be quick about it," said Cade, turning back to Ritter after Carson had gone. "Leave the body here. We can come back for it later."

They went through the door at the back of the church into an open area that evidently served as the vestry. An old white surplice was hanging from a hook on the far wall beneath a dirty window, and a pile of hymn books was stacked on a low table. A rope hanging down through a hole in the middle of the plaster ceiling was obviously connected to the bell at the top of the tower that Ritter had noticed earlier, when they were walking up the hill to the church. Rocard should have rung it when he heard the firing coming from down the drive, thought Ritter. Somebody might have come to save him, but it was too late now.

There was a staircase in the corner of the vestry with stone steps going up and down. Cade took a torch out of his pocket and started descending. He had obviously come prepared.

The stairs were narrow and curved round on themselves, and Cade and Ritter had to keep a firm hold on their prisoners to make sure they didn't fall over. Rocard's wife seemed to be in a state of shock, and the old man could hardly walk.

They stopped at the bottom of the stairs, and it took a few moments for Ritter to realise the scale of the room that he had now entered. The crypt ran the whole length of the church, and each wall was lined with tombs. Some were plain stone coffins, while others were surmounted with life-size sculptures of their occupants, but each tomb seemed to have an inscription on the wall beside it. Names and dates that were illegible in the torchlight.

"Who are they?" asked Ritter. He had never seen a place like this before and never wanted to again. It reminded him of the Nottinghamshire mines that he had run away from to join the army when his father died.

"Abbots, mostly. There was a monastery here once. The church is pretty well all there's left of it."

The anger had gone out of Cade's voice and his tone was businesslike as he lit a paraffin lamp hanging down from the centre of the ceiling.

Then, at the colonel's direction, Ritter pulled two chairs out of a corner and sat the Frenchwoman and the old man down under the lamp. It was still swinging slightly from when Cade had lit it, and it felt to Ritter for a moment like they were in the bowels of a ship. Ritter had always hated the sea.

The old man was mumbling incoherently, and Rocard's wife seemed almost lifeless. Cade tried smacking her again, but it had no effect. Bruises were already beginning to come up around her eyes, and her cheeks were red weals.

"This is useless," said Cade. "Give me your whisky flask, Reg. Maybe that'll work."

Surprisingly it did. Ritter held the woman's head back while Cade dropped the alcohol into her mouth. After a moment she began coughing and spluttering, and the anger and grief reappeared in her eyes.

Cade began talking to her in French. His face was inches from hers, and he kept repeating that same word that Ritter had heard him use outside the house.

"Où est le roi?" Or was it "Où est la croix?" But the Frenchwoman just shook her head from side to side like a metronome. It was as if she had lost the energy for words.

It went on like this for a minute or maybe two. Cade's unanswered questions echoed off the stone walls, so that it seemed to Ritter like the dead monks were mocking them, until finally Cade fell silent and walked away into a corner of the crypt, where he stood leaning against the wall.

"There's no time for any more of this. And the bitch probably doesn't know anything anyway." Cade spoke softly, and it was as if he was talking to himself rather than to Ritter. He still had the whisky flask in his hand, and now he raised it to his lips and took a hard swallow before passing it back to the sergeant.

"Finish it," said the colonel. "We've got dirty work to do."

Cade had the German pistol in his hand, and the Frenchwoman began to tremble, remembering how he'd held it to her temple outside the house. The vicious little round opening pressed into her flesh, the sound the gun had made when he killed the dog.

Cade leant over her shoulder, whispering in her ear, while he let the gun play back and forth over her body. Ritter could feel her fear, but still she said nothing, just shook her head from side to side. Perhaps she was too frightened to talk, or perhaps she didn't have any answers. It didn't matter. Cade had had enough.

Abruptly he stood up to his full height, and her eyes followed the gun as he turned it away from her and on to the old man.

"Dis-moi," he said. "Tell me." But she didn't. And Cade pulled the trigger.

She tried to get up from the chair, but Cade pushed her back, holding her down with one hand, while he pointed the gun at her head with the other.

"Où est la croix?" Cade spoke slowly, pronouncing each word separately so that Ritter, standing by the doorway out of the way of flying bullets, understood the question quite clearly this time. But it was impossible to say if the Frenchwoman did. She seemed beyond speech, and Ritter wondered afterward if she had had some kind of stroke or heart attack before Cade finally killed her.

"They had to die," Cade said in a matter-of-fact tone of voice as they went back up the narrow stairs. "Once you killed the Frenchman, there was no choice. You see that, don't you, Reg?"

And Ritter did. He accepted the responsibility. He'd have killed them himself if the colonel had asked him to, although he'd have chosen somewhere else. Anywhere would have been better than this God-forsaken church and its black crypt.

Back upstairs, Ritter stooped to pick up Rocard's body, but Cade stopped him with a gesture of his hand.

"That's where the Germans killed him," he said. "Leave him be. It's the trucks that we need to move. After that you can radio in, and then we can search the house while we're waiting. Maybe we'll find something there, although I doubt it somehow. If either of them knew anything, they'd probably have told me."

It was a sort of forgiveness, and Ritter felt an almost irrational gratitude, which he knew better than to express. There was no time anyway. The firing began before they got to the door. Two rifles, it sounded like. One answering the other. Backward and forward, and then silence.

Ritter and Cade stood behind the door of the church, listening to the footsteps approaching. God knows who was outside. Friend or foe. The truth was that they weren't ready for either. The Germans would kill them, and the British would find them with the Germans' guns.

It was almost dark in the church now, and Ritter could only just make out the outline of Rocard's body on the floor behind him. He cursed the whole sorry business under his breath and felt that he would give almost anything to get outside into the open. The church was bad luck. That much was obvious.

Suddenly the door began to move. Ritter and Cade flattened themselves against the wall behind them, holding their guns out with both hands in readiness, and Ritter would probably have shot Carson if he hadn't called out the colonel's name before he came into view. Instead Ritter reached forward and pulled him roughly inside.

"What was that?" asked the colonel. "Who was firing out there?"

"Me. There was someone in the house and he took a couple of potshots at me. Almost hit me too." Carson spoke in a rush, and his hands were shaking.

"So where are they now?"

"I don't know. I think maybe I got him. There was a lamp in one of the windows, and I saw someone moving behind it. I fired two or three times and he didn't shoot back after that."

"All right. Let's take a look."

Cade led them outside, and then almost immediately began running down the hill toward the house. There were flames leaping up in two of the ground-floor windows, and by the time he reached the door, they had spread to a third. Ritter was slower than the colonel even though he was the younger man, and he didn't follow Cade inside. He was too busy catching his breath. And it didn't take long for Cade to come back out anyway.

"The place is going up like a fucking tinderbox," he said. "I can't stop it."

"What about whoever it was that shot at me?" asked Carson, who'd arrived outside the house last.

"It was an old woman. Probably the wife of the old man. And she's dead. Or if she isn't, she will be in a minute or two. Burnt up with the house and all its contents. Courtesy of Corporal Crackshot here. You're a fucking idiot, you know that, Corporal. A fucking idiot." Cade didn't raise his voice, but Ritter could sense how angry he was. The colonel rarely swore.

"What was I supposed to do?" said Carson defensively. "How was I supposed to know it was some old woman?"

"You weren't. But it doesn't take a genius to know what happens if you shoot a rifle at a kerosene lamp."

Cade turned away before Carson could think of a reply.

"This inferno's going to be visible for miles around," he said to Ritter. "We've got to move the trucks and put the guns back. There's no time to lose."

They began jogging down the drive.

"You too, Corporal," Cade shouted back over his shoulder at Carson, who had hung back, watching the flames spread upward into the higher storeys of the house.

And that was how it had ended. They'd waited for the troops to arrive, and then shown them what the Nazi bastards had done. It was a pity that they hadn't got there in time to save the people in the house, Cade had told them, but that was what happened in wartime. It was just bad luck.

The bells of St. Paul's rang out the hour of two, and Ritter stretched, rous-

ing himself from his reverie. He could have told the silent jury and the jour-
nalists with their itching inky fingers all about Marjean and Jimmy Carson.
He had stories to tell that would make their hair stand on end, but instead he
had lied. And he had lied well. He wasn't going to be some sideshow that
Stevie's devious lawyer could use to shift the blame. Cade's death had nothing
to do with Marjean. It was simple greed that had driven Stevie to kill his father, and Ritter hated him for it. He hated the son as much as he had once
loved the father, and he wanted him dead. Hanging on the end of a rope.

Ritter walked quickly back toward the court. He didn't want to miss even
one minute of his wife's evidence. He had coached her well, and he expected
her to be a credit to him.

THIRTEEN

Adam Clayton was worried. No, it was worse than that. He was scared. He'd felt awkward ever since he'd got to the courthouse at ten o'clock on the dot that morning, following the directions that he'd written down so carefully on a piece of paper back at the police station in Oxford. He felt secure there, but here he couldn't rid himself of a sense that he didn't belong. He'd worked hard to become a detective, but now he wished himself back in uniform again and out of the black pinstripe suit that had felt fine yesterday but now seemed too tight all over. Even before Bert Blake had sat down opposite him in the cafeteria, Clayton had had a feeling that something was going to go wrong, and now it had. In spades. This was Clayton's first big trial, but he knew enough about the criminal law to be sure that policemen weren't supposed to go round talking about sensitive exhibits in front of important prosecution witnesses, and that was exactly what he'd just done.

He'd turned around in time to see the look of anguish on Mrs. Ritter's face as she got up and hurried out, leaving her fat husband licking the coffee from his black moustache. The photographs had been of one of the other women in the house, Cade's assistant, Sasha, and Clayton couldn't understand why his conversation with Blake should have had such an effect on Mrs. Ritter. Perhaps it hadn't. Perhaps he was just being paranoid, and her husband had said something to upset her. Clayton had never liked the look of the man, even though he was the prosecution's most important witness, the one who'd caught the defendant red-handed. But Clayton was sure that his gut instinct was right. It was his conversation with Blake that had sent Mrs. Ritter running from the room. He remembered how the people at the other tables had gone silent as he and Blake had raised their voices. God, he was an idiot. Clayton smacked the side of his head in irritation. It was his own fault for talking to Blake. The photographer had worked him out for just what he was: green behind the ears and a bit of a prude, and it had taken Blake less than five minutes to get a rise out of him. It was rotten luck that the Ritters had been sitting at a table right behind his back, but he should have known better.

Clayton looked at his watch and realised he'd been walking the halls for over an hour. Now he stopped outside the entrance to Court number 1. From this vantage point, he could see virtually nothing of what was going on inside, and so he leant on one of the high swing doors slightly to get a better view. It didn't help, but the muffled voices inside suddenly became clearer, and Clayton could hear Ritter giving his evidence. It'd be his turn soon, once Ritter and his wife had finished, and perhaps he'd find himself answering questions about his error of judgement in the cafeteria. Clayton turned away with a shudder, and Trave had to stop suddenly to avoid colliding with his junior officer as he came out of the court.

"What the hell are you doing, Clayton?" he asked angrily. "You're not allowed to listen to the evidence until after you've given your own. You shouldn't need me to tell you that."

"I don't, Bill. I was . . ."

"Not Bill. Inspector Trave."

"Sorry, Inspector. I was looking for you. That's why I'm here." Clayton stammered over his words, shaken by Trave's insistence on being addressed by his rank. They'd been on first-name terms before, back on the day of Cade's postmortem, when Trave had kept him on his feet and bought him a whisky.

"There's something that's happened, that I need to tell you about," he went on after a moment, and then stopped, at a loss for words.

Trave looked at Clayton for a moment, and his expression softened.

"All right," he said. "Let's find somewhere to talk. This isn't the best place. They'll all be coming out in a minute."

They went outside, turned left and left again, and Clayton suddenly found himself trying to keep up with Trave as he turned this way and that, seemingly at random, through a succession of tiny side streets under the shadow of St. Paul's, until the inspector stopped under a freshly painted pub sign and disappeared into the dark interior of The Lamb and Flag Public House.

"You certainly seem to know your way around here," said Clayton, admiringly, as they sat down at a table near the bar.

"An old friend of mine took me here for lunch, when I was starting out just like you, and he was an old inspector who'd seen better days. He's been dead awhile, and I doubt anyone really remembers him now."

"Except you," said Clayton, picking up on a note of sadness, or was it bitterness? in the inspector's voice.

"Except me," said Trave, smiling. "I remember him just like it was yesterday, sitting where you are now, and saying, 'Best bread and cheese in London, son,' as if it was an article of faith. And he was right too. It still is the best."

Adam Clayton began to feel better. He did not know whether it was just getting out of the courthouse or Trave's company or the pub food, which did turn out to be really good, but his conversation with Bert Blake didn't seem to be so terrible after all, even if Mrs. Ritter had got herself upset about it. And Trave agreed with him.

"I wouldn't worry about it if I was you, Adam," he said. "It isn't as if they were photographs of the Ritter woman herself, and her evidence isn't exactly controversial, you know. I remember taking her statement the day after it happened. It was funny. She was very specific about what she remembered, but she didn't remember anything of any real significance. They're like that sometimes." Trave laughed, remembering the look of rapt concentration on Jeanne Ritter's face as she told her story.

"I don't think she has a very good time," said Clayton.

"Her husband, you mean. Yes, he's the one that I've got a problem with," said Trave musingly. "He's not telling the truth about that place in France. Silas had no reason to lie about what he and his brother overheard. Something terrible happened there. I feel sure of it. And I don't know if it's got any bearing on this case. Perhaps it doesn't. Perhaps it was this man, Carson, who shot Cade when he went back there and wrote him that letter afterward. I don't know. I just think I should have gone over to France and asked some questions. Poked around a bit. If it hadn't been for that blinkered barrister in there, I probably would have done."

"Why don't you? There's still time," said Clayton, feeling slightly surprised by the inspector's obvious antipathy toward the prosecutor. He'd not been aware of it before now.

"No, it won't work," said Trave hurriedly. He felt surprised at himself for having said so much. It was what came from keeping so much bottled up inside. He liked Adam Clayton, but he knew he shouldn't be talking to him like this. Clayton was too junior, and besides he hadn't yet given his evidence.

"Why won't it work?" asked Clayton. The inspector's anxieties about the case had begun to trouble him too.

"Because there's no time. The prosecution case'll be over by tomorrow or the next day. And then it'll be up to the other side. I'm sure they'll have made their own enquiries. The defendant's barrister doesn't look like he's anyone's fool. And we're not here to do his job for him. He won't thank us for getting in his way," Trave added as he got up to go. He gave the impression of having talked himself out of his earlier uncertainty, and he avoided any further reference to the court case on their way back to the Old Bailey.

They parted company in the main hall.

"Don't wear your shoes out walking up and down, Adam," said Trave smiling. "Everything'll be fine. I promise you."

"Where are you going to be?" asked Clayton, feeling suddenly nervous again.

"In court. I want to hear what Mrs. Ritter has to say. And if you're still here at the end of the day, I'll drive you back to Oxford."

It was almost two o'clock, and most of the main actors in Stephen Cade's drama were already in their places. The public gallery was packed full of spectators just like it had been in the morning, and Trave noticed Ritter and Silas sitting in opposite corners. There was no way of knowing if they were conscious of each other's presence, but Silas certainly looked ill at ease. He kept fidgeting with his tie, running his hand through his thin sandy-coloured hair. The sergeant, on the other hand, looked more than satisfied with the world around him, and several times Trave saw him rubbing his pudgy hands together.

Suddenly the whispering and fidgeting stopped, and everyone got to their feet as Judge Murdoch swept into court. He looked even more foul tempered than usual, thought Trave. Rumour had it that the judge's digestive system was shot to pieces after years of overindulgent lunches. Certainly the afternoon was not the best time to get on the wrong side of him.

"All right. Who's next?" the judge growled at Thompson, once he was ready.

"Jeanne Ritter," said the prosecutor, clearly unperturbed by the judge's irritation. Most of the time Thompson actually felt stimulated by Murdoch's permanent bad temper. He thought of it as a sort of righteous rage against all criminals, and Murdoch was clever as well as angry. He'd already made some well-timed interventions that friend Swift hadn't had an answer to.

After a few moments the door at the back of the court swung open and Jeanne Ritter followed the usher up the aisle to the witness box. She took the oath in a quiet voice that Trave, sitting at the back of the court, could hardly hear, and then the judge made her do it all over again.

"Louder this time, young woman," he said. "This isn't a boudoir, it's a court of law."

Ritter's wife was obviously nervous, but there was also a determination about the way that she vowed to tell the truth that made Trave prick up his ears. It wasn't how he remembered her, back on the day after the murder, when he went out to Moreton Manor to take her statement. She'd been nervous and quiet then too, but most of all apologetic that she couldn't help the police because she'd seen nothing at all. Trave remembered how anxiously insistent she'd been about that. He'd wondered about it at the time, but then he'd put it down to her being a foreigner and highly strung. Anyone married to Sergeant Ritter would've had reason enough to suffer from anxiety.

She'd been crying. That much was obvious. Her eyes were swollen, and there were red blotches on her cheeks left by the little white handkerchief that she now had entwined in her fingers. She wore her long auburn hair tied up behind her, and the black dress with long sleeves and high collar gave the impression that she was here for someone's funeral. She looked haggard and awful but pretty too, and her husky French voice stumbling over unfamiliar

English words made Trave understand why Ritter had always seemed so pleased with his possession of her.

"Please tell the court your full name," asked Thompson.

"It is Jeanne. Jeanne Ritter."

"And you are married to Mr. Reginald Ritter, from whom we have already heard?"

"Yes." Jeanne's voice sounded sad, as if her marriage was a source of lasting regret, and Trave noticed Ritter stir impatiently in his seat in the public gallery.

"How long have you been living at Moreton Manor House, Mrs. Ritter?"

Jeanne closed her eyes, and Trave wondered for a moment if something was wrong. But as it turned out, she was just thinking, calculating time.

"Seven years. Perhaps eight," she said. "We came after the lady died. She didn't want to know Reg. Not like the professor did."

"I see. And after you came, what did you do at the manor house?"

"I was the housekeeper. I looked after the house, and Reg, he looked after the professor."

"So did you have keys to the various doors?" Thompson asked, looking interested in his witness for the first time since she started giving evidence.

"Yes, of course. The professor had one set, and I and my husband, we had another."

"What about the internal door to the professor's study? Did you have a key to that?"

"I am sorry. I do not understand. Which door do you mean?"

"The one inside. The one leading out into the corridor."

"Yes, I had the key to that one too. But I never used it."

"Why not?"

"Because the professor, he never locked that door. Only the one that goes outside. Sometimes he locked that one."

"Thank you, Mrs. Ritter," said Thompson, looking pleased. "Now I want to ask you, please, about what happened on the night that Professor Cade was murdered."

"Yes, that is what I want to tell you about. About what I saw," said Jeanne, suddenly gripping hold of the edge of the witness box with both her hands. She looked frightened and determined all at the same time, reminding Trave of a suicide that he'd failed to talk down from the top of the University Church two years earlier. The face had stayed with him, imprinted on his mind.

"What did you see?" asked Thompson, sounding puzzled. There was nothing in the woman's statement about seeing anything special. In fact, she seemed to have been pretty insistent that she saw nothing at all. She'd told the police that several times.

"I saw Silas Cade in the courtyard. It was before the shouting started. And he was going from the study to the front door. I saw him go inside."

"Where were you?"

"I was at my window, doing my hair. I had not gone to bed. My husband had. He was waiting for me."

"But he told us you both went to sleep," interrupted Thompson, countering with the first thing that came into his head. He'd left his prepared questions behind, and now he was in uncharted territory.

"He may have been asleep. I don't know. It doesn't matter. It's what I saw outside that is important," said Jeanne. It was as if it hadn't occurred to her that she wouldn't be believed. "I could see everything because there was a moon. How do you call it when the moon is big?" she asked.

"A full moon," said Thompson.

"Yes. That's it," she said eagerly. "There was a full moon, and Silas, he was coming from below me, walking quickly. Very quickly. Soon I found out why, but then I did not know."

"How could you be sure it was him? Did you see his face?" asked Thompson.

"No. I saw him from above, and from behind. But I know it was him. He was wearing his own black mackintosh and his hat. I have seen him wearing them many, many times before."

Thompson seemed at a loss for words. He had been completely unprepared for Mrs. Ritter's revelations. He'd just wanted her to corroborate her husband's evidence about the study key, which she'd done. Perfectly. And if only that had been the end of it. But instead, here she was, pointing the defendant's brother out as the murderer. And the worst part of it was that Silas *was* the only other person with a motive. The same motive as Stephen. Disinheritance.

But the woman was lying. She had to be. Otherwise she'd have told the truth in her statement. Thompson just needed to find out why she was trying to put a rope round Silas Cade's neck. There had to be a reason.

"I'd like to address your lordship in the absence of the jury," said Thompson, turning away from his witness with a look of disgust.

"Yes, Mr. Thompson. I thought you might be wanting to do that," said Judge Murdoch. "Just step outside for a minute, ladies and gentlemen, please. This shouldn't take long."

The jurors filed out, looking puzzled. Some of them even seemed irritated. And who could blame them, thought Trave. They were being sent out just when the trial was getting interesting. The Frenchwoman looked like she'd got plenty more to say about Silas Cade. Trave glanced over at the public gallery and noticed that Silas had disappeared, although Ritter was still there, looking like thunder. Trave considered going after Silas, but then thought better of the idea. There was no way of knowing where he'd gone, and Trave needed to hear the rest of the Ritter woman's evidence. It was his case, after all.

The door at the back of the court closed behind the last juror, and the judge turned to the witness.

"Sit down, young woman," he said coldly. "I need to talk to counsel."

Jeanne obeyed. She looked terrified now, like someone who has jumped headlong into the water and found it to be far colder and deeper than she'd expected.

"There's nothing of what the witness has been saying about this man in the courtyard in her witness statement. That's your point, isn't it, Mr. Thompson?" asked the judge.

"Yes, my lord. And I need to ask her why. The jury needs to have the full picture."

"Yes. And I am sure defence counsel will agree with that proposition. Am I right, Mr. Swift?"

"Yes, my lord," said Swift. Mrs. Ritter had entirely changed her story, and there was no basis on which he could object to Thompson's application. Besides, he wanted to know what else she would say. Perhaps she would implicate Silas even further.

"Very well," said Murdoch. "The prosecution's application to cross-examine their witness is hereby granted. Let's have the jury back. And you can come back into the witness box now, Madam," he added. "There'll be some more questions for you."

"You remember making a statement to the police, Mrs. Ritter?" asked Thompson, once the jurors were back in their places.

"Yes, I remember," said Jeanne softly.

"Good. Let me read you a bit of it then. This is what you said: 'I went to sleep quite early with my husband, and I wasn't aware of anything unusual until the sound of someone shouting woke me up.' That's what you told the police. You were asleep until you heard the shouting. Not a word about anyone in the courtyard."

"It's not true. What I said there isn't true."

"But that's not what you said at the time, is it, Mrs. Ritter?" said Thompson, with a smile. "Look, you signed a declaration saying that your statement was all true. You even agreed that you could be prosecuted if it wasn't." Thompson held up the last page of the statement for everyone to see, with his finger pointing at Jeanne Ritter's rather laborious-looking signature at the bottom.

"I was lying. I wanted to protect Silas."

"Why?"

"Because I loved him." Jeanne almost shouted the words, glorying in the momentary sense of complete release that they gave her. "I loved him, and I thought he loved me. But he didn't. He never loved me at all."

"And that's why you've made up this story about him. Isn't that right, Mrs. Ritter?" asked Thompson, scenting victory. "It's revenge you're after. Not the truth."

"No, I'm telling you the truth now."

"But you were lying before."

"Yes, can't you understand?" Jeanne was crying now, and her words came out in short rushes between the heaves of her body. "I was downstairs in the hall, and Reg was shouting about the colonel, about him being dead, and I knew what I had to do. First of all, I locked the door. Then I picked up the mackintosh and the hat, and I hung them up so that no one would see. And afterward I told the policeman that I saw nothing. Nothing at all. But it wasn't true. I saw him, and I know what he did."

"So you say, Mrs. Ritter," said Thompson. His icy calm was a sharp contrast to the obvious distress of his witness. "But it's what you would say, isn't it, now that Mr. Cade has rejected you?"

"No," said Jeanne weakly, but it sounded more like a protest than a denial. She felt suddenly terribly tired, drained of all emotion. Thompson was staring at her, making no effort to hide his contempt, and it took an enormous effort of will to turn away from him. She scanned the courtroom, looking for a friendly face, but everyone seemed indifferent to her. Except Stephen. She could not bear the look in his eyes. "You protected Silas and you condemned me," he seemed to be saying. "And it's too late now. Too late for you and too late for me."

Thompson was asking her more questions, pressing her to tell the jury the story of her adultery, but she couldn't answer anymore. She was no match for the mean little barrister with the effeminate voice or the judge who talked to her like she was so much dirt. Suddenly she felt an intense longing to see her father again, coming whistling up the lane at twelve o'clock with the mailbag over his shoulder and a present for his own little girl in the pocket of his black serge uniform. She could feel the hair of his thick moustache against her cheek as he picked her up and told her that everything was going to be all right, because she'd cried a lot back then as well. Before any of the bad things happened. Before her father died. And her mother too. Before Reg Ritter came to claim her. She needed everything to have been different, but it wasn't, and something inside her, deep inside her vital organs, seemed to snap, and her legs buckled beneath her as everything faded away. The policeman told her afterward that she was lucky to have been standing in the witness box. The side of it apparently broke her fall.

By the time she regained full consciousness of her surroundings, the judge had disappeared from off his dais, and the people in the courtroom were moving around, gathering up their possessions.

The policeman who'd taken her statement was leaning over her, encouraging her to drink from a glass of water he had in his hand. She remembered his big hands with the bitten-down fingernails and his sad, sympathetic pale blue eyes. She hadn't found it easy to lie to him on that June morning when he'd come to see her at the manor house. But now everyone knew she was a liar and an adulteress. The shame of it, the sense of the spectacle that she must have made of herself in front of all these people, was almost more than she could bear. She closed her eyes, and Trave leaned forward instinctively and loosened her high collar.

"What happened?" she asked. She found it difficult to speak, and the words came out in a whisper.

"You fainted. And the judge left you to it," Trave said with a smile.

"So please, can I go?" Jeanne asked, getting unsteadily to her feet.

"Yes. But they want you back tomorrow, I'm afraid. Have you got somewhere to stay? I don't think you should go back to Moreton."

"Yes, I can find somewhere. There are places up near Baker Street where I was living before. I'll be all right."

In truth, Jeanne had no idea if she would be all right. All she knew is that she wanted to be alone, far away from anyone who had seen her in court, but the police officer was persistent. He wouldn't let her go so easily.

"What about money?" he asked.

"I've got enough."

"Well, I'll walk you to the tube."

Trave felt frightened for the woman. Either tonight, that she'd do something to herself, sitting on the side of the bed in some ill-lit cheap hotel room in the early hours with bottles of pills lined up on the dresser, or tomorrow, when Ritter found her. There was no sign of him anywhere in the courthouse or in the street when they got outside, but that didn't mean that he wasn't lurking somewhere, ready to grasp his wife in his thick pudgy hands as soon as Trave's back was turned.

But there was nothing Trave could do. That much was obvious to him as his companion hurried down Blackfriars Road toward the underground station, intent only on getting away from him. He couldn't guard her if she didn't want to be guarded, and even if she did, it was probably outside his job description.

The station was crowded, and she had to queue for a ticket.

"Are you sure you'll be all right?" he asked, as if in need of some kind of blessing for leaving her alone. But she didn't answer. She was looking in her purse for coins, and Trave felt as if he'd already been left behind.

At the foot of the stairs, Trave turned back, hoping to get a last glimpse of her at the turnstiles, but she was gone, swallowed up into the throng of afternoon travelers, and so he climbed back up into the day and walked out onto Blackfriars Bridge.

The great grey river washed against its stone banks, too dirty to reflect the solid nineteenth-century buildings rising up on either side. And, despite the sunshine, there was almost no river traffic. Just a police launch approaching fast from the east, looking for something or someone. London was an easy place to end your life, if that's what you had in mind.

Trave felt the old familiar depression settle down onto his shoulders, although there was no return of the pain in his chest that had brought him to his knees on the first day of the trial. He'd almost have welcomed it, because the sense of desolation told him a different story. He'd live for many more years yet in his big old North Oxford house, thinking about his son who had died and his wife who had left him for another man. He'd hear the echo of things that had gone forever until he couldn't stand it anymore. The echo of playing the piano in an empty room or mowing the lawn in an empty garden. Keeping going for no good reason at all.

Trave's work had been his salvation ever since his son died. He was good at it, and it had kept his demons at bay, for most of the time at least. But this case had changed things. Standing, looking down into the grey river, Trave realised that now. He'd begun to make mistakes. He should have pressed Ritter's wife more when she made her statement. He should have had enough experience to know if she was lying to him. Stephen's guilt was too easy an explanation, but he'd ignored the personalities and concentrated on the facts. It didn't matter how strong the evidence was. He should have known better. He should have kept an open mind. Instead he'd got it wrong. And now a boy might hang for something he probably never did. And a woman might die tonight. And it seemed like there was nothing he could do.

Trave turned away from the river with a sense of despair, but then thought better of stopping at the pub on the corner for a whisky. He had work to do, and he needed a clear head. First of all, he had to find Adam Clayton, if he was still in the courthouse. The gossip in the witness room was clearly what had driven the Frenchwoman to change her story. And of course Clayton's evidence about what had happened that afternoon would help Gerald Thompson persuade the jury that she'd invented her new account on the spur of the moment, in order to punish Silas by accusing him of the murder. Clayton would help put the rope back round Stephen Cade's neck, and Trave understood himself well enough by now to know that he would do almost anything to save the boy. Anything except not do his job. His duty was to provide the evidence, not to withhold it, and then it was for the jury to decide who was guilty and who was not.

Perhaps Jeanne Ritter had told him the truth back on that late summer's day when he had gone to visit her at Moreton and they had sat so awkwardly at either end of the heavy mahogany table in the dining room, never once making eye contact. In court today, he'd believed her, but now he wasn't so sure. She'd been angry as well as desperate until Thompson had got the better of her. There were questions that still needed answers. Had she seen Stephen coming back into the study just before his brother crossed the courtyard? She'd have been at the window because she was doing her hair, but would she have seen him? If he'd come along the side of the house, he'd have been out of her view—and maybe out of her hearing too if the window was closed. There was a wind, and she'd never said she heard the gunshot. But then again, perhaps she hadn't mentioned Stephen because he never did come back. Perhaps he was in the study all the time, killing his father, and the rest was just a figment of the Frenchwoman's overactive imagination.

Trave shook his head from side to side, as if to rid himself of his thoughts. His mind was going round and round in circles, posing questions to which he had no answers. But at least Adam Clayton hadn't gone. He was waiting for the inspector outside the courthouse.

"Where have you been?" he asked, sounding nervous and excited all at once. "People in there were saying that Ritter's wife fainted and that's why the court rose early."

"Yes. I've just been taking her to the underground. She'll have to come back tomorrow."

"But that can't be right," said Clayton, clearly surprised. "She just went by here only a couple of minutes ago. She was with her husband. He was shouting at her, calling her names."

"What names?" asked Trave, looking horrified.

"He called her a whore. And a bitch too, I think. He was pulling her along, and so I didn't get to hear much. Perhaps I should have stopped him, but I didn't, because she is his wife, after all," Clayton ended uncertainly.

"No, I'm the one who should have done that." Trave realised what a fool he'd been. Why hadn't he seen her onto a train? Instead he might just as well have handed her over to her murderous husband. Ritter had obviously followed them down into the underground station, and then calmly waited until Trave had left before taking hold of his wife and dragging her back the way she'd come, while Trave gazed down into the River Thames, wallowing in self-pity. God knows where they were now.

"Did Ritter say anything else?" Trave asked.

"He said she was going to show him. Whatever that meant."

"Show him," repeated Trave, sounding puzzled, and then suddenly he understood. "Come on," he shouted. "He's taking her back to Moreton. And he's driving. Otherwise he wouldn't have come back here."

"How do you know it's Moreton?" asked Clayton, speaking between panting breaths, as he struggled to keep up with the inspector.

"Because that's where she betrayed him with scrawny Silas Cade. He's probably going after him too."

FOURTEEN

The Rolls-Royce glided down the fast lane of the motorway, headed for Oxford. Silas was driving at close to one hundred miles per hour, but the car showed no sign of stress. Cocooned inside, Silas's mind was racing. He had very little time to make a plan, and he needed something that would work.

Jeanne's evidence had come as a complete shock. Only the day before she'd been her normal self. Ritter had gone into Oxford and they'd met in the trees by the west wall. And afterward she'd clung to him, fantasising about a future he knew they would never have. But it didn't matter. He'd let her get on with it, building her castles in the air. Ritter would take her away once the trial was finished and Silas was the undisputed lord of the manor. In the meantime, there was no need to rock the boat.

But then she'd got up in court and practically accused him of murdering his father. She must have found out about the photographs of Sasha. There was no other possible explanation. Somebody must have told her about them. But who? Silas had asked himself this question a hundred times or more since he'd slipped out of the back of the courtroom in the middle of Jeanne's evidence, but forty miles down the highway, he was still no nearer to an answer.

He'd known from the first that the photographs were his Achilles' heel. He should have had the sense to destroy them before the police searched the house. But they had been very understanding when he'd gone down to the station in Oxford to ask for them back. They'd got their man, and the pictures weren't relevant to the case. He'd burnt them when he got home, but that didn't mean he could erase them from people's minds. The whole bloody Oxfordshire police force must have been laughing at him for months, thought Silas bitterly—calling him a voyeur, a dirty little peeping Tom. But it didn't matter. What mattered was that now, thanks to Jeanne, he was a murder suspect. He needed an alibi. And there was only one person in the world who could provide him with one. Silas looked up into the empty afternoon sky and prayed to a god in whom he didn't believe that just this once Sasha would be home.

He found her in the manuscript gallery on the second floor. He hadn't seen her at first. The high polished oak bookcases, which the professor had had specially constructed by a firm of Oxford craftsmen a decade earlier, divided the gallery into self-contained aisles, connected by several open archways. The central aisle was the widest, but those at the sides had tables set under the high leaded windows, to enable the professor and his assistants to work using natural light. Sasha was sitting at one of these now, poring over some Latin text or other. She had turned on a green reading lamp, but a few final shafts of late afternoon sunlight still penetrated the library, illuminating motes of dust in the still air, picking out the gold titles on the spines of the old leather books on the highest shelves.

Silas had come quietly up the central aisle and now stood watching the woman he wanted from the other side of the archway between them. She had taken off the jacket of her grey suit and pushed her hair back over her shoulders. With an imaginary hand, he traced the line of her soft white neck down beneath her starched white shirt, on to the high mound of her right breast, and then round, behind, to where she was most vulnerable. Forgetting himself, Silas moved slightly, adjusting his weight from one foot to the other, and Sasha looked up, startled. Surprise and then irritation replaced the previous expression of rapt concentration on her face, and then, almost immediately, she reached back and put on her jacket. It was always the same. She could never rid herself of the consciousness of her disfigurement, and Silas imagined that it must itch her all the time, like eczema.

"What are you doing? Something interesting?" he asked, glancing down at the papers spread out on the table between them. There was no time, but he needed her calm before they talked.

"Just work. It wouldn't interest you." Sasha was ruder than she intended, unable to keep the annoyance out of her voice. Silas always seemed to appear out of nowhere, as if he'd been watching her for a while before he finally approached.

"Why not?" he asked. "Maybe I know what you're looking for."

Sasha suddenly became very still while her mind raced. What was he talking about? Perhaps Silas did know something about the codex. Perhaps he'd seen something. What a fool she'd been, allowing her dislike of the man to get the better of her common sense. If anybody could be relied on to pry out people's secrets it was Silas, and yet she'd spent the last six months trying to avoid him.

"I've been watching you, Sasha," he said. "I've seen what you do, late at night down in my father's study, when you think no one is looking. Opening this, opening that, tapping on walls. And all the time what you're searching for is sitting right there in front of your eyes."

Silas laughed, but Sasha forced herself not to respond. His tone angered her as much as his words. She hated the thought of his knowing her so well, but she needed to know what he was going to say.

"It's the book you're after, isn't it?" he said. "The one that my father stole from those people in France." Silas knew there was no time left to fence about. He needed to engage Sasha, and all the time he was listening with one ear for the sound of police cars screeching to a halt outside. Jeanne's evidence made it inevitable that they'd be coming after him.

"What is it you want, Silas?" asked Sasha, trying to keep the excitement out of her voice. At that moment there was almost nothing she wouldn't have done to get her hands on the codex.

"I want to make a trade," he said.

"A trade?"

"Yes, that's what they call it in the secret service, you know. We each have something the other one wants. We make an exchange, and then we both live happily ever after. That's how it works."

"And what have I got that you want?" Sasha asked warily.

"Evidence."

"Evidence." She repeated the word as if she didn't understand it. It was not the answer she had been expecting.

"Yes. I need an alibi."

"For what?"

"For killing my father."

It was Sasha's turn to laugh. The thought of Silas as the Moreton Manor murderer had never even occurred to her. Silas was like Hamlet without the speeches. He never *did* anything. He just took photographs.

"Oh, don't worry," he said. "I didn't do it, if that's what you're thinking. We've got my brother to thank for that. No, I've just been accused of it, that's all."

"By whom?"

"Jeanne Ritter. She gave evidence today. Said she saw me crossing the courtyard from the study to the front door, just before Stephen started shouting."

"And did you?"

"No, of course not. I was up in my room, like I told the police." Silas lied easily. It was something that came naturally to him.

"So what's the problem?"

"She's the problem. It's my word against hers. And they're going to believe her because I've got no one to back me up. Unless you help me."

"Help you how?"

"By saying we were together before the shooting started. It doesn't matter if we say we were in my room or yours, provided we agree on it before we make our new statements."

Silas spoke confidently, but then his voice trailed away as he caught the instinctive look of disgust written so plainly across Sasha's face.

"What about Stephen?" she asked.

"What about him?"

"Jeanne's evidence might save him."

"And put the noose around my neck?"

"Maybe."

Sasha turned away, biting her lip. She liked Stephen. She'd only met him twice, but both times he'd gone out of his way to be friendly toward her, asking her about her work on the manuscripts, and she had appreciated his efforts at the time, realising the pressure he must have been under, seeing his father again after so long. But did that oblige her to try and save him? Did it mean that she had to give up the codex when she had worked so hard, had given up so much to find it? Leave it to Silas, who had no use for it? No, surely not. Providing the alibi might save Silas, but it wouldn't condemn Stephen. His guilt was for the jury to decide. With a visible effort Sasha beat her conscience into submission. She had to have the book because that was the way to the cross, which was worth paying almost any price to obtain.

"So what were we doing in my room or yours?" she asked, making no effort to hide the contempt in her voice.

"Having an affair. And we made false statements because we didn't want your Catholic mother to know about us."

"How do you know I've got a Catholic mother?" asked Sasha, surprised.

"Because she came here once to visit you, don't you remember? She arrived unexpectedly, and you weren't happy about it. Took her straight off into Oxford. But I was the one who opened the door to her. She was complaining about her journey, and I got her some of my mother's smelling salts that never got thrown out. Your mother said they smelt like something in her church. Her Catholic church."

"Well, you're right about one thing. I wouldn't want my mother to know. Or anyone else either," said Sasha.

Silas looked exasperated. "Oh God, does it matter?" he said. "It's not like I'm asking to have an affair with you, can't you see that? I just want you to say we did have one and to explain why you lied about it before. That's all."

"And for this I get what?"

"The book. But only after you've given evidence. Until then you'll have to trust me."

"No." Sasha turned away and began gathering her papers together. She calculated that Silas needed her at this moment more than she needed him. And she was right. It didn't take him long to give in.

"All right," he said. "You can have it once you've made a statement to the police. At least you'll be committed then."

"Show it to me first," she countered. "Then the statement." It was the first time in his life Silas could ever recall Sasha's smiling at him like she was now. He knew the reason, of course. He wasn't stupid. It was the first and probably the last time that he had ever had anything she wanted. But still he wished he could stop the ornate clock that ticked away so loudly and relentlessly above the entrance to the library. He wondered for a moment if she would let him kiss her to seal their agreement, but then he realised that he would never have the courage to ask. Women frightened him, and Sasha most of all.

"It's in the study," he said.

"Well, at least I knew that much," said Sasha, going past him. She was unable to keep the excitement out of her voice. She'd forgotten Stephen now that the codex was about to fall into her hands, just when she'd been on the point of giving up on it for good. She wondered as she went downstairs if all this was meant to be, but then laughed at herself softly. She'd studied religious history long enough to know that there was no such thing as Divine Providence.

In the study she turned to face Silas. One of the tall green leather armchairs was between them, and she stood with her hands lightly touching the brass studs in its back, watching him in the doorway.

"So show me," she said. Her face was flushed and her lower lip trembled slightly.

"That's the chair in which he died, you know," said Silas, ignoring her demand. "Where he was most comfortable. I've got photographs of him sitting there. In life and in death. Before and after. I look at them sometimes up there in my room, wondering what it all means. Do you do that, Sasha?"

"What?"

"Think about him. I do. All the time. This whole house rotated round him like a clock, and now it's stopped. I spent my whole life trying to make him notice me, and I don't think he ever really did. Not even once."

"You were adopted," said Sasha brutally. Silas wasn't the only one who'd had a bad time growing up.

"Yes. But that wasn't it," he said. "No one really existed for him. Except maybe my mother."

"I never knew her."

"And she wasn't really my mother."

Silas smiled, but Sasha stamped her foot, unable to contain her impatience any longer. Perhaps Silas was bluffing her about the codex. She had to know one way or the other.

"Where is it, Silas?" she said. "It was a deal, remember?"

"You're looking at it," he said. "You've been looking at it all the time."

Sasha looked down at the low table between the chairs, but all she could see were several old magazines and the professor's chessboard with the old ivory pieces set out in battle formation, ready to play.

"Don't play games with me, Silas," she said. "I've no time for them."

"Which is probably why you never found your precious book," he said, as he bent down over the table and began to remove the chess pieces from the board. "My father was brilliant at this game, you know. He'd have done well as a Soviet grand master, although perhaps he didn't have the imagination to be the best. I wonder if that's why he never played competitively," Silas added musingly, as he held the now-empty board up to the light. His earlier agitation had disappeared, now that Sasha had agreed to give him what he wanted.

"It's a beautiful thing," he said. "So simple and yet so clever. Of all my father's possessions it's the one I like the most. Even more than the Rolls-Royce, I think, sometimes."

"It's a chessboard," said Sasha, looking bemused.

"Yes, but it's more than that. Much more. It's also a hiding place." Silas held the board just above the top of the table and began to press down on two of the diagonally opposing corner squares with his thumbs.

"I saw him doing this through my telephoto lens," he said. "He was in a hurry for some reason and forgot to close the curtains. It was unlike him."

Slowly, the base of the board divided down an invisible central seam, and the two sides opened. But the book stayed inside, kept in place by two small clips, until Silas turned the board upside down and lifted it out.

"I think he had it specially made, although I don't know where," he said. "And I don't understand why he chose the two queens' rooks for the squares to press. Perhaps there's no significance."

Sasha wasn't listening. She'd seized the codex from Silas's hands almost as soon as he had it out of the box, and now she found it hard to turn the pages with her shaking hands. But it didn't take her long to know that it was the real thing. The tooled leather binding was an eighteenth-century addition, there to protect the ancient vellum on which the old French monk had inscribed the gospel of St. Luke. It was not long. Not many pages. But the painting was magnificent. Red and black and gold. The colours were richer than any that Sasha had ever seen.

But would it tell her the secret of the cross, or was that just an old wives' tale in which John of Rome had too-credulously believed? Cade must have spent years trying to find the answer, but there was nothing of his inside that she could see, except a small sheet of notepaper between the last two pages with a series of numbers written in columns that made no immediate sense to her. Was it a code? Sasha thought of trying to remove it from the book, but there was no time as Silas pulled the codex back out of her hands.

"I can hear them coming," he said. "Remember what we agreed."

Sasha did not hear anything immediately. The windows were closed, and Silas's hearing was much more acute than hers, but soon the sound of a car approaching fast up the drive became unmistakable.

"Christ, it's not the police; it's Ritter. And he's got Jeanne with him," said Silas a moment later. He had moved over behind the window and was looking out into the courtyard, where a blue estate car had just driven up.

"Well, what's so weird about that? She is his wife," said Sasha.

"Shut up and get over here."

Sasha had never heard Silas speak to her so rudely, but something in his tone made her do as he said. Out in the courtyard, Ritter and his wife were still in their car arguing. But then the driver's door flew open, and Ritter got out. He was clearly enraged. It was obvious from the way in which he pulled open his wife's door and hauled her out.

She seemed limp and held on to the car for support when he let her go, and her face was obviously bruised around the eyes. She looked a mess, with her hair in a tangle and her dress crumpled. Below the hem her stockings were torn, and there appeared to be dried blood as well as dirt on her shins, as if she had fallen over. Or been pushed.

"What a pig!" said Sasha. "He's not going to get away with it this time. I'm going out there. Right now."

She moved toward the french windows, but Silas took hold of her arm and pulled her back before she could open them. It was the first time he had ever laid hands on her, and for a moment she was paralysed with shock.

"Keep quiet, Sasha," he said, speaking through his teeth. "Do you want him to kill us too?"

"What the hell are you talking about?"

"He kills people. That's what he does. The family in France who owned this book that you care about so much. And a man called Carson. Others too probably that I don't even know about."

"But why would he kill us?"

Silas didn't answer. Outside Ritter was hitting his wife, holding her up with one hand and smacking her across the face again and again with the back of the other.

Leaving Sasha by the window, Silas crawled over to his father's desk on his hands and knees and put his hand up above his head to lift the telephone receiver down from off its cradle. Laboriously he dialed 999.

"Show me," Ritter kept shouting at his wife out in the courtyard. "Show me where you fucked him, you cheap little whore."

"Fire, police, or ambulance?" asked the operator at the other end of the telephone line.

"Police," whispered Silas. There was no risk of Ritter's hearing him, but fear had taken his voice away, and Silas had to give the address twice before the operator was able to tell him that help was on its way.

Outside, Ritter was getting no reply from his wife. That much was obvious. It didn't look like Jeanne was still conscious, and, quite soon, Ritter let go of her and she slumped to the ground. It was only then that he seemed to take in the presence of the Rolls-Royce for the first time. He went over and pulled the door open as if he thought someone might be hiding inside, and then, finding nothing, he suddenly shouted out Silas's name, causing its owner inside the study to drop the telephone receiver on the ground like it was a hot coal.

"Where are you, Silence?" he called up at the empty windows of the house. "You're in there. I know you are. Snot pouring out of your fucking oversized nose and your legs shaking. Knock, knock, knock. I can hear them knocking down here, Silence." Ritter laughed.

A minute or two passed before he started shouting again. "Look out here, boy," he called. "I've got something to show you." Ritter had picked up his wife from off the ground, and now he held her up like she was some kind of puppet. There was blood on her face. Around her nostrils and trickling down from the corner of her mouth.

"Don't like the look of her now, boy? Damaged goods. Is that it?"

It was as if Ritter knew that Silas was at one of the windows watching, and the thought seemed to reinvigorate him. Ritter was like a man who had burnt all his bridges and was now looking for the bloodiest possible ending.

Inside the study, Silas had seen enough. He needed to get to the back door before Ritter found him. What a fool he'd been not to put the Rolls in the garage. But he had never dreamt that Jeanne would be fool enough to tell her husband about their affair. Or perhaps it had come out in court. In front of everyone. If Ritter found him, he'd never find out what had happened.

"Come on," he said to Sasha, but she didn't move, and so he pulled her out into the corridor. The door he needed was in the kitchen at the back of the house, but the only way to get to it was through the main hall, and turning the corner, Silas saw that his route was blocked. Ritter was just at that moment coming in through the front door, hauling his wife along beside him. Silas stepped back like he'd been burnt and clapped his hand over Sasha's mouth.

For what seemed like forever, they stood flattened against the wall of the corridor, listening to the sound of Ritter running water in the kitchen, but in fact it was only moments later that somebody cried out with shock. Ritter must have thrown the water in his wife's face. He obviously hadn't finished with her yet.

Silas's mind was racing as he calculated the odds. Upstairs Ritter definitely had one gun in his room, maybe more. But Silas didn't know where they were kept, and he couldn't face the idea of the big man finding him in there while he was looking. Escape was still the better option. If he could just get the Rolls started before Ritter found him, he could easily beat the sergeant's old car in a race on the open road.

With Ritter busy in the kitchen, the best way was back through the study. There was no point in taking Sasha if she didn't want to come. She'd only slow him down, and besides Ritter's quarrel was not with her. They had a deal, and Silas still had the book. He looked at her one last time, realising it was his obsession with her that had brought all this down on their heads. The events of the afternoon had temporarily freed him of his inhibitions, and he leant forward and kissed her on the lips. But she didn't respond, and he couldn't read the expression in her dark eyes. He left her where she was.

In the study Silas softly opened the french windows and looked out, but there was no sign of Ritter. He must still be in the kitchen. Crouching low, and clutching the codex in his hand, Silas ran across the courtyard to the Rolls and opened the door. His hands were trembling, and he had difficulty fitting the key in the ignition, but at last it was there. He turned it, waiting for the roar of the engine, but instead he heard nothing. Just a dull click. Again and again the car didn't respond, until finally he gave up, falling back against the seat in despair.

Opening his eyes after a moment, Silas looked out the window, wondering whether to make a run for the main gate, and that's when he saw Ritter, standing at the front door, laughing. He was holding the distributor cap in his hands, and there was no sign of his wife.

Silas had no time to think. It was pure instinct that got him out of the car and through the open french windows of the study. Then, picking up speed, he ran down the corridor past Sasha and up the stairs. At the top, he stopped to catch his breath and hesitated for the first time, looking to his left, down toward the closed door of Ritter's room. But a moment later he'd made his decision, and he went on into the manuscript gallery in front of him. There was a hiding place there, although he hadn't been in it since he was a child. It used to be the best one in the whole house, behind the tallest bookshelf in the corner. Ritter wouldn't find him there. All he needed was to buy a little time before the police arrived.

Downstairs, Ritter felt a strange contentment. It was like he was floating on air, watching everything and everyone from a distance. He knew what he was going to do. He'd known it ever since he'd taken his wife out of that underground station in London. But Silas's running around like a frightened cat had increased the pleasure. The little creep couldn't get away. Let him wait instead, shaking and sweating in some upstairs closet until Ritter found him. The sergeant rubbed his hands around the distributor cap, imagining the feel of Silas's neck between his fingers. He'd shoot him first, and then strangle him afterward. Strangulation was an art. There was nothing more intimate in the whole world.

But there were other things to do first. Abruptly Ritter went back into the hall and bent down over the body of his wife. She had collapsed again after her brief revival in the kitchen, and now Ritter put her over his shoulder and carried her up the same staircase that Silas had just climbed. In his room he slung her down on the bed and then went over to a cabinet in the corner and unlocked one of the drawers. When he turned back to the bed, he had a gun in his hand.

"Wake up, you bitch," he shouted at his wife. "You can sleep forever in a minute, but first of all you're going to hear what I've got to say."

Above and below, Silas and Sasha could hear everything. But neither of them moved. They were both frozen in a sort of terrible complicity.

On the bed, Jeanne was only half-conscious. Her husband was shouting something, but she didn't understand what it was. She wished he would go away and leave her alone, so that she could be back with her father again, as he leant over her little white bed to look at her in the early half-dark morning before he went to work. He didn't think she was awake, but she was. She just had her eyes closed, pretending to be asleep.

"Stop fucking pretending," shouted Ritter, throwing another cup of water at her that he had just got from the sink in the corner.

She opened her eyes and saw the gun, and she screamed. Again and again. But no one came. Not her father or her mother or anyone.

"Don't kill me, Reg," she whimpered. "Please don't." She wanted to tell him that it wasn't supposed to be this way, that it wasn't what her papa had told her would happen when she grew up and the right man came along. Another postman, perhaps, like her father, or somebody with a shop. Somebody to look after her when he was gone. But she couldn't find the words, and Reg was shouting again.

"This is where you fucked him, isn't it, you bitch? This is the place. Tell me, you slut. Tell me."

And suddenly Jeanne had had enough. Life was too hard, and she was too tired. Everything hurt too much. In the end it was always easier to give Reg what he wanted. There was no point in resisting him.

"Yes," she said. And he shot her.

The sound of the gunshot reverberated round the house, and in the silence that followed, Silas knew that Jeanne was dead. Leaning over, he retched into a corner of the narrow hiding place, but it was just a momentary relief from the fear that was gripping his stomach. He wished now that he had run off into the trees instead of going back into the house. Maybe he wouldn't have made it to the gate with Ritter coming after him in his car, but at least he would have been outside, moving. Here he could do nothing but just stand and shiver and wait for Ritter to find him. He remembered the feel of the sergeant's pudgy hands when they squeezed him in his father's study all those years ago. The fear paralysed him, and Silas realised with a terrible shame that he would probably die without putting up a fight.

The sound he was dreading began. Footsteps walking in the aisle. Just a few feet away. Then silence. Ritter was close. Silas could feel him. Standing, listening, weighing the air.

"You're near, aren't you, Silence," he said softly. "Hiding somewhere. Trying not to breathe. I can feel you, Silence. I can feel how frightened you are. Because you know I'll kill you, don't you? Just like I killed Jeanne a minute ago. You can't stop it, Silence. You can't stay quiet forever. You know that, don't you?"

Silas's back and legs hurt terribly from standing so still. He had only a few seconds left before he had to adjust his position, but when he did, it didn't matter. Ritter was no longer listening. A car had pulled up in the courtyard outside, and Silas could hear the sound of voices down below. It had to be the police. Sasha would tell them what had happened, and then it would be Ritter's turn to be hunted down.

The footsteps receded. Ritter must be looking out the window, thought Silas, deciding what to do. A minute or two more, and he would be safe.

Downstairs, Trave had left Sasha with Clayton. Now he forced himself to go up the stairs. He was breaking every rule in the book. He knew that. Ritter was armed and desperate, and Trave had no gun. He should be waiting for the police reinforcements to arrive, but by that time everyone might be dead. Sasha was sure that she had only heard one shot.

At the top, Trave turned to his left and tiptoed down the corridor toward Ritter's bedroom. He had no clear plan, except to run in and jump on the man before he could fire. Surprise was the only weapon he possessed. But when he crashed through the half-closed door, Trave found no sign of Ritter. Just his wife laid out on the bed, killed with a single bullet. She looked quite peaceful, and perhaps she was better off, Trave thought, as he bent down instinctively to close her eyes. He couldn't at that moment imagine a fate worse than being married to Reg Ritter.

But there was no time to think. Over toward the centre of the house, Ritter was firing his gun. Five shots, and then a pause while he reloaded. Trave looked round the room madly. Ritter had to have got his gun from somewhere, and here was the obvious place. Trave noticed the cabinet in the corner just as the sound of the shooting began again. In the open drawer at the top was the rest of the sergeant's private arsenal—a pistol, rounds of ammunition. Trave took the pistol and loaded it as he ran.

In the gallery, Ritter was firing indiscriminately into the shelves of books. One came through into the hiding place, ricocheting off the wall just above where Silas was standing. He had to get out. It was a physical necessity. He forced himself to wait until the sound of the shooting was farthest away and then pushed the bookcase just far enough back to enable him to squeeze out. He left the codex behind. It was the best place for it.

Ritter was nowhere in sight and the gallery was suddenly quiet, except for the ticking of the gold clock above the entrance. Had Ritter stopped shooting because he had heard the shelf move? There was no way of knowing.

Silas crossed quickly to an archway leading to the main aisle. On either side tall leather books climbed to the ceiling, with labels on the shelves written in his father's careful script. It was almost too dark to read them now, and, on the other side of the gallery, beyond the opposite archway, the light from Sasha's reading lamp was a luminous green pool in the gathering gloom.

Silas could hear voices again, talking down below. If he could only get to them, he'd be safe. They were so close. Just a few yards to run to the door at the far end of the gallery, and then down the stairs to safety. It was now or never. Silas stepped out into the main aisle. And Ritter fired.

Lying facedown on the polished wooden floor, listening to the heavy footsteps approach, it took Silas a moment or two to realise that he wasn't hurt. It must have been the shock of the gunshot that had caused him to stumble and fall. He could have made it if his legs had carried him, but they hadn't. And now he was going to die. For what? For nothing. For a little lust that had left him even more lonely than he was before. It didn't seem possible that he would end. He couldn't accept it, that he would never be again. Silas's mouth filled with his own vomit, and he could hardly get out the words to beg Ritter for his life.

"Please," he said. "I'll do anything."

"All right," said Ritter, standing over him with an expression on his face that seemed almost like happiness. "All right, Silence, you can do something. You can crawl."

On his hands and knees, Silas edged toward the half-open door. Perhaps he would escape after all. Miracles happened all the time. But behind him Ritter laughed.

"You're a snake, Silas," he said, "and you know what we do with snakes, don't you? We shoot them."

The bullet went straight through Silas's left foot and lodged in the wooden floor below. The pain was unbearable. He screamed, and somewhere inside he could hear himself screaming, could feel his lungs uselessly contract and expand, as he watched Ritter reloading his gun. He looked up into the barrel and saw his own extinction, and then, just as he closed his eyes, the room exploded again, and Ritter fell down almost on top of him. Trave had aimed for the sergeant's chest and had ended up shooting him in the head. Ritter was dead before he hit the ground.

Trave felt shocked—shocked to his core. The obvious necessity for his action didn't change its significance. He felt a great emptiness inside; he felt Ritter's weight on his soul.

But for now he didn't have to think. He pushed Ritter's big body away and leant down over Silas, removing the remains of his shoe and sock. The foot was a mess, and Trave tied his handkerchief around the wound to try and stop the bleeding. He couldn't think of anything else he could do.

"Is he dead?" Silas asked. His voice was very faint.

"Yes." Trave was sure of it. He'd turned on the lights in the gallery, and he could see Ritter's eyes gazing sightlessly up at the ceiling. They hadn't moved at all.

"Thank you," Silas whispered, and Trave felt oddly touched. He had saved Silas's life. It didn't matter that Silas had probably killed his father.

"Stay quiet," he said. "The ambulance'll be here soon."

But Silas had something else he needed to say. Something that wouldn't wait.

"I didn't tell the truth," he said. "About when my father was killed. I was with Sasha. I didn't want to say before. But now it's different."

"Why?" Trave was shaken, unprepared for what Silas was saying.

"Because of Jeanne. She was jealous. That's why she said those things in court."

Silas's voice trailed away and he closed his eyes. Trave wanted to shake him, wake him up, cross-examine him about this new story, because he didn't believe it. Not for a moment. It was too damn convenient.

Trave forgot the poignancy of Ritter's death and Silas's survival. He was a policeman again, with a mission to ferret out the lies and extract the truth. But at the last moment he pulled back his hand, knowing he had to let Silas be. Nothing he said now could be used in evidence. A statement could wait until after the doctors had done their work. Silas wasn't going anywhere.

On the floor, the wounded man was no longer conscious of the policeman leaning over him or the dead man behind his head. The pain in his foot was still there, but it seemed to belong to someone else. Not just the gallery, but the whole house was full of bright blue water. His arms were strong, and he swam through the rooms like an arrow. Upstairs and downstairs, he could go where he pleased. Until the ambulancemen bent down to put him on a stretcher, and he came rushing back up to the surface and remembered who he was and how much everything hurt.

But worse than the pain was the knowledge that he'd lost something while he was underwater. It was on the edge of his mind but he couldn't grasp it. Trying to reach it only made it seem further away. With a supreme effort of will, Silas concentrated his mind and realised it was why he'd lost consciousness upstairs. He was missing something. It was about Sasha. She was standing at the bottom of the stairs, and he was floating down toward her. He wanted to shout to get her attention, but all that came out was a whisper. It didn't matter. She came over and stood by him for a moment. She wanted to know where the book was, but he shook his head. He wasn't going to tell her that. Not yet. He needed to be sure of her first. And now it came to him what it was he'd forgotten.

"My room or yours?" he asked, but he couldn't be sure that she had heard, and there was no time to repeat the question. He was going forward out into the dusk, and she was staying behind.

Now they were at the back of the ambulance opening the door, and suddenly she was there again, on the edge of his vision. He could hardly hear what she was saying. It sounded like "mine." Silas raised himself on the stretcher, and she said it again. "Mine." It was all right. They understood each other. And Silas sank back into the blue water again as the ambulance drove away.

PART TWO

FIFTEEN

Once again Trave stopped at Moreton Manor on his way to London, but he was coming to see Sasha this time, not Silas who was still in hospital, recovering from the surgery on his foot.

It was a grey overcast day, and the manor house seemed more desolate than ever. The shootings were still fresh in Trave's mind, troubling his sleep, and he would have preferred not to come, but he felt he had no choice. Sasha had been so impassive as she'd given her statement at the police station two days earlier, just as if she was reciting lines she'd stayed up too late at night to learn, and he wanted to see if he could shake her, crack this alibi of Silas's. It made no sense. Why would Sasha want to protect Silas of all people? He might have saved the man's life, but in his current mood even the mention of Silas's name made Trave shudder.

A maid answered the door, and as she took Trave's hat and coat, he thought of Jeanne Ritter hanging another man's hat and coat on this same stand four months earlier. If only she had told the truth from the outset she might be alive today, Trave reflected bitterly.

"Miss Vigne's in the library. Would you like me to take you up?" asked the maid. She'd become nervous, her hands twitching, ever since Trave had shown her his badge on the doorstep.

"No. I'd prefer to see her down here, if you don't mind," he replied quickly. "Anywhere'll do." The thought of going upstairs made Trave grimace. He had no wish to revisit unnecessarily the place where Ritter's body had fallen so heavily to the floor, and he wondered at Sasha's cold-blooded ability to stay on at the manor house after what had happened. But then his eye alighted on three brown suitcases standing in the corner of the hall and he realised he'd been wrong. He'd got here just in time.

Sasha came slowly down the stairs, patting her elaborately coiffured brown hair into place, and Trave was struck by how pretty she looked: her radiant brown eyes sparkled against her pale complexion, and her generous mouth, dimpled chin, and full figure invited admiration. And yet at the same time Trave remembered her disfigurement and realised forcibly that this was the opposite of the impression she intended to give. Her body was taut and her expression severe: she meant to repel attention, not attract it.

"I'm sorry to bother you, Miss Vigne. I know you're busy."

"I'm not busy. I'm leaving," Sasha said brusquely, pointing at her bags standing by the front door.

"Well, I'll try not to delay you too long," said Trave, adopting a friendly tone. "Is there somewhere we could talk?"

Reluctantly, Sasha gestured toward a small parlour next to the kitchen, and Trave followed her in. In contrast to the rest of the house, this room was sparsely furnished and had the air of not having been used in a long time. Two button-backed Victorian armchairs stood on either side of an empty fireplace, and a single framed photograph hung over the simple wooden mantelpiece. It was a picture of Stephen and Silas and their parents taken outside the manor house nine years earlier: the date 1950 was written in black ink in the bottom right-hand corner. John Cade was resting his hand on his wife's shoulder, and he was looking at her with pleased proprietorship as she gazed determinedly ahead, straight at the camera. The boys were in front, standing on the lower step, dressed in identical tweed suits, but it was obvious that they were not real brothers. Stephen looked just like his mother. He had her bright blue eyes and fair straw-textured hair, and he was smiling unself-consciously, expecting the best of the world in contrast to his brother, who stood awkwardly, keeping his grey eyes turned downward to the ground. Nothing had changed. So what was it that made Sasha do Silas's bidding? Trave asked himself for the hundredth time since Silas had announced his alibi in a trembling voice as he was being carried out to the ambulance in the aftermath of the shooting.

"Happier times," said Trave, pointing up at the photograph.

"Perhaps," said Sasha. "Some people aren't born lucky, I guess." Her tone was guarded and she sat perched on the edge of her chair as if ready to make her escape at the slightest provocation.

"Maybe," said Trave. "But Stephen isn't where he is because of luck. You know that, Miss Vigne. Someone's put him there."

"No, I don't know that, Inspector. He put himself there. He shot his father."

"But I don't believe he did. And that's why I'm here. I want you to help me."

"How?"

"By telling the truth. About Silas Cade; about what happened that night."

"I have told the truth," Sasha said angrily. "You've got my statement."

"Yes, I do. And I don't believe it. Not a word of it."

"That's not my affair."

"Your affair! Your nonexistent affair with Silas Cade, you mean. What would a woman like you want with someone like him?"

Sasha flushed. For some reason she felt touched by the policeman's compliment, perhaps because it was so obviously unintended.

"I'm sorry, Inspector. I don't think I can help you," she said quietly, adjusting her dress as she prepared to get up.

"No, wait. Please wait," said Trave quickly, putting out his hand in an almost pleading gesture as he silently cursed himself for his stupidity. This was not how he had intended the interview to go at all. He was more upset by the place, by what had happened than he'd realised. That was the problem.

"Look, I know this is difficult," he said. "I just want you to think about what you're doing. That's all. Before it's too late."

Sasha didn't respond, refusing to meet his eye.

"Too late for Stephen," said Trave, pointing up at the photograph. "They'll hang him, you know. If he's convicted."

Sasha grimaced, biting her lip. The thought of the hangman frightened her, and she screwed up her eyes, trying to suppress it.

"Maybe he won't be. I'm not accusing him of anything, am I?"

"No, you're just exonerating his brother."

Again Sasha didn't respond, but Trave's mind was racing in the silence, searching for a way through.

"How did it happen?" he asked, changing tack. "Who did it to you?"

"What?"

"Your neck," he said, pointing. "Who did that?"

For some reason that Sasha couldn't understand she wasn't angry. Perhaps it was because she knew that Trave wasn't repelled by her, that he wanted to connect.

"A man," she said. "A teacher at my school. He tried to touch me and I pushed him away. It had happened before. Lots of times. There was water boiling on the stove, and he threw it at me. I suppose I was lucky it didn't hit my face."

"I'm so sorry," said Trave. He wished he could think of something else to say. It seemed so unfair, so unjust that a person's life could be spoilt so quickly, so completely. For nothing.

"What happened to him?" he asked.

"He was put away. Somewhere in the country. A place for crazy people who do things like that."

"It doesn't help, though, does it?" said Trave.

"What?"

"The punishment."

"No, you make your own life. That's all. Make sure you're not dependent anymore."

"Dependent on whom?"

"On men I suppose. Not you, Inspector. You seem different somehow. I don't know why."

"Perhaps because I've lost something too."

"Perhaps. But I can't help you, you know. I wish I could, but I can't."

Trave detected a note of sadness, almost regret, in Sasha's voice—a chink in her armour perhaps. He had to try again.

"Why?" he asked. "What is it that you owe Silas Cade? At least tell me that."

"It's not what I owe him. It's what I owe myself. My life has a meaning too, you know. I matter." There was defiance in Sasha's voice. Trave felt her moving out of reach.

"Of course you do," he said. "But the truth matters too. Why won't you tell the truth, Miss Vigne?"

"I have told the truth. I had an affair with Silas Cade, and he was in my room on the night of the murder. I hold to my statement, Inspector," said Sasha in a flat voice, getting up.

"He knows something or he has something, something you want. It must be that," said Trave, following her across the hall. It made no sense to him: this alibi in which he could not believe.

Standing on the front steps in his hat and coat, Trave turned to try to get through to Sasha one last time, but she held up her hand, forestalling him.

"Do you know what my mother told me, Inspector, after I got burnt?" she asked.

Trave shook his head.

"She said it was a blessing, God's blessing. Now that I was ugly I would have no more use for the world, and I could happily become a nun and contemplate God's great mercy."

"That's crazy. You're not ugly."

"Maybe; maybe not. But I'm no nun. I have things to accomplish in this world, Inspector. Other purposes."

There was a faraway look in Sasha's eye as she closed the door that Trave didn't understand. More than ever he felt that there was something he was missing. It was as if he could only see one half of the puzzle and didn't know where to look for the other pieces.

Trave was early. His meeting with the prosecutor was fixed for twelve o'clock, but it was only just after eleven thirty when he parked his car in an underground garage across the river from the Temple and crossed Waterloo Bridge, heading toward Gerald Thompson's chambers.

As he passed through the gate at the back of the Queen Elizabeth Building, Trave felt as if he was entering enemy territory. It was the same each time he came here. As representatives of the Crown, the lawyers and he supposedly shared a common purpose, but it didn't make him trust them. All they seemed to care about were each others' opinions. The rest of the world, policemen and criminals alike, were a sort of underworld that they had to visit from time to time, in order to earn their bread and butter. The barristers in their robes and horsehair wigs made Trave uncomfortable and even angry sometimes, and he knew himself well enough to realise that this arose from a fundamental feeling of inferiority. There was no basis for it. Trave had got a perfectly reasonable university degree, and he could just as easily have set out to become a lawyer all those years ago, but instead he had wanted to be a policeman. The job made sense. He was trying to bring order to a disordered world. Barristers were hired guns. Men without principle, available to whomever could afford their inflated hourly rates. But still, sometimes Trave felt that he was in the wrong job. The lawyers had the final say. Prosecuting innocent men and letting the guilty ones go. Maybe if he'd got a promotion, he'd have had more clout. But he had never been good at making people like him, particularly superior officers. He had remained a middle-ranking detective inspector for fifteen years, marooned on a rate of pay that had had his wife, Vanessa, on his back almost every week until she had left him. He got good work to do, because everyone knew that he was one of the best detectives on the force, but the final decisions were out of his hands.

And this case had begun to trouble him more than any he had ever worked on, until now it was almost an obsession. He had killed Reg Ritter, but it was the man's wife whom Trave couldn't forget. He kept seeing her lying dead on her bed in the manor house. She had seemed so small and abandoned, laid out in the centre of the white counterpane with little pink flowers that just reached all the edges of the mattress beneath. She was obviously a person who cared intensely, almost disproportionately, about the way things looked, and she had made her bed so neatly before she left for London with her husband in the morning. Little did she know then that it was her deathbed she was preparing and that the counterpane would be her winding sheet.

Trave shook his head and tried to forget all the dead faces: Ritter and his wife and Cade himself and, soon, if Thompson would not listen, Stephen as well, dangling on the end of a rope somewhere in Wandsworth Prison.

Trave was now inside the enclosure of medieval buildings known collectively as the Temple. Some of it had been bombed during the war, and rebuilding was still continuing in various places. But much of it was unchanged since Dickens's day. Little alleyways opened unexpectedly into grand squares with fountains and tall beech trees and distant views of the river. Hare

Court, Pump Court, and Doctor Johnson's Buildings. Everywhere the Temple was a hub of activity: barristers coming and going, their clerks tottering down the cobbled lanes under mountains of papers tied up with different-coloured ribbon. Red for defence work and white for prosecution. Most barristers defended and prosecuted, but Tiny Thompson was an exception. The government had secured his exclusive services, and he only prosecuted capital cases. He got results too. The hangman was busier than ever.

Trave had taken a roundabout route to kill time, walking up to Fleet Street and past Temple Bar, where the authorities displayed the heads of executed criminals as late as the eighteenth century. But he was still ten minutes early when he knocked on the door of Number 5 King's Bench Walk and was shown into a waiting room in which a coal fire was giving off very little heat. The scuttle was empty, and there was no sign of any wood.

Trave picked up a magazine off the table in the centre of the room and flicked the pages, but he could not concentrate. He was remembering a day when he and Vanessa and Joe had come here just after the end of the war. God knows why they had chosen the Temple, unless it was just that it was one of the few places that Trave knew in London. But Joe had loved it, running ahead of his parents and jumping out of hidden doorways to scare them. Until they turned a corner and found that he had completely disappeared. Trave had shouted for his son, but he wasn't really worried. He knew Joe couldn't have gone far. But Vanessa didn't see it that way. The look of abject terror on her face had shaken Trave at the time, and now, in retrospect, it seemed like it was a premonition. Trave remembered how they had gone to a tea shop on the Strand afterward, and he had tried to console her while Joe ate his way through an entire chocolate cake. But her confidence had snapped, and she hadn't touched her food. And then, at the end, just as he was paying the bill, she'd taken his hand and told him what she felt, and the words had stayed with him ever since.

"We're walking on ice, Bill. All the time on thin ice, and we just don't know it. We think it's solid ground, until it breaks."

And ten years later the ice had broken. Joe had died and now Vanessa had left Trave for another man. It was as if she held him responsible for what had happened. She'd given him the son he craved, and he hadn't protected that son. He'd failed her, and so she'd left him.

Trave's contempt for his own self-pity didn't make him feel any better or more prepared for Gerald Thompson, who now appeared in the doorway of the waiting room, looking down at Trave over gold half-moon spectacles that he wore forward on his nose, enhancing a naturally supercilious expression.

But to Trave's surprise, the barrister seemed disposed to be friendly. He shook Trave's hand quite warmly, before guiding him down a corridor into his office. It was a beautiful room with light wood-paneled walls and a roaring fire in the corner, a marked contrast to its counterpart in the waiting room.

Thompson went to the door and called to an invisible assistant to make coffee, while Trave took in more of his surroundings. Everything was neat: books arranged in descending order of height on the shelves and papers tied up with ubiquitous white ribbon. The big kneehole desk with drawers on either side was devoid of photographs, but, between two of the bookcases, a six-foot-high mirror had been set into the wall, and Trave imagined Tiny Thompson in his robes, preening himself in front of it, standing slightly on tiptoes to achieve the best effect.

"You're quite a hero, Inspector," said Thompson, returning to his seat on the other side of the desk. "It's not every day that I get to drink coffee with a man of action like yourself."

Trave forced a smile, uncertain how else to respond to being complimented on killing another human being. Even if it was a man like Ritter.

"I hear you felled friend Ritter with just one shot." The prosecutor spoke in the same clipped, almost feminine, voice that had so grated on Trave's nerves during the trial, and his words were laced with irony, but Trave was nevertheless grateful that Thompson was not hostile before he'd begun. Maybe the barrister would listen to what he had to say.

"Thank you for seeing me, Mr. Thompson," he said. "I appreciate it's short notice."

"Gerald, please," interrupted Thompson, smiling.

"Gerald." Trave found it hard to get the name out. It would have been easier to call the prosecutor Tiny. "Gerald, I wanted to talk to you about the case."

"Yes, I imagined you would," said Thompson. "It's going well, I think. I've had the new statements from Sasha Vigne and Silas Cade, saying they were together in her room on the night of the murder. Obviously Silas will have to be recalled now that he's changed his evidence, but I don't see that as too much of a problem."

"So the trial's going ahead? There won't need to be a new jury?" Trave sounded surprised—shocked, even. It was not what he had expected.

"No. No need for one. I spoke to friend Swift yesterday. He doesn't want to start again. He'd lose the evidence of poor Mrs. Ritter if he did. The defence'll obviously be attacking Silas for all they're worth from now on, but I doubt it'll do them much good. His injuries should make him more sympathetic to the jury. Not less."

"But what about the prosecution?"

"What about it?"

"Don't you want to start again?"

"No, I'd lose my star witness if I did that."

Trave looked perplexed, and Thompson laughed.

"Come on, Inspector. You should know who I'm talking about. You're the one who got rid of Sergeant Ritter, after all. I'm just glad that you waited until after he'd given his evidence."

"I had to do it. It wasn't a choice," said Trave, unable to contain his irritation at being depicted as some sort of trigger-happy gunman. The prosecutor's evident amusement at his discomfiture only increased Trave's annoyance.

"It's all right, Inspector. I know you only did what you had to do, as they say. Like I said outside, everyone thinks you're quite the hero. Me included." Thompson laughed and picked up his cup of coffee. Trave noticed with surprise that it was an antique, made of a delicately painted bone china. Thompson blew into the liquid several times before he took his first sip. It was like he was preparing a kiss.

"It's in both our interests to carry on, you see, Inspector," he said after a moment. "The defence have Mrs. Ritter, and we have her husband. The jurors may not have liked him, but they believed his evidence. And the key turning in the lock is the jewel in our crown, particularly when you add in the fingerprint evidence. No, I'm content. I understand your anxieties after what happened at the manor house last week, but you can rest calmer now, Inspector. We're still on course."

Trave stirred uneasily in his seat. The interview was not going at all as he'd anticipated. It was as if the prosecutor was deliberately misinterpreting the reason for his visit. Trave wasn't worried that Stephen Cade might be acquitted; it was the precise opposite that concerned him. After all that had happened, he felt sure that the boy was innocent, and he'd come to London to try to persuade Thompson that the prosecution should stop for good. Obviously he should have realised before he set out that it would be a wasted journey, but still, he was here now, and it was his duty to try.

"You say the defence have Mrs. Ritter, but what do you think about her evidence?" he asked. "What about the man in the courtyard?"

"I don't really see her as a problem, to be honest with you, Inspector," said Thompson patiently. "The Crown takes the view that the poor woman can no longer be seen as a witness of truth. It's quite clear that she changed her evidence and perjured herself at the last moment, because of what she overheard in the cafeteria just before she went into court. Your colleague Detective Constable Clayton has provided us with a most helpful statement about what happened, and you yourself heard the Ritter woman admit her feelings for Silas when she was giving her evidence.

"Of course, it's really unacceptable that prosecution witnesses aren't kept isolated from one another in important cases like this. It's something I've already raised with the people in charge over at the Bailey, although I doubt I'll get anywhere. The court staff tend to be a law unto themselves. More coffee, Inspector?"

"I don't think you understand what I'm trying to say, Mr. Thompson," said Trave, ignoring the offer. "I actually believe Mrs. Ritter did see a man in the courtyard crossing to the front door. Her evidence fits with Stephen Cade's interview. And Silas had a motive. He stood to be disinherited. Now, if we carry on, he'll get everything. I don't believe a word of his alibi, Mr. Thompson. Not a word of it."

"Well, I'm sorry to hear that, Inspector," said Thompson, taking off his glasses and fixing Trave with a cold stare. "Fortunately, however, you're not the one conducting this case. That task has been entrusted to me. And I'm carrying it out without fear or favour, as is my duty. Perhaps you should bear that in mind, Inspector. You seem to have become rather clouded in your judgements recently, if you don't mind my saying so."

"What the hell do you mean by that?" asked Trave angrily.

"I mean that you appear to have developed something of a personal interest in the defendant in this case," Thompson replied evenly. "I understand that you lost your only child in a motorcycle accident several years ago and that he would have been the same age as young Mr. Cade if he'd lived. It must have been terrible for you, Inspector."

There was no sympathy at all in the prosecutor's voice to match his words, and he continued to stare coldly at Trave across his desk.

"My son's got nothing to do with it," said Trave, trying to sound sure of himself, although he couldn't prevent a flush of colour rising to his cheeks. The prosecutor's well-directed thrust had cut right through his defences.

"Perhaps. Perhaps not," said Thompson, with a thin smile. "Let's just say that a reminder of where your duty lies should not go amiss, Inspector."

"I am doing my duty and obtaining this statement was part of that," said Trave, drawing two sheets of folded paper from the inside pocket of his jacket and banging them down on the desk so that the two cups rattled in their saucers.

"Please, Inspector. This isn't one of your police stations," said Thompson, injecting a note of contempt into his voice, designed to irritate Trave even further. "You'd better tell me what this is," he said, nodding at the documents without picking them up. "I hope you haven't done something you're going to regret."

"I've done my job. That's all," said Trave, finding it easier to regain his composure, now that Thompson had become so obviously rude. "The statement was made to me yesterday by Esther Rudd. I wrote it down and brought it to you, which is correct police practice, I think."

"Who's Esther Rudd?"

"She was a housemaid at Moreton Manor at the time of the murder."

"Ah, yes. Now I remember. One of your colleagues took a statement from her. It wasn't very helpful, as I recall. All about how she was a heavy sleeper and only came downstairs shortly before the police arrived. Have you helped her remember something else, Inspector? Is that what all this is about?"

"She's saying that when she got to the top of the stairs, she looked down and saw Mrs. Ritter in the hallway by the front door with a man's hat in her hand," said Trave, ignoring Thompson's accusation that he'd manipulated the witness. "There was no one else in the hall, and Mrs. Ritter hung the hat on the coat stand."

"Whose hat was it?"

"She can't say. She went straight to the east wing when she got to the bottom of the stairs because that's where all the shouting was coming from. There was no reason for her to worry about Mrs. Ritter and a hat."

"Which is, I suppose, why it didn't find its way into her first statement."

"Yes. But what she says now backs up Mrs. Ritter's account. If Silas came running into the house after committing the murder, then he might well have dropped his hat on the floor before he went to his room."

"If he went to his room. He says that he was with Miss Vigne in her room, and she backs up his account. Remember that this is not the only new statement that we have, Inspector," said Thompson tartly. "Anyway, I better read what this Rudd woman has to say."

It didn't take the prosecutor long. He carefully put his glasses back on and held the statement between his thumb and forefinger as he read it, as if it was something offensive that it pained him even to look at, and then when he was done, he dropped the two sheets of paper back onto his desk with a look of derision.

"So the good Esther saw Madame Ritter with a hat," he said, with a sneer. "She can't say whose hat. Only that it was a hat. But with no coat to accompany it, as we might have hoped for. And she says nothing about anyone locking the front door. You remember Mrs. Ritter's evidence, don't you, Inspector? She saw Silas come inside, and so she went downstairs and put his hat and coat back on the hat stand and locked the front door. I don't really think that any of this helps your friend in Wandsworth, Inspector. What's missing from the statement is more significant than what's in it."

"Mrs. Ritter could already have locked the door," said Trave. "The statement at least puts her in the right place at the right time. And why would she have the hat unless she was trying to cover for Silas?"

"I don't know, Inspector. Perhaps because Mrs. Ritter was the housekeeper and didn't like things lying around on the floor. And, more important, I don't understand what you mean by 'the right place.' It was Stephen Cade who was in the right place, complete with gun and key and his dead father. He killed his father, and he's going to have to pay for it. It's as simple as that. And now I'm afraid I've got work to do, even if you haven't," said Thompson, getting up from his chair.

"So you're not going to do anything about this?" Trave stayed where he was, meeting the prosecutor's stare across the desk.

"I'm going to send Esther Rudd's statement to the defence, and they can do with it what they will. Or perhaps I should leave it to you to take it round to them. Swift's chambers are only four doors down the lane. After all, you appear to have become a fully paid-up member of the defence team, Inspector," added Thompson sarcastically.

Trave could think of nothing else to say. All he seemed to have achieved was to increase Thompson's determination to get his man. Trave picked up his hat and coat and turned to go, but at the door, the prosecutor called him back.

"I think you said that Esther Rudd *was* a housemaid, Inspector."

"That's right."

"So she isn't any more?"

"No. Not at the manor house."

"Did she leave, or was she fired?"

"I think she said that she was asked to leave a few months ago. She's got another job in Oxford now."

"I'm glad to hear it. But that's not the point of my question, Inspector. Who asked the good lady to leave? Do you know that?"

"I believe it was Silas Cade," said Trave after a moment.

"Yes, I thought that might be the case," said Thompson, smiling again. "Part of me wonders whether friend Swift will even want to call the good Esther to give evidence. I shall certainly enjoy cross-examining her if he does."

Trave tried to think of an answer, but he gave up almost immediately. The prosecution case against Stephen Cade was like a runaway train, and there seemed to be nothing he could do to stop it. His gut instinct counted for nothing in the face of overwhelming evidence. Trave turned away, but Thompson hadn't yet finished.

"You had no business interfering like this, Inspector," he said angrily. "It's nothing short of professional misconduct. I shall write to your superintendent telling him what has occurred, and he will no doubt take whatever action is appropriate. But in the meantime, stay out of my way, Inspector. Do you hear me? Stay out."

The prosecutor had come out from behind his desk as he was speaking, and now he took a final venomous look at Trave and then shut the door hard, leaving the policeman alone in the corridor.

Outside it had begun to rain, and Trave pulled the collar of his coat around his neck and hurried away toward the river. He didn't look back, and so he missed the sight of Thompson gazing down at him from above, with a look of utter contempt written across his curiously hairless face.

Then, once the policeman had disappeared from view, Thompson crossed over to the fireplace and added another perfectly shaped log to the blaze.

SIXTEEN

There were dark circles under Mary's eyes, and her hands were in continual motion, with the nails bitten down to the quick. Obviously Stephen wasn't the only one feeling the strain of the trial. The visits to the prison were taking a visible toll on his girlfriend. She longed for everything to be over.

"So why doesn't he visit you?" she asked. They'd been talking about Silas for ten minutes already. He had been the only topic of conversation since Mary had first come into the visits hall and Stephen had fanned the new witness statements out across the table between them.

"Because he's not allowed to," said Stephen.

"Why?"

"Because he's a prosecution witness."

"But he didn't need to be, did he? I didn't make a statement to the police. They wanted me to, but I didn't."

Stephen stared intently into a space just above Mary's head. He was unable to make his mind up about what to do.

"You know, he didn't look at me once all the time he was giving his evidence," he said after a moment, remembering the bent, averted head of his brother as Silas slowly answered the barristers' questions. "It was like he couldn't bear to."

"Well, he can bear to drive your father's Rolls-Royce. I've seen him in it, gliding up and down the High Street in Oxford like he owns the place," said Mary.

"Why are you so against him suddenly?" asked Stephen, picking up on a vehemence in his girlfriend's voice that he hadn't heard before.

"Because you've got to save yourself. And this is the only way."

"Save myself! I still might be acquitted, you know. I mean, I am innocent—in case you hadn't noticed."

Stephen bit his lip, fighting to control his emotions. Months inside Wandsworth Prison had taught Stephen to live in the present and not think about the fate that awaited him if he was convicted. It was the only way to survive, although he wasn't always successful.

"I know you're innocent. But that's not enough," said Mary, refusing to give ground. "You can't leave this to chance, Stephen."

"I'm not leaving it to chance. I'm going to tell the jury the truth. The whole truth and nothing but the truth. That I couldn't kill anyone even if I wanted to, let alone my own flesh and blood. I'm simply not that kind of person. The whole thing's completely crazy: I mean, why would I have sat there playing chess with my father if I was going to shoot him in the head at the end of the game? You know, Mary, sometimes I feel like Alice in bloody Wonderland, like I've gone through the looking glass backward."

"I know you do. I can understand that. But the trouble is that murderers do crazy things. And you were there in the room with him. That's the problem. I know you don't want to hear it, but I think the jury is going to need someone else to blame if it's going to let you off."

"And that someone's my brother. I know. But if I'm so up against it, why didn't you push me to accuse Silas before? Why now?"

"Because of Mrs. Ritter and the maid. The new evidence gives you an opportunity that you didn't have before. And I don't want you to die, Stephen. You're running out of time. Can't you see that?" asked Mary, with sudden passion.

But Stephen was silent, gnawing his knuckles.

"Swift wanted to go for my brother from the first, you know," he said eventually. "But I wouldn't let him."

"Why not?"

"Because I didn't believe Silas killed our father. I couldn't believe it."

"But what did that matter if you got acquitted?" asked Mary impatiently. "He's not the one on trial."

"No. But he might be. Afterward. And I wanted to do what was right. It must seem mad to you, Mary, but I felt—I still feel—I owe him something. I suppose it's because he's adopted and I'm not. It's like I came along and took everything away from him. My mother always preferred me. She was like that. She did what she wanted without thinking too much about other people. And Silas got a raw deal. I was at home, and he was away at school, and during the holidays nobody took any notice of him except to point out how much better I was at everything.

"But I never knew what he was thinking. He always kept everything to himself. And then, when I was sent away to school after my mother died, he didn't spend much time with me. He was a lot older, and I suppose there was no reason for him to."

"Except that it would've been kind," interjected Mary.

"Yes, but still it wasn't unusual. No, what sticks in my mind is something that happened near the end of my first term. There were some boys in my class who were picking on me, making my life miserable, and one day I came round a corner and Silas was with them. I don't know if he was telling them to stop or encouraging them to carry on. I never asked him because the bullying stopped soon after that, but I often wondered.

"And then there was another time. We went to the movies with my mother to watch a film called *The Way to the Stars*. In it, there's a young American pilot with engine trouble flying over this village, and he has to decide whether to eject and hope for the best or steer the plane onto somewhere safe and then go down with it in a ball of flame."

"So what does he do?"

"He stays with the plane, of course," said Stephen, smiling. "This was a war movie, and that's what war heroes do. But afterward Silas and I had this big discussion about it. And he said that he'd have bailed out because, chances are, nothing would have happened and the plane would've crashed beyond the village anyway."

"But you voted to go down with the plane?"

"Yes, although there's no virtue in that. It was just a conversation. Why I'm telling you about it is because Silas was so cold-blooded about the whole thing. He was only interested in calculating the chances. It was obvious that concepts like honour and sacrifice didn't mean anything to him. And I was thinking before you came that that's the kind of mind-set you need to have if you're going to sit down and plan out how to kill someone."

"I suppose so," said Mary. "I don't know."

"No, of course you don't. You're not like that. I'm just saying that maybe my sense of guilt has got in the way of my seeing Silas for who he really is."

"A cold-blooded killer?"

"Yes. Maybe. My father was certainly that. I keep thinking of what he did to those people in France. I can't get the place out of my mind. I wish I'd never gone there. It feels like a curse, like something I've got to pay for. Not just my father, but me as well."

"Don't be silly," said Mary uneasily. "Curses didn't kill your father. And they won't kill you."

"Maybe not. It's just it was something about that place. It was so desolate. It was like that ruin near Oxford that you took me to. What was it called?"

"Minster Lovell?"

"Yes. A locked church and a fallen-down house and a sense that time was standing still. Like it was frozen. Waiting. Marjean was like that, but even more so."

"But there's no forbidden lake at Minster Lovell," said Mary, making an effort to lighten the conversation. "The Windrush is a beautiful river. There were children swimming in it when I went there the first time."

"How do you know about the lake?" asked Stephen, looking up. "I never told you about a lake at Marjean."

"Yes, you did," said Mary. "You described it all to me in your rooms in Oxford the night before we went to see your father, so that I'd be prepared. That's what you said. Don't you remember?"

"No. I don't know. I suppose I must have done. I'm sorry, Mary. I'm so confused," said Stephen wearily. "It's being in here that does it to me."

"It's all right. I understand. You need to concentrate on your trial now. That's what matters. And your barrister is right. You should go after Silas, because he's the one who killed your father. Everything points to him. Not just Mrs. Ritter and the maid. Remember the way he got you to go out to your father's house?"

"But that wasn't just him. It was you too. You needed the money for your mother."

"Yes, but it's not me who wrote the letter to your father. Don't you remember him standing behind you at the desk, suggesting what would be the right words to use? And his alibi is so convenient. Didn't you see the way that he gazed at Sasha when she wasn't looking that night at dinner?"

"Which night?"

"The night of the murder. Maybe it's something only women can see. He was watching her so hungrily, and she looked at anyone except him. They weren't sleeping together. I'd bet my life on it."

"Would you?"

"Yes, I would."

"What about my life though? Would you bet *that* on it?" asked Stephen.

Mary hesitated before she replied. She looked up at the clock at the back of the visits hall and swallowed hard before she looked back at her lover.

"Yes, I would," she said. "You've got no choice, Stephen. You can't go down with the plane this time."

Stephen visibly relaxed. "All right," he said. "You've convinced me. Let's see what Swift can do tomorrow. Perhaps it's not too late after all."

Mary smiled back, but as she got up to go, she felt her heart beating hard against her chest and tears starting in her eyes. She turned away suddenly without saying good-bye, and half ran toward the exit at the far end of the hall, without looking back at Stephen. Then, once she was outside the prison gates, she took a moment to compose herself, breathing the free air deep into her lungs, before she got into her car and drove away.

Overhead the sun had disappeared behind thick clouds and there was an icy bite to the wind. And yet Mary kept the windows wound down all the way back into London. The winter air blew all her thoughts away, granting her a temporary oblivion that Stephen couldn't even begin to hope for. Back in his cell he lay quite still on the wafer-thin mattress of his bunk bed, concentrating hard, trying to shut out the banging of heavy doors and the anonymous shouting, the constant noise of the prison that seemed never to go away. There was something on the edge of his memory, just out of reach. It had come to him for a moment while he was talking to Mary and then disappeared. Something that she'd said, something about Silas. And now he had it. Silas driving their father's car—the Rolls-Royce, the beautiful car in which his mother died. But Stephen was remembering a time long before that, just after the end of the war when he was no more than seven or eight. A hot summer's day with his big brother home from school for the holidays. Silas wore long trousers and Stephen wore shorts, and he only came up to just above Silas's elbow. Silas walked round through the elm trees to the big brick garage at the back of the house, and Stephen followed him at a respectful distance. They were going to look at the Rolls-Royce Silver Wraith, their father's pride and joy.

It was cool inside, a relief from the hot sun, and Stephen took out a wrinkled linen ball that had once borne some resemblance to a pocket handkerchief and wiped his forehead, while he blinked, getting used to the half darkness. Gently he ran his hand down the gleaming black side of the car and then up over the curve of the great round headlamp to where the silver lady knelt above the radiator grille. Stephen loved the Rolls-Royce mascot, the girl with her arms outstretched behind her, holding her flowing gown, her silver hair flying in the wind. And last time they came here, Silas had told him the lady's real name. She was called the Spirit of Ecstasy. It was just right, thought Stephen. That was exactly what she was.

But that was last time. This time was different. Silas had brought a key. Stephen knew it was wrong, but he was too excited to protest when his brother opened the doors and invited him into the red morocco interior, sitting next to his brother as Silas handled the wheel, shifted the gear stick, and flicked the indicator up and down, up and down, until the door opened and their father pulled them out of the car one by one, dragging them by their collars out into the sunlight.

Stephen remembered how frightened he'd been at that moment, but as it turned out, his fear had been groundless. His father didn't touch him; John Cade's rage was focused entirely on his elder son. Cade let go of Stephen, adjusted his hold on Silas's collar, and with his free hand smacked Silas across the face one, two, three times. And then, pulling Silas close, Cade spoke through his teeth into his son's frightened eyes: "Don't you ever do that again, boy. You hear me? One more time and you'll be gone for good."

Silas was white as a sheet, the colour entirely drained from his face, but Cade hadn't finished.

"Do you hear me?" he shouted.

"Yes."

Silas barely got the word out through his chattering teeth, but it was enough. Cade pushed him away, letting go of his shirt, and Silas fell back onto the Tarmac drive. And by the time he'd picked himself up, his father was gone.

Silas was a mess, bleeding from the nose and with tears running down his cheeks, and his breath came in strangled gasps. Stephen felt shocked. It was his first experience of violence. Unable to think of any other way to comfort his brother, he offered him the dirty handkerchief that he still had balled up in his hand and then stood there uncertainly while Silas wiped away the blood and tears.

And then, catching his brother's eye, Stephen realised that Silas wasn't frightened anymore; he was angry, angrier than Stephen had ever seen him.

"I'll kill the bastard," said Silas. "I swear it. When I'm old enough, I'll get a gun and I'll shoot him. Like a dog."

Silas held Stephen's gaze for a moment and then handed him back his handkerchief before he turned and walked away, limping slightly as he made his way back toward the house. But Stephen remained rooted to the spot, trying to find some way to absorb the trauma of his experience.

And perhaps he'd been unable to, Stephen thought to himself, sitting on the bed in his prison cell fifteen years later. And perhaps that was why he'd forgotten the day in the garage for so long. Until now. The return of the memory seemed like a sign. And Silas's words spoken all those years ago seemed no empty threat; they seemed like a promise.

SEVENTEEN

The courtroom was full of people but entirely silent as Silas slowly maneuvered himself up the long aisle from the entrance door to the witness box. The only noise was the sound of his crutches hitting the parquet floor as he made his way past the press box and the barristers' table. Gerald Thompson wore a solemn expression, but inside he felt a glow of satisfaction. Everyone had their eyes fixed on the injured man. He was an object of sympathy even before he'd opened his mouth to speak.

Silas grimaced with pain as he settled himself into the chair that had been specially provided for him beside the witness box, but the truth was that he had been lucky. Ritter's bullet had not inflicted any lasting damage, and the doctors had assured him that he would walk again before too long. In the meantime, he was under strict instructions not to put his injured foot to the ground. And Silas was no fool. He knew the value of his injury as well as the prosecutor. Lying in his hospital bed, he had felt the finger of suspicion moving inexorably in his direction. Inspector Trave had made no effort to hide his disbelief when he came to take the alibi statement. But Silas knew that it didn't matter what the policeman thought as long as he could get the jury on his side.

He approached his evidence with a determination that had been completely absent the first time around. He kept his eyes up and didn't hesitate when he gave his answers. Jeanne Ritter was dead, and he was not going to let himself be pulled down by her bitter ghost.

"Tell us how you got your injury, Mr. Cade," asked Thompson, understanding the need to satisfy the jury's obvious curiosity at the outset.

"I was shot in the foot by Reginald Ritter. We were in the library of my father's house. He'd have killed me if Inspector Trave hadn't shot him first."

"Why did he shoot you?"

"Because he'd found out that I'd been seeing his wife. It sent him crazy. He killed her in their bedroom before he came after me."

"Before her death, Mrs. Ritter told this court that she saw a figure dressed in your hat and coat cross the courtyard to the front door of the manor house, just before the shouting started on the night of the murder. Did you do that, Mr. Cade?"

"No, I did not," said Silas, emphasising each and every word. "I never went into the courtyard that night."

"Where were you, then?"

"I was with Sasha Vigne. Upstairs in her room. We were in a relationship together."

"Now, you will recall that when you gave evidence before you said you were in your own room. Not Miss Vigne's."

They had come to the part of Silas's evidence that Thompson had prepared most carefully. But he kept his voice even and methodical, as if he was dealing with a mundane part of the prosecution case that the jury did not need to worry about too much. Silas, however, could not hide his nervous anxiety.

"Yes, I lied," he said eagerly. "I shouldn't have, but I did. Sasha wanted to keep our affair a secret. She has a Catholic mother, and I didn't see any harm in saying that I was in my room rather than hers. After all, it had nothing to do with what happened on the other side of the house."

"That's not for you to say," interrupted the judge angrily. "Perjury is a serious offence. Not something to be taken lightly. Mr. Thompson, you must make the police aware of this matter."

"I certainly will, my lord," said the prosecutor, who was secretly resolved to use all his influence to ensure that no action was taken against the elder Cade brother, if he could only secure the conviction of the younger one.

"Do you know of any reason why Mrs. Ritter would've said you were in the courtyard if you weren't, Mr. Cade?" he asked, turning back to his witness.

"Because she found out about Sasha. It's the only possible reason."

"Yes, I see. Now, you should know that the jury has already heard evidence this morning from Detective Constable Clayton about a conversation that he had in the cafeteria, which was overheard by Mrs. Ritter just before she gave her evidence. The officer talked about certain photographs of Miss Vigne which were taken by yourself without her knowledge. Did you take those photographs, Mr. Cade?"

"Yes. I'm not proud of it. But Sasha knows about them now and she's forgiven me," said Silas, lowering his head as if in contrition. "I didn't think she would, but she has."

"Yes, thank you, Mr. Cade." Thompson sat down. He knew that, injured or not, Silas was never going to look good. He'd admitted perjury and confessed to being a voyeur. But that didn't make him guilty of murder. Mrs. Ritter had a powerful reason to lie about Silas on the day she gave her evidence, and Sasha Vigne would support Silas's alibi. Nothing had happened to change the main picture. Silas's character defects didn't take the gun or the key out of his brother's hand. That was what mattered when all was said and done.

John Swift got slowly to his feet. Now that he at last had the green light from his client to accuse Silas of the murder, to run the case as he had wanted to from the outset, it was difficult to know where to begin. And he wished that Silas wasn't sitting down. It didn't play well to the jury to attack a witness whose head was level with his waist, particularly when that witness had been shot in the foot less than a week before.

"I want to take you back to the day when you were last in this courtroom, Mr. Cade," he began, speaking in an apparently friendly tone. "It was last Wednesday, and you were sitting in the public gallery. I don't know if any of the members of the jury saw you like I did. Perhaps not. You were at the back, after all, near the exit, and you didn't stay for all the evidence."

Silas watched the defence barrister intently, but he remained silent, determined to say nothing until he had to. The judge was less patient.

"You're here to cross-examine the witness, Mr. Swift, not to give evidence yourself," he said, in a tone of angry rebuke. "Now what's your question?"

"It's simply this, my lord," said Swift, keeping his eyes fixed on Silas. "Why did you leave the court in the middle of Mrs. Ritter's evidence, Mr. Cade? Was it something she said that upset you?"

"I left because I knew I had to tell the truth about where I was when my father was killed. I couldn't lie about it anymore."

"Why not? You'd done so up to then. You'd lied to the police and to this court. Why not carry on lying?"

"Because Jeanne was practically accusing me of murdering my father. I had to defend myself."

"You needed an alibi?"

"I needed to tell the truth."

"Then why didn't you ask to see a policeman? Inspector Trave was in court. He could've taken a further statement from you. That would've been the proper thing to do, wouldn't it?"

"I don't know. Maybe. I was upset at the time. I needed to explain to Sasha why I couldn't keep our relationship a secret anymore. I wanted her to understand why we had to tell the truth about where we were that night."

"Come on, Mr. Cade. Are you really asking this jury to believe that you snuck out of this court and drove all the way down to Moreton in the fast lane because you were concerned for Miss Vigne's feelings?"

"I wanted to do what was right."

"No, you didn't. You wanted her to give you an alibi that would take you out of the courtyard. And out of your father's study as well. Because that's where you went that night after you saw your brother leave. Isn't that right, Mr. Cade?"

Swift had raised his voice as he accused Silas of the murder, but Silas held his gaze, and his voice remained firm and clear as he denied it.

"No, I was never in my father's study," he said. "I swear it."

"Just like you swore last time you were in the witness box that you were alone in your room."

"That was to protect Sasha."

"From what?"

"Her mother. She didn't want anyone to know that she was sleeping with me."

"And you're seriously telling this court that you were so worried about Sasha's Roman Catholic mother that you were prepared to commit perjury to stop her finding out about you and her daughter."

"Yes."

"Perjury is a serious offence, Mr. Cade. You can go to prison for it. You knew that already though, didn't you? You didn't need his lordship to tell you."

"I knew it was wrong to lie. I did it because Sasha asked me to, and I didn't think that it mattered that much. It had nothing to do with my father's death whether I was in my room or Sasha's."

"Unless you were in neither," said Swift with a smile. "Mrs. Ritter said you were in the courtyard."

"She made that up because she was jealous of me."

"She loved you. That's why she hung up your hat and coat in the hall. To cover for you."

"I wasn't wearing them."

"The maid, Esther Rudd, saw her hanging them up."

"No. What Esther Rudd saw was an opportunity to get at me after I dismissed her."

"She's got a grudge against you, in other words?"

"Yes."

"Just like the late Mrs. Ritter?"

"Yes."

"Are you still having an affair with your father's personal assistant?" asked Swift, changing tack without warning.

"No, we ended it soon after my father died."

"I see. And how long before your father's death did you start sleeping together?"

"A month. Maybe two. I'm not sure exactly."

"But the photographs of Miss Vigne seized from your room were taken only two weeks before the murder. That's what you told the police when they asked you about them."

"Well, then, that must be right."

"Good. Perhaps then you could explain to this jury why you felt the need to take long-distance photographs of Miss Vigne through her bathroom window, if you were already enjoying carnal knowledge of her in her bedroom."

Silas didn't answer. His cheeks flushed red and his eyes performed a rapid circuit of the courtroom until they ended up fixed on the judge, who looked like the personification of moral outrage.

"Come on, Mr. Cade," he said angrily. "Answer the question."

"It's hard to say," said Silas, in an almost inaudible voice. "It's just that I found taking the photographs exciting. I shouldn't have, but I did."

"Speak up," said Murdoch, looking down at Silas like he was some insect specimen that he'd just skewered on the end of a fork.

"I found it exciting," repeated Silas, raising his voice a little. "Looking at her when she didn't know I was looking. I've always found that exciting."

"It's not exciting. It's disgusting," said the judge with finality.

"Yes," said Silas softly. "I know."

"You're a photographer by trade, Mr. Cade. Isn't that right?" asked Swift, turning to a new page in his notes.

"Yes."

"But I understand you've closed your shop in Oxford."

"Yes."

"Why?"

"I don't need to do it anymore."

"Because of all the money you've inherited from your father?"

"That's right," said Silas defiantly.

"But you wouldn't have got any of that if he'd lived long enough to see his solicitor, would you?"

"No. But neither would Stephen."

"Except that he's not going to get any of it if he's convicted. It'll all go to you then, won't it?"

"I suppose so," said Silas slowly. "But that's not my fault."

"No. Unless, of course, you planned the whole thing. From start to finish."

"Don't be ridiculous."

"But is it so ridiculous? After all, you're the one who's been pulling the strings in your family for a long time now."

"I don't know what you're talking about."

"Don't you? Well, let's go back to the blackmail letter addressed to your father that you opened. It was you who insisted on reading it to your brother, and then, just a few weeks later, you were the one who got him up in the middle of the night to eavesdrop on your father and Sergeant Ritter while they were making their plans to kill Mr. Carson."

"Stephen had a right to know."

"Maybe. But it certainly mattered to you that he did. And then every time he went to confront your father, you hung back."

"I couldn't face it. I've already told you that."

"Yes. But wasn't that rather convenient for you? Stephen ended up out in the cold, while you stayed home taking photographs of your father's manuscript collection."

"I'm not saying what I did was right," said Silas slowly. "Or that my father was a good man. But I didn't have to quarrel with him if I didn't want to. I had a choice just like Stephen."

"Of course you did. But what were your motives in making that choice, Mr. Cade? Was it that you hoped to get Stephen disinherited while he was out of the way, so that you'd get everything when your father died? He was a sick man, after all."

"I didn't think about that. I didn't want him to die. And it was me who persuaded Stephen to go back when I heard my father hadn't got long to live. Why would I have done that if I wanted to cut my brother out?" asked Silas, suddenly confident, as if he felt he'd won the argument.

But Swift was ready with his answer. "Because your first plan hadn't worked," he said. "Your father was in the clutches of Reg Ritter, and you'd found out he was going to disinherit you as well as Stephen."

"Stephen had a right to know what he was going to do."

"Yes. But it was the same pattern as before, wasn't it?"

"What pattern? I don't know what you're talking about."

"Yes, you do. You were pushing Stephen all the time behind the scenes—delivering letters, arranging visits. But yet you never stuck your head up above the parapet with your father. Not once."

"I didn't push Stephen to do anything."

"Oh, yes, you did. You practically drafted his letter to your father."

"I helped him write it. There's nothing wrong with that."

"Maybe not. But then you just happen to see the entry in your father's diary about seeing his solicitor. Blackburn. Three o'clock. You remember that, Mr. Cade?"

"Of course I do. But I didn't just happen to see it. Both Stephen and I agreed that it was important to watch what our father was doing, given what I'd heard him say to Ritter."

"About the will?"

"Yes."

"Well, you were certainly the one for the job, weren't you? Always reading people's mail and listening at their windows in the middle of the night. You led your brother along every inch of the way, telling him he was the one who should talk to your father, because you were adopted and he wouldn't listen to you."

"That's true. He wouldn't have."

"Do you understand what I'm putting to you, Mr. Cade? You inflamed your brother to just the right level and then you kept him there. Until you were ready to arrange his final meeting with your father."

"I didn't arrange it. Stephen did."

"But you told him to ask for it. Because you realised that you'd run out of time. You had to get rid of your father before he saw his solicitor, and you needed someone to take the blame."

"No," protested Silas angrily, but Swift ignored him.

"And who better than your brother?" he went on relentlessly. "You hated him because he took your place. Once he was there, you could never forget that you were adopted, that you were second best."

"I wasn't second best," said Silas. Tears had welled up in his grey eyes and his knuckles were white from clutching the sides of his chair.

"You felt you were, though," countered Swift. "He took your mother away from you, after all. And you hated him for it, didn't you?"

"No. I loved him. He's my brother."

"You're lying, Mr. Cade," said Swift, relaxing suddenly. "You set your brother up for your father's murder so that he'd be the one who paid for it and you'd inherit everything: the house, the art, the car, the money. The whole shooting match."

"Damn you. Damn you to hell," shouted Silas, finally losing his temper in the face of Swift's taunts.

But the barrister ignored him. He hadn't finished yet. "You waited for Stephen to leave the study that night, and then you walked in there quite calmly and shot your father in the head. Maybe the fact that he wasn't your real father made it easier. But anyway, you only needed one bullet because you were already a very good shot, and you'd been practising. Hadn't you, Mr. Cade?"

"No. I bloody well hadn't. I don't even own a fucking gun."

Silas looked like he had plenty more to say, but the judge didn't give him the opportunity. "Control your language, young man," he said, almost spitting out the words. "Do you hear me? Any more swearing and I'll hold you in contempt. This is a courtroom, not some bar."

"I'm sorry," said Silas, biting his lip. He had tried to get up from his chair as he answered Swift's last question and had inadvertently put pressure on his injured foot. Now he was breathing deeply, trying to control the pain. Beads of sweat stood out on his pale face.

"You didn't expect your brother to come back into the study when he did," said Swift, resuming his attack. "But you kept your nerve. You waited behind the curtains while he picked up your gun and you slipped out just before he started shouting. It was just bad luck that there was a full moon and your mistress happened to be looking down into the courtyard when you went over to the front door."

"I didn't. I was nowhere near the courtyard."

"So you say, Mr. Cade. So you say."

But Silas wasn't prepared to leave it at that. Something in him rebelled against the lawyer's self-assurance.

"It's not just me who says it," he shouted across the court. "It's Sasha Vigne as well. And you didn't accuse me of murdering my father when I came here before. Why not, if that's what you and Stephen believed. Why not?"

"I'm not here to answer your questions, Mr. Cade," said Swift quietly. "It's you who must answer mine."

"And I have. But they're not my prints on the key and they're not my prints on the gun. They're my brother's. My bloody murdering brother," said

Silas, pointing toward Stephen in the dock. Silas was crying now, and his voice had broken.

"That's enough," said the judge, banging his table hard with his fist. "I've already warned you about your behaviour, sir. Any more and I'll put you in the cells. Do you understand me? Have you any more questions, Mr. Swift?" he asked, turning to the barrister.

"No, my lord," said Swift. He'd got what he needed from Silas. There was nothing to be gained by any further exchanges.

All in all, the cross-examination had gone even better than he'd hoped, Swift thought, as he sat back in his chair, allowing himself to mentally unwind. He'd known he'd be able to show the jury that Silas was a liar and a pervert who had both motive and opportunity to kill his father. The evidence was there for all these allegations, and Silas couldn't deny it. The bonus was that Silas had finally cracked and lost his temper. That had been the missing ingredient up to now. Without it the jury might not believe that Silas had the stomach for the crime. And now they might. And *might* was enough— enough for a verdict based on reasonable doubt.

But that outcome depended on Stephen's not cracking himself when it came his turn to give evidence. Because God knows he'd had motive and opportunity too. And, as Silas had said, Stephen's prints were on the key and the gun. Swift glanced behind him at his client. Stephen's fists were clenched around the rail of the dock and his eyes were bright with anger as his brother limped past him down the aisle. He'd have to control himself in the witness box if he was to have a chance. And yet he was so headstrong and there was no barrister in the business better at riling a witness if he wanted to than Thompson. And Tiny would have the judge on his side as well. Swift felt his own fists clenching involuntarily as he glanced up at Old Murder sitting so self-righteously up on his dais.

Briefly Swift reconsidered the possibility of not calling his client. Stephen didn't have to give evidence after all, but he was desperate to do so, and, in all conscience, Swift didn't feel able to keep him out of the witness box. The prosecution case was too strong. That was the trouble. It needed an answer.

But giving an answer opened Stephen up to Thompson, waiting like a hawk on the other side of the court, circling over his prey.

Swift drummed his fingers on his table, trying in vain to find an outlet for his frustration. He was damned if he called his client, and damned if he didn't. That was the truth. He needed a drink, he thought suddenly. A double or even a triple whisky. And another after that as well.

EIGHTEEN

Sasha settled herself into her window seat and breathed a sigh of relief as the train pulled out of Paddington Station, and yet within moments she was twisting and turning again, trying to get comfortable. It wasn't her immediate surroundings that were causing her distress. The compartment was half-empty, and there was room to stretch out her legs. No, it was the memory of Stephen's face as he'd stared at her across the courtroom while she gave her evidence that was troubling her. She'd tried to avoid his gaze but there had not been one moment when she'd not felt his eyes boring into her, pleading with her to tell the truth. And yet she'd lied, over and over again and without hesitation. Why? Looking out the train window at the passing suburbs, Sasha realised that she didn't really have a satisfactory answer. She already had the codex, after all. She'd gone to the hospital and made Silas tell her about its new hiding place at the back of the manuscript gallery as soon as she'd given her statement to the police. Because that had been their agreement. And perhaps that was why she'd lied to the court today. Because she'd given her word. Keeping her promises was rapidly becoming her only virtue, she reflected bitterly.

Sasha screwed up her eyes in a vain effort to suppress the picture of Stephen in his prison cell waiting for the executioner to come. But that wasn't inevitable, she told herself, just as she had so many times before. Perhaps

Stephen would get off. All he needed was reasonable doubt. It was like she'd told the policeman: she hadn't pointed the finger at Stephen; all she'd done was help to exonerate his brother. And yet in truth Sasha knew that nothing would've stopped her from doing whatever was necessary to secure the codex once she'd found out that Silas had it. It was no excuse that she felt herself in the grip of a force more powerful than she was: that didn't stop her hating herself for what she'd done back in Courtroom number 1, but she knew that the decision to give Silas his alibi had never really been in her hands.

And the jury had believed her. She felt sure of it. Stephen's clever barrister had certainly done his best, taking her through her first statement to the police line by line, but she had been ready with an explanation for her change of story that—try as he might—he couldn't shoot down. Because no one knew her mother like Sasha did. The old bitch was more Roman Catholic than the pope. Sex was a bad thing that could just about be tolerated if it was for the purpose of manufacturing Catholic babies, but pursued for pleasure outside the confines of marriage it was a mortal sin. It led to ruin, just like what had happened to Sasha's father when he chose to fornicate with his students rather than teach them medieval art history. Sasha had had no difficulty describing to the jury how her mother would have reacted to hearing about her affair with Silas, because that is exactly how she had reacted when Sasha phoned her the day before to tell her what she was planning to say in court. Sasha had held the receiver away from her ear for at least a minute while the old woman shouted herself hoarse. She'd obviously not told the jury that her mother had long since ceased to have any hold on her.

Sasha didn't want to admit it to herself, but part of her had almost enjoyed her sparring match with the defence barrister, at least while it was happening. The point about lying was that it took practice, and God knows she'd had enough of that. She'd worked with John Cade eight hours a day, five days a week, for more than eighteen months, and he'd never once guessed who she really was. Perhaps it was because he needed to trust her. There was, after all, nobody else at the manor house who understood the significance or the value of what he owned. And she was his lifeline to the outside world. He never went outside the gates himself, and so he had to rely on her to go to libraries and visit the auction houses. At the end, she was all he had to rely on in his long, hopeless search for the jewelled cross of St. Peter, and so he had had no choice but to trust her. It was as if he had been taken in by all Ritter's boasts about his state-of-the-art security system. Cade viewed everything and everybody outside his gates with a distrust bordering on paranoia, but once someone had got inside the enclosure, his suspicions seemed to vanish. Ritter and his wife had been quite right when they testified that Cade never locked the internal door of his study.

Once or twice Sasha had come close to exposing herself, although it was Ritter, not Cade, whose watchfulness she feared. The worst time had been only a month or two before Cade's death. They had been sitting at dinner in the big dark dining room. It was a dismal place with shadowy portraits on the walls and heavy mahogany furniture that had long since lost its shine. The lights in the half chandeliers overhead were always too dim, and conversation was a struggle against the silence. Except for Ritter. The dining room was where he was at his most animated. Because it was the one room from which Silas could not escape. It guaranteed Ritter a victim and an audience for at least half an hour every day.

But on this particular evening Ritter went too far. Perhaps he had drunk too much, but his insinuations about Silas's sexuality turned to outright accusation, and Cade pulled the sergeant up short.

"You're out of line, Reg," he said. "Silas may not have the balls to say 'boo' to a goose, let alone a girl, but that doesn't make him queer. If he was, I'd kick him out of here without thinking twice about it."

Ritter was silenced. He couldn't respond, not even when Silas shot him a look of triumphant hatred across the table. And meanwhile, Cade was warming to his theme. He was usually silent in the evenings, letting Ritter run the conversation, but tonight was different. He'd got two bottles of vintage red wine up from the cellar, and the food had been less heavy and stodgy than usual.

"Queers are all the same, you know," said Cade, sitting back in his chair at the end of the table and twirling his glass of wine in his hand. "They've all got one thing in common."

"They can't be trusted," said Ritter, trying to recover his employer's approval.

"That too. But what they really can't do is control themselves. I had first-hand experience of this before the war, you know."

"Where?" asked Ritter.

"Here in Oxford. There was a fellow over at Worcester College. Blayne, he was called. Taught medieval art just like me and put himself forward for the university professorship when old Spencer died in thirty-seven."

"At the same time as you?" asked Silas.

"That's right. Anyway, we were both being considered by the selection panel when one of Blayne's students came forward and said that Blayne had been having relations with him."

"You're joking," said Ritter, laughing.

"No, I'm not. At three o'clock every Tuesday. Once a week for three months. During their one-on-one tutorials. That was the end of Blayne's candidacy, of course."

"I should hope so," said Ritter.

"Yes. But my point is the man couldn't control himself. He knew how important it was to stay out of trouble when he was applying for the professorship, but he just couldn't keep his hands off the first pretty boy that came along. And why not? Because he was queer. That's why."

Cade smiled complacently and poured himself another glass of wine, and it was all that Sasha could do to stop herself reaching over and throwing it in his mottled corrupt old face. Instead she bit her lip until the blood flowed inside her mouth, and, unseen, she stabbed her nails into the palms of her hands under the table. But, when she looked up, she saw Ritter staring at her and felt for a moment entirely naked under his gaze, as if he knew exactly what she was thinking.

"Are you all right, Sasha?" he asked. "You look very pale all of a sudden."

"I'm fine," she replied, answering a shade too quickly. "It must have been quite convenient for you, Professor," she said, turning to Cade.

"What?"

"This Blayne man turning out to be a homosexual. Didn't it get rid of your rival for the professorship?"

"I suppose so," said Cade languidly. "But he wasn't really a rival, you know. He'd published very little and what he had was rather second-rate. He didn't have the same reputation as me."

"I'm sure he hadn't," said Ritter, laughing. "He was a nancy boy, wasn't he?"

"Yes. But he had a wife and daughter too, you know, although whether that was for cover or because he couldn't acknowledge the truth about himself, I don't know."

"What happened to them?" asked Sasha, unable to resist asking the question, although it cost her an almost superhuman effort to keep her voice steady.

"The wife left him. And he lost everything. His fellowship too. The last I heard he was lecturing miners' sons in South Wales."

"Well, he'd better watch himself if he tries molesting them," said Ritter. "Or he'll end up underground for good."

Sasha couldn't stand it anymore. While Cade and the sergeant were still laughing, she got up, pushing her chair back against the wall behind her.

"I think maybe the sergeant's right. I'm not feeling so well after all," she said, holding her napkin up to her face to hide the tears that were starting in her eyes. "I think I'll go and lie down for a while."

"You do that, my dear. And I hope you feel better soon," said Cade benevolently. "We've got important work to do tomorrow."

Sasha hated Cade more than ever after that evening. She could not look at him without thinking of her father shambling around Oxford in his old unmended clothes. In the evenings, Cade would sometimes lean on her shoulder as they came down the stairs from the manuscript gallery, and she would think how easy it would be to push him forward and watch him break up like an old doll as he turned and turned, bouncing off the bannisters until he hit the ground at the bottom with a final thud.

But she did nothing. The stakes were too high, and Cade was her only hope of finding the codex and the cross. And so she watched herself even more closely than before, burying her hatred beneath a cool, professional exterior that deceived even Ritter. He was the one that she always feared. She couldn't rid herself of the sense that he suspected her. But perhaps he had that effect on everyone. There was only one person he had ever been loyal to, and that was Cade. Still, they were both dead now. And Jeanne too, although Sasha didn't want to think about Jeanne. It was too horrible what had happened. She wished she could've done something more to protect the poor woman from her monstrous husband, but at the same time she realised her own impotence. The sense of defeat that she had felt after trying to confront Ritter in the kitchen was still fresh in her mind. The man was a force of nature, and she was glad he was dead.

And she had the codex. That was what mattered. She'd fulfilled her bargain with Silas, although more than once in the last few days she'd considered throwing him over. The thought of his watching her from a distance, taking pictures of her body, revolted her. She remembered how his eyes had always been drawn to her disfigurement. That was what he'd photographed. She didn't need to see the pictures to know that. Silas had told her that he'd burnt them. He'd given her his word about that, and she was minded to believe him. But still they had existed. Policemen had leered at them together. She knew they had. And all because of Silas. Sasha hated him almost as much as his father, but yet she had given false evidence for him. She'd given him his alibi and possibly condemned his brother to a horrible death, she thought bitterly.

It was all too much. She'd think about Stephen some other time, she told herself. When she was feeling stronger. But in her heart she knew that the only way to survive was to cut him out of her consciousness forever. It was a small price to pay for the codex, even if it meant diminishing herself, and she knew that there would almost certainly be other even more difficult sacrifices she would have to make if she was ever to get her hands on the cross of St. Peter.

The train drew into Oxford, and Sasha gathered her things together. The railway station reminded her, as it always did, of the time she'd come here as a little girl to visit her father. She'd been too young to travel alone, and so her mother had accompanied her on the journey. But her mother had made her feelings clear by dressing in black, complete with a veil, just as if she was going to a funeral, and she had ignored her daughter all the way, immersing herself instead in a thick book of Catholic sermons. When they got to Oxford, her father was waiting on the platform in the rain. He looked bedraggled and unkempt in an old mackintosh, and his thinning hair stuck to his skull in clumps. Sasha had been looking forward to seeing him for weeks, but when she saw him she felt ashamed. She didn't run to him when he recognised her but instead hung back, taking her cue from her mother's look of contemptuous disdain.

Sasha understood now, all these years later, how important that day had been for her, which is why she remembered it so clearly. She had been hoping that the train taking her mother and her toward Oxford would also reunite them with her father. But it had been a childish dream. On the platform,

Sasha's mother would not go near her husband, not even to pass the time of day. Sasha remembered how her father had taken a few hesitant steps toward them until his wife's evident antipathy stopped him in his tracks. Sasha's mother said nothing. She didn't need to. The arrangements had already been made by letter. She just looped Sasha's hand around the handle of her small tan suitcase and pushed her forward toward her father. It had been like crossing a border between enemy countries, Sasha thought now as she stood in the same place where she had been twenty years earlier. She'd been too young for such an ordeal.

Her father had been working at an obscure art college in the suburbs, filling in for somebody else for very little money. He had no car and there were no buses at the station, so they walked for what seemed like hours through the rain, with him carrying her suitcase, until they got to the dingy little flat that was his temporary home. The next day Sasha woke up on a camp bed with a fever and had to go back to her mother's early. Soon afterward Sasha's visits to her father had stopped altogether and her mother had not seen fit to even inform her absent husband when Sasha was assaulted by the teacher at her school. In fact, she had even found a way to blame Sasha's father for what had happened, and in later years it became an article of faith for Sasha's mother that the vivid burn mark covering her daughter's neck and shoulders had been put there by God as a punishment for the sins of her husband.

Sasha also believed that the burn was no accident. But unlike her mother, she didn't think it had anything to do with her father. The disfigurement made her different from other people, and she believed that she had been singled out because it was her destiny to achieve something special. She was going to find the cross that should have been her father's. She had known from the first that it would not be easy, but she was determined that no one would stand in her way. Cade deserved exactly what he had got: a bullet in the head. And now she had the codex. It was the key to the cross's hiding place. She was certain of it. She would make better use of it than he ever had.

Sasha hailed a taxi outside the station and gave the driver an address in North Oxford. It was good to have a place of her own at last, even if it was only a bed-sit in someone else's house. She had left the manor house immediately after Inspector Trave's visit, while Silas was still in hospital, and had rented the room under an assumed name. It felt safe. No one would find her there.

She told the taxi to wait and went upstairs. The book was where she had left it, hidden among her clothes, with Cade's mysterious sheet of notepaper tucked inside. She put it in a briefcase that she'd bought for the purpose and went back down the stairs. Twenty minutes later she was standing outside the door of her father's room. There was no reply to her knock, and so she turned the key and went inside.

Andrew Blayne was sleeping in his chair. His head had fallen forward onto his chest, and his mouth was slightly open. His breath was uneven, and Sasha, watching from the doorway, felt for a moment like she was waiting for him to die. There seemed no good reason why another breath should come to rattle his thin, fragile frame. Except that it did. Again and again. His body's mechanism would tick on until everything was worn away. It seemed cruel to Sasha. At least his trembling hands were still while he slept. Better perhaps that everything should be still and that her father's pain should end forever.

The room was cold, and Sasha went over to the fireplace and tried without much success to stir the coals back into some semblance of life. The noise woke her father.

"Half your books are missing. And where's the gramophone?" she asked, but she already knew the answer to her question. There was a pawnbroker's ticket on the mantelpiece next to where she was standing. "I've got money," she said. "For God's sake, let me give you some, Daddy."

"No, I'll be all right," said Blayne. "It was only to tide me over until the end of the month."

Sasha wondered if he would last that long, but there was nothing she could do if he would not let her help him. She leant over and pulled the codex out of the briefcase, placing it in her father's trembling hands.

"Here's something to take your mind off your troubles," she said. "Beautiful, isn't it? It's the real thing."

"The codex of Marjean." Blayne said the words like they were a prayer or some magical incantation. Tears stood out in the corners of his watery blue eyes as he slowly turned the thick vellum pages.

"Where did you get it, Sasha?" he asked. There was fear in his eyes now, supplanting the first look of wonder.

"Cade had it all the time," she said. "It's a long story, and I can't tell it to you now. I need you to look at this."

Carefully, Sasha opened out the folded sheet of notepaper with the series of numbers in columns that she had first seen in Cade's study, when Silas had taken the codex out of his father's chess box.

"This was inside the codex," she said. "I need to know what it means."

"It's Cade's handwriting. I recognize the way he wrote his sevens. They were always distinctive," said Blayne, examining the paper. "It must be his key to the code."

"I know that," said Sasha impatiently. "What do you think I've been doing for the past three days? I've tried everything, but they're numbers, not letters. You can't read numbers."

"The numbers must be telling you the position of the letters in the codex," said Blayne quietly. He was holding the piece of paper in one hand and comparing it with the first page of the codex. "How extraordinary," he went on after a moment. "It must have taken him more than ten years to get this far."

"How do you know?"

"Because of the dates. We can assume Cade got possession of the codex in 1944, and then he went to France and got shot in 1956. Twelve long years. And all the time he can't have known that there *was* a code to break at all. He was in the dark. The frustration must have been terrible."

"You don't know it was twelve years. It's just a guess that he went to Marjean in 1956 because of the codex."

"Maybe. But it's a good guess."

"I don't care what kind of guess it is," said Sasha, unable to contain her irritation. "I haven't got twelve years. I need to know what these numbers mean now."

"Well, the first thing you need to do is stop thinking like that, Sasha. Good codes are like the insides of old clocks. You have to work on them slowly. And you need to get inside the mind of the man who made the code in the first place. He didn't think like we do."

Sasha clenched her fists, trying to hold back her exasperation, and her father smiled.

"You used to do that when you were a child," he said. "Look, don't despair,

Sasha. We have Cade's key. And with it the knowledge that there is a code and that it can be cracked. There will be pleasure in this for me. It will make me forget my landlady for a little while. I'm very grateful to you."

Sasha couldn't help laughing. She felt relieved: if anyone could decipher Cade's key, it would be her father. She could tell from the look in his eye that his curiosity was aroused. She didn't need to worry that he wouldn't do his best.

She got up to leave, but at the door he called her back. There was a look of anxiety on his face, and he had put the codex back on the table. His hands were trembling more than ever.

"What if I do crack this code, Sasha? What will you do then?" he asked. His voice was full of fear.

Sasha stood in the doorway without answering. She didn't need to. Blayne knew the answer to his own question.

"You'll go to France just like he did, won't you?" he said. "And something terrible will happen to you."

"No, it won't. I can look after myself."

"How? You're a woman on your own, and he had that man Ritter with him. From what you tell me, he was lucky to come home alive."

"I'll be more careful. I've told you before, Daddy. I've come too far to stop now."

"Maybe. But I haven't. I don't need to look at this book," said Blayne, making a show of pushing it away.

"Ah, but you will," said Sasha with a smile, "I know you too well. It's in your blood. And whatever you find out, you owe it to me to tell me."

"So you can kill yourself with my blessing?"

"No, I won't kill myself," said Sasha, crossing over to her father and putting her hand on his shoulder. "I tell you what I'll do. If you crack the code, we'll decide what to do with it together. And, in the meantime, you must take this, and I'll go to the pawnbroker and get your things back."

Sasha had put three ten-pound notes on the codex as she spoke, and now she picked up the pawn ticket and kissed her father on the crown of his head before turning to leave.

"It probably won't matter anyway," he muttered. "The codex didn't take Cade to the cross, and he cracked the code."

Sasha opened her mouth to respond, but then thought better of it. Let her father console himself with such reflections if he wanted to, she thought. They did no harm. And there was no reason why she needed to tell her father how much she believed in the codex. The book would take her to the cross. She was sure of it. Cade's failure didn't deter her. He had simply taken a wrong turn somewhere. That was all.

At the door she glanced back into the room and saw that he had picked up Cade's sheet of notepaper again and was running his shaking finger up and down the list of numbers.

The sight renewed Sasha's optimism, and she took the stairs two at a time. Outside she made for the High Street. She could get a bus there to take her home. She smiled at the word. A bed, a chair, and a wardrobe didn't make a home. But the room was safe and warm. And she could close her eyes and go to sleep, secure in the knowledge that Silas and his cameras were far away and that she had got from him all that she had ever wanted.

She leant against a recess in the wall opposite Queen's College and idly watched the passing cars. It was the rush hour and the traffic was moving slowly in both directions. Soon a red light farther down the road brought the flow on her side to a complete halt, and her eyes rested on a black Jaguar that had stopped almost parallel with where she was standing. There was a man driving, and a woman beside him in the passenger seat. They were obviously arguing. The woman was gesticulating almost violently with her hands, and the man kept twisting around toward her to deliver a flurry of angry words before turning back to check the road in front of him.

With a start Sasha recognised Stephen's girlfriend, Mary. She hadn't seen her since the night of the murder. And now here she was, arguing with this strange foreign-looking man inside an expensive car. There was something about his high cheekbones and narrow eyes that made Sasha uneasy. Of course there was nothing wrong with Mary's finding another man to spend her time with, given where Stephen was heading. But the choice seemed strange. Mary had struck her as so sweet natured and devoted to Stephen when she had visited the manor house in the week before Cade's murder, and yet here she was now with this hard-looking man. He looked capable of anything. Involuntarily, Sasha turned away from the car and faced the wall, pretending to look for something in her empty briefcase. Without knowing why, she realised that she didn't want Mary to see her. The ploy seemed to have been successful, for when she turned back a minute later, the Jaguar had disappeared from view, and her bus was coming up the road toward her.

Sasha settled herself into a corner seat and thought of the Marjean codex open on her father's table. He would translate Cade's numbers into letters. She was sure of it. And the letters would tell her the way to St. Peter's cross. Cade had failed to find it, but she wouldn't make the same mistakes. It was her destiny to have it. She knew it was. Closing her eyes, Sasha pictured the cross in her hands. The wood was ancient, cut from one of the oak trees that used to grow in such profusion on the hills around Jerusalem. Jesus Christ had been nailed to it by the Jews, and Simon Peter had worn it around his neck until the Romans crucified him too. The jewels had come later. They authenticated the cross and made it heavy, too heavy to wear according to the old authors. They spoke of great uncut rubies and emeralds, sapphires and diamonds, and Sasha imagined the lights of the gemstones mixing together in the candlelight of Charlemagne's church to create a precious rainbow, an earthly representation of the lights of heaven. Sasha longed for the cross. It was a wonder of the world, worth nothing less than everything to obtain.

By the time she got back to her room, Sasha had entirely forgotten about Mary Martin and the man in the car. As so often happened, the thought of the codex and the cross had driven every other experience right out of her head.

NINETEEN

Above all Stephen felt a sensation of weight. The air itself seemed heavy, pressing down on his chest, making it difficult to breathe. It wasn't at all how he had imagined it was going to be. He had pictured the witness box as an opportunity, his chance to convince the doubters, to win them over to his side. But it was nothing like that. He directed his answers at the jury just as his barrister had told him to, but the jurors' faces remained impassive. There were no connections to be made. He was surrounded by people hanging on his every word, and yet he was completely alone.

Swift had let him tell his story. It was the same one he'd told the police on the day after his father died. And time hadn't made it any more credible than it had been then. If only he hadn't gone back to the study. If only he hadn't picked up the gun. Every choice that he'd made had taken him further down the wrong road. And Stephen didn't need to be told where that road led. It was why everyone was here. To see if he was going to live or die.

The moment had arrived. Gerald Thompson got to his feet and gazed at Stephen over the top of his gold-rimmed half-moon spectacles, allowing the silence to build around the accused. Standing in the witness box, waiting to be attacked, Stephen felt a curious sense of disassociation from himself. It reminded him of a scene that seemed to happen so often in the war movies he had watched insatiably as a child. The man from the gestapo would come into the interrogation room, carefully removing his black leather gloves as he approached the table. It was always immediately obvious that he was an entirely different species of man from the soldiers that had been asking the prisoner questions up to then. For a start, he wore no uniform. Just an immaculately pressed double-breasted suit under his heavy tan mackintosh, with a small swastika on the lapel. He carried a small briefcase and looked just like a businessman arriving for a company meeting. There was nothing strong or hardy about him, and he never raised his voice. But the battle-hardened soldiers all instinctively shrank away from the new arrival. They knew that he was capable of things that they would prefer not to even imagine, and the cinema audience was left in no doubt that it was all over for the brave British airman sitting handcuffed to the chair with his back to the door. Thompson would've gone far in the gestapo, thought Stephen. He looked over at the prosecutor and realised with a shudder that the little man desired his death just as much as he himself wanted to live. It pushed Stephen onto the back foot before the cross-examination had even begun.

"How would you describe your relationship with your father in the last two years of his life?" Thompson began at last. There was a measured deliberation about the question, as if it was the first move in a long-planned game of chess.

But Stephen answered immediately without considering his reply. "We were estranged," he said. "We had no relationship."

"And that was because of your anger against him, yes?"

"It was more shame than anger. I couldn't cope with what he had done. He'd killed people in cold blood. And it was obvious he felt no remorse."

"And your feelings were strong enough that you cut off all contact with him?"

"Yes. I felt I had no choice."

"So you left. Stayed away for two whole years. Did your father make any effort to contact you all the time you were away?"

"No, I think he was glad to be rid of me. He blamed me for my mother's death. It was like he hated me."

Stephen cursed himself as soon as the words were out of his mouth. It was what Swift had told him not to do. To volunteer information, to provide openings. Thompson wasn't slow to take advantage.

"And you'd done nothing to deserve your father's hatred," he said. "The injustice must have made you very angry."

"I tried not to think about it."

"But did you succeed? Isn't the reality, Mr. Cade, that as the months passed and turned into years, you became more angry with your father, not less?"

"No. Like I told you, I didn't think about him."

"I see. Well, why then did you go back to your father in the middle of last year, if you'd been so successful in putting him out of your mind?"

"Because of what Silas told me. That he didn't have long to live. Knowing that made everything seem different."

"Yes. Particularly if you were going to be disinherited. That was the real reason you went back to Moreton, wasn't it? To stop your father from chang- ing his will. By any means possible."

"No," said Stephen. "The will was only one of the reasons."

But Thompson didn't let him finish. "You'd had enough, hadn't you, Mr. Cade?" he went on, pressing home his advantage. "Two years of thinking about the injustice and the rejection, and then your brother tells you that your father's going to disinherit you. It made you want to kill him, didn't it? You'd had enough."

"No, I wanted to talk to him. That's all."

"Are you sure about that? Remember what you said to Inspector Trave in your interview. That you told your father he deserved to die. Is that what you said?"

"Yes. But I didn't mean it."

"Didn't you? It's just a coincidence then that your father was murdered that evening?"

"Yes; I didn't kill him."

"So you say. But then who did?"

"Silas—it had to be Silas." Stephen couldn't keep the desperation out of his voice. "He must've hid in the curtains and slipped out after I came back. Jeanne Ritter saw him in the courtyard."

"So she said. But she had a reason to lie. And so do you, Mr. Cade. From the outset you've tried to blame everybody but yourself. First of all it was the mysterious man in the Mercedes, and then you changed your mind and said it was your brother. Who will it be next?"

"I just know it wasn't me."

"Because you were there. Well, perhaps you better tell us again what happened between you and your father that evening."

"We talked."

"About what?"

"The will. Him dying. He said he wouldn't discuss those things with me. I asked him for money for Mary, my girlfriend, because her mother needed to have an operation, but he refused to give it to me. He said I was lying to him. That I needed the money to pay debts, but that wasn't true at all. He was just being cynical like he always was. So we argued, and then he said that I could have the money if I beat him at chess. It was ridiculous. He was just playing with me, like he used to do when I was a kid. He'd be black and play without one of his pieces, but he always won. And that evening was just the same. I don't know why I went through with it. Perhaps I thought he'd do the decent thing for once."

"And lose?"

"Yes. I know I was stupid."

"And how did you feel when he didn't do the decent thing?"

"I was upset. Obviously. The money meant nothing to him and everything to me."

"Why everything?"

"Not everything. I'm exaggerating," said Stephen nervously. "Mary said she'd have to go and look for work up in London if I couldn't get the money from my father. I didn't want her to go."

"Because you were in love with her?"

Stephen didn't answer, and the judge was quick to intervene.

"Answer the question," he demanded, fixing Stephen with an unfriendly glare.

"Yes, I loved her," said Stephen finally. "I still do."

"So the game of chess was for high stakes?" asked Thompson, carrying on where he'd left off.

"I suppose so. It didn't make me do any better, though. My father was black and without a knight, but he still beat me. Easily. I should never have played him."

"Because it just made you angrier than you'd been before, when he refused to give you the money in the first place."

"Yes. It's not a crime to be angry, is it?" said Stephen defiantly. But Thompson ignored the question.

"What happened after you lost the game?" he asked.

"He grinned at me. Said, 'better luck next time,' or something sarcastic like that. I told him that I'd had enough, that I'd expose him, make everyone know what he'd done. I meant it as well. It wasn't like before."

"This wasn't the first time you'd threatened to expose him then?" asked Thompson. As he had anticipated, Stephen's desire to talk about how he had been treated had got the better of the unnatural reticence that his barrister had forced on him. All Thompson had to do was to nudge him along, and Stephen would soon reveal the full depth of his rage against the dead man.

"No, it wasn't the first time," said Stephen. "I said I'd do it when I first found out what he'd done to those people in France. Silas and I were listening outside the window of the study, and he and Ritter were gloating about it. How they'd left no survivors, and so it had to be Carson who'd written the blackmail letter. I made my father promise to stop Ritter going after Carson, and I left it at that. He was telling me how it would disgrace the family name if I went to the police and how he was too ill to cope with a trial. He had a way with words, but I shouldn't have listened to him."

"And so then two years later you threatened to expose him again. How did he react?"

"He laughed at me. He said there were no witnesses now. Nobody except him and Ritter. Then he went over to his desk and got out a newspaper cutting about Carson's death. It was from a few months before, and it was obvious that Carson hadn't fallen off a train. Ritter had pushed him. And my father had lied to me again. He hadn't done anything to stop Ritter from murdering Carson. It probably just took them longer to find him than they'd first thought. Maybe if I'd gone to the police when I first found out about Marjean, Carson would still be alive."

"And all this went through your mind when your father showed you that cutting, didn't it, Mr. Cade?"

"Yes, of course it did," said Stephen, leaning forward in the witness box and throwing caution to the winds. "He disgusted me, sitting there looking so smug with all that blood on his hands. People's lives meant nothing to him. Nothing at all."

"Yours included?"

"Yes."

"And that made you angry?"

"Of course it did."

"Very angry?"

"I don't know." Stephen's voice was suddenly quiet as if he had just realised where his answers had led him.

"I suggest you do know," said Thompson, switching seamlessly on to the offensive. "You were angrier with your father than you'd ever been in your life before. Everything suddenly came together. The changing of his will, his refusal to give you the money for your girlfriend, the way he'd toyed with you over the chess game, the shame that he'd brought down on your head, and all the lies he'd told you." Thompson ticked off John Cade's sins on his fingers one by one, but he left the worst for last. "Above all, you couldn't stand his smug indifference to everything you cared about," he said. "It drove you crazy, didn't it, Mr. Cade?"

"I was angry, like I said before. I wasn't crazy," said Stephen doggedly.

"Are you sure about that?" asked the prosecutor. "It was after your father showed you the newspaper cutting that you told him that he deserved to die. Isn't that right?"

"I don't know. I must've been referring to what Silas told me. That my father had said to Ritter that he didn't have long to live. I was saying that that's what he deserved."

"No, you weren't," countered Thompson. "You're the one who's lying now, and you know it. You said in interview that you shouted at your father that he deserved to die. *Shouted*, Mr. Cade. You shouted because you'd lost your temper. And that's when you took the gun out of your pocket and shot your father dead."

"No."

"Yes. You murdered him. And then you locked the door to give yourself some time to think."

"No, I didn't," shouted Stephen, losing his self-control. "I never locked the door. And I never killed my father. I left him sitting in his armchair and I walked down to the gate. And when I came back, he was dead. That's what happened." Stephen was breathing loudly now, and his knuckles were white from gripping the top of the witness box with his hands. Thompson's tactics had paid off. Stephen would never have reacted to the accusation with such obvious emotion if he had been hit with it straightaway.

"You're angry now, aren't you, Mr. Cade?" asked Thompson with a smile. Perhaps it was intentional. The prosecutor's smugness reminded Stephen irresistibly of his father. The half-moon glasses they wore were the same too.

"Of course I am," he said. "You're accusing me of something I never did."

"But they're your fingerprints on the gun. No one else's."

"I saw it on the floor when I came back in. It was a natural thing to do to pick it up."

"But the truth is that you never left the room in the first place, did you? If you had, you'd have taken your hat and coat with you. Unless you're seriously suggesting that you intended to go back for them after your walk."

"No, of course not. I forgot them. That's all. I was angry and upset and I just wanted to get out in the air. I wasn't thinking about my hat and coat. And it had stopped raining so I didn't need them anyway."

"You never went to the gate, Mr. Cade," Thompson went on relentlessly. "You just made that up to try and escape responsibility for what you'd done."

"No."

"You had the motive, you had the anger, and you had the gun. Your fingerprints tell their own story. You are guilty of this crime. Guilty as charged," said Thompson with finality. He sat down without waiting for Stephen to respond.

Too late, Stephen thought of all the things he had wanted to say. That he was a terrible shot, that he wouldn't have played chess with his father if he'd brought a gun to kill him with, that he wouldn't have opened the door to Ritter if he'd committed the crime. He'd have tried to escape. But it was too late now. Thompson had played him like a prize-winning angler with his catch. He'd let Stephen do his work for him, and then pulled him effortlessly ashore and left him exposed and struggling for breath. Waiting to die, thought Stephen, as he made his slow way back to the dock. Waiting to die.

TWENTY

The trial was virtually at an end. Thompson and Swift had argued for and against Stephen's guilt to the jury, and hardly anyone in the press box felt able to say which way the verdict would go. Some speculated that the jury would be unable to reach a verdict and that the trial would have to begin all over again. Others wondered aloud whether the jurors would be able to stomach sending such a young man to the gallows. But, then again, the case against Stephen Cade was strong, and everyone was frightened of guns. There were scare stories in the papers every day about armed gangs roaming the streets just like they did in New York or Los Angeles. No one was safe in their beds.

The last word lay with the judge. It was his right to comment on the evidence in his summing up, and in a case like this Old Man Murdoch was unlikely to keep his powder dry.

"Members of the jury, you are the only judges of the facts in this case," he began, leaning back in his high-backed chair and allowing his eyes to travel up and down the jurors as if he was a general inspecting his troops before they went into battle. "The verdict is yours and yours alone. So you should ignore any comments that I make on the evidence if they do not assist you. Use them only if they help you. It is your opinion that matters, not mine."

Swift could not help admiring the judge's false modesty. He made the jurors listen to what he had to say by flattering their importance. He didn't need to remind them that he had the experience of presiding over hundreds of the most serious criminal trials. He had seen it all before. It was their decision, but they would be fools to ignore the help that he had to offer them.

"So let us begin with the Crown's case against this defendant," said Murdoch. "Is it strong or is it weak? Has it been undermined by the defence? Remember, the Crown must make you sure of his guilt. Nothing less will do. Put another way, you must have gone beyond reasonable doubt. We can start with what is agreed. Stephen Cade and his father were estranged for the two years leading up to the murder. There is no dispute about that. The defendant has told you that he felt ashamed of his father and also harboured strong feelings of rejection. Whether he was right to do so is not what matters. You are concerned with his state of mind.

"At the end of this two-year period the defendant suddenly asks to see his father again. Why, members of the jury? I suggest that this is a vital question for you to answer. Was he concerned about his father's failing health as he claims, or was he inflamed by the news brought by his brother, Silas, that he was about to be disinherited? Professor Cade was clearly a very rich man, and the defendant faced the loss of all his prospects at a stroke of his father's pen.

"It is also apparent from the defendant's evidence that this bombshell could not have come at a worse time. Young Mr. Cade had particular need of money last summer if he was going to keep his girlfriend, Miss Martin, from leaving Oxford. You will need to bear these matters in mind, members of the jury, when you come to decide what Stephen Cade's intentions were when he sought a private interview with his father on the fateful night of the fifth of June. Was he quiet in his mind or had he had enough, as Mr. Thompson put it? And did his father's insensitive behaviour with the chess pieces drive his son over the edge, or merely exasperate him to the point where he felt the need for a little evening air to cool his understandable annoyance?

"Nobody can read a man's mind, members of the jury. Science cannot help you. No; what you must do is look at the evidence and use your common sense to draw inferences. There is quite enough material before you, I would suggest, to enable you to reach clear conclusions about what was in this defendant's mind on the evening of the fifth of June, and those conclusions should help you decide what happened when Professor Cade won their rather one-sided game of chess.

"Remember that the defendant has admitted shouting at his father that he deserved to die. Was he referring to his belief that his father would soon be dead through natural causes, or was it at this point that he produced the murder weapon from his pocket? You must use you common sense to decide which explanation is correct. It is not for me to say. It is your verdict.

"And then there is the fingerprint evidence for you to consider. Of course Mr. Cade does not deny that he handled the gun and the key. He would be laughed out of court if he did. But he says that he did so innocently. Do you believe him, members of the jury? Would you pick up a gun at a murder scene, or would you leave it well alone, knowing that it would be vital evidence for the police to examine when they arrived? And what about the defendant's hat and coat on the other side of the dead man's body? Did he forget about them in his rush to get outside, or did he never go outside at all?

"The defendant says that someone must have come into the study and shot his father while he was out walking in the grounds. But who is this alternative assassin? Was it a passenger in the mysterious Mercedes that the defendant claims to have seen parked across from the gate on two occasions that evening? Certainly the first officers to arrive saw a car parked by the phone kiosk, and a Mercedes was stopped for speeding between Moreton and Oxford later that night. However, you must bear in mind that there was no breach of the manor's security system that evening and that there is no one to corroborate the defendant's account that the main gate was ever open. And if it was an intruder that killed Professor Cade, then what was his or her motive? It was clearly not robbery, for nothing appears to have been taken from the study, but what about revenge? It may well be that a man called James Carson hated the professor to the point that he tried to kill him in France in 1956, but this Carson was already dead by the time of the actual murder. He couldn't have been the man in the Mercedes.

"I need to say a few words to you at this point about the evidence you have heard during this trial relating to a place called Marjean in northern France, where certain people died back in 1944. I allowed that evidence to go before you because I did not know at the time where it would lead. However it is now apparent that there is no connection whatsoever between the Marjean

deaths and the murder of Professor Cade earlier this year, and in these cir-
cumstances I am issuing you with a formal instruction to set aside all the
evidence relating to Marjean. It is irrelevant and cannot help you reach your
verdict.

"So I go back to my earlier question. Who killed Professor Cade if it was
not the defendant? Interestingly, the defence appears to have shifted its ground
on this question during the course of the trial. At first its case appeared to be
that it was an intruder, but now it points the finger at the defendant's brother,
Mr. Silas Cade. The defence relies on the evidence of Mrs. Ritter, who told
you that she saw a figure wearing his hat and coat cross the courtyard beneath
her window just before the shouting began down below. If true, this evidence
clearly goes a long way toward exonerating the defendant. But is it true? Can
you rely on Mrs. Ritter? Do not be swayed, members of the jury, by her unfor-
tunate and untimely death. You must be objective. Remember what she said
about Silas Cade. She felt betrayed by him, and it seems almost certain that
she had only learnt of that betrayal minutes before she entered this courtroom
to give evidence. Detective Clayton has told you about his ill-advised conversation with Mr. Blake in the cafeteria, and the way in which Mrs. Ritter ran
from the room. It is not difficult to imagine her anger and distress, but did it
lead her to lie?

"The question can be put another way. Was Silas Cade in the courtyard, or
was he with Sasha Vigne in her bedroom? They both admit that they lied to
the police, and Silas says that he lied to you when he first came here to give
evidence. Perjury is a very serious offence not to be taken lightly, but both
these witnesses have explained why they lied. Do you believe them? Again it
is a matter for you, members of the jury. Silas told you that his fingerprints are
not on the gun or the key. His brother's are. And it was Stephen Cade who
told their father that he deserved to die. You must decide who is telling the
truth about this and the other questions that I have posed for you. And the
answers should guide you down the road toward reaching a verdict on which
all of you must be agreed. You shall have all the time you need for that purpose."

The judge nodded to the two jury bailiffs who had taken up a position at
each end of the jury box. Now they in turn held up a copy of the King James
Bible and swore to keep the jury in a private and convenient place and not to

ask its members anything about the case except if they were agreed upon
their verdict.

And suddenly it was over. The jurors gathered up their notes and filed out
of court, soon followed by the judge, who disappeared through a door behind his dais. There was a sound of chairs being pulled back and of conversations starting up in different corners of the courtroom as Stephen was led
down the stairs at the back of the dock into the subterranean world of clanging gates and fluorescent lighting, where he would have to sit and wait for as
long as it took for twelve strangers to decide his fate.

The jury was silent all afternoon, and at half past four Judge Murdoch
called an end to the trial for the day and sent the jurors to a hotel for the night.
Stephen went back to Wandsworth, and after walking up and down in his cell
for the best part of an hour, he threw himself down on his bunk and fell into a
fitful sleep. But he got no rest, tossing and turning all night in the grip of
nightmares and apparitions. He dreamt he was back at home, searching for
something. He knew it was there, but he couldn't find it. He went from room
to room turning the furniture upside down, but there was nothing. His father
was dead downstairs and the murderer was still in the house, but Stephen
couldn't find what he was looking for.

There was shouting coming from down below. People were running this
way and that. The housemaid, Esther, was at the top of the stairs. She was
bleary with sleep, pulling a nightgown around her shoulders. And looking
past her down the stairs, Stephen could see Jeanne Ritter picking up a hat and
coat and hanging them on the stand by the door. He had no trouble recognis-
ing them. They belonged to his brother. But where was Silas? Here. Running
across the hall. He looked up for a moment, and Stephen saw the expression
on his face. The self-contained mask had slipped. Stephen saw fear and panic,
but was Silas frightened because of what he knew or because of what he did
not know? Where had he come from? Had he gone to his room after drop-
ping the hat and coat? Or perhaps someone else had worn Silas's clothes?

There was no time to try and understand, because here was Sasha Vigne
coming down the stairs. She didn't look like she had been to bed. Always so
immaculately dressed. Trouser suits and high collars. And it was no different
now. Who was she? Just his father's personal assistant or something more?
She'd said very little on each of the times that Stephen had been out to

Moreton. But she had looked watchful at dinner. Was she waiting for an opportunity?

And lastly Mary. God, she was beautiful. Her chestnut-brown hair was tousled, framing the perfect oval of her face, and Stephen longed to put out his hand to stop her, but she passed beside him, almost through him just as if he wasn't there.

The hall was empty now, and the shouting had died down. Stephen walked to the end of the hall and turned right into the corridor leading to his father's study. There were people in the doorway, but he passed through them. Ritter was by the desk talking on the telephone. He was heavy—heavy and hard. And his hands were balled up into big fists like slabs of old meat. Stephen felt the stinging pain on his cheek where the sergeant had hit him as he effortlessly joined his shadow to himself and stood hopelessly by the french windows, looking down at his dead father and a game of chess.

What he was looking for was here in this room. Stephen was certain of it. It was right in front of him, but he couldn't see it. Desperately he ran his eyes across the study. Past the hat and coat that he had left behind in the far corner, over by the window where Silas and he had eavesdropped two years before. Past the green reading lamp on the desk and the big black telephone. He saw the gun on the table by the door and the key that he had turned in the lock. He smelt the scent of jasmine on the air coming in from outside, and he examined the small round bullet hole in the middle of his father's head.

The newspaper cutting lay on the low table beside the big chess box where his father had left it. Man fallen from train. Sudden death outside Leicester. And all around were the chess pieces spread out over the board and the table. Taken pieces and untaken pieces. Stephen had never realised how beautiful they were. The delicate carving of the knights' heads and the queens' crowns. The feel of the ivory between the fingers, and the richness of the black-and-white colours. It was another language. One his father spoke like a native but he and Silas could never learn. They had never understood one another. They had never been a family at all.

The police were coming. Stephen could hear the sound of a car on the drive. Jeanne Ritter left the doorway and walked away toward the front door. She was the housekeeper, after all. It was her job to let them in. There was no time left. Stephen couldn't bear it. He looked at the chess pieces again. They held the key to what he needed. He was sure of it. But what key? Stephen couldn't work it out and suddenly he felt too tired to think anymore, too tired to move. He leant against the wall for support and took hold of one of the thick curtains that were half drawn across the french windows. And then he stood there swaying, waiting for the police to come and take him away.

Stephen was fully awake now. In truth he had only ever been half asleep, and the feeling of frustration stayed with him, although the details of his dream faded. He felt more certain than ever that he had missed something. It was just beyond his reach, but try as he might, he couldn't get to it.

Somewhere out in the half darkness the bells of Wandsworth Church rung out the hour of six. It was the beginning of another day, and Stephen wondered not for the first time how many he had left before the hangman came for him. But still there was hope. Stephen felt momentarily buoyed by the grey early-morning light seeping through his cell window. There was surely enough doubt for the jury to let him off. If it wanted to. But that was reckoning without the old judge, who seemed to want to squeeze the life out of him just because he was young. Stephen couldn't understand it. Thompson too with his mean, pitiless little eyes. They had got to the jury. Stephen felt sure of it. Thompson had pushed him back and back until he'd done just what Swift had told him not to do. He'd lost his temper. And then Murdoch had gone in for the kill. The old judge was clever. Everything seemed fair and evenly balanced, but that was an illusion. He'd told the jury what to do as much as if he'd given them a written order to convict.

But maybe they'd refuse to do what they were told. There was hope yet. Summoning up all his energy, Stephen washed, brushed his hair, and put on the black suit and tie that his lawyers had brought to the prison before the trial. Then, on the way out, he glanced over at his reflection in the small mirror hanging over the sink. But just as quickly he turned away, trying to escape from the unwanted thought that he looked exactly like a man on the way to his own funeral.

They came for him at just after three.

"It's a verdict," one of the gaolers said. It was their custom. The jury could come back to ask a question or to receive a direction from the judge. Men awaiting their fate should be able to prepare themselves as they walked down the basement corridors and then up the steep stairs that led to the courts.

Emerging into the dock, Stephen felt the sudden force of the silence in the courtroom. Downstairs there had been constant noise: keys turning in old locks and gates clanging, the screws' shouts echoing off the damp, white-washed walls. But here there was silence. There must have been nearly a hundred people in the courtroom, but not one of them spoke. They were still as statues, waiting for what was to come. It was always like this just before a verdict came in on a capital charge, but Stephen wasn't to know that. The tension frightened him. It was like ice on his soul.

Everyone was staring at him. He could feel their eyes. He closed his own, but it made him sick. When he opened them again, the jury was filing back into court.

"You've got to watch if they look at you. If they do, it's all right." A prisoner in the cell across from him at Wandsworth had told Stephen this the night before like it was gospel truth. And several of the jurors did. They definitely glanced in his direction as they took their seats. There was no mistaking it. Stephen felt a sudden hope soaring inside him. It could all be over in a few seconds. Two words, and he would be going home. To Mary and the sunlight.

"The defendant will stand," said the clerk of the court. But it was hard. Stephen's legs felt like dead weights. He had to hold on to the front of the dock to pull himself up.

"Members of the jury, have you reached a verdict upon which you are all agreed?" asked the clerk. Stephen swayed gently from side to side.

"Yes, we have," said a dapper little man with a bow tie who had got to his feet at the far end of the jury box. He was not one of those that had looked at Stephen as they came in.

"On the single count of murder, how do you find the defendant? Guilty or not guilty?"

The moment of crisis: Caesar's thumb suspended in midair, and Stephen trembling in the dock with his eyes fixed on the lion and unicorn above the judge's head. *Not guilty, not guilty, not guilty,* he prayed. The two words filled his head like a drumbeat, but the foreman of the jury couldn't hear them. He was too far away.

"Guilty," he said. Just one word and Stephen's fate was decided.

The judge nodded. It was almost imperceptible, but it conveyed all the steely satisfaction that Murdoch felt inside. He looked straight into the eyes of the broken young man in the dock, and he felt no pity at all.

"Stephen Cade," he said in a harsh voice that filled the courtroom. "Have you anything to say why sentence of death should not now be pronounced upon you?"

Stephen tried to speak, but the words stuck in his throat. It was too dry, and there was no time.

"Because I am innocent," he eventually managed to say in a hoarse whisper. "I didn't kill my father."

"You are not innocent," said the judge flatly. "You have been convicted by this jury of a heinous crime. The sentence is prescribed by law."

A tall thin man in a frock coat stepped out from behind the judge's chair. There was something in his hands. A small square of black silk. Delicately he placed it on top of the judge's wig and then stepped back into the shadows, leaving Murdoch to speak the final words.

"Stephen Cade, you are sentenced to be taken hence to the prison in which you were last confined, and from there to a place of execution where you will suffer death by hanging, and thereafter your body shall be buried within the precincts of the prison, and may the Lord have mercy upon your soul."

The judge spoke the words slowly and deliberately. It was at these moments he felt most alive. He became the law in all its cold majesty. He personified it.

But Stephen didn't hear his sentence. His legs gave way beneath him, and the prison officers on either side had to support him until the judge had left the courtroom, and it was time to stumble down the stairs at the back of the dock and begin his journey into oblivion.

PART THREE

TWENTY-ONE

Sasha visited her father six times during the two weeks after she first brought him the Marjean codex and Cade's sheet of mysterious numbers. The visits were not a success. He didn't have any answers to give her, and she found it almost impossible to contain her frustration. And her eagerness to crack the code alarmed him. He feared what would happen to her if she went after St. Peter's cross. Cade's search had ended with a bullet. Why should Sasha fare any better? And yet Andrew Blayne could not resist the lure of the codex for very long. It was such a beautiful thing, and in his heart he wanted to know its secret as much as his daughter did. It was as if the monk who had painted the Latin words on to the calfskin all those hundreds of years before was trying to talk to him across time, trying to make him understand. Alone in his attic room, Blayne stayed up night after night, poring over the Gospel of St. Luke, using up all his reserves of physical energy until he looked like a ghost of himself. His hands shook more than ever, and there was a white pallor to his face that Sasha was too preoccupied to notice.

On her last visit, Blayne had become angry with his daughter. It was unlike him, and the experience shook her. She had taken the codex away to the sofa and was trying in vain to make some connection between Cade's list of numbers and the Latin text in front of her when, without warning, Blayne came up behind her and snatched the book out of her hands.

"Why don't you leave me alone, Sasha?" he shouted. "You're in my way. Can't you see that? How can I work when you're in my way?"

Sasha *had* left him alone after that. He had her address, and she felt confident he would get in touch when he had something to tell her. She felt angry too, bruised by the change in her father. And the need to break the code blinded her to almost every other consideration. If leaving him alone was the way to get what she wanted, then she would do just that. She didn't go back to see her father for a week, and when she did, he was gone.

She realised something was wrong as soon as she got to the top of the stairs and found the door to his room ajar. It was quite late in the evening, and she could feel the force of the cold air even before she went inside. The window over the bed had blown open, and her breath hung in the air like so much white smoke.

Her father wasn't in the room, and yet he never went out after dark. Fighting down the mounting panic that she felt inside, Sasha ran down to the antiquated bathroom on the half landing below. But it was empty except for her father's shaving kit and his old green toothbrush planted in a white enamel mug above the discoloured sink. The sight of it made her cry out her father's name, even though she knew inside that he was nowhere in the house, and the noise brought the tenant of the bed-sit on the floor below to her door. She was a young woman with a wrinkled face, whom Sasha dimly remembered from several previous encounters on the stairs. A baby was crying somewhere in the background.

"Are you all right?" asked the woman, looking up at Sasha, who nodded, unable to speak for a moment because of a sob that was stuck in her throat.

"You're his daughter, aren't you? I've seen you here before."

"Yes. Do you know where he's gone?"

"They took him to hospital this morning. I was the one who went for the ambulance. He was out on the landing when I was going out to buy my milk, and he called down to me. It gave me quite a shock, I can tell you."

"Why did he call down to you? What was wrong with him?" asked Sasha, hanging on to the stair rail for support as the woman's words sank into her consciousness.

"Some sort of stroke is what they said. Meant he couldn't get down the stairs. Strokes do that, you know."

"Do what?"

"Paralyse you all down one side. I reckon that's what happened to your dad."

"You don't know that," said Sasha, suddenly angry at the woman's morbid assumption of the worst. "It might just be something temporary, for all you know."

"Well, I know he couldn't hardly move himself," said the woman defiantly. "He's been overdoing it, if you ask me, and that's what's brought this on. I've heard him every night this week, pacing up and down, and he's looked awful. But you wouldn't know, of course. You haven't been round here for a while, have you?"

Sasha swallowed hard, refusing to rise to the woman's spiteful challenge.

"Which hospital did he go to?" she asked. "Do you know that?"

"Radcliffe Infirmary. That's what they said."

"Thank you," said Sasha. "And thank you for calling the ambulance." But the woman had already closed her door, leaving Sasha alone on the landing in the semidarkness.

Outside the front door Sasha remembered the codex. But she didn't go back. She felt clutched by a terrible guilt. The woman was right. She *had* neglected her father—set him a task that was always going to be beyond his powers, and then left him to it. Alone in a cold attic room with no coal for the fire and no food in the fridge. She'd pretended that her search for the codex and the cross was for his benefit, but that had been a lie, an excuse for neglecting him when he was too old and sick to look after himself. The search was a curse. She'd sacrificed Stephen and now perhaps her father to its demands, and all it had given her in return was an old painted book and a dead man's list of meaningless numbers.

All these thoughts and more rushed through Sasha's mind as she headed across Oxford in the back of a taxi. And then at the hospital she had to sit in a cavernous reception area on the ground floor, crossing and uncrossing her legs for what seemed like hours, before a young Indian doctor appeared as if out of nowhere and told her that, yes, her father was still alive but that he couldn't offer her what she wanted to hear. He couldn't offer her any hope at all.

He said it was something called a hemorrhagic stroke. A blood vessel had burst somewhere in her father's brain some time during the previous night and now the blood was seeping slowly but surely through the cerebral lobes, shutting her father down little by little, like he was a machine. He was still conscious, but for how much longer the doctor couldn't say.

A strange calm descended over Sasha as she followed the doctor down the hospital corridors, turning this way and that until they arrived at a door marked "intensive care." Perhaps it was a reaction to the roller-coaster of emotions that she had been riding during the previous hour, but now she felt a soft sadness settling down on her like an invisible dust.

Her father was lying in the hollow of two hospital pillows, connected to a myriad of tubes and machines, and his slow death was being charted on two grey screens positioned on trolleys behind his head. He smiled when he saw his daughter and reached out his right hand for her to hold. His left hand and arm lay stretched out motionless on the white sheet, and Sasha knew without being told that he wouldn't be moving them anymore.

"How are you, Dad?" she asked, regretting the inane question as soon as it was out of her mouth.

"Dying," he answered succinctly, with a trace of a smile hovering around his pale lips. "Apparently it all started on the right side of my brain, but it's my left side I can't move. Mysteries of the organism, Sasha. Incomprehensible to the likes of you and me."

"Yes, Dad," said Sasha, trying her best to return her father's smile. She'd read somewhere that humour was the language of the brave. Only now did she realise the essential truth of the observation.

"They've been very kind, you know," Andrew Blayne went on after a moment. "One of the doctors explained it all to me when I asked. I'm like a submarine after the water's come in. The crew are battening down the hatches, but there are no iron walls in my brain, I'm afraid. And blood is thicker than water. Unfortunately."

Sasha understood her father's need for irony to face his situation, but try as she might, she could no longer keep her emotions in check. "I'm so sorry, Dad," she said through her tears. "I'm just so sorry."

"About what?" Andrew Blayne sounded genuinely puzzled.

"About everything. About leaving you alone. About not looking after you properly all these years." The words caught in Sasha's throat, and she turned her head away.

"It's not true, Sasha. Do you hear me? You mustn't blame yourself." Suddenly there was urgency in Andrew Blayne's weakened voice, and he squeezed his daughter's hand, commanding her attention. "You're everything I could've asked for. I wouldn't have wanted it any other way."

"I shouldn't have given you that book," cried Sasha, refusing to listen to her father. "It's cursed. It's all my own bloody fault."

"No, it's not. It's a beautiful book. One of the most beautiful I've ever seen. And I'm happy that I lived to see it. I never thought I would. But I did. And that's down to you, Sasha."

The effort to speak obviously cost Blayne a great deal, and he laid his head back on the pillow as soon as he had finished and half closed his eyes.

"I should go," said Sasha, uncertain of what to do. "They said you had to rest, and I'm not helping." But her father kept hold of her hand, and she stayed where she was.

Neither of them said anything for a little while, and Sasha fought hard to control herself. She hadn't cried for years, and these tears had been torn from her body, leaving her with a sense of rupture that she couldn't erase. She didn't hear her father the first time that he spoke, and he had to squeeze her hand to get her attention.

"I solved it, Sasha," he said in a whisper. "It was last night I understood. Just before all this happened. It was so simple. I should have seen it straightaway. But that's always the way of it, isn't it? Everything is easy once you have the answer."

Sasha's heart raced. She felt excited and guilty about being excited all at the same time. She remembered how she had stood wavering outside her father's door less than two hours earlier, uncertain of whether to go back for the codex, before she'd turned away and made for the hospital. And she remembered the years she had spent searching for St. Peter's cross while she took instructions from the man she hated most in the whole world or sat in cold deserted libraries searching through the lumber rooms of the past, looking for the key that her father now held in the palm of his hand.

"I don't know whether to tell you," he said. "I don't know what will happen to you if I do. I don't know what is right."

Sasha heard the uncertainty in her father's voice, but she was tongue-tied, unable to help him make up his mind. Irrationally it seemed to her that demanding to know the secret from her father on his deathbed would be to acknowledge that the codex mattered more to her than he did. And yet telling him to stay silent meant giving up all that she had worked for and dreamt about. Unable to make a choice, she said nothing, leaving it to her father to decide.

"You'll carry on searching whatever I do, won't you, Sasha?" he said sadly. It was almost as if he was talking to himself. "It's in your blood, just like it's in mine. Looking backward, searching for secrets in dusty places. It's no life for a beautiful young woman."

"I don't care about being beautiful or young or a woman," said Sasha passionately, and then stopped, biting her tongue. She had no right thinking of herself while her father was dying in front of her eyes.

"I care about secrets," she said quietly after a moment. "And about the past. You taught me that. I suppose I believe that dead men sometimes still speak."

"Like the monks of Marjean spoke to me last night, you mean," said Blayne. "Yes, you're right. In the end that is what matters. The voices of the dead. And the soon-to-be dead," he added with a weak smile.

Sasha smiled back at her father through her tears, and for a moment there was a complete understanding between them. Then, when the moment was over, he told her what he knew, pausing to muster his failing strength at the end of almost every short sentence.

"The codex is unusual," he said, "and not just because it's beautiful. In one way it's almost unique."

"In what way?" asked Sasha when her father didn't go on.

"Well, you know that generally only the first letter of the chapter headings is decorated in medieval Gospels, but in the Marjean codex it's different. The beginning letters of certain other paragraphs are embellished as well. I counted how many times it happens. The answer's twenty-six."

"And there are twenty-six numbers on Cade's list," cried Sasha. "You count from the start of each paragraph and that gives you the letters. Is that how it works?"

"Almost, but not quite. Cade encoded his own numbers. But that wasn't too difficult to break. And then I had the answer without knowing how I'd got there, which wasn't good for my vanity." Andrew Blayne laughed, which brought on a coughing fit. His face was momentarily twisted by a spasm of violent pain, but he fought it down and carried on where he had left off. "In the end I made the connection by thinking about the codex itself. The Gospel of St. Luke. One of the books of the New Testament. And without Revelation, but counting all the letters of St. Paul, there are twenty-six books in the New Testament. And the number of letters in each book is how far you go from each decorated initial. It's as simple as that."

"So what do the letters say? What is the message?" asked Sasha, unable to contain her impatience any longer.

But her father didn't answer her question. "I'm so tired, Sasha," he said after a moment. "I have to sleep a little. Just a little. And then we can talk some more." His voice was faint and seemed to come from far away. He closed his eyes, and in the silence Sasha noticed the shallowness of his breathing. There was a tremor too in his right cheek. The lines on the screens behind her father's head rose and fell as before, but she couldn't remember if they were higher or flatter now than when she had first come in.

"Isn't there anything you can do?" she asked, turning to the young doctor who had appeared in the doorway on the other side of the bed.

"We can do quite a lot to stop the pain. But not the bleeding, I'm afraid. I can't tell you how long it will take. An hour, a day. It's better if he rests. There's a room down the hall where you can get a cup of coffee, and one of the nurses will call you when he wakes up."

Sasha got up and looked down at her father. She felt suddenly uncertain about whether she should kiss him. Would it disturb the flow of electronic signals running from his body to the machines behind his bed? She glanced over at the doctor, and it was as if he could read her mind.

"Go on," he said. "I'll be outside if you need me."

Sasha gently brushed away two stray locks of her father's straggly white hair and thought back on his life. It had promised so much, only to descend into sickness and poverty once John Cade had intervened. The professor's cold, cruel face flashed across Sasha's consciousness, and she involuntarily clenched her fists. Given the chance, she'd have murdered him herself all over again at that moment. But instead she willed herself to forget Cade and the codex and to remember her father instead. He had loved her all her life. Even when they were separated through so much of her childhood, Sasha had never doubted him. And now he was going to leave her forever. A terrible premonition of her own future loneliness swept over Sasha and she turned away, groping a path toward the door through the mist of her returning tears.

In the little room at the end of the hall, she was too tired to get coffee. She just sat down on a chair in the corner, closed her eyes, and within less than a minute was asleep. She dreamt that Cade and Ritter were alive again. They knew who she was and everything she had done. She was walking in Oxford, and they were following her down this lane and that through the warren of narrow cobbled streets behind the Cornmarket. Their footsteps echoed off the thick stone walls, and she could feel them gaining on her all the time. She looked up at the overcast sky and gargoyles with ghastly faces grinned down at her from the rooves of churches and colleges. Breathless, she turned into the run-down courtyard where her father lived and ran up the stairs to his attic room. She took them two at a time, but it was no use. Cade and Ritter were right behind her now. She could almost feel their hands on her clothes, on the ravaged, burnt skin under her shirt. She opened the door and the air was cold as ice, forcing her to a standstill. There was an old crackly record of *The Threepenny Opera* playing on the gramophone. "Well, the shark has pretty teeth, dear," sang a German voice singing English. And over on the bed in the corner alcove, her father was stretched out, dressed in a shiny black suit and tie. His patent leather shoes looked strange lying on the starched white bed sheet, and it took Sasha a moment before she noticed the silver half-crown pieces placed over his eyes. She bent down to take them away, but a voice behind her, the sergeant's voice, told her to leave the coins alone. Andrew Blayne belonged to them now. He wasn't her father anymore.

Sasha woke with a start. The doctor was gently shaking her shoulder, trying to get her attention.

"A bad dream?" he asked, smiling.

"Yes. It doesn't matter. How's my father?"

"He's slipping away, I'm afraid, and so I thought I should wake you. I've had to give him more painkilling drugs, and that makes it less likely that he'll regain consciousness. But I don't know. He might."

"Mysteries of the organism," said Sasha.

"Mysteries of what?"

"I'm sorry. It was just something funny he said when we were talking in there before. How long have I been asleep?" she asked, rubbing her eyes with the back of her hand.

"An hour. Maybe a little more."

Sasha followed the doctor into her father's room. Immediately she could see that he was worse, much worse. His breathing was very laboured now, and she sat holding his hand until the end came less than twenty minutes later.

Just before he died, he opened his eyes and looked at her. She was sure he knew who she was, and it seemed like he was trying to say something, but the words would not come. He gave up, and she leant over and kissed him on each sunken cheek.

"Thank you," she whispered. "Thank you for being my father."

She didn't know whether he had heard her or not, and a minute later the lines on the screens flattened out, and she knew that he was gone.

And that was the end of it. She sat by her father's corpse for another fifteen minutes and then got up to go. But at the end of the corridor, the doctor called her back.

"You're forgetting something," he said. "Your father brought a bag with him. The ambulance men packed it for him before he came here. There's what looks like a valuable book inside it. I don't think you should leave it here."

Sasha mumbled her thanks. The doctor deserved better for his kindness, but for now she was too preoccupied to talk, and he seemed to understand. Was this what her father had been trying to say at the end when the words would not come? she asked herself as she went down the hospital stairs. That the codex was in his bag, or was he telling her to leave the book alone? She would never know. He had chosen to tell her the book's secret, and knowing what it meant would be their last connection.

She was too impatient to wait until she got home. It was nearly midnight, and the big reception area of the hospital was half-empty. She sat down beside a tank of somnolent tropical fish and opened the codex on her knee. There was no sign of Cade's list, but she didn't look for it. It wouldn't be right to use a crib, and besides her father had said that Cade had encoded his own numbers. It was easier to spell out the Latin names: The four evangelists and then the Acts of the Apostles and the letters of St. Paul to the Corinthians and the Thessalonians and to Timothy. As the letters slowly emerged, Sasha wrote them down one by one. After nine books she had the first two words: "Crux Petri," "The cross of Peter." A shiver ran down her back.

Slowly and methodically she carried on, reading the old monk's code under the hospital's strip lighting, oblivious to the murmuring voices of the sick men and women around her. A few minutes later, and she had the message complete. "Crux Petri in manibus Petri est," it read. "The cross of Peter is in the hands of Peter." What could it possibly mean? Who was the second Peter, and where were his hands?

Leaving the last decorated initial behind, Sasha read the last page of the Gospel of St. Luke to herself. Jesus led them out as far as Bethany and blessed them, and while he blessed them, he parted from them and ascended into heaven. "Ascendit in caelum." She turned the page, and there was Cade's list of numbers tucked into the back of the book, and at the bottom in her father's handwriting was a list of his own under the heading, "Abbots of Marjean." There were four names and four sets of dates: Marcus 1278–1300. Stephanus Pisano 1300–05. Bartholomeus 1306–21. Simeon 1321–27. The last name was twice underlined. Simon, abbot of Marjean. Was he the second Peter of the coded message? Peter after all was Christ's name for the apostle Simon. He called him *petrus*, or *stone*, because Simon was the rock on whom Christ chose to build his church—the same Simon Peter who betrayed Christ three times before the cock crowed on the day of the crucifixion.

Was St. Peter's cross lying in the hands of Simon, abbot of Marjean? There was a crypt under the church with tombs on either side. She'd been there and seen it all two years earlier. The church had not been damaged by the fire that had gutted the château at the end of the war. Could it be possible that the cross had lain undetected in a stone tomb for nearly seven hundred years before Cade went there in 1956?

The thought of her father's nemesis brought Sasha back to earth. Even forgetting that it made no sense that Cade had taken so long to break the code, she could not ignore the fact that he had gone to Marjean in 1956 and had come away empty-handed. He hadn't found the cross, or he wouldn't have hired her eighteen months later to search for it everywhere except where it ought to be: beneath the church at Marjean. Unless he had missed something. She had to go and look for herself. She must bury her father, and then she would take the ferry to Le Havre and hire a car. Her father had all but told her where to go, even though he knew the dangers. As she had told him weeks before, when she first brought him Cade's diary: She had gone too far to stop now.

The radio was playing in the taxi that took Sasha home from the hospital. Late-night news repeated every hour. The second item was the Moreton Manor murder. "Stephen Cade's appeal due in court tomorrow," announced a toneless voice from the dashboard. "Will death sentence be upheld?"

Sasha felt suddenly sick. She leant forward in her seat, clutching her knees as the world turned over. She was powerless to stop her brain from summoning up the same image that had come to her before: the image of Stephen sitting alone in his cell in the early morning, watching the clock for the appointed hour, waiting for the hangman to come. Her sense of responsibility clutched her like a vice. She thought fleetingly of telling the taxi driver to turn round, to take her to the police station so she could confess her sins to that weathered old policeman who had come to visit her at the manor house, pleading with her to tell the truth. But she knew she couldn't. It was too late now. Perjury in a capital case was a serious crime: she didn't need a lawyer to tell her that. They'd imprison her for what she'd done and the prize would slip from her grasp. She'd never find out what lay "in manibus Petri." And anyway it would do no good. What was done was done. Stephen was beyond saving and her father was dead. The only way was forward: She had to go on.

Exhausted, Sasha wound down her window and lay back in her seat, letting the cold night air play over her face. The headlines were over on the radio, and she finished her journey to the accompaniment of an American called Elvis Presley singing something loud and insistent called rock and roll.

"At least it keeps you awake," said the taxi driver, apologetically, as he took her money.

"Yes, it does that," agreed Sasha with a thin smile, before she turned away with the bag containing the codex and its deciphered code held tightly in her hand.

TWENTY-TWO

Someone tapped Trave on the shoulder as he was waiting outside the Court of Appeal. It was John Swift, ready once more to go into battle. It wasn't the first time the two had spoken: Swift had written Trave a note to thank him for the statement from the maid, Esther Rudd, and they had had a drink together after the verdict to commiserate on what had happened.

"Don't get your hopes up, Inspector," said Swift. "This hearing isn't about the facts, remember, it's about whether everything was done legally over at the Bailey. And Old Man Murdoch's no fool. He kept everything on the legal side of bias just like he always does. We're firing blanks, I'm afraid."

Trave would've responded, but just then Tiny Thompson bustled past them through the door of the court, looking outraged at the spectacle of the officer in the case locked in discussion with his opposite number.

"Someone looks happy this morning," said Swift, raising his eyebrows, and turned to follow Thompson into court. The case had been called on.

Trave barely had time to settle in his chair before the hearing began, and he was soon struck, just as he had been so many times before, by how remote everything seemed. There were no witnesses, no defendants being cross-examined—just lawyers arguing the legal rights and wrongs of what had already happened elsewhere. The three black-robed law lords sat far away on a high dais with shelves of antique lawbooks rising from floor to ceiling behind them, and green-shaded reading lamps threw pools of light on their old hands as they listened to the arguments of Thompson and Swift. It was a duel of words—cut and thrust, back and forth, which was obviously almost entirely incomprehensible to Stephen as he sat biting his nails in a caged dock at the side of the court. And to Trave too, except that he had the advantage of Swift's warning of the likely outcome, which proved before the end of the day to be entirely accurate. It was still quite early in the afternoon when the Lord Chief Justice dismissed the appeal, upheld the mandatory sentence of death, and disappeared with his two colleagues through three separate polished mahogany doors at the back of the court.

Fifteen minutes later Trave and Swift stood on the courthouse steps and watched the prison van turn out into the Strand, ready to take Stephen back to Wandsworth Prison for the last time.

"God help him," said Swift. "I need a drink."

They ordered double whiskies in the pub across the road, and then Trave bought them two more. Swift was visibly upset, shaken by Thompson's taunts in the robing room and his own sense of failure. Trave, as always, was doing a good job of keeping his emotions in check.

"They're the worst, these kinds of cases," said Swift.

"Which kind?"

"The ones where you know the defendant's innocent and yet you can't get him off, however hard you try. And when it's a capital case it's almost unbearable. Makes me want to give it all up sometimes."

"It's not your fault," said Trave. "The evidence was overwhelming. That's why I had to charge him in the first place."

"Yes, but too overwhelming," said Swift. "Too neat. Someone else committed this crime and set Stephen up. I know they did."

"Yes, someone did," agreed Trave flatly. "And his name's Silas Cade."

"Maybe; maybe not," said Swift, sounding unconvinced. "He's the obvious candidate, I agree. But part of me doesn't buy it. He just didn't feel guilty for some reason when I was cross-examining him. Scared and defiant, yes— but not guilty."

"Well, he felt guilty to me," said Trave, having none of it. "And his alibi's rubbish. I know that much."

"But that doesn't mean he killed his father. The jurors sure as hell didn't think he did or they'd have acquitted Stephen."

Trave didn't respond, and they were both silent, each turning over the evidence in their minds.

"What about the home secretary? Can't you get him to grant a reprieve?" asked Trave, changing the subject.

"I'll try. Of course I'll try. But don't count on it. We're in the court of public opinion now and hanging Stephen'll be a lot more popular with Joe Public than showing him mercy. You can be sure of that. Stephen's not one of them, remember. He was born with a silver spoon in his mouth. Much good that it did him."

"Mercy! These bastards don't know the meaning of the word," said Trave bitterly, suddenly overwhelmed by disgust at the whole situation.

And yet as he spoke, he knew that it wasn't disgust that was tearing him up inside. It was powerlessness. It reminded him of how he'd felt when his son died.

Trave's depression lasted through the weekend, and Sunday evening found him out on the golf course, walking alone in the twilight. His head sunk in thought, he cut across the seventh fairway, making for the gate in the hedge. He had been thinking more often recently about getting a dog, a companion for his lonely evening walks across the deserted course. But he feared the attachment even more than he desired it, and he could always think of reasons to hold back from making the commitment. The dog would get bored sitting at home in the empty house, waiting for his master to return. He would bark at the neighbours and cause a nuisance, or he might wander out in the road and get run over. And Trave would be left alone all over again. Being alone was one thing; being left was quite another. Lifting the latch on the gate, Trave thought that he had had quite enough of being left behind for one lifetime.

The evening was cold and windy, and Trave had only come out because he felt so restless indoors. Sundays were always hard, but this one was worse. He'd gone out in the garden after he got back from church, but then the rain had driven him back inside. It was the Lord's day, but he'd given into the need for alcohol by mid afternoon and taken a bottle of whisky into the front room and sat in the threadbare armchair, looking up at the framed photographs of Joe and Vanessa on the mantelpiece. What was she doing now? Making a new life with a man called Osman over on the other side of Oxford. It was all that Trave could do to resist the impulse to throw his glass at the wall. And so he'd got up and gone out, walking the golf course without dog or clubs, trying not to think about his wife or his son or Stephen Cade, sitting in his prison cell up in London, waiting for the executioner to come.

Now that Stephen's appeal had been dismissed, Stephen would be moved into the Wandsworth death house, a two-storey red-brick building over by the perimeter wall. He had ten days left to live unless the home secretary granted a reprieve, which Trave agreed with Swift seemed unlikely with the government wanting to stay popular and law and order such a prominent issue. People needed to be protected from guns, and what crime could be worse than killing your father in his own home? It was a cold, premeditated act, and the murderer had shown no remorse.

Starting from tomorrow, the hangman would be visiting the gaol every other day, watching his subject through the eyehole in the cell door, measuring weight and drop with a trained scientific eye. The whole assembly line of death was now in motion. Its wheels were turning in nondescript offices all over London. Warrants and orders were passing backward and forward between the Court of Appeal and the Home Office and the prison at Wandsworth. All stamped with the right stamp and signed by the right person. Everything that needed to happen before a modern British hanging could go ahead.

Trave had always hated the death penalty and its attendant machinery. He didn't bring murderers to justice to see them murdered. His church said it was wrong to take life, and that at least was something he had no trouble believing. And yet he realised now that he had never really confronted the implications of his own role in the process. Death sentences were not as common now as they used to be, and he had not doubted the guilt of those men whom he had brought to justice, those who had gone on to pay the ultimate penalty. But Stephen Cade was different. And not just because he was young and reminded Trave so forcibly of his own lost son. In his heart, Trave was sure Stephen was innocent, and yet there seemed to be nothing he could do to save him. The trial was over, and Trave had no authority to ask the witnesses any more questions. He had saved Silas from Ritter when he should have saved Ritter's wife, and now Silas was sending Stephen to his death when Silas should be going there himself. Silas. It had to be Silas, whatever Swift said. He was the one who had the motive, and Jeanne Ritter had seen him in the courtyard. And his alibi was a lie. The jurors were fools to have been taken in by it.

Trave turned the corner and stopped dead in his tracks. The man he was thinking about was standing on the pavement just outside his house, illuminated by the light from a streetlamp overhead. Silas was off the crutches but seemed to be leaning heavily on a tall walking stick for support.

"What are you doing here?" Trave asked furiously as soon as he had got level with Silas. The anger that had been boiling up inside him as he walked home overflowed in this sudden unexpected encounter with the man he held responsible for everything that had happened.

But Silas didn't seem to notice the animosity in the policeman's voice. He was too preoccupied with the reason for his visit.

"I found your name in the book," he said breathlessly. "And I didn't want to wait until tomorrow. I don't know why. I needed to know what you think." Silas blurted his words out in such a rush that Trave found it quite difficult to understand what he was saying.

"Think about what?" he asked, his anger half giving way to curiosity.

"About what I've found. Photographs. I need to show them to you."

Silas held up an old briefcase that he had been holding in his left hand, which Trave had not noticed until then.

"You better come in," he said grudgingly. Trave didn't like visitors. His house was where he kept his grief, and he didn't want to share it with anyone, least of all sneaky Silas Cade. But he felt he didn't have any option. It was beginning to rain again, and they could hardly examine photographs under a streetlight in the wet, with Silas wobbling unsteadily on his walking stick.

In the living room, Silas sat down awkwardly on the edge of the chair where Trave had been drowning his sorrows in drink less than an hour earlier. Trave remained standing on the other side of the empty fireplace, refusing to provide his visitor with any kind of welcome.

"Is that your boy?" Silas asked, pointing at a photograph of Joe aged thirteen on the mantelpiece. It was Vanessa's favourite, but Trave had insisted on keeping it when she left.

"He's not here," said Trave shortly. "Perhaps you better show me whatever you came here to show me, Mr. Cade. Sunday's my day off, and I've got to work tomorrow."

This time the hostility got through to Silas.

"I shouldn't have come," he said. "I know what you think of me. You're like Stephen. You think I killed my father."

"What I think doesn't matter," said Trave. "It's the jury's decision that counts."

"But you believe it was the wrong decision, don't you?" said Silas, refusing to be put off. "You think I should be the one with my head in the noose. Not my precious brother."

"I've got concerns. Yes. But they're my affair. Not yours."

Silas met the policeman's stare for a moment and then dropped his eyes. "I'm here because I don't think Stephen killed our father either," he said in an almost inaudible voice. "I used to, but I don't anymore. And I don't want him to hang for something he never did. I was hoping that the appeal would work, but it didn't, and now I've got to do something."

"Well, I'm sure he'll be pleased to hear that," said Trave sarcastically. "But just how do you propose to stop them hanging your brother, Mr. Cade? Are you here to make a confession? If so, you'll have to wait while I go and get a pen and some paper. It shouldn't take long."

"No," said Silas angrily. "I didn't kill my father any more than Stephen did."

"That's not what Mrs. Ritter said."

"I know," said Silas slowly. "I thought she was lying at first. God knows she was angry enough to say anything once she got in that courtroom. But now I'm not so sure. I think someone did go into my father's study after Stephen left it and then slipped away across the courtyard after he came back."

"Yes. And that person was you."

"No. Not me. Someone wearing my hat and coat, pretending to be me. Jeanne never said she saw my face, remember? You were in court for her evidence."

"All right, maybe she didn't," said Trave grudgingly. "But who was it she saw in the courtyard if it wasn't you? Who else had a motive to kill your father?" Trave made no effort to keep the disbelief out of his voice.

"I don't know," said Silas. "I wish I did, but I don't."

"You don't know. And yet you're the one with the motive and the alibi that I've never believed in for one second. How much did you pay Miss Vigne to say you were sleeping together, Mr. Cade? It must have been a lot, but I suppose you can afford it now that you're the lord of Moreton Manor."

Trave had had no intention of discussing the case with his visitor, but his anger toward Silas had got the better of him. Now he just wished Silas gone so that he could nurse his bitterness in peace.

"Why would I be here talking to you if I were the murderer?" asked Silas, refusing to give up now that he had come so far.

"I don't know. Perhaps you've got a guilty conscience."

"Oh, come on, Inspector. You can do better than that." Silas had started to get to his feet while making this angry outburst, but now he sank back into the armchair, and his brow creased as if he was suddenly deep in thought.

The brass clock on the mantelpiece ticked loudly, and Silas nervously fingered the catch on the briefcase that he was holding across his knees.

"It's not easy for me," he said, breaking the silence. "Helping to exonerate my brother is just going to make you point the finger at me even more. It's hardly an incentive. I was a lot better off when I believed that my brother did commit the murder."

"What made you change your mind?" asked Trave. He was not in the business of making deals with murderers. If Silas had something to say, he should say it. Let the evidence point where it will.

"Jeanne's dying and my almost getting killed by Ritter shook me up. Changed me more than my father's death, I think. But in the end it was photographs," said Silas. "Photographs and a name. They made me change my mind."

"What name? What photographs?"

"The ones I have here. In my bag. If I show them to you, Inspector, will you do one thing for me? One small thing."

"What thing?"

"Keep an open mind about who killed my father. That's all I ask. Just keep an open mind."

Trave was not won over. The pleading edge to Silas's voice annoyed him. But the request was a reasonable one. If he'd had more of an open mind at the outset, he might not have been so quick to hand Stephen over to Gerald Thompson. And Silas was right. There was no reason for him to be here if he was the murderer. He would be undoing his best-laid plans just as they were coming to fruition.

"All right," Trave said grudgingly. "I'll keep an open mind. Now show me your pictures."

Silas didn't need to be asked twice. He opened the briefcase and took out two large colour photographs. Then, moving Trave's whisky bottle out of the way, he laid them out side by side on the low coffee table in front of the fireplace.

Trave sat on the sofa as far away as he could from Silas and studied the pictures. It was obvious that one photograph was simply a blown-up section of the other. In the first the murdered man sat in his high-backed green leather armchair with the bullet hole in his forehead and the game of chess laid out on the table in front of him. In the second there were only the big heavy chess board and the hand-carved ivory pieces. Some were on the board and some were on the table, some still in play and some taken.

"Well, what's the point?" asked Trave. The irritation was back in his voice. There was nothing new to see. Cade had played chess with his younger son before he died. Everyone agreed that that had happened. According to Thompson, the loss of the game was one of the things that drove Stephen over the edge.

"Can't you see?" asked Silas.

"No, I can't. And I don't know how you got these photographs either. They're a crime scene, for God's sake. And that man's your father."

"Was my father. I took quite a few photographs when the policeman you'd put in the study had his back turned. It was the same one who told Jeanne all about me and Sasha at court. What was his name?"

"Clayton. Adam Clayton. And he didn't tell Jeanne anything."

"She overheard him. Yes, I know. But it still had the same effect. Anyway, the second picture, the one with the chess pieces: I developed that off the first one about a week ago. I did it because of what I heard my brother say when he was giving his evidence."

"About what?"

"About the chess pieces. You were in court too, Inspector. I saw you. But perhaps you didn't listen. Too busy building a case against me, I expect."

Trave felt an almost irresistible desire to punch his visitor, to literally kick him out of the house. But he did resist. He swallowed his anger and waited for Silas to continue.

"Stephen said that our father told him he could have the money he wanted if he won a game of chess. And then a little later he said that Dad played black and without a knight, but he still won easily. All that struck a chord with me, Inspector. It was the sort of thing my father did. He liked to show off his superiority, and he had a sadistic streak. It was there all the time when we were children, but it got worse after my mother died—much worse."

"In any case, what Stephen said about the chess game jogged something in my memory. And so I went back to the photographs I'd taken in the study, and that's when I saw it."

"Saw what?"

"That black didn't win. Look. It's the black king that can't move. And the white queen's attacking him down the rook file. White won in the photograph, Inspector. Not black."

"And so he must have carried on playing chess with himself after Stephen walked out. Really serious players do that, don't they?" said Trave, suddenly excited. "Your photograph shows that Stephen must have left the study like he said. And Cade replayed the game or some of it before his killer came in."

"Dressed in my hat and coat."

Trave ignored Silas's denial that he was the murderer. The photographs entranced him. They were like a laser beam shining back through time toward the truth, and yet they were not enough. Trave had realised that almost as soon as he had understood their significance. They supported Stephen's case only if he was telling the truth about his father playing with the black pieces. Of course he had no reason to lie. But the evidence was self-serving. It wouldn't be enough to reverse the conviction or save Stephen from the hangman. More was needed. Some independent evidence exonerating Stephen of the crime. But where was it to come from? There was so little time left, and Trave didn't know where to begin.

"Is this all you've got?" he asked. "It's good but it's not enough. Or maybe you know that already."

"I know we need more, if that's what you mean," said Silas. "The photographs are important for me because they made me change my mind, not because they'll save Stephen."

"So, have you got anything else?" asked Trave, trying to contain his irritation.

"Not much. Somebody changed the chess pieces back to their starting positions. I found them that way when I came downstairs in the morning a couple of days after the murder. I don't know who did it, but everyone in the house denied responsibility. Especially Esther, the housemaid. She got quite angry when I asked her, as if I was accusing her of something. We never got on after that, and I had to get rid of her. She was too much trouble."

"You think it was the murderer who came back and changed the pieces."

"Maybe. Except I don't know how he'd have known what happened in the chess game without Stephen telling him. I only realised when Stephen gave his evidence."

"Unless Stephen said something while he was still in the house."

"What? You mean before you arrived?"

"Or after. But we're clutching at straws. And straws won't save your brother."

Silas looked over at Trave quickly. He'd picked up on the policeman's use of the word "we." Perhaps Trave would keep an open mind after all.

"There's one other thing that might help," he said slowly. "Do you remember the Mercedes that got stopped outside Moreton on the night my father was killed?"

"Yes. How do you know about that?"

"You gave evidence about it, and there was a report in one of the newspapers. Anyway, the driver gave his name as Noirtier. Well, I don't know if it means anything, but look."

Silas bent down and took an old book out of his briefcase. It was an atlas, and he quickly turned to the page he wanted. A map of northern France. He pointed to a black dot a little way south of Rouen.

"Do you see the name?" he asked.

The light was bad, and Trave had to bend down close to the page so that his head almost touched Silas's.

"Moirtier," he said. "Moirtier-sur-Bagne."

"An *m* for an *n*," said Silas. "It's close enough. And Marjean is less than three miles down the road. Maybe it's a coincidence, but maybe not."

"You think your father's murder had something to do with what happened in France?"

"Yes. I don't know why, but I feel sure of it. Ritter and my father did kill those people, you know. Stephen and I heard them talking about it. Things like that don't go unpunished."

"In war they do," said Trave. He felt suddenly as if Silas was trying to lead him somewhere, and his natural obstinacy combined with his policeman's suspicious mind to hold him back. And yet he had always felt he should go to France and ask some questions, look in the record books, see what he could find. He remembered Swift's question to him at the trial: "Why didn't you go to Marjean to investigate for yourself who shot Professor Cade in 1956 and sent him the blackmail letter the following year?" "It was a prosecution decision," he had said. But it hadn't been his decision. And he could still go. To Moirtier. It didn't sound like a common name. It didn't sound like a coincidence.

And yet why would Silas want to send him to France? Perhaps he wanted him out of the way until his brother was safely executed and the case was closed forever. Trave remembered what Swift had said to Silas when he cross-examined him the second time: "You're the one who's been pulling the strings in your family for a long time now." Silas was the one with the motive, and Silas was the one with the false alibi. It had to be false. Trave remembered Sasha Vigne's suitcases standing in the hall at Moreton Manor. She'd been in a hurry to leave because she didn't want to be in the house when Silas got out of hospital. She had never slept with him. Trave was sure of it.

Trave walked over to the front window and looked out into the dark empty street. He felt confused and uncertain—a man in search of a sign. Unless the sign was on the map lying open on the table behind him, where Silas had just put his finger. Moirtier-sur-Bagne, the place was called. Less than three miles from Marjean.

"I'll go with you if you like," said Silas, breaking the silence. "There's nothing to keep me here." It was as if he'd been reading Trave's mind.

"No," said Trave more harshly than he had intended. "I can't go if you go. Surely you can see that."

"Because I'm still a suspect, you mean," said Silas, laughing mirthlessly. "What more can I do to convince you, Inspector?"

"Nothing. There's nothing you can do other than what you have done. Nothing at all. I'll go alone, and I just hope I'm doing the right thing."

Hearing himself, Trave realised that he had already decided what to do before he had even known of his own decision. He was going to follow his instinct. That was what had deserted him in this case. Perhaps it would take him in the right direction now. He'd take a leave of absence. With luck he could be in Rouen by Tuesday evening.

Silas went back to the manor house in a taxi. His injured foot made it impossible for him to drive the Rolls-Royce, which had stood parked in the garage behind the house since the day the Ritters died. The road to Moreton was full of landmarks: the bottom of the hill where his mother died, the place where the unknown driver of the black Mercedes was stopped by a traffic policeman and gave the name Noirtier and a false address in Oxford. But Silas was not looking out the window. He had taken the photographs back out of his briefcase and was gazing with rapt attention at his father's last game of chess. So many secrets. The Marjean codex hidden inside the board and the black king mated. Under attack and with nowhere left to go, just like Silas's brother up in London. Alone in his cell, awaiting the coup de grâce.

TWENTY-THREE

Early the next morning, Trave went to his police station in the centre of Oxford. He itched to be on his way now that he had decided to go to France, but he couldn't leave without getting the superintendent's blessing. There should be no problem with his cases. They were mostly quiet, and Adam Clayton could look after them while he was away. All in all, Trave didn't anticipate Creswell making any objection. The superintendent had only a few years left before his retirement, and he was content to let Trave and the other two inspectors get on with their jobs without too much interference, as long as their activities didn't add to his own workload.

"I need a leave of absence," said Trave almost as soon as he was inside the superintendent's office. He was in too much of a hurry to take in that Creswell looked like thunder.

"Why?"

"I want to go to France for a few days. I'll be back by the end of the week."

"So tell me, has this sudden desire to go south got something to do with the case of Mr. Stephen Cade?" asked Creswell, leaning back in his chair and giving his subordinate a look of unconcealed distaste.

"Why do you say that?" asked Trave, taken aback. Silas hadn't mentioned talking to anyone else about his suspicions.

"Let's just say it's an educated guess," said Creswell acidly. "You'd better sit down and read this. It's from that barrister up in London. He doesn't seem to like you very much."

Tiny Thompson had certainly made good on his promise to write a letter of complaint. On two pages of closely typed paper, he had portrayed Trave as having been engaged in a sort of guerrilla operation to sabotage Stephen Cade's prosecution almost from the outset. The last straw had been the maid's statement that Trave had taken to Thompson's chambers after the Ritters died.

"Well?" asked Creswell once Trave had finished reading the prosecutor's diatribe.

"It's rubbish. Every word of it. I haven't done anything wrong."

"Maybe not. But it doesn't look good, does it? I don't need this Thompson character causing me grief. Or you making it worse. And this trip to France isn't going to help, is it? Why've you got to go?"

"Because I think there might be something over there that everyone's missed up to now. I just don't believe Stephen Cade killed his father. I haven't done so for a long time now. And I don't want him to hang for something he never did."

"Well, if you've got evidence that he's innocent, you should take it to the powers that be. And they're in London, not France. What you shouldn't be doing is slinking around trying to undermine your own case just because you've got some kind of hunch about it. You're not the damned jury, Bill, do you hear me? It's done its job. Now you get on and do yours."

Trave remained silent, but the stubborn scowl that had formed around his mouth was more expressive than any mere words could be.

After a moment, the superintendent sighed and pushed Thompson's letter to the side of his desk, where it joined a growing pile of unanswered correspondence.

"I can't stop you from taking a holiday, Bill," he said resignedly. "You're due for one. But remember this: It's your trip and not mine. You're not taking anyone else down with you if down is where you're going. I'll see to that. And don't claim any expenses," he added as Trave got up to go.

Trave nodded. "Thank you, sir," he said, and he meant it. Creswell could have made it a lot harder for him if he'd chosen to, although it wouldn't have stopped his leaving. Trave had made his mind up, and he'd have disobeyed a direct order to stay in Oxford if he'd had to. But that didn't stop him from being grateful it hadn't come to that.

Trave took Clayton out to lunch at a nearby pub. In recent weeks he'd warmed to the young man. He made mistakes, but there was an innocent, wide-eyed enthusiasm about him that Trave had grown to like. Clayton asked questions and worked late because he was doing what he'd always wanted to do, not because he had his eyes set on the next promotion, like so many of the other young detectives on the force. And there was a human side to the boy that made Trave feel almost fatherly toward him. He hadn't forgotten Clayton's sudden nausea at Cade's postmortem or his panic outside the courtroom in London. The memory of these episodes made Trave smile as he paid for two pints of Oxford bitter and took them over to a table by the fire.

"There's something that I want you to do for me while I'm away," he said, wiping the froth of the beer away from his lips after taking his first sip.

"Sure. Shoot."

Trave smiled at the Americanism. Clayton had clearly been watching too much television on his days off. "It's about one of the exhibits in the Cade case," he said. "The key to the study door."

"The one with our man's fingerprints on it?"

"Yes. That's the one. Not surprisingly, our friend Mr. Thompson attached a great deal of importance to it at the trial, because Sergeant Ritter heard Stephen turning the key in the lock before he opened the door. And both the Ritters said that the professor never locked the internal door of the study, so the jurors were left to infer that Stephen must have done so himself sometime before he unlocked it to let Ritter in. Pretty incriminating on the face of it, you have to admit."

"Unless someone else locked the door after Stephen left the room and then didn't have time to remove the key before Stephen came back," said Clayton slowly.

"Yes, exactly," said Trave, pleased by Clayton's understanding. "Neither of the Ritters ever said anything about Cade's leaving the key in the door, and in fact there's no reason for him to have done so if he never locked it. He was an orderly man, and so he'd have kept the key on the ring in his desk drawer. And that's not all. This murder was premeditated. I know it was. You don't bring a gun to an interview unless you're intending to use it. This killer didn't lose his temper, Adam. He did what he came to do. And if he locked the door to stop anyone from following him in, he wouldn't have relied on there being a key in the door waiting for him to use. He'd have brought one with him."

"Which he would've had copied before."

"Yes. Using either Cade's key or Mrs. Ritter's for the purpose. It's a long shot, Adam, but what I want you to do is get hold of Cade's key ring. It should still be with the other exhibits up at the Bailey. If one of the keys on it fits the study door, then the one with Stephen's prints on it is a copy, and you'll need to start checking with all the locksmiths in the area. I'll call you tomorrow evening after I've arrived, and you can tell me how you've got on. But keep your enquiries quiet. The superintendent isn't exactly wild about what we're doing."

"How long are you going for?" asked Clayton.

"I don't know. It would help if I knew what I was looking for. I told Creswell that I'd be back by the end of the week, but maybe it'll take longer. Not much, though, or there won't be any point. Stephen Cade'll be dead."

"When's the execution fixed for?" asked Clayton, feeling his blood run suddenly cold as the reality of the situation got through to him.

"Nine days' time is what I've heard. Wednesday week at eight in the morning. We're his only hope, Adam, if Swift can't get the home secretary to come through with a reprieve, and I wouldn't hold your breath over that happening. This is the most right-wing government we've had since the war."

"Jesus Christ," said Clayton, feeling slightly sick as he finished his drink.

"And all his saints," agreed Trave. But his mind was already looking ahead, thinking about his journey the next day. Although many of his colleagues would have taken Trave for the epitome of a little Englander, he was in fact surprisingly widely traveled, and he spoke French quite well for a man who'd learnt the language off long-playing records on weekday evenings after work.

It was French, in fact, that had first brought Trave and his wife together. They'd met at a class that he'd taken for a while when he'd gone as far as he could with the records. The teacher had divided her students into pairs so that they could practise talking about a day on the beach or visiting the cultural sites of Paris. Some pairings were more successful than others, but theirs was inspired. Trave and Vanessa never changed partners after that first day. The class became the highlight of their weeks. They laughed at each others' mistakes and encouraged each others' efforts, and slowly but surely their laboured conversations turned into actual plans. They visited Paris first and then went south in search of the sun, and as soon as the first holiday was over they were planning the next one. Those were the happiest days of Trave's life. They'd scrimped and saved and gone third class on trains, camping out at night under the stars and waking in the mornings with the cathedrals of Chartres or Tours or Rheims waiting for them on the horizon. They'd fallen in love with France and fallen in love with each other, and the experience had brought Trave out of himself, temporarily expunging his natural shyness. And it occurred to him now, as he prepared to return to a country that he hadn't seen for more than four years, that he had been in headlong retreat from himself since Joe's death, putting back up the shutters that he had first taken down when he started going to French classes at the Lycée on the Banbury Road all those years ago.

Trave could have flown to Paris, but he had opted instead to go on the ferry to Le Havre and then drive across Normandy to Rouen, and now, standing on deck, feeling the sea spray flying up into his face, blown on the back of a big southwesterly wind, Trave felt pleased with his decision. He disliked aeroplanes. Perhaps it was the memory of the bombers flying high across the skies of southern England during the war or just that he liked to physically travel his journeys, measuring the passage of earth or water beneath his feet. Whatever the reason, he always found an excuse to avoid air travel if he possibly could, and he enjoyed ferries or trains all the more because he wasn't up in the air.

And he had no wish to see Paris again. Vanessa and he had gone there more times than he could remember, visiting the same little restaurants down side streets in the Latin Quarter until the proprietors got to know them by name or sitting under café awnings in the Jardins du Luxembourg, listening to the jazz players in the late afternoon. Paris belonged in the past with a thousand other memories, thought Trave, as the north coast of France rose up toward him out of the sea mist. There was no going back.

Rouen. Vanessa and he had never been there. God knows why. It was less than an hour from the capital on the train, and they had both always loved Monet's pictures of the cathedral in the sunset, with the architecture dissolving into blue and gold. It was just one of the places that they'd happened to miss, and Trave was glad of that now. It allowed him to concentrate on the job in hand. His instinct told him that there was a connection between this tract of northern France and what had happened in the old English manor house outside Oxford five months earlier. What it was he didn't know. Everything was murky. He had a hundred different questions but no answers. Who, for example, was the man in the black Mercedes parked opposite the manorhouse gates on the night of the murder? Trave was sure that he wasn't a figment of Stephen's imagination. Clayton had seen a car there, after all, when he responded to Ritter's emergency call. But was the driver the man who shot John Cade? Or was he just waiting for the murderer to come out? Was the Mercedes a getaway car to be used if needed? And was that why the door of the telephone box was wedged open—so that the real killer could telephone through instructions to his accomplice from inside the house? But no telephone calls had been made that evening. Trave had had the log printed out and there was nothing until Ritter called the police at ten forty-six.

Was Silas the man on the inside? Now that almost two days had passed since their evening interview, Trave's doubts about the new owner of Moreton Manor had started to resurface in abundance. As he had told Clayton the day before, Trave felt certain that Cade's murder was premeditated. And Silas fitted the profile of a cold-blooded killer. He had found his father murdered in his chair, and his first reaction had been to go and get his camera. Except of course that John Cade hadn't been Silas's real father. Silas was adopted. Patricide had to be an easier crime to commit when there was no biological link between the killer and his victim. And Trave remembered how shifty Silas had looked in the witness box the second time around, when Swift had gone for the jugular. His alibi was false. Trave had always been certain of that. And if he hadn't been with Sasha Vigne, then where had he been on the night of his father's murder? Waiting to enter the study as soon as his brother had left it, with a key in one gloved hand and a gun in the other? Hiding behind the thick green curtains when Stephen unexpectedly returned, and then slipping away across the stone courtyard unseen by anyone except his lover as she sat brushing her hair at the upstairs window while her fat husband lay snoring in the bed behind her?

Was this how it had been? What was it that Swift had called Silas? A puppet master. Perhaps Silas already knew that there had been no survivors of what had happened at Marjean Château in the summer of 1944—no survivors and no relatives of those who had died. Perhaps there was no French connection. Trave was hit by a sudden wave of anxiety that he had been sent on a wild-goose chase. He'd spoken to Swift before his departure about the investigation work that the defence team had done in Normandy, and it was clear that their man had done a thorough job. Perhaps the best he could hope for would be the same blank answers to his questions from unhelpful French officials, while Stephen's last days on this earth would drain fruitlessly away on the other side of the Channel as his brother sat in Moreton Manor valuing his ill-gotten gains.

It was almost enough to make Trave turn back. And perhaps he would have done so if he hadn't thought of the atlas that Silas had opened on his table. Moirtier-sur-Bagne. Three miles from Marjean. And almost the same name that the Mercedes driver had given when he was stopped on the road to Oxford. An alias given on the spur of the moment or a signature on the night's events? Whatever it was, Silas had not made up the name. It was in the policeman's notebook. Trave had to go on. Rouen first, to look at the records, and then on to the towns themselves. Moirtier and Marjean. There was still time, and he had to follow his instincts.

Trave got to Rouen early on Tuesday evening and put up at a cheap hotel called the Jeanne d'Arc, down by the docks. The expenses for this trip weren't going to be repaid, and he needed to watch his money. The centre of Rouen around the cathedral had already been extensively rebuilt, but down by the Seine the effects of the Allied bombing were still everywhere to be seen. It was a barren, ruined landscape for which Trave had been ill prepared. He slept uneasily in his dingy room and dreamt that Joe was still alive, running from German soldiers across the churned-up land, dodging bullets among the broken buildings. There was nothing that Trave could do except watch them gaining on his son, and he was shamed by the sense of relief that he felt in the morning when he woke up covered in sweat and realised that Joe was dead and buried, gone beyond the reach of evil men.

The records office in Rouen opened at nine o'clock on the dot, but that was where its efficiency ended. Certificates of birth, death, and marriage had to be requested from an unseen holy of holies deep inside the building, and Trave was told that it would take at least a day to process his application. Waving his police badge in front of the expressionless bureaucrat in the front office was a complete waste of time. The procedures were inflexible, and Trave soon gave up the argument.

He had even less luck finding any contemporary documents. Rouen had been occupied by the Germans until two days after the killings at Marjean, and local news reporting in the summer of 1944 appeared to have been virtually nonexistent. Trave could find no account anywhere to either contradict or support the British military report that Cade had shown Stephen after the arrival of the blackmail letter at Moreton Manor two years earlier.

Trave wandered around feeling depressed and frustrated. Even the cathedral failed to lift his spirits, and in the evening he drank too much red wine on an empty stomach, sitting in the corner of a deserted riverside café until it finally closed its doors for the night. Afterward he walked unsteadily back to his hotel through the unlit backstreets, and narrowly avoided being run over by a speeding motorcycle as he missed his footing on the edge of a broken pavement.

There was a message from Adam Clayton pushed under his door, asking him to call when he got in, but it was past midnight and Trave decided to wait until morning. His head was throbbing when he got up, and the phone line was bad. Standing in the hotel lobby, Trave had to shout to make himself heard, and the other residents eating their breakfast in the hotel's miniature dining room glared at Trave until he turned his back on them. Above the crackling Clayton sounded almost ebullient. He'd found Cade's key ring, and one of the keys on it did fit the study door. Trave felt a tremor of excitement. It was as if he had uncovered the footprint of an invisible man. His instinct had been right. The key with Stephen's fingerprints on it had been a copy. The question was, Who had made it? Trave was about to tell Clayton what to do next but Clayton preempted him. He had already started making the rounds of Oxford locksmiths.

Buoyed, Trave packed his bag and drove over to the records office. But he didn't get the death certificates that he'd applied for the previous day until the afternoon. There were four of them, each neatly typed and signed and edged with a black border. Henri Rocard, aged forty-eight; his wife, Mathilde, aged

fifty-two; and an old servant called Albert Blanc were each described as having been shot by the enemy in Marjean Church on August 28, 1944. The
fourth victim, Marguerite Blanc, clearly the wife of Albert, had been burnt
by the Germans in the château on the same day.

There was also a copy of a letter with the certificates in which the chief
registrar in Rouen informed the lawyers for Stephen Cade in London that all
the existing records had been checked, and they disclosed no evidence that
either the Rocards or the Blancs had any close living relatives at the time of
their deaths.

Existing records. Trave asked the man behind the desk why that word had
been used. Why not just *records*? He was a different official from the day before. More helpful but just as self-important. He explained, in slow French
for Trave's benefit, that the records for 1938, 1939, and early 1940 had been
destroyed when the Germans invaded northern France, but those before that
had survived because they had been kept in a secure archive immune from
enemy bombing. A disaster of this kind would not happen again, added the
clerk in a self-satisfied tone, because procedures had improved since the war.
It was almost as if he was expecting the Germans to start bombing Rouen
again anyday now.

Trave drove out of the town, gripped with a sense of mounting frustration.
He'd half known, of course, that the records office wouldn't help him. Swift's
man had been there already after all. But his policeman's instincts had told
him to be thorough, and now he regretted his decision. He should have gone
straight to Moirtier and Marjean, but as it was, he had wasted nearly two
days and was no further forward, while all the time the clocks in Wandsworth Prison ticked remorselessly on.

Moirtier-sur-Bagne called itself a town, but really it was little bigger than
a large village, built on either side of a tiny tributary of the Seine. There was
one hotel with a café on the ground floor, which faced the mayor's office and
police station across the village square, where a group of men in berets were
playing bowls under the plane trees in the late afternoon. Trave bought a glass
of wine and sat down near the game, watching the black balls being tossed
through the air to land in the sandy dirt. The players hardly ever spoke and
showed no apparent interest in Trave, even when he tried unsuccessfully to

strike up a conversation with them. Eventually, despairing of an opening, he asked them outright if they knew anything about the killings at Marjean Château fifteen years before. But this just made things worse. They shook their heads and turned their backs on him, muttering to one another in a fast French that he could not understand, until he gave up and went inside.

It was the same with everyone he approached in Moirtier both that day and the next. The reactions ranged from incomprehension to outright hostility, and he fared little better in Marjean itself, which turned out to be an even smaller place than Moirtier, a few houses built around the crest of a low hill surrounded by vineyards, with a view across a long dark lake to a ruined house and church encircled by encroaching woods.

The police station in Moirtier was closed on the day of Trave's arrival, but the following morning, a Friday, he found a young gendarme sitting behind an iron desk, laboriously typing out something official on an ancient typewriter.

"You make me feel like I'm at home again," said Trave with a smile.

"Seventeen Hill Road, Oxford, England," said the young man, without looking up.

"How do you know that?" asked Trave, astonished.

"Your registration card at the hotel," said the young man, waving it in the air like a conjuror. "They pass it on to us, and we make a record in triplicate. One stays here, one goes to Rouen, and one to Paris. Don't ask me why. It's the law and I do what I'm told. Fortunately, I don't have to do it too often. Not too many foreigners put up at the Claire Fontaine these days, particularly in the winter."

The young man's friendliness was a welcome change after the reticence Trave had encountered from the other villagers. "I'm here for a reason," he said.

"So I hear. Asking questions and getting no answers. This is a small town, Mr. Trave. People don't like outsiders."

"But you don't feel that way?"

"You're a policeman and so am I. We have something in common."

"Not enough, I'm afraid," said Trave with a smile. "You're too young to be able to help me."

"With what?"

"The real story of what happened at Marjean Château fifteen years ago. You'd still have been in school in 1944."

"But that doesn't mean I can't help," the gendarme said. "It's no great secret. It's the same as I told the lawyer's man who came out here from London a few months back: the owners were killed by the Germans. Some people here say they were collaborators, but even if it's true, they didn't deserve to die that way. Herded into the church and shot like animals. The Nazis burnt the house too. It's a ruin now."

"I know all that. But I'm here because I need to find out whether there were any survivors, anyone who saw what happened. It's important. Somebody's life depends on the answer."

"That's what the other man said. But, as I told him, I've never heard of there being any survivors. Still, as you say, I was only a boy back then. You could ask my inspector, I suppose. He'd know one way or the other. He's been here since before the war."

"Did the man from England talk to him?"

"No. He was away then. It was during the summer. Everyone deserves a holiday some time, don't they, Inspector?" said the gendarme, smiling.

"Where is he now?" asked Trave, smiling in agreement.

"Gone to Lille to see his sister. She's not well and he visits her most weekends, but this time he's taken the Friday off as well. He'll be back on Monday. You can talk to him then."

"Can't we call him? Doesn't his sister have a telephone?"

"No. She lives outside the city. No telephone, I'm afraid."

"What about a telegram?"

"I don't have the address. Come back on Monday morning, Inspector. You can talk to him then."

"Monday's too late."

"I'm sorry." The gendarme opened his hands in a gesture of deprecation, and then turned away to resume his typing.

Trave realised that he had gone as far as he could. Perhaps the inspector's sister did have a telephone, but the gendarme was not going to tell him the number. He was probably under strict orders not to reveal such information. Trave would have to wait until Monday. There was no point in going back to

England before then anyway. Clayton didn't need his help to visit a few locksmiths' shops. And Stephen's execution was not until Wednesday morning. There would still be time to get back to England and go with Swift to see the powers that be, as Creswell called them, if he found out something useful on Monday. At present he didn't have anything. He didn't need a lawyer to tell him that. Stephen could have copied the key, and the name in the atlas was just a curious coincidence.

The next day Trave drove to Marjean, parked his car at the foot of the hill, and walked out to the ruined château along the side of the lake. It was a longer distance than it had looked when he set out, and the path was muddy in places, forcing him to take detours through the adjacent scrub. There was a glassy darkness to the water, an absence of movement on its surface that Trave found oddly disquieting. Several times before he reached the end of the path, he thought of turning back, and only his natural obstinacy kept him going.

Eventually he found himself standing on the far side, looking up at the grey stone church and bell tower built on the top of a small hill, sloping up from where he stood at the water's edge. Beyond the church the ground ran down again to the ruins of what had once been the château. It was sadly dilapidated. The glass in all the windows was broken and most of the roof had fallen in. It was a desolate place, but incongruously, unexpectedly, a white truck was parked in front of the main door, which hung precariously off its hinges, swinging backward and forward in the slight breeze.

As Trave stood looking at the car, wondering who it might belong to, two people came out of the church and began walking quickly down the path to the house. They had their backs to him, but Trave could see from their dress that they were male and female. The man was carrying what looked like two crowbars and the woman was holding a piece of paper. It was impossible to be sure as long as her back was turned, but Trave had the sense that she was angry about something. She was gesticulating with her hands, and her walk seemed unnaturally fast. There was something vaguely familiar about her figure, and Trave ran along the side of the hill toward the house, eager to see who she was. Just before she reached the car, the woman must have become aware of his approach, because she turned round to face him. Trave recognised her straightaway. It was Sasha Vigne.

He stopped dead in his tracks, and so for a moment did she. But she recovered more quickly than he did, covering the last few yards to the car in a few rapid strides, before she yanked open the passenger door and joined her companion inside. Trave could hear her shouting at the man to drive: "Vite, vite." The car's motor gunned into life just as he reached her door, and the car shot forward toward the church, throwing him out of the way, before it turned half circle and disappeared down a track that seemed to lead straight into the woods. Trave ran after it a little way but then stopped with his hands on his knees, panting. His heart was racing but so was his mind. Sasha Vigne was the last person that he had expected to meet in this lonely place, far removed from all civilization.

He needed to find her again, but he had no car. Cursing his decision to walk to the château, Trave turned back the way he'd come and started to walk quickly down the path towards Marjean village, shimmering on its hilltop in the last of the winter sunshine.

TWENTY-FOUR

Sasha had been the only mourner at her father's funeral, which took just under twelve minutes to complete in Chapel number 2 at Oxford Crematorium's Garden of Remembrance. She was given the last slot before lunch, and the minister was already running late when her father's turn came around. There was thus little time available for meaningful reflection before the big red curtain was drawn electronically around the light oak coffin and Andrew Blayne made his final invisible journey down the crematorium's carousel toward the central furnace, which had been belching smoke when Sasha arrived and was belching smoke when she left with her father's ashes in a small white plastic urn half an hour later.

Andrew Blayne had left no instructions on whether he wished to be burnt or buried, but in the end Sasha had found the choice surprisingly easy to make. Sitting in his room on the day after his death, Sasha had tried to puzzle out what he might have wanted. But then a sudden breeze blowing through the open window had made up her mind for her, as it picked up the last scents of her father and dispersed them forever. The wind was like fire. Clean and quick and true. Not like the earth. The thought of her father's body slowly decomposing in the wet soil had made Sasha sick to her stomach. God knows, he had known enough decay while he was still alive. The end was the end.

Sasha had never believed in the resurrection of the body. Not even when she was a little girl and her mother took her to church twice on Sundays.

And so she had made her booking with the undertaker and ended up outside the crematorium's iron gates on a cold November day with a sense of complete isolation from everyone else in the world. But that of course was just what she wanted to feel. Her grief for her father was an event waiting to happen, but for now she was almost glad of his absence. Without him, there was nobody to deflect her from her purpose.

First thing the next morning, she cleared out her bank account and changed her money into French francs. She had already given notice to her landlord and packed her belongings into two suitcases. One she deposited in the left-luggage office at Paddington Station, and the other she took with her on the boat train. The codex was wrapped inside her clothes, and the urn was in an outer pocket. She had not yet found a place to scatter her father's ashes, and it didn't seem right to leave what was left of him behind. After all, she didn't know when she would be coming back.

She got to Marjean late on Friday evening. Nothing had changed since her last visit two years before. There were no new houses, and just as few people in the narrow streets. The same single-track road wound down through the vineyards to the blue-black waters of the lake, and in the distance Sasha could just make out the silver-grey bell tower of Marjean Church, fading in the last rays of the sun.

She checked in to the small inn on the edge of the village where she had put up before. The landlord was an old man with a brown weather-beaten face, and he made no comment as he took down the details from her passport, filling out the registration form in laborious block capitals. But a passing alertness in his pale blue eyes made her think that he recognised either her face or her name, and he smiled when she gave the purpose of her visit as tourism. It made her slightly uneasy, but the sensation was transient, and she forgot about the old man almost as soon as he had shown her to her room and left her with the key.

Underneath her buttoned-up exterior, Sasha could hardly contain her excitement. But she knew that darkness would come quickly once the sun had set, and she had no option but to wait until morning before driving out to the church.

She was restless at dinner and drank too much of the local red wine, trying not to think about John Cade, who had been this way already, armed with the same secret that she had worked so hard to discover. And yet he hadn't found the cross. Just a bullet in the lung fired from a high-velocity rifle. Sasha remembered what her father had said when she first brought the codex to his attic room in Oxford: "You'll go to France just like he did. . . . And something terrible will happen to you." Sasha shivered. The words seemed like a prophecy.

She wanted to believe that she had begun a completely new chapter in her life, that she had left the past entirely behind her on the other side of the English Channel, and yet unbeknownst to her, less than four miles down the dark road, Trave was pacing up and down in another hotel room, thinking just like Sasha about Marjean Church and what may or may not have happened there.

At first light she drove out of the village, looking for the wrought-iron gate in the wall that ran along the right side of the road. She remembered it clearly from two years before, but now it had disappeared, and the entrance was virtually indistinguishable from other openings where the wall had fallen down and local people had carried away the stone for their own construction works. Sasha went straight past the gateway the first time and only realised her mistake when she found herself coming into Moirtier-sur-Bagne. Turning the car round, she drove back toward Marjean at a snail's pace until eventually she found what she was looking for. She knew it must be right because the two white prancing horses on top of the gateposts were just visible beneath the fast-growing ivy. Beyond, the track was half-dark with overarching trees cutting off most of the sunlight, but there were no serious obstructions to her progress. Mass was still said at Marjean Church, and the curé made sure that his parishioners kept the way clear for his car.

There was no opening in the woods on either side. Once Sasha thought she saw the head of a deer flashing between two tree trunks, but it was gone as quickly as it had appeared. And then there was nothing until the track turned to the right and she came out suddenly into the light. The ruined house was in front of her, and beyond it Marjean Church occupied a low ridge with the lake as a backdrop. Sasha parked at the bottom of the path leading up to the church, but she didn't get out for a moment. The dead seemed to be all around her: the abbots and their monks who had worshipped God in this place for centuries, proud of their library and their church with the jewelled cross of St. Peter that hung sparkling above the high altar. Sasha closed her eyes and heard the night bells, summoning the tonsured monks from their dormitories to come shuffling through the candlelit darkness to the church for vespers, compline, prime, and lauds. There was nothing left of the monastery now except the remains of a few low walls in a clearing beyond the château. And nothing left of the monks' library except the codex that lay wrapped up in her clothes back at the inn. And the cross—that was why she was here. To see if she could bring it back from the past, out of the hands of dead men.

With a renewed sense of purpose, Sasha climbed the hill to the church. There was an old rusty padlock securing the door, but she had come prepared for that. She broke it easily with a pair of bolt cutters that she had bought in Le Havre the day before and went inside, crossing quickly to the vestry area at the back. And then down a winding, narrow staircase to the crypt. She had brought candles, but she didn't need them. A power cable had been run down the stairs since her last visit, and with a flick of a switch the grey stone tombs of the abbots of Marjean were suddenly bathed in the cold electric light of the twentieth century.

"Crux Petri in manibus Petri est." Sasha took Cade's list of numbers out of her pocket, looking for her father's words at the bottom of the page. "Abbots of Marjean," he had written in his own distinctive shaky Parkinson's-affected script. "Marcus 1278–1300. Stephanus Pisano 1300–05. Bartholomeus 1306–21. Simeon 1321–27." They were probably the last words he had ever written, before the stroke knocked him to the ground.

Slowly, Sasha walked the length of the crypt, concentrating her attention on the tombs on the left-hand side. The inscriptions on the wall showed that these were the most recent. Seven from the end, she came to the name "Marcus" with the date 1278 written underneath: the same year that he had become abbot of Marjean. Like so many of his predecessors, he had been immortalised in stone. Except that the details of his face had been worn away with time, so that the expression was now unreadable. Sasha remembered that Marcus had also been Bishop of Rouen for a time. He had ruled the city with an iron hand, burning heretics in the cathedral square on an almost daily basis until the townsmen had had enough and petitioned the archbishop in Paris to have him removed. This abbot certainly had no right to rest in peace, but it was not him with whom Sasha was concerned.

Beyond Marcus, the remaining tombs were sarcophagi without sculpture or adornment. These held the last abbots before the monastery was wiped out by the Black Death in 1352, little more than half a century after the death of Marcus in 1300.

The names on the wall above the tombs corresponded exactly to Andrew Blayne's list, and Sasha read them out loud as she passed each one. Stephanus Pisano, 1300; Bartholomeus, 1306; Simeon, 1321 1327. Her voice echoed off the thick walls of the crypt, and she could hear it trembling just like her hands as she came to a halt in front of the tomb of Abbot Simon. It was strange that there were two dates for him, whereas all the others only had one, but still, the dates were the same as those that her father had written down and under-lined twice. She needed to open the tomb and see what was inside. It was not that she really expected to find the jewelled cross lying in the dead abbot's hands. Cade had been here before, after all, and come away empty-handed. It was rather that she hoped for some sign that would take her forward. Some-thing that Cade had missed.

But try as she might, she couldn't move the stone lid of the sarcophagus. She pushed as hard as she could, but it was useless. She needed help. A man with a crowbar could do it if she had one too. Sasha swallowed her frustration. Getting help meant taking someone into her confidence, and Sasha trusted no one. But this time she knew that she had no choice. She quickly turned over her options as she drove back down the track to the main road. People in Mar-jean used this church. They had kept it open since the end of the war, even though the château was a ruin and the church was a mile's walk from the vil-lage. They were hardly likely to want to help a foreigner open up tombs in its crypt, however much money she offered them, and they probably wouldn't just refuse. They'd go to the curé or, worse still, the police, and that would be the end of any chance she had of finding the cross. No, she needed to go farther afield to find someone without any local loyalties.

Half an hour later she thought she had found the man she was looking for. She had driven through Moirtier-sur-Bagne and stopped at a café on the outskirts of Rouen. There was a builder's truck parked outside, and she took it as a sign. The owner was at the bar, slightly the worse for drink. His wife had left him and his business was failing, and the café proprietor looked like he had had enough of listening to the man's complaints. He cursed everybody and everything and seemed to hold Jesus Christ and the Virgin Mary equally responsible for his troubles. Sasha shook out her long brown hair and took a seat beside the man at the bar. His name was Jean Marie, and he was like clay in her fingers. She puckered her lips and showed him some of her French francs, and twenty minutes later she was sitting beside him in his truck, giving him directions in her slow, grammatically correct French. Behind her on the backseat there were two crowbars under a blanket, and Sasha felt a warm glow of anticipation as they turned down the track leading to Marjean Church.

But the man's enthusiasm quickly waned once he'd got out of his truck. A stray dog was barking somewhere inside the ruined château and a light rain had begun to fall out of the grey, leaden sky. Down in the crypt under the cold electric light, Sasha could hardly get him to stay. Cursing Jesus Christ and the Virgin Mary in a roadside café didn't make Jean Marie an unbeliever, and he seemed to have no doubt that digging up the abbots of Marjean was a blasphemous act, for which he would suffer on both sides of the grave. Sasha had to double and then triple the money that she had already given him in the café before he was prepared to fit his crowbar under the lid of Abbot Simon's tomb and join her in levering it up and around to the point where there was enough space for her to shine her torch down into the interior. The tomb was not empty. The pale white skull and bones of the once-holy abbot were there, but that was all. There was no cross, no jewels. Just the empty eye sockets of the dead man, staring up at Sasha in silent mockery.

It was what Sasha had expected, but not what she had hoped for. There was something she was missing, but she did not know what it was. She needed time to think without this half-drunk Frenchman whining in the corner of the crypt. It was all she could do to get him to help her replace the stone cover of the tomb. Outside the church, he ran down the hill to his truck, and she had to call to him to stop, worried that he would leave her behind, even though she had only paid him half his money. Then, just as she got level with the château, she became aware of someone slightly below her, to her left. She turned to see who it was and stopped dead in her tracks. It was Inspector Trave, the policeman from Stephen's trial, the one who'd come to visit her at Moreton to try to get her to change her evidence. He seemed as shocked as she was. Behind her, Jean Marie was already in the truck, and she knew he wouldn't wait. Pulling herself together, she launched herself across the few remaining yards, pulled open the passenger door and told him the word that he most dreaded to hear. "Police," she shouted. "Drive now. Quickly. Quickly. Go."

The truck's engine roared into life, and it jumped forward, almost stalling. But it didn't. Instead Jean Marie took it around in a screeching 180-degree turn and then accelerated away into the woods, leaving Trave shouting uselessly in the dust that the truck had left behind.

As they careered up the track leading to the road, Sasha tried to persuade the hysterical Frenchman to take her back to Marjean. She cursed herself for having left the codex in her room, but it was too late now, and she had to go back. But he wouldn't listen. Instead he drove like a madman down the road to Rouen and practically threw her out of his truck when they got to the café where they had first met less than an hour before. Her car was still in the parking lot, and she drove back to Marjean as fast as she could. With luck she'd still get there before Trave. There had been no car outside the church. He must have walked, and it was over a mile along the side of the lake. He looked too old to be able to run very far, and besides, the path was muddy. He'd fall in the water if he tried to go too fast.

She parked outside the inn and took the stairs to her room two at a time. There was a note that had been slipped under her door. She almost missed it, and there was no time to read it when she picked it up. She just threw everything into her bag and headed out onto the landing. At the top of the stairs, she heard Trave down below, asking the way to her room. She was sure that the landlord hadn't seen her when she came in. He'd been in the cubicle at the back of the reception area talking on the telephone. Trave was coming up on the off chance. He didn't know she was there. She backed away into the semidarkness at the back of the landing and watched him come down the corridor toward her. But he wasn't looking in front of him. His eyes were on the door of her room. He knocked twice before he tried the handle. When it turned, he went inside and the door swung to behind him. There was no time to lose. On tiptoe she ran across the landing, down the stairs, and out the door.

Trave was standing at the window of her room looking down into the street when he saw her. He didn't move. There was no point. She had already started her car, and he pursed his lips, cursing softly as he watched her drive away.

TWENTY-FIVE

Sasha had forgotten her coat. It hung forlornly in the wardrobe. The pockets were empty, and Trave left it where it was. Downstairs, the landlord appeared unconcerned by his guest's sudden departure.

"She ran away because of you," he said flatly. "Not because of the money. She will send me what she owes. The English, they always pay their bills."

Trave didn't argue. After all, the landlord was right about why Sasha had left. There was an implied accusation in his tone, however, that Trave felt obliged to answer. And the old man might know something. It wasn't as if Trave could afford to leave any stone unturned.

"I'm a policeman," he said. "From Oxford in England. Someone was killed near there, murdered, about six months ago, and I think it may have something to do with what happened here at the end of the war."

"Nothing happened here."

"No, I don't mean here in the village. I mean over on the other side of the lake. In the church."

"The Germans killed the people that lived there. They did the same everywhere. They were Nazis."

The old man seemed entirely satisfied with his three-word explanation for the atrocity, but Trave persisted.

"The lady who was here, Miss Vigne, was at the house where the man was killed. And now she is here. Do you know why?" he asked.

The old man looked Trave full in the eye and then shrugged his shoulders. It was a gesture of contempt. He might just as well have spat on the floor. Trave felt certain that he knew something but equally certain that he was not going to talk about it. He turned away exasperated, but at the door the landlord called him back.

"Mr. Policeman," he said, "you tell me your name and your telephone number, and if I think of something, then I will call you. Okay?"

Quickly, Trave wrote his details down on the back of a registration form and put it in the landlord's calloused hand. But then he didn't let go of the piece of paper. Instead he leant across the counter, bringing his face up close to the Frenchman's.

"A boy is going to hang for something he never did," he said softly. "If you think of something, think of that."

Then, without waiting for a reply, Trave walked out of the door and made for his car. He was angry, and he didn't look back. If he'd done so, he might have seen the landlord disappear back into the cubicle behind the reception area and pick up the telephone. He dialed a long-distance number, waited for a reply, and then began talking in rapid French to the person on the other end.

Trave drove out of the village. Sasha had disappeared, and he knew instinctively that he wouldn't find her again. And even if he did, he had no authority to ask her any questions. He was outside his jurisdiction, and he didn't have any basis to invoke the help of the French police. And yet there was so much that he wanted to know. What was she doing here? Outside the church, she'd looked like someone who'd been searching for something and failed to find it. But that wasn't the same as having a relation to the Rocards or their servants, having some reason for wanting revenge on John Cade for what he'd done here in 1944.

She'd given Silas the alibi, or was it the other way round? Was she the one who'd killed her employer in his chair and then escaped across the courtyard in Silas's mackintosh and hat? She had had the opportunity, and she was certainly cold-blooded enough to plan such a crime. But what was her motive, and why was she in the backwoods of Normandy now, looking for something she couldn't find?

Trave stopped at the church on the way back to Moirtier, but he couldn't see anything unusual beyond the severed padlock hanging uselessly from one handle of the big oak door. A notice by the entrance advertised Holy Mass at nine o'clock every Sunday, and Trave decided to come back the next day. Perhaps the curé would know something. God knows, his luck had to change soon.

In the evening he called Adam Clayton from the hotel. The young man sounded excited.

"I found the locksmith," he said. "He wasn't in Oxford. He was in Reading. Our friend went halfway to London to copy the key. But he did it, Bill. You were right. It was four days before Cade's murder. A Frenchman in his late twenties, early thirties, calling himself Paul Noirtier and speaking very poor English. Walked in off the street with three wax casts and came back the next day to collect the keys. I'm assuming he got one for the french windows to the study as well as the internal door, and the last key's probably for the front door of the house. And there was also one duplicate apparently, although I obviously don't know which door that one's for. He paid cash apparently. I've got a description: tall, short black hair, clean shaven, and no glasses. Doesn't tell us much. The locksmith says he didn't like the look of him, but that's probably because he doesn't like foreigners." Clayton laughed.

"Was the man alone?" asked Trave.

"I asked about that. The locksmith's pretty sure there was a woman waiting outside the shop in a Mercedes, but he can't describe her, and none of the photographs jogged his memory."

"Did you show him Sasha Vigne's picture?"

"Yes. I showed him pictures of everyone who was in the house. Like you said I should. And he drew a blank on all of them. Why Sasha Vigne particularly?"

"Because she's here."

"Where?"

"In bloody Marjean. And I don't know why."

"Can't you ask her?"

"She's disappeared."

Clayton whistled. "There's bad news about the home secretary, I'm afraid," he said after a moment. "The defence barrister rang here yesterday, looking for you. He called to say the minister refused the reprieve. He seemed pretty upset—said something about the old bastard not knowing the meaning of the word. The execution's on Wednesday morning at eight. Same as before."

"Can't we take this statement from the locksmith to the Home Office?" Clayton asked anxiously when Trave stayed silent at the other end of the phone. "The name and the car link up with the Mercedes that was stopped on the murder night."

"It's not enough," said Trave flatly. "The man in the Mercedes could just as well have been Stephen's accomplice as anyone else's. I've got a couple more people to talk to here, but if nothing comes of that, I think we've had it, Adam. There's no point in pretending. We're damn near played out."

"Don't say that. Something'll turn up."

Trave said nothing. He suddenly realised that he wanted to cry, but he couldn't. He'd felt the same after Joe died. It made him hate himself.

"I'll call you on Monday," he said finally and was about to put the phone down, when Adam spoke again.

"When are you going to come back?" he asked. "Creswell wants to know."

"Tell him Monday night," said Trave. "I'll know one way or the other by then."

After the call was over, he stayed by the telephone, tempted to ring the airlines and book the earliest flight home. But he didn't. He knew that there was nothing to be gained by going back. Only evidence could help Stephen. And he felt sure that there was evidence here, if only he could find it in time.

Trave remembered his father telling him when he was a boy that there was only one way to untie a knot, and that was to go back to the beginning. And the beginning was in one of these towns. Moirtier or Marjean. He felt the thread just beyond the tips of his outstretched fingers, but try as he might, he couldn't get hold of it. The Frenchman and his accomplice were out there somewhere, waiting for the final chapter to unfold, and he was here, alone and confused, with three days left to find out who killed John Cade. And one of these days was a Sunday.

Trave sat at the back of Marjean Church during the Mass. It was in Latin and the liturgy was far removed from the Book of Common Prayer that he was used to in his Anglican church at home. Unexpectedly, it lifted his spirits. *Deum de deo. Lumen de lumine. Deum verum de deo vero.* The singing reached into the rafters, mixing with the incense, muffling the sound of the rain beating against the windows, and Trave prayed to this unfamiliar Latin God to show him the way, to save an innocent boy from another Calvary. At the end he put a coin in the iron box by the door and lit two candles, one for Joe and one for Stephen, and then he waited while the congregation filed out into the rain and the curé changed out of his lawn-green surplice in the vestry.

He was a young man in his early thirties with a long, angular face and wide open, bright blue eyes: a complete contrast to the shifty-looking landlord of the village inn on the other side of the lake. And he appeared entirely unruffled by the presence of an English policeman in his church who had obviously come to ask him questions. Without needing to be asked, he told Trave about the padlock on the door that had been cut the day before, but he had no idea what the intruder had been looking for. Nothing was missing from the church, and he had never heard of a young Englishwoman called Sasha Vigne.

The curé insisted on giving Trave a guided tour of the church.

"It's one of the oldest in Normandy," he said. "And we get people coming from all over France to look at the tombs. But then the château is a disgrace. It just falls down stone by stone, and no one lifts a finger to stop it. They say the government owns the place, but they're not interested. Until some child gets killed by a falling mansard, of course. Then they'll do something."

"Where are the tombs?" asked Trave, in an effort to distract the curé from the subject of the ruined château, which was obviously his personal bête noire.

"Down in the crypt," said the curé, leading Trave through the vestry and down the narrow, winding stairs. "There was a monastery here once and this is where they buried their abbots."

"And isn't it true that the owners of the château were killed here at the end of the war?" asked Trave, interrupting. He wondered whether he had shown too much eagerness to move the conversation on to what he really wanted to talk about, but the curé seemed perfectly happy to change the subject.

"Yes, it was a terrible thing. Madame Rocard and the old manservant were killed down here," said the curé, pointing to the middle of the stone-flagged floor. "Her husband died upstairs. He was probably trying to stop the Germans from bringing them down here, although I've never understood why they wanted to do that in the first place. Maybe the Nazis wanted to ask them questions, turn the place into one of their torture chambers. But they'd been camped out in the house for the best part of two years. Plenty of opportunity to interrogate the Rocards in that time, instead of waiting until the day of their departure when the British and Canadians were just up the road."

"What were they like? The Rocards?" asked Trave. Suddenly they seemed very close. He didn't know why, but he felt more certain with every passing day that the murder of this middle-aged French couple in the summer of 1944 was the key to everything else. It was as if he needed to find out who killed them if he was ever going to discover who murdered John Cade fifteen years afterward.

"I can't tell you much about them, I'm afraid," said the curé apologetically. "I only got appointed to this parish two years ago, and so they were before my time. And no one seems to want to talk about them for some reason. I don't know why. Maybe people think they were collaborators. Memories tend to be long in places like this."

"Did the Germans kill everyone? Were there any survivors?" asked Trave, trying to keep the eagerness out of his voice. This was after all the question he'd come to ask.

"No, I don't think so. The Rocards had a little girl, but she died with the servant's wife in the house when the Germans set fire to it before they left."

"What about any other relatives? Anyone who might bear a grudge because of what happened?"

"No. None that I know of. Of course, it's not the only time there's been violence here. An Englishman was shot just outside the entrance door three years ago. But they never found out who did it, or whether it had anything to do with what happened here before. The inspector over at Moirtier said that the victim and his friend weren't exactly helpful, but I don't know the details. You know, he's the man you want to talk to if you want to find out more about the Rocards. Marcel Laroche is his name. He's been a policeman in this area since before the war. There's very little that happens in Marjean or Moirtier that he doesn't get to hear about. And now I've got to go, I'm afraid. I say

Mass in Moirtier at eleven. Having two churches to look after doesn't make my life that easy sometimes, although I mustn't complain. This is a beautiful church."

The curé ushered Trave out the door with a smile and then bent down to attach a brand-new padlock to the handles.

"That ought to keep the vandals out," he said in a satisfied tone as he raised a big clerical black umbrella above their heads, sufficient to shelter Trave as well as himself from the heavy rain. They went down the hill in a huddle, and the curé held the umbrella up high for Trave as he got into his car.

"It *is* beautiful, isn't it?" the curé said, pointing with a sweep of his hand at the ruined château and the old grey stone church and, beyond them, the blue-black lake whose surface was now a mass of silver raindrops. "But it's a strange place too. There's an atmosphere here. Something you can't quite put your finger on. I suppose if I believed in ghosts, I'd expect to find them here."

A faraway look had appeared in the curé's eye for a moment, but he recovered himself with a laugh. "You must forgive me for being foolish," he said. "Priests aren't supposed to talk about ghosts. Go and see Marcel Laroche if you have time. You'll like him, and maybe he can help you with some of your questions."

In the afternoon Trave walked out beyond Moirtier into the Norman countryside. The rain had stopped and the cold air smelt surprisingly fresh and full of promise, even though it was winter and the trees were black and leafless. A few cars passed every so often, and once a tiny aeroplane flew out toward the Channel, leaving a white line drawn high across the blue cloudless sky, but for most of the time everything was silent, and Trave walked to the sound of his own footsteps on the road.

It had turned into a beautiful day, but Trave took in very little of his surroundings as his mind turned over and over the words of the curé back at Marjean Church. "The Rocards had a little girl, but she died." Why then had he found no trace of her at the records office in Rouen? He remembered now. The clerk had said that the records for the two years before the invasion had been destroyed by enemy bombing. If the Rocards' daughter had been born in 1938, then there would be no birth certificate in Rouen. And no wonder Stephen's lawyers hadn't looked any further for missing children. Madame Rocard had been childless up to the age of forty-five. There was no reason to think that she wouldn't stay that way. The girl was a war child. Had Cade missed her too? Stephen had said that his father wanted something at Marjean. A valuable book. Even if he had gone there before the war to try to get it, he still wouldn't have been able to go back until after D-day. A gap of four years or more. Perhaps Cade never knew about the Rocards' little daughter.

But the curé had said she was dead. And yet there was no death certificate. She hadn't just died—she'd disappeared into thin air. Unless that was deliberate. What if all record of her had been removed so that she could grow up invisible, biding her time until she was ready to revenge herself on John Cade, who had killed her father and mother in cold blood? What if the elusive Frenchman in the Mercedes was her accomplice, waiting by the telephone box outside Moreton Manor in case he was needed on that Friday night back in June when Cade had been shot through the head? Executed with a single bullet.

And who had been inside the manor house for eighteen months before that night, learning how everything worked, preparing for the appointed day when Cade would get his just deserts? Sasha Vigne. And it was Sasha who had run away the day before. She'd done that because she had something to hide, and she was still here somewhere. Trave was sure of it. Gone to ground in one of these little towns or villages, waiting for Stephen Cade to die and Trave to go home. Because with Stephen's execution, her revenge would be complete. Father and son would have paid for the murder of her own mother and father. An eye for an eye and a tooth for a tooth. Old Testament justice.

A car horn sounded suddenly close behind Trave, shattering the peace of the day. He had unconsciously drifted into the middle of the road while he built his theories up like castles in the winter air, and now he had to step quickly back onto the verge to let a builder's truck go by. For a moment he thought it was the same white van in which Sasha and her friend had accelerated away from Marjean Church the day before, but he soon realised his mistake. This truck was far bigger. The one yesterday had looked like a very run-down vehicle. And the frightened driver hadn't been Trave's idea of a cold-blooded conspirator who drove a Mercedes round the English countryside, plotting the murder of an Oxford University professor. No, he wasn't Mr. Noirtier, and Sasha was probably not the Rocards' daughter either. Because that girl was almost certainly dead. Burnt to death in her family home in the late summer of 1944, just like the curé had said.

Whatever happened, this wild-goose chase would have to come to an end soon. He'd told Clayton that he'd be back in England by Monday evening, and Trave intended to keep to that. He'd see the policeman, Laroche, in the morning, and after that he could do no more. Enough was enough. Turning back toward Moirtier-sur-Bagne, Trave realised with a start that the sun had almost set, and he had gone much farther down the road than he had intended. The temperature was colder now, and he would have to hurry if he was going to get back to his hotel before dark. He shivered, pulling his inadequate coat around him, and inside he felt the onset of a black despair. He'd been in France for almost a week now, and he'd accomplished nothing except to fritter away what little time was left before Stephen's neck was broken. He cursed and swore, and his angry words made little volleys of white smoke in the thin, cold air, until he finally desisted, realising what a comical figure he must seem, a middle-aged man with unkempt hair and crumpled clothes scurrying through the deserted French countryside on a Sunday evening, swearing in English at nobody at all.

Marcel Laroche was an imposing figure. He was six foot four and carried himself militarily erect even though he was in his late fifties. But it was more than sheer physical size that gave him such a commanding presence. He had fought with the Free French in North Africa during the first years of the war and had then been parachuted into northern France to help the Resistance around Caen in the preparation for D-day. He had seen things that others hadn't, and his wartime experiences seemed to have given his character an unusual depth, which Trave found oddly attractive.

He was expecting Trave, and as soon as the Englishman came through the door of the police station, Laroche picked up his hat and coat, clapped his subordinate on the shoulder, and took Trave across to the café on the other side of the square where they sat drinking hot black coffee by the open window.

Laroche seemed genuinely touched when Trave asked after the health of his sister in Lille. "She's dying," he said simply. "But we don't discuss it. And she won't give in, which makes it harder. I hope for her sake that it will end soon. But you're not here to talk about me, Inspector," he added with a smile. "My deputy told me that you're interested in the Rocards."

"Yes. A young man in England says that his father killed them, not the Germans."

"Well, that's simply not true," said Laroche, surprised. "The Nazis did it. Everyone knows that. The British just didn't get to Marjean in time to stop them. That's all they did wrong."

"Were you here when it happened?" asked Trave.

"No. My unit didn't come this way. We were with the Americans, farther south. But I came back here after the war, and obviously I heard about what had happened. In detail. There were German bullets in the bodies."

"What about the Rocards' little girl? What about her body?"

"That was different. She was burnt in the fire at the house. The housekeeper was in there too, and they both died. It doesn't bear thinking about."

"There's no death certificate for the girl in Rouen," said Trave baldly. "I checked."

"Well, I can't explain that. Except that it was near the end of the war, and a lot of documents went missing everywhere. It couldn't be helped."

"People disappeared."

"Yes. There was chaos for a while, particularly around here. It was more stable in the south, in Vichy, where there was a handover of government. We didn't have that in the North."

"This boy in England is going to be executed on Wednesday for killing his father," said Trave. "And I don't think he did it. In fact, I'm sure he didn't. I think his father's death has got something to do with what happened here in 1944. I don't know if it was a survivor or a relative of someone who got killed, but whoever it is murdered this boy's father, and I need to find him. Or her. Before it's too late."

"Or her," said Laroche, repeating Trave's words. "You're talking about the girl, aren't you? The Rocards' daughter."

"Yes, I'm interested in her. There's a woman who was in the house when this boy's father was murdered. And she was at Marjean Church the day before yesterday."

"You think she might be the girl?"

"Maybe."

"What's her name?"

"Sasha Vigne."

"I've never heard of her," said Laroche, shrugging his shoulders.

"But you know something about the girl, don't you?" said Trave. He had noticed an alertness in the Frenchman ever since he first mentioned the Rocards' daughter, as if Laroche was keeping something back all the while that he was insisting that she had died in the fire.

"It's probably nothing," he said. "It was about three or four years after the end of the war. I can't be sure of the date. A young man came into the police station. He can't have been more than sixteen or seventeen. Called himself Paul Martin and said that he was originally from around here but had moved away when he was small. I found out afterward he was telling the truth about that. His uncle was old Père Martin, who used to be the priest of Marjean. He died a couple of years ago. He was a good man.

"Anyway, the boy claimed to be a friend of Madame Rocard, who was killed by the Nazis. Said the little girl had survived the massacre at the château, but she was too scared to come forward unless we guaranteed her safety."

"From whom?"

"From the people who'd killed her parents. Paul said that she'd told him three English soldiers had done it. That's why I looked at you the way I did when you said the same thing a minute ago. It wasn't the first time I'd heard someone say that."

"Did you believe him?"

"No, I didn't. I thought he was a gold digger. The Rocards had left no will and no relatives, and so their house went to the state. That's the way the law works in this country. You've seen the château. It's a ruin. But there's the land it's built on. There would still have been a financial incentive for pretending to be the Rocards' daughter."

"So what did you do?"

"I told him that I couldn't help him. Not unless the girl came into the station, and I could check out who she was. And that was the last I ever heard of Paul Martin. I don't know what became of him."

"He fell in love with an actress," said Trave softly. "One last question, Inspector. Do you happen to know the first name of the Rocards' daughter?"

"Marie," said Laroche without hesitation. "She was called Marie Rocard. And may she rest in peace."

Trave got up quickly and shook his companion's hand.

"You've been very helpful," he said. "More helpful than you can know. Can I use your telephone?"

Luck was on Trave's side. Clayton was in his office and answered almost immediately.

"Put out an alert," said Trave. "For the arrest of Mary Martin and a man calling himself Paul Noirtier, although he's probably changed his name by now. There's a photograph of her on the file that you can use. You'll have to use the locksmith's description for him. Not that it's much good. They're both likely to be armed and they're very dangerous."

"Why Mary Martin?" asked Adam, sounding perplexed at the other end of the line. "I thought you said it was Sasha Vigne whom you'd seen in Marjean."

"It was. But I got it wrong about her. It's Mary Martin we're after. She's the Rocards' daughter and she planned everything. From start to finish. With the help of this man Paul. It would've been her in the Mercedes when he went in to get the keys from the locksmith in Reading."

"What if we don't find her?"

"Then Swift'll have to have another go at the home secretary tomorrow. You better call him now and fill him in on what's happened. Maybe Swift can get the old bastard to grant a stay, but I wouldn't hold your breath. I've got enough to convince myself that it's her and not Stephen who killed John Cade. But a right-wing politician who doesn't want to know? I'm not so sure. We have to find her, Adam."

"All right. I'll get on to it," said Clayton, sounding nervous. "Where are you now, Bill?"

"I'm still in France. But I'm flying back this afternoon. And then I'm going straight home. I don't know why, but I'm dead beat, and I need to get some rest. I'm hardly a more likely candidate to find our lady than the entire British police force. It's wait-and-hope time now, Adam."

"Somebody called asking for you at lunchtime," said Clayton. "Sounded foreign. I said you were getting back today." But he didn't go on. The dull, unchanging tone on the other end of the line made him realise that Trave had already hung up, and Clayton had no number to call him back on.

The aeroplane was delayed leaving Paris, but Trave still got back into London by early evening, and from there he took the train back to Oxford and picked up his car at the station. He had told Clayton the truth about being dead tired. He couldn't remember when he had last felt so exhausted. It must be the stress, he thought, as he drove home, because the journey had not been that difficult. He was thinking no further ahead than a bath and change of clothes. Mary Martin still had to be found, but Trave remained buoyed by what he had discovered in the morning, and he had a strange feeling that the future would take care of itself.

As he turned the key in the door, he thought of how he had found Silas standing like an apparition under the streetlight nine days earlier and how he had resolved that evening to go to France and find things out for himself. Well, he had done that, and now he was home again. Home, sweet home. In the hallway Trave put out his hand to switch on the lights and felt instead a cold hand on his wrist and the muzzle of a gun thrust up against his heart.

"Hello, Inspector," said a voice that he recognised from a long time ago. "We've been expecting you."

TWENTY-SIX

On that same Monday morning that Trave sat down with Inspector Laroche to drink coffee by the front window of the Claire Fontaine Hotel in Moirtier-sur-Bagne, Stephen Cade was led across the exercise yard of Wandsworth Prison to the visits hall, where Mary Martin was waiting for him.

The warders were quiet, almost respectful, now that Stephen's execution date was so close, and he was put in a special room off the main hall with just one prison officer sitting on a chair in the corner to ensure that nothing was passed to or from the condemned man.

Stephen had been up all night, and there were rings of tiredness around his unnaturally bright blue eyes. He was moving all the time, squirming in his seat, and he talked in a rush, jumping haphazardly from subject to subject. Anything to fill the silence.

"Swift came to see me on Friday," he said. "Told me about the reprieve, or lack of one. He says it's because they want to make an example of me. Show the youth of this country what happens if you shoot people. And I'm just what they want, apparently. Tailor-made for their requirements. A member of the privileged classes, born with a silver spoon in my mouth. The idea being that if someone like me ends up dangling from the end of a rope, then nobody can expect to get away with using a gun. I'm the government's

Christmas message to the criminal classes, Mary. Guaranteed front-page material."

Stephen laughed bitterly, and his anger beat against his old girlfriend, forcing her away from him, up against the back of her ugly wooden chair. In truth she looked little better than Stephen. Her nails were bitten to the quick and the tightness of her facial muscles showed the strain she was under as she fought to keep hold of her usual composure. All the day before Paul had tried to make her stay away from the prison, but she'd insisted on coming. Stephen had a right to know what they had done to him, she'd said; he had the right to an explanation, but now that she was here the words wouldn't come, and every passing minute made it more difficult to find a way to begin.

The truth was that it had all turned out wrong. Stephen hadn't deserved any of this—she realised that now. It had just all seemed so much simpler before, when she was still in France and it was all about her parents, about getting them justice. Closing her eyes, Mary summoned up the image of her mother looking up at her in the window of the tower as she crossed the nave of Marjean Church for the last time. It was the memory that had haunted Mary and sustained her for the last fifteen years. Her own mother leaving behind her dead husband, slumped on the stone-flagged floor of the church, as the two Englishmen, Cade and Ritter, pushed her and old Albert through the door of the vestry and down the narrow winding stairs to the crypt. Mary had waited for them to come back, but instead she had heard the shouting and the cries of pain and the gunshots and the silence afterward. Always the silence that went on and on and on forever. It demanded retribution; it required the oath that she had sworn with Paul on the deserted hill outside Dijon all those years ago.

They had watched and they had waited, dreaming of a just revenge. And killing John Cade had been just that. She'd not felt one moment's remorse for what she had done that night at Moreton Manor. She still rejoiced in it, when she wasn't thinking about what had happened since, but almost from the outset this slow judicial murder of Cade's son had begun to make her sick, until now she couldn't stand it any longer. It was too cold-blooded, and Stephen wasn't just Cade's son anymore, either. She knew him too well, and, however hard she tried, she hadn't been able to stay entirely detached from the part she'd played with him in the months before his arrest. The trouble was that he had nothing to do with what had happened to her at Marjean. It wasn't his fault that John Cade was his father. God knows, Stephen had walked away from the man because of what he'd done to her parents.

Mary had hoped that he'd be acquitted at the trial, but it hadn't happened. The jury hadn't bought Silas as the murderer, and now she could only save Stephen by exposing herself. And Paul wouldn't hear of it. Not because he was frightened. That wasn't in Paul's nature. No, it was because of the plan. Always the plan. An eye for an eye and a tooth for a tooth—not just Cade but his son as well, which was fine when you were far away, working out details on a piece of paper. It was very different when Cade's son was a man who loved you, a young man with his whole life in front of him, a life that you were trying to take away.

It was funny how Paul's determination to carry out the plan to the letter seemed to have grown in direct proportion to the waning of her own enthusiasm for it. She and Paul had always been like brother and sister, but that didn't mean that he hadn't become jealous of Stephen. Looking back, even Mary had to admit that there had been times in Oxford when she had forgotten that she was an actress playing a part. But that was in the past. All Mary knew now was that the time had come to change the script, with or without Paul. She'd already worked out what had to be done, but first she owed it to Stephen to tell him the truth, and that was the difficult part, she now realised; the rest would be far easier.

"It's not over yet," she said lamely, trying to buy time before she began her confession, but the remark infuriated Stephen.

"Yes, it is," he shouted. "Over and out. I'm going through that trapdoor on Wednesday unless the real murderer comes forward, and I don't think that's very likely. Do you?"

"I don't know. Maybe . . ."

Stephen shook his head violently, and Mary's prepared speech died in her throat as she glimpsed the depth of his despair. He swallowed hard and looked up at the ceiling, fighting to keep back his tears. Brutally, he rubbed the back of each hand across his face, and then, blinking, he seemed to see Mary for the first time since he had come into the room.

"You know, this is probably the last time we'll ever be together," he said, in a suddenly quiet voice. "Unless you believe in the afterlife, which I don't. Since I was moved to the new cell, I've been reading the Bible at night when I can't sleep. Trying to make sense of all this and failing. All that cursing and begetting. But I was wondering last night if that's what all this is about."

"What?"

"Being cursed through the generations. Like I'm dying, not for what I've done, but to atone for what my father did. As if his death wasn't enough. It needs more blood to even up the scales."

"Your father was an evil man."

"Yes. But I'm not. I've always tried to do the right thing. And look where I've ended up. You know, I've always thought that this is about what happened to those people in France all those years ago. You and Swift persuaded me to accuse Silas, but I never thought he was capable of killing anyone, let alone our father. And I don't think accusing him helped me at all in the end. It looked like opportunism, which is exactly what it was."

"You had to try it," said Mary defensively. "The stuff about Marjean wasn't working. You know that."

"No, I don't," said Stephen stubbornly. "That car was parked outside the gate for a reason that night. There was something about it. You'd know if you'd seen it. And the name the driver gave the police turns out to be almost the same as the next town up from Marjean. That's not a coincidence. I know it's not."

"How do you know about the name?"

"It's always been in the evidence. I just didn't make the connection."

"Who did?"

"Silas. He came to see me. I'm glad he did too. He said he didn't believe I killed the old man anymore. He's found out the chess pieces were changed after I left the study. Somebody else did that. And it wasn't Silas."

"Who was it?"

"I don't know. Silas says the policeman in charge of the case has gone to France to ask questions. Maybe he'll find out something."

Stephen's face lit up as he clutched at this straw of hope.

"You've been good to me, Mary," he said. "You've always believed in me. Not like everyone else. You were all I ever asked for, and then this happened. It seems like such a waste. You know what I can't stand? If I've got to die, I'd like to die for a reason. Not for nothing at all. I'm twenty years too late. That's my problem. I remember the Spitfires and the Hurricanes up in the sky when I was a boy. Dogfights in the air. Pilots flying head over heels. They were real heroes. Dying for a reason. Not like this. Trussed up like a turkey, hanging on the end of a rope."

"I'm sorry, Stephen," said Mary. "I'm sorry about what has happened. It wasn't what I . . ."

"No, Mary" interrupted her ex-lover, reaching out his hand. "Don't say that. It's not as if it's your fault I'm here. You've nothing to be sorry for. Nothing at all."

Over on the other side of the exercise yard, Henry Crean, the Queen's hangman, waited patiently while a warder made unusually heavy work of finding the right key to open the door of Stephen's cell. Inside the prison he often seemed to have this effect on people, making them nervous and uncomfortable, but he knew that there was nothing he could do about it even if he had wanted to. It came with the territory. Anyway, his mind was focused on what lay beyond the door. Usually he prepared the gallows on the day before an execution, but his assistant, a young Welshman called Owen Jones, was new to the job, and in this instance Crean had decided that two dry runs were required before he sent Stephen Cade to his maker.

Crean was a quiet, orderly man in his mid fifties, who took a professional pride in his work, and the thought of something going wrong was abhorrent to him. Press reporting of executions had long since been abolished, but news of a botched hanging had a way of leaking out, particularly in a case like this, where the public had got themselves so worked up about the condemned man. He was young and handsome, and the tabloid newspapers had recently taken to calling him Pretty Boy Cade. But Crean was oblivious to the character of his victim. In fact, he took pride in his detachment, knowing that pity made for hesitation and increased the risk of mistakes. In the last few moments of his life, the condemned prisoner's best friend was a cold, quick executioner who knew exactly what he was doing.

Stephen had been weighed every day for the past week, and most mornings Crean had watched him as well, pacing up and down the condemned cell, through the enlarged eyehole in the big iron door. Now, with two days left to go, Crean was confident that the Italian hemp rope was adjusted to just the right length to do what was required of it.

Stephen had known for over a week that he was scheduled to die at eight o'clock on Wednesday morning, but he had no idea that the prison gallows were set up less than twenty feet from where he slept, divided from his bed by no more than a thin partition. He'd been moved to his new cell immediately after the trial was over, and at first he had not been unhappy with the change. It was a larger room than he had before, on the second floor of a separate block, with more of the sky visible from the high barred window. But the biggest difference was that there were no other prisoners anywhere near, so that the cell was almost silent at night, which for some reason made it much more difficult to sleep. Time passed, and Stephen remained unaware of the fact that he was now living on the top story of a death house purpose built according to standard specifications issued by the Ministry of Works in Whitehall. The wooden wardrobe on the far wall was designed to turn on its base, revealing a concealed door that led straight onto the gallows, and below the trapdoors was another room known as the pit, where Stephen would hang suspended in midair until the prison doctor pronounced him dead and Crean and his assistant came in to cut him down and take him to the autopsy room next door. The whole block was an assembly line of death, with the prisoner in his cell unaware of what lay beside and beneath him until the moment of his execution arrived.

Once the wardrobe had been turned aside, Crean wasted no further time, leading his assistant through the door in the wall and out to the trapdoors. There was a *T* chalked in the middle to show where Stephen would need to be positioned, with warders standing on boards on either side to hold him in place.

"That's in case he faints," said Crean. "They do sometimes. Anyway, I've already pinioned his wrists behind his back right at the start, and so this is where you strap his ankles, just like I showed you before. Quick as you can, while I put the hood over his head. Then the noose goes nice and tight under the jaw. Check everything's okay, and I release the doors. And he's gone." Crean snapped his fingers to underline the quickness and totality of the fall.

One by one, he held up the various pieces of the hangman's equipment as he instructed his assistant. The brown leather straps for wrists and ankles and the white cotton hood. It looked incongruous in Crean's big hands, just like a small pillowcase.

"Why not hood him before?" asked Jones, sounding puzzled. "Before he comes in here and sees all this."

"We used to do that, but it didn't work so well. You wouldn't think it, but they tend to be more frightened not knowing where they are, and so there's more risk of them falling over. And it'd take longer. Twenty seconds from going in the cell to turning them off. Anything more is a failure. That's what Pierrepoint used to say. And he was right."

"Twenty seconds?" The assistant looked incredulous.

"Yes. You'll see. Once we're inside the cell, we're in charge. No signals from the governor. Nothing like that. He's just here to see it's done right. And it will be. Believe me."

Above the gallows, the rope hung coiled from a chain that was bolted to the ceiling, and with practised hands Crean attached a sandbag weighing just as much as Stephen to the end of it. Then he turned and removed the safety pin from the base of the operating lever behind him and pushed it forward to release the doors. The bag fell with sudden, ferocious force and jerked at the end of the rope.

Jones took a step back and almost lost balance. It was an instinctive reaction, and Crean grinned.

"You'll be all right," he said, clapping the younger man on the shoulder. "Just you wait and see. Now, we'll let that bag hang there until tomorrow."

"Why?"

"It stretches the rope out. If that happens at the hanging, then the force on the neck's less, and he'll end up strangling to death. We've got to break his neck, Owen. That's what we're paid to do."

Jones nodded. Somewhere inside he felt disgusted with himself, but he quickly stifled the emotion. An execution was something important. Particularly this one. Everyone was talking about it. And assisting at it made him important too. Owen Jones from Swansea puffed out his chest a little as he helped Crean turn the wardrobe back in front of the door to the gallows.

A minute later and they were gone. Stephen's cell was just as it had been before. His black suit hanging in the wardrobe. The photographs of Mary and his mother standing on the shelf below the high window through which the bright winter sun was shining, filling the room with a transient light. It didn't seem like such a bad place if you didn't know what was on the other side of the wall.

"God, I feel so hot," said Stephen, fiddling with the top button of his prison-issue blue shirt. "Are you hot, Mary?"

She shook her head. It was the end of November, and she had kept her outside coat on.

"The worst part is knowing what's going to happen," said Stephen. "Measuring out the time. Animals know too, you know. We're not the only ones. People say they don't, but they do. I remember there was this butcher's shop in Moreton when I was a boy. Sawdust on the floor, a china pig in a blue and white apron inside the window. My mother used to buy our meat there. 'Price and Sons, Family Butchers since 1878.' That's what it said over the door. I can see it now." Stephen closed his eyes for a moment, remembering. "They did their own slaughtering in an abattoir out back. I went once with Silas. Hid and watched. The calves and cows were in these pens going from one to the other, and each one was narrower than the last, so that halfway to the shed they couldn't turn round at all. And they knew then. I don't know how, but I could tell they did. They were pushing and bellowing, climbing on top of each other, trying to go back, but they couldn't. Maybe they could smell what was coming, because they couldn't see inside. But we looked in and there was Price's eldest son with a big white apron over his fat stomach. He had a great steel knife in his hands, and he slit this calf right down the middle. He was about ten feet away from us, and I saw the whole thing. And then I was sick. More sick than I've ever been. Silas had to pull me away while I was still retching, or otherwise they'd have seen us.

"And I never went back after that. I stayed in the car when my mother went meat shopping. I could see her getting served by Price's son. He was really friendly, you know. A nice man. He always gave my mother the best cuts." Stephen laughed hollowly. "The point is that those animals knew what was coming. I could see they did. And now I know what they felt, Mary. The walls are getting narrower all the time and every hour he's getting closer. I can almost feel his breath on my skin." Stephen shuddered.

"Who?" asked Mary. "Who's getting closer?"

"The hangman. I don't even know his name, but he knows me. Sometimes I think he's watching me through the eyehole in the door, and I stand up against the wall so he won't see me, but it's useless. I can't get away from him, and he knows that."

"Yes, you can," said Mary, looking Stephen in the eye for the first time since they'd started talking. "The policeman'll find something and it'll be okay. You'll see. It'll be okay."

But Stephen didn't seem to hear her. "I just wish I knew why," he said with a suddenly renewed anger. "There's someone out there who killed my father and now he's going to kill me, and I don't know who it is. I'll go to my death not knowing. Every night I lie in my cell with my eyes closed, not sleeping, just thinking about the past, trying to make sense of all that's happened. And then you keep coming into my mind for some reason. Like last night. There was a full moon outside, and it made me remember that evening when I first saw you in the cloister at New College. And you said nothing. Just stood up and walked away into the night. What were you doing there, Mary? Were you waiting for me?"

"Things don't always turn out as we intend them," said Mary, getting to her feet and wiping away the tears that had begun to form in her eyes. She was ashamed of herself, of her inability to say what she had come to say. "I told you, Stephen. The policeman will find something," she repeated. "You're going to be okay."

"How do you know that?" asked Stephen, suddenly turning white as he began to take in the meaning of her words.

"I just know it," she said quietly. "Leave it at that. I came here to tell you something, but I can't seem to find the words, and I'm sorry for that, Stephen; sorry for everything I've done to you. More sorry than you can know. I should have stopped this a long time ago. I see that now. But what's done is done, and now I've got to go. And I won't ever see you again. Do you hear me? This is over, and it's important you understand that. So don't come looking for me. You're young, Stephen. You'll get over all this."

It was a strange thing to say. Mary was actually a few months younger than Stephen, but now it seemed like she was years older. It suddenly seemed to him as if all he had ever really known of her was the actress.

He had sat in a state of shock while she was speaking, and it was only now, when she was almost at the door, that he made a move toward her. But his anger was too obvious, and the burly warder got up and stood in his way, pushing him back and preventing him from following Mary out of the room.

TWENTY-SEVEN

Two strong hands pushed Trave deep down into his own armchair, and a moment later the light went on overhead. Mary Martin was sitting opposite him on the other side of the fireplace with a pistol in her hand.

She held the gun trained on the centre of his forehead, but for a moment he didn't take it seriously. It made him angry to be manhandled, threatened in his own house. It was a violation, and he started back up out of the chair in instinctive protest. But he was hardly able to take a step before the man by the door pushed him back, pinning him down with one hand while he smacked him twice across the face with the back of the other.

Trave stroked his stinging cheeks and looked his attacker in the eye. He had never seen him before. He'd have remembered if he had. Paul Martin's narrow grey eyes were completely cold. The violence had been switched on and off quite effortlessly, and once it had achieved its desired effect, he returned to his original position by the door.

"I'm sorry about that, Inspector," said Mary, glancing angrily toward her accomplice and looking genuinely pained by what had just happened. "Paul has a tendency to overreact, but he won't touch you again, I promise, if you don't do anything stupid."

"What do you want?" Trave demanded, refusing to be mollified. "Why are you here?"

"Isn't it usually the one with the gun that asks the questions?" she countered quietly. "Even if you are the policeman."

Mary's voice was unnaturally calm, and it struck Trave that she was in fact making a supreme effort to keep control of her emotions. However, the only outward sign of her inner turmoil was the way in which the gun shook slightly in her hand.

"All right," said Trave, breathing deeply to regain his composure. "Have it your way. What do you want to know?"

"How was France?" She made it sound as if she was asking about a recent holiday, not a police investigation.

He didn't answer at once, partly because he was so shocked by the change in the woman he had once known as Mary Martin. At the time of Cade's murder she had been part of the background. Never more than that. She was obviously attractive, but she didn't seem to have anything very interesting to say. She answered all the police questions without any fuss, but she didn't volunteer any information. Really the most significant thing about Mary Martin had been her lack of significance, and Trave was shocked now by how stupid he had been to accept her at face value. She was an actress, and Stephen Cade was infatuated with her. That ought to have been enough to make him want to find out more, but instead he'd done nothing, seduced by the mountain of evidence against her boyfriend. What a fool he'd been!

Her clothes were more expensive than he remembered—a black Chanel dress and a cashmere coat that hung down below her knees—but otherwise she was the same. Except that now, for the first time, he was aware of the force of her personality. She was no longer a shy young girl; instead she was a woman capable of premeditated murder. The change left Trave temporarily off balance, at a disadvantage in their conversation.

"All right, let me put it another way," she said after a moment. "How much did you find out while you were away?"

"I found out who you are," he said, rising to the challenge.

"I'm impressed. So who am I?"

"Marie Rocard. And you're wanted for the murder of John Cade at Moreton Manor House last June."

"Wanted for questioning?"

"That's right."

"Because, without my help, you haven't got enough to save Stephen from the rope. That's the truth, isn't it, Inspector?"

"I don't know," said Trave, trying not to sound defeated. "Maybe."

Mary looked over toward Paul, and Trave was again aware of the tension between them.

"Paul doesn't think we should be here at all," she said. "But don't worry, Inspector. Paul and I have had our argument, and I've won the day. This is my party now. Paul'll make us some coffee. Won't you, Paul?" she asked, slowing down her English to speak to her companion.

Trave could sense the Frenchman's reluctance to leave the room, but finally, without a word, he moved away from the door, and Trave could hear him farther down the hall, opening drawers and cupboards in the kitchen.

"I saw Stephen today," said Mary, biting her lip, and Trave couldn't help noticing the break in her voice.

"That must've been interesting," he said noncommittedly.

"No, it was horrible. I'm not proud of what I've done to him, you know."

"Well, I'm sure it'll be a comfort to him to know that."

"Don't be stupid. Of course it won't. He hates me now, which is as it should be, but for some silly reason I wish he didn't. We were happy together for a while before all this happened."

"How could you be happy? You were using him to get to his father."

"Yes, and I don't regret that. I had no choice. It was framing him afterward that was wrong. I didn't realize that until after Stephen was arrested, but planning something isn't the same as watching it happen. Paul thinks I'm crazy, but I'd give almost anything to put the clock back."

"Would you spare John Cade?"

"No, not that. I said almost anything," said Mary with a half smile.

"In my experience murderers always blame their accomplices," said Trave, refusing to believe in Mary's sincerity.

"But I'm not blaming anyone. Paul didn't kill John Cade; I did. It had to be me, because it wasn't a murder; it was an execution, an act of justice. If any man deserved to die, it was that bastard—surely to God you can see that."

Mary stopped suddenly, realising that anger had got the better of her, and then breathed deeply, reasserting her self-control. "Well, let's not quibble over words. You did well, Inspector. Better than I expected. It's one thing to discover that my parents had a daughter, quite another to find out that she survived John Cade and turned into me."

"I got lucky," said Trave, making a conscious decision to be less confrontational. If Mary was here to help him save Stephen, he wasn't going to discourage her. "Your friend in the kitchen complained about Cade to the police in Moirtier, and one of them told me about it," he explained.

"Laroche, you mean. That was more than ten years ago, and I thought Paul gave him a false name. Still, whatever he said, he shouldn't have gone to the police. We both realised that afterward. But it was early days, and we were naïve back then. We thought somebody might help us, that the world was a fair place. And Paul thought I should have my inheritance. Not that I ever wanted it. A burnt-out house with bad memories and a few outbuildings. *La belle France* is welcome to it, as far as I'm concerned."

Trave noticed the bitterness that had crept into Mary's voice as she was speaking. It was like the cover of a deep, empty well had been momentarily removed, revealing the unplumbed depths of black cynicism that lay underneath.

"You see, neither of us understood back then that my nonexistence was my greatest advantage. Cade never knew about me until the second before he died. I hadn't been thought of when he first came to the house, and my mother was upstairs, seven months pregnant, when he came back at the end of 1938 and my father kicked him out."

"But what about in 1944? What happened then?" asked Trave.

"I was in the church tower, and so they didn't see me watching them. Cade and Ritter and stupid Jimmy Carson. If they'd asked questions afterward, people would've said I died in the fire with sweet old Marguerite. That was the story my friends spread about. But they had no reason to ask questions. Not then and not later. Cade always thought it was Carson who took a shot at him in 1956 and sent him that blackmail letter a year later. He never knew it was me because I didn't exist. My birth certificate was destroyed by the Germans when they attacked Rouen, and there was never a death certificate because I didn't die. It was easy. Stephen's lawyers never found out about me either. They sent a man out there to ask questions, but I guess he didn't get lucky like you did.

"Anyway, from the church, I got as far as a friend's house, and he sent me on to Paul's father. Hundreds of miles away. I wasn't even six, but I didn't forget. And Paul looked after me after that. He made me what I am."

Trave decided against asking Mary whether she thought this was a good thing or a bad thing, because Paul was back now, leaning against the wall by the door, and although he continued to remain silent Trave had no idea how much he understood of the conversation.

"What do you want me to do?" Trave asked.

"Write my statement over at that table," said Mary. "Then when we're done, I'll sign it, and you can take it up to London in the morning. Give it to Stephen's barrister. He'll know what to do. They can't hang Stephen if I've confessed."

Trave wasn't so sure, but he picked up the mug of black coffee that Paul had put in front of him and went over to the table where he'd got slowly used to eating his meals alone in the months since Vanessa left him. Just as he'd finished sitting down, the telephone rang. Instinctively he put out his hand to answer it, but Mary's voice stopped him.

"I'll shoot you, Inspector, if you do that," she said in a flat, hard voice. "I don't want to, but I will."

Trave wasn't sure he believed her, but there was no way he was going to put her assertion to the test. Not with the cold-eyed Frenchman standing behind him. The telephone rang on unanswered for nearly a minute, and then, when it had stopped, Paul put pen and paper in front of him, and Trave began to write down what Mary was telling him. After a few sentences she gave the gun to Paul and began walking up and down the room as she dictated her statement, speaking quickly and with little hesitation. It seemed obvious to Trave that she had prepared a great deal of what she had to say in advance, but a growing passion that crept into her voice as she told her story made him realise that she'd been waiting for this moment for a long, long time.

"My name is Marie Rocard," she began, "and I was born on January third, 1939. My parents, Henri and Mathilde Rocard, were killed by John Cade and Reginald Ritter on August twenty-eighth, 1944, at Marjean Church in Normandy. There was a third man called Carson who kept watch outside. They killed our servants, Albert and Marguerite too, and they set fire to our house, and then they blamed it all on the Nazis, who'd been using the château as a headquarters since 1942. Cade believed that there were no survivors because he never knew that my parents had a child.

"Afterward, with the help of friends, I escaped to another part of France and took on a new identity, and then, when I was old enough, I planned out how to punish John Cade for what he'd done. For as long as I can remember I thought of nothing else, but I also knew it wouldn't be easy. In 1956 I enticed him to Marjean and shot him with a rifle but he recovered from his wound, and after that I couldn't find a way to get him to leave his house, however hard I tried. He was a rich man who lived behind high walls and electronic gates, and a break-in was simply not practical. I had to get close to him to make sure he died, but that meant that someone else in the house would have to take the blame for the murder. I decided on Cade's son, Stephen, who was a student at Oxford University. He would be my passport into Moreton Manor House, and then the state would hang him for what I'd done. Back then I held the whole Cade family responsible for the father's crime. But I was wrong. I wish now that I acted differently after the murder, that I didn't stand aside and watch Stephen suffer as he has. But what's done is done. I cannot make amends. All I can do now is save him from the gallows."

"What about Ritter?" asked Trave, interrupting. "You said it was Ritter as well as Cade that killed your parents."

"He would've come afterward. But you saved me the trouble, Inspector." Mary smiled briefly, as if acknowledging a debt. "And Ritter killed Carson. Pushed him from a train outside Leicester. But you probably know that already, don't you?"

"I guessed," said Trave, picking up his pen and trying to avoid looking at Paul, who still had the gun trained on his head. Unlike Mary, his hand was entirely steady.

"Where was I?" said Mary. "Oh yes, Stephen. Always Stephen. He was twenty-one years old when I first met him and very impressionable. And he was estranged from his father, which was always going to make him the prime suspect. It didn't take him long to fall in love with me. That was the easy part. And then, when he couldn't do without me anymore, I told him that my mother was sick and I needed money for an operation. He believed me. He had no reason not to. How was he to know that my mother was well beyond medical help, rotting in her grave on the other side of the Channel?"

Mary laughed harshly, allowing Trave another glimpse of the angry bitterness that lay just beneath the smooth surface of her personality. But he said nothing, waiting for her to continue her story.

"I told him that I'd have to go and look for work up in London or even Manchester if I couldn't find the money, and of course there was only one person whom he could go to for it. But still, it wasn't easy for him to ask his father for anything, and maybe he wouldn't have written to the old man at all if I hadn't got lucky. Just when I was beginning to put the pressure on, Silas arrived and told Stephen about the will. It was Silas who practically dictated the letter that Stephen wrote to his father, asking to be allowed back. And, you know, at the time it didn't seem like luck at all. It felt like fate was on my side, as if I'd been chosen in some way."

"Like you were the wrath of God?" asked Trave.

"Yes, if you like," said Mary, ignoring the irony. "It certainly hardened my resolve—helped me use the son to get at the father. Anyway, the letter worked and we went out to the manor house for lunch with the man I hated most in all the world."

"How was that?"

"Not easy. No, almost unbearable since you ask. But I got through it somehow and then, in the afternoon, I slipped away and took a tour of the rooms that I needed to know. I found Cade's keys in his desk drawer. There was one that fitted the door between the study and the east-wing corridor, and I took a wax impression of that one and also of the ones that opened the french windows to the study and the front door of the house. Afterward Paul arranged to have copies made. One for the front door, one for the french windows, and two for the door to the study."

"Why two?"

"For the fingerprints. I held one of the keys in Stephen's fingers while he was asleep. And I used the other to lock the door after I'd killed his father. Then I took it out and put the one with Stephen's prints back in the lock so that it'd look like he locked the door himself. I needed two keys because locking the door with the first key would've wiped away his prints. And I did the same with the guns. There were two of them as well. One that he'd held in his sleep, and one that I used to kill Cade. I fired the one with Stephen's prints on it the day before I put it in his hands."

"Why didn't he wake up?"

"I'd given him some sleeping powder. It wasn't difficult. And so that was the plan. Wait for Stephen to leave the study, follow him in, kill Cade, and lock the door behind me before I went out through the french windows. Go back in the house through the front door and then wait for someone to find the body. And then when the police came, the gun would be in Stephen's room with his prints on the magazine."

"He'd have known it was you. Nobody else could have put his prints on the gun. Or the key."

"Possibly. But, in any case, nobody would have believed him. He was the one with the motive, not me. And I hadn't been in the study. He had."

Trave nodded. "So what happened?" he asked. "When you went back?"

"Things turned out differently than I expected," she said. "Just like they always do. After dinner I went down the drive and opened the gate. Paul had his car parked over by the phone box on the other side of the road, so I could call if anything went wrong, and then he would come and get me. It was a fail-safe. Nothing more than that. I didn't expect to need to run away.

"Stephen had arranged to see his father at ten o'clock, and once he was inside the study, I went to get his hat and coat from his bedroom. I was going to wear them to cross the courtyard afterward, you see, so anyone looking down would think I was Stephen. Not that I expected anyone to see me. I hoped that all the lights would be out by then, and I had a silencer for the gun. But the hat and coat weren't there. It was only afterward that I found out that Stephen had put them on to go for a walk up the drive before he saw his father. So I didn't know at the time that he'd closed the gate and seen the Mercedes, and I'm glad I didn't. It might have made me lose my nerve."

Trave thought this unlikely, but he didn't say so. He had his work cut out trying to write down everything that Mary was saying. She was speaking quicker now that she was reliving the events of the murder night, and Trave's pen raced backward and forward across the paper. He tried not to think of Paul over by the door with the gun still aimed at his head.

"I ran downstairs from the bedroom," Mary went on, "and I took Silas's hat and coat from off the stand in the hall. I needed a disguise, and something was better than nothing. Then I went into the little book room off the east-wing corridor next to the study and waited. There was the sound of talking, but I couldn't really make out any of the words until about thirty minutes had gone by. Then, suddenly, the voices got louder, and I could hear most of what Stephen was saying. He did tell his father that he deserved to die. And, you know, Inspector, it made me smile, standing waiting in the darkness on the other side of the wall, ready to kill that bastard just as soon as his son had gone on his way.

"Stephen went out through the french windows pretty soon after the shouting started, and I hadn't expected that. I don't really know why. I'd just anticipated him coming past me down the corridor. And he didn't go across the courtyard to the front door either. I looked out of the window in the corridor and I didn't see him, so he had to have walked away down the drive or out into the grounds. Either way, there was obviously a risk that he might come back, but I had to accept that. I'd gone too far to pull back with Cade a few feet away and the gun ready in my hand. I didn't know when the chance might come again, now that he'd quarreled with Stephen. And I couldn't hold myself back any longer. All the years of waiting came together in that moment when I went through the door of his study and there he was, bent down over his stupid chess game with his big wet tongue flicking round his lips, like he was some horrible bloodsucking insect that needed to be stamped on, put an end to, destroyed."

Mary punched her clenched fist into the open palm of her other hand to give emphasis to her words, and then suddenly stopped short, as if realising that her narrative had carried her away. It struck Trave that she hadn't just come to confess to Cade's murder. She was also dictating a sort of testament.

"I didn't shoot him straightaway," she said after a moment, in a quiet, more measured voice. "I waited until he saw me. Because I needed him to know why he was going to die. That was important. So I let his watery pale blue eyes come up level with mine, focusing through his little gold half-moon glasses, and then I told him who I was. It took him a second or two to register the information, and then I shot him just as he opened his mouth to shout. One bullet right in the middle of his big shiny forehead. And it was done. Revenge for my parents; revenge for Albert and Marguerite. Good people who never did anyone any harm. It was the best moment of my life.

"But I didn't lose my concentration; I didn't waste any time. The plan was what mattered. I locked the door with the first key I'd copied, and then I took it out and replaced it with the second, the one with Stephen's fingerprints on it. And I was just about to go over to the desk to remove Cade's key from his ring when I heard footsteps outside. It was Stephen coming back. I couldn't believe it. I was beside myself. I hid behind the curtains over the french windows, and he walked straight past me into the room. He never saw me at all. But I still made a mistake that could have cost me everything. Obviously I realised I had to change the plan now that Stephen had come back. I couldn't put the gun in his room. He had to have it with him in the study. Otherwise nothing would make sense. But I didn't have time to think it through. He started shouting for help, and I needed to get out of there. So I slid the gun in my hand, the wrong gun, out into the room, and then I walked quickly across the courtyard to the front door. Stephen didn't hear me. He was too busy shouting. And until Ritter's wife came to court and said her piece, I thought no one had seen me.

"Anyway, I unlocked the front door with the key I'd had made, closed it behind me, and it was only then, when it was too late to do anything about it, that I realised what I'd done. The gun I'd left behind was the one I'd killed Cade with. There were no fingerprints on it because I'd worn gloves. But Stephen wasn't wearing gloves. A clean gun would be as bad as no gun at all, but there was nothing I could do about it. Nothing at all.

"I threw Silas's hat and coat in the general direction of the hat stand and ran up the west-wing stairs to my room. I didn't try to compose myself because it didn't matter. Everyone was going to be upset. I came back down just in time to see Ritter's wife in the hall. I must've missed with the hat and coat because she was hanging them up on the stand. I had no idea that she was protecting Silas. I thought she was just doing her job, being the housekeeper. She must've locked the front door too. I walked straight past her and down the corridor to the study. The door was open, and Ritter was inside with Stephen, smacking him across the face, and I could see the gun. It was on the side table by the door. Someone had picked it up off the floor and put it there. And for some reason I knew it wasn't Ritter. He was a psychopath but he wasn't stupid. It had to be Stephen. And I knew then that I was safe. The plan had worked better than I could have hoped for. Now that he'd touched the gun and the key, there was no reason for him to suspect me at all. All I had to do was visit him in Wandsworth Prison once a week and watch him getting ready to die.

"And, of course, that's what I hadn't reckoned with," said Mary, with a bitter laugh. Her voice had been confident, proud even, as she told the story of the murder, but now her fluency deserted her as she returned to Stephen and the present.

"Don't worry, Inspector, the irony hasn't escaped me," she went on after a moment. "I'm here because everything went too well. If the plan had gone as I'd anticipated and Stephen hadn't come back to the study, then he'd probably have ended up suspecting me, just like you said. He'd have known that some-body had put his fingerprints on the gun and the key, and that person was likely to be me. And if he'd accused me of the murder, then I'd never have carried on visiting him in gaol and ended up feeling like this. I'd just have left justice to take its course."

"Not justice," said Trave. "Injustice. And, if you ask me, I don't think you'd have left him to hang, whatever you say. You're not as cold-blooded as you like to pretend, Miss Martin or Rocard or whoever you are. You'd have regretted what you'd done to that poor boy, whether you'd gone to see him once a week, twice a week, or not at all."

Mary was about to respond, but the sudden harsh ring of the doorbell stopped her short. Paul was the first to react. He crossed the room as quickly and noiselessly as a cat and pressed the revolver up hard against Trave's temple. His free hand was clamped over the policeman's mouth. Mary stood by the door into the hall, listening. There was silence. And then the bell rang again. Longer this time. Afterward they could hear the sound of someone stamping their feet on the step. It was cold outside, and perhaps the visitor would go away. But instead he knocked on the door with his fist and called out for Trave to let him in. It was Clayton, and he obviously believed Trave was inside be-cause of the light on in the living room. But Trave didn't move a muscle. He wasn't going to give the silent Frenchman any excuses. And after a moment they could hear footsteps receding down the road and a car engine gunning into life. Paul let go of Trave's head and moved away toward the window.

"Who was that?" asked Mary.

"Someone who works for me," said Trave.

"Will he be back?"

"I don't know. It depends on what he wants."

"Well, we're not going to wait to find out. Is what you've got there enough if I sign it now?"

"I don't know. I hope so. Confessions are usually best if they come with the people who make them."

"Well, you can't have everything, Inspector," said Mary with a half smile. "This should make the difference, though, if those men in Whitehall need further persuading."

Mary opened her bag and took out a rectangular black velvet case. Inside, spaces had been hollowed out for two revolvers. One was empty, but there was a little silver snub-nosed gun in the other. Trave recognized it immediately. It was an exact match for the one that he'd seized from Cade's study on the night of the murder.

"I got them as a pair," she said. "They're an exact match. I can't see them arguing with that. You can look if you want. It's not loaded."

But Trave didn't take up the invitation. Not while the Frenchman still had him in his sights.

"Good. Now give me what you've written so I can see if you've got it all right before I sign it," said Mary, picking up the papers. "Paul'll make us some more coffee and then we can go."

"We?" repeated Trave, surprised.

"Yes. You too. I'm not leaving you here to put out a general alert as soon as we've gone round the corner. What do you take me for?"

Mary went over to Paul and took the gun out of his hand. It seemed as if she whispered something as well, but Trave couldn't be sure. It was too quick, and he was tired, dog tired. He needed the coffee if he was going to stay awake. She read the pages methodically, one by one, looking up at frequent intervals to check that Trave hadn't got up from the chair Paul had moved him to in the far corner of the room, and then signed the statement at the end in the name of Mary Martin, formerly Marie Rocard. Trave witnessed her signature underneath.

"Why did Cade kill your parents?" he asked, finishing the coffee that Paul had put in front of him. "Stephen said it was about a book."

"Yes. My father wouldn't sell it to Cade and so he stole it. Then he killed everyone to cover his tracks."

"It must have been some book. People don't commit murder for nothing."

"You're probably right, but it was stolen when I was too young to know anything about such things. And I've never seen it since. Books don't concern us, Inspector. That's not why I'm here."

Trave had other questions he wanted to ask. Questions about Sasha and Marjean Church, but for some reason he couldn't find the words. His head was swirling, and he felt strange inside. It was like he was in a rudderless boat going up on the highest waves and down into the deepest troughs. It was more than fatigue. He knew that for a fact as he rolled in and out of consciousness, losing his unsuccessful fight with the drug that Paul had stirred into his coffee minutes before. Mary was still in the room when he fell down onto the floor, but he didn't know if it was she or Paul who carried him over to the sofa and laid him out under a blanket.

"It's all right. You'll just sleep for a while," she said. "And then when you wake up, you can go to London and save Stephen from the gallows. You'll be a national hero. And I, I'll be gone."

She was by the door now, but her voice came floating through the air toward him one last time.

"Good-bye, Inspector," she said. "Tell Stephen I'm sorry."

He didn't hear the door close.

TWENTY-EIGHT

Sasha woke up, blinking in the sunlight of a new Paris morning. Outside, the varied noises and smells of a fruit and vegetable market in the street below rose up toward her through the half-open window of her room, and for a moment she was still unaware of the significance of the day. But then her eye fell on the crumpled piece of paper lying spread out on the bedside table, and she immediately resumed the train of thought that had occupied almost every waking minute of her time since she'd driven away from the inn at Marjean three days earlier.

"If you want to see the cross, bring the codex to the church on Tuesday at three o'clock. Tell no one." The note was handwritten, and there was no date or signature. She'd picked it up off the floor inside the door of her room when she had returned to the inn for the codex with Trave hot on her heels, and she still had no idea who had left it there. Each day since her arrival in the capital, she had walked up and down the long tree-lined avenues of the Bois de Boulogne, oblivious to her surroundings while she debated whether or not to keep the appointment. But deep down she had always known she would go. The desire for the cross had become a physical longing, gnawing at her insides. The lust for it consumed her.

She was frightened of going alone, but she possessed neither the capacity for trust nor the money to go out and recruit an assistant, even if she had known where to find one. The Frenchman she had enticed out of the café on the road to Rouen had turned out a useless coward. He'd have left her to Trave if she hadn't got to his truck in time. No, she was better off on her own. But that didn't mean that she wouldn't go prepared. The day before she had found a man in Montmartre who was willing to sell her a gun. There was nowhere to fire it, but she had practised the mechanism again and again before going to bed, and now she felt confident that she could use the revolver to good effect if she had to. It gave her a sense of security, knowing that it was in the shoulder bag by the bed, wrapped up in her clothes with the codex.

She kept the book with her at all times now after what had happened before, but it really didn't interest her much anymore. It was a means to an end. Nothing more. The cross was somewhere in Marjean Church. Sasha was sure of it. She could think of nothing else.

She dressed carefully, settling her hair down over the upright collar of her padded jacket so that the livid burn mark on her neck was almost invisible, and then went downstairs to eat a late breakfast. An hour later she had paid her bill and was on the road north. She hummed a tune to herself as she came out into the open fields of the Norman countryside and then realised with a start that it was *The Marseillaise*. She was filled with a sudden rush of optimism and pressed her foot down on the accelerator, taking the Citroen speeding down the road, like an arrow between the winter hedgerows.

This time she had no difficulty finding the gateway, but the sudden descent into semidarkness as the car passed under the overhanging trees filled her with a sense of foreboding, and it was a relief to get back out into the light. She parked beside the ruined château and immediately began walking up the path to the church. She was early and there was no one in sight, but that didn't mean she wasn't being watched. The church made her feel that way. It dominated the surrounding landscape with a brooding presence, and Sasha was not the first to be unnerved by it. The gun in her pocket felt more reassuring with every step she took.

There was a new silver-coloured padlock on the door, but for some reason it was already open and there was nothing to keep her from walking inside. She stopped at the beginning of the nave to get her bearings and then froze to the spot when an apparently disembodied voice spoke to her from only a few feet away.

"You're standing just where my father died," said the voice. "There used to be a bloodstain on the stone, but it's gone now."

For a moment Sasha could not see who was speaking, but then a figure she recognised stepped out from behind a grey stone pillar in the south transept and began walking across the nave toward her. It was Mary Martin, but a different Mary from the one Sasha remembered. She was dressed in a leather flying jacket and a pair of blue jeans, and the slightly masculine effect of her clothing was accentuated by the easy authority with which she moved. She made Sasha feel like an intruder.

It had to be Mary who had sent the note. And Mary was Rocard's daughter. Somehow she must have survived the massacre of her family at the end of the war.

"You killed Cade," said Sasha, blurting out the accusation a second after the idea had entered her head. "It wasn't Stephen at all. It was you."

"That's right. It was me," said Mary, acknowledging her guilt with an easy smile. She was standing close beside Sasha now and looked her straight in the eye until Sasha dropped her gaze. The experience was disconcerting. Sasha felt as if Mary was looking inside her, and she backed away toward the door, resisting the temptation to take the gun out of her pocket.

"I'm glad you killed him," she said. "You saved me the trouble of doing it myself."

"Why do you say that?" It was Mary's turn to look surprised.

"Because of what he did to my father. Cade took everything from him: his work, his family, his position in society. And then he laughed about what he'd done. I heard him one night at the manor house." Sasha made no effort to hide her bitterness as she remembered the last poverty-stricken years of her father's life spent in the cold tenement room in Oxford while Cade lived in the lap of luxury only a few miles away.

"Well, we've certainly found something we agree about," said Mary, looking Sasha up and down with a new regard. "You know, I wasn't even six when he and Ritter killed my parents. But I still knew it meant nothing to Cade. And he didn't just kill them either. He tortured my mother and our old servant before they died. I heard him shouting at them down in the crypt before he shot them." Mary spoke in a flat, even voice that was strangely at odds with the terrible events she was describing. It was as if she was talking about something that had happened to somebody else, not to her at all. Perhaps that was the only way she could cope with such terrible memories.

"Where were you?" asked Sasha.

"When they came into the church? I was in the tower. There are windows on the stairway, and I spent a lot of time up there when I was a kid, watching the Nazis down below. I liked seeing them when they couldn't see me. Most of the windows look outside, but one of them faces down into the church. You can see it over there," said Mary, pointing to an opening halfway up the back wall. "I had a grandstand view. And then, after I heard the gunshots, I ran up to the top of the tower and stood there, watching our house burning up in the twilight. It's funny: if they hadn't done that, they might have found out about me. And Cade might still be alive."

"But he isn't," said Sasha harshly. "He's dead, and you've got what he was looking for. I know you have."

"The cross, you mean," said Mary, staring Sasha straight in the eye.

"Yes. You said in the note that you'd show it to me."

"Only if you've got the codex. That's what I said."

"How did you find out I've got it?"

"It wasn't hard to guess once I heard you'd come back here again. I have friends in the village, you know. This was my home once upon a time."

"The codex is here," said Sasha, tapping her bag. "Now show me the cross."

"So you can steal it? Have it for yourself? Is that why you want to see it?" asked Mary, making no effort to conceal her contempt.

Sasha said nothing. She bit her lip, and her hand trembled on the gun in her pocket.

"What would you do to get it, I wonder?" asked Mary, smiling. "Would you kill defenceless men and women, execute old people like Cade did? How much is it worth to you, Sasha?"

Sasha's temper finally snapped. There was clearly only one way to get what she wanted, and that was by force. She should have seen that at the outset, instead of wasting time talking. Taking a step back, she took the gun out of her pocket and pointed it at Mary's chest.

"Give me it," she said. "You know what I'll do if you don't."

For a moment Sasha felt a sense of power rush through her veins, but then doubt set in. Mary didn't seem in the least frightened of the revolver, and the odd air of authority that she carried with her was in no way diminished.

"You better follow me," she said in an even voice. "It's down here." Then, without any hesitation, she turned her back on Sasha and the gun, went through the door into the vestry, and began climbing down the winding stairway to the crypt. Sasha followed a little way behind, listening to Mary's voice coming back up to her from below.

"The curé who was here before this one, Père Martin, was my father's best friend. He took me in when my parents died, and afterward he helped me escape to another part of France. But before I left he gave me a locket that my father had entrusted to him when the Nazis came, to give to me if anything happened. There was a picture of my parents in the front and the code was written inside the back."

"Crux Petri in manibus Petri est."

"That's right. I don't know if my father knew what it meant. Père Martin certainly didn't."

"But you know, don't you?" said Sasha, retraining the gun on Mary now that she had reached the bottom of the stairs. "Tell me what it means."

"It means just what you think it means. Simon Peter's cross is in Simon Peter's hands."

"Abbot Simon's hands?"

"Yes. Of course it wouldn't have taken Cade long to work that out, but he had to crack the code first," said Mary, who continued to seem entirely unfazed by the gun. "He didn't come back here for four long years after 1944, and when he did, he found nothing."

"Why?"

"Because he looked in the wrong place. Just like you did. And then he got impatient and opened up all the tombs, and still he found nothing. He tore the place apart, and that's when Père Martin found him down here among all the skulls and bones, beating his head against the wall in frustration. I wish I could've seen him," said Mary, with a faraway look in her eye.

"Cade told Père Martin he was looking for a jewelled cross that the Nazis had hidden somewhere in the church. Of course Père Martin knew it was a lie. He was the one who'd told me about the legend of the Marjean cross years before when he gave me the locket. But he said nothing. Just waited until

Cade had gone, and then he told me everything that had happened. I already knew that Cade was after the cross. After all, I'd heard him torturing my mother for it before he killed her. And after Cade came back, I made the connection between the Peter in the code and the Abbot Simon who was buried down here. But I didn't need to open his tomb to know that the cross wasn't there, because I knew from Père Martin that Cade had already done that. I realised the answer was somewhere else, but it still took me a long time to work it out."

"So what is the answer? Where is the cross?" demanded Sasha, unable to contain her impatience any longer. But Mary ignored the questions. It was as if she was determined to tell the story her own way, and neither Sasha nor the gun were going to deflect her from her purpose.

"I found the cross and Cade didn't," she said, "because I knew this place a great deal better than he did. That was the difference between us. You probably haven't noticed, but down beyond the house there are a few old broken-down walls. They're almost disappearing in the long grass now, but I played there a lot when I was a child, spying on the German soldiers as they went backward and forward from the house. And one day I was digging, making a tunnel to Australia, and I found an old moss-covered stone buried in the ground with a Latin inscription indented in its surface. It was square, the wrong shape for a tombstone, and I never told anyone about it because it was my secret, my lucky stone, and I kept it covered up with leaves and grass. It was only much later, years after I'd left this place, that I realised it was the foundation stone of a chapter house for the monastery, laid by Simon, Abbot of Marjean, in the year of our Lord 1328."

Mary spoke slowly, emphasising the date, but Sasha just looked perplexed, and Mary had to say the year again.

"1328, Sasha. Doesn't it mean anything to you?" she asked pointedly. "It was the year after Abbot Simon died according to the dates on the wall over there. Except that that's not what the dates mean. The foundation stone made me realise that. Look. You see the same thing all along both these walls. One date for each name. And the date is the year they became abbot. But Simon is different from everyone else. He has two dates. 1321 and 1327. Why's that?"

"Because there are two Simons," said Sasha breathlessly, suddenly beginning to understand.

"Yes. Two. And the second one died within a year of his promotion. That's why the next abbot, Josephus, has the year 1328 under his name. And the beauty of the whole thing is that there's no record anywhere of this second Simon. Nothing except the foundation stone lost under the grass. The monks who hid the cross must have seen to that. And so no one knew about his existence except me. That is, until I told Cade all about him in the summer of 1956."

"Why? Why would you do that?" asked Sasha, shocked. It was the last thing she'd expected to hear.

"To lure him over here so I could take a shot at him. Give him back a little of what he'd done to my parents. The curé helped me, although perhaps he wouldn't have done so if he'd known what I had in mind. But still there was no need to spell it out. Back in 1948 Cade had promised him a reward for any new information that might lead Cade to the cross, and so the opening was already there. Everything went perfectly. The curé wrote to him about the foundation stone, and less than two weeks later he was here with Ritter. I waited to see him come out empty-handed before I fired. That was part of what I'd promised myself. But I wasn't brave enough, or perhaps I was just nervous. I shot him from too far away and he lived to tell the tale. Until I got inside the manor house last summer, that is, and did what I'd failed to do four years ago."

"So the cross was in the tomb until he came. You had it all the time," said Sasha. Her agitation was plain to see. The gun was trembling in her hand. But the threat of it still seemed to have no effect on Mary. She smiled and said nothing.

"Where is it now?" demanded Sasha, finally losing her self-control. "Tell me where it is or I'll kill you."

"It's where it always was," said Mary evenly. "I know of no better hiding place than the one the monks made for it six hundred years ago."

Mary crossed over to Abbot Simon's tomb. The lid was still slightly off centre, resting in the same position that Sasha had left it in the week before. But Mary ignored the top of the tomb. Instead she took a small chisel out of her pocket and chipped away the stone-coloured plaster in a line halfway down the side. It came off easily, and Sasha could see that it had only recently been applied. Soon a clear dividing line was visible, and it was obvious that there were two tombs, one on top of the other. When Mary had finished removing the plaster, she pushed with only moderate force against one end of the lower sarcophagus, and the other end came swinging out into the open.

Sasha looked down into the open tomb and saw what she had been searching for all her life. The cross of St. Peter. It was lying between the two skeletal hands of the dead man, and the red rubies and green emeralds embedded in the ancient wood drew Sasha forward as much as the hollow eye sockets and empty mouth repelled her. The cross was bigger than she'd imagined and glowed with a kaleidoscope of colours, so that the wood of first-century Palestine was almost invisible underneath. The jewels were there because this object was as close as men could get in this world to the Son of God. Nothing was more precious than the true cross on which the Saviour had redeemed the sins of mankind and given back to a fallen race the hope of everlasting life.

Sasha remembered Sir Galahad, who had been the only one of Arthur's knights worthy to drink from the Holy Grail. She was different too. Unique and separate. She leant forward and claimed the cross of St. Peter for her own.

Mary could have taken the gun from her then. It would have been easy, but she chose not to. Instead she went first up the stairs, leaving the crypt behind, crossed the main body of the church, and opened the door. Sasha looked out from behind her, checking there was no one in sight. She had already decided what to do. She pressed the revolver between Mary's shoulder blades and pushed her back into the dusky interior.

"I'm going to lock you in," she said. "I'll phone someone to come and let you out once I'm far enough away."

Mary didn't react or resist. Her face remained inscrutable, and for a moment Sasha wondered why it had all been so easy. But not for long. She had the cross in her bag and nothing else mattered. She shut the heavy church door behind her and secured it with the padlock. There was no other way out. Mary couldn't come after her. She walked out of the porch, heading for the path down to her car, but she had only gone a few steps when she felt the barrel of a rifle in the small of her back, forcing her down onto her knees. Her pistol spilt out onto the ground, and the flinty sharp stones cut into her skin, causing her to cry out. She looked up at Paul Martin through the tears that had welled up in her eyes and realised what a complete fool she had been.

Too late, she remembered that day in Oxford when she'd last seen Mary. She'd been in a Jaguar with this same man. Sasha recognised his cold narrow eyes and the strange high cheekbones that accentuated the boniness of his face. How stupid she had been to assume that Mary was alone. The cross had blinded her to what should have been so obvious. Mary had planned it all from start to finish. Even the padlock. Paul opened it now with a key and stood aside to let Mary pass.

But perhaps it was not too late. Sasha reached out toward the pistol lying on the ground, but Paul was watching her. With a quick movement he fired past Sasha's outstretched hand, and the revolver exploded in a rain of metal fragments. Sasha froze in shock. She cowered against the wall of the church while Paul reloaded again and again, took aim with an unerring accuracy, and shot out the tires of her car one by one. The shots reverberated around the empty landscape, losing their final echoes in the encircling woods as the car subsided down onto its useless wheels.

Quite gently, Mary unlaced Sasha's fingers from around the handle of her bag, and then extracted the codex and the cross from inside.

"You've had what we agreed," she said. "You've seen the cross of St. Peter. Now I'm taking what is mine, paid for with my parents' blood. Don't try to follow me. You understand me, don't you, Sasha?"

Sasha nodded. She had no doubt about what Paul would do if they met again. She'd seen the way he used the rifle. Now he was pointing it at her again, and instinctively she obeyed its command, backing away into the church.

Mary looked her in the eye one last time, and then she closed the door. A moment later Sasha heard the snap of the padlock and the sound of footsteps walking away down the path. She was a prisoner inside the church.

For several minutes she remained where she was, numbed by the shock of her unexpected defeat. But then she remembered what Mary had said about the windows in the tower. She needed to see outside. Maybe there would be somebody she could call to, somebody who would help her escape. She took the steps two at a time. The first window was the one looking down into the church that Mary had shown her earlier, and the second had a view toward the house. She looked down, but there was no one in sight. Just the car with its exploded wheels, a wreck beside the ruined house. Round the corner she came to the window on the other side. It was an extraordinary view. The ground sloped down toward the blue-black lake where a thin rowing boat was gliding across the still water toward the red tiled rooves of Marjean village. It was already too far away for Sasha to distinguish the faces of the two occupants, and soon it was barely more than a speck, almost invisible against the rays thrown by the bright winter sun as it sank toward the western horizon.

Marjean Church had given up its secret, and now Sasha was left alone with its ghosts. The silence weighed down on her as the light began to fade, and she felt a grey timeless despair settling down on her like so much dust. Sitting at the end of one of the pews in the centre of the nave, she stroked the scar tissue on her neck and shoulders and waited for the coming of the night.

TWENTY-NINE

Trave arrived at the pub first. He took his beer and went and sat down by the river. There were snowdrops and wild crocuses in the grass running down to the water, and there was a charge in the air that seemed to promise that winter would soon be over. The inspector felt changed by all that had happened, and yet everything was still the same. He still lived alone without any real hope of promotion, and it seemed now like Vanessa would never be coming back. There were even days when he didn't think about her anymore. Not today, however: It was his son's birthday, and Trave felt confused by the intense emotions that the anniversary had summoned up inside him. Birthdays were for the living: a celebration of continued life. You did not celebrate the birthdays of the dead, but did that mean that Joe's day no longer had any significance except as an occasion for solitary recollection of half-forgotten presents and parties, fleeting moments that could never really be captured in the black-and-white photograph albums now gathering dust in a pile under the stairs? Trave had no answers. Time made him no wiser; its passing only helped dull the pain.

"Hullo, Inspector. I'm sorry I'm late." Stephen Cade's voice broke in on Trave's reverie, and he was startled to realise that he had forgotten the reason he was here. Stephen had asked for the meeting, and Trave had agreed to it with some trepidation. He had done his best to save the boy from the gallows, but without Mary's confession he would probably have failed. He was too honest not to admit this truth to himself.

Stephen seemed different from the young man that he remembered from before. The intensity hadn't disappeared from his bright blue eyes, but it was cloaked in a new watchfulness. Trave noticed that he was drinking whisky, and the glass shook slightly in his hand. Several times while they were talking, Stephen looked over his shoulder, as if he was expecting some enemy to come looking for him. Prison had clearly left its scars.

"How have you been?" asked Trave, sounding falsely jovial. "How's life as a free man treating you?"

"Not too bad," said Stephen with a forced smile, but it didn't last. "No, why lie? I can't sleep and I can't eat properly. I'm a bundle of nerves. I went up to London two days ago to see my barrister and tie up some loose ends, and, you know, I couldn't go through with it. I got halfway to his chambers in a taxi and then I had to turn around. I had no choice. The ride along the river reminded me of the prison van. I rang him from the station and got on the first train home."

"Was Swift understanding?"

"Yes, completely. He couldn't have been nicer. Said he'd come and see me at the manor house next week. And he wrote me a letter after the pardon came through saying it meant more to him than any verdict he'd ever achieved. I was touched by that."

"Yes," said Trave. "He told me the same. He's a good man."

"Like you, Inspector. I've been lucky."

"I wouldn't say that," said Trave. It felt like a serious understatement.

"No, perhaps not," said Stephen with a wry smile. "All I seem to be able to do at the moment is drink too much and put off making any decisions about my future. The university says I can go back, but I can't face it at the moment. All the students looking at me, pointing me out to their friends in the street. Like I was some weird exhibit at the circus. I'm nervous enough as it is. Still, I suppose it's what you'd expect from someone who's come so close to being strung up. The doctor says I'll take time to heal. But you know, Inspector, I'm not sure that's true. Sometimes I feel like there's something broken inside me. Something final."

Stephen's sadness cut Trave to the quick. It was how he'd felt after Joe died. He felt responsible for what had happened.

"I'm sorry," he said. "I should have believed in you. I wish I'd gone to France when it all started. Then you might never have had to go through any of this."

"Don't say that," said Stephen. "You did your best when it mattered. That's why I wanted to see you. To thank you. And as for what happened before, if my own brother didn't believe me until after I'd been sentenced to death, what were you supposed to think?"

"What's happened to Silas?" asked Trave, genuinely curious. He'd heard nothing more from Stephen's brother since the night that he came to the house with the old atlas and the photographs of his father's last game of chess.

"He's better than he was. Less reclusive, more at ease with himself somehow. It's like, I don't know, like he was ashamed of himself before, but he's not now."

"Well, he shouldn't be," said Trave. "It took a lot of courage for him to do what he did. You know he came to see me, don't you? He was the one who got me to go to France."

"Yes, he told me," said Stephen with a smile. "He said you needed quite a lot of persuading."

"That's true. I thought he was the murderer," said Trave ruefully. "I was sure of it."

"I know. I tried to think the same for a while. Mr. Swift wanted me to, but deep down I could never really believe it," said Stephen meditatively. "The truth is I don't think Silas is capable of killing anyone, not even if he wanted to. He's a watcher at heart, my brother, not an actor. It's why he's such a good photographer."

"Perhaps that'll be his redemption," said Trave hopefully. "His way out."

"Maybe. He's certainly making a good job of photographing my father's manuscripts. He's got a darkroom rigged up in one corner of the gallery now and he seems to spend most of his time in there. The pictures will make a beautiful book if he can find the right publisher, but I think sometimes that it's more than that, that he's really doing it to keep a connection going with our father. He never gave up on loving the old man, you know. Not even when he found out who our father really was."

"Perhaps he never had anything else to hold on to."

"Perhaps. Although I can understand how he feels. Our father's still our father, whatever he's done. Except that there can be no forgiveness now because he's dead—gone for good. There's not a day goes by that I don't wish I'd saved him."

"There was nothing you could do. You know that. What you need is a new start. Somewhere completely different. Away from all these memories."

"You're right. If I had my way, I'd like to sell the house and put all the manuscripts up for auction. But Silas won't hear of it, even though the money would make us rich. Sometimes I think they're more his ghosts than mine at home. The Ritters and Sasha and the old man. He stands in their rooms sometimes with his eyes half closed, and I don't know what he's thinking."

"Well, it can't be easy for either of you being together," said Trave sympathetically. "You both thought that the other one had committed the crime. You can't take that back."

"No, you can't. But it's also like the experience has brought us together as well," said Stephen slowly. His brow creased as he tried to find the right words. "You see, it's not just Silas who has suffered now; it's me as well. I'm not the lucky one anymore. You could search pretty hard to find two people who are more unlike one another, and yet we are brothers. We weren't before but we are now, and I don't think that'll change."

"He told me the truth about his alibi the other day," Stephen went on after a pause. "It was like he felt he had to."

"That it was false?"

"No. More than that. It turns out he wasn't in his room that night at all. He was out in the grounds taking photographs of Sasha. That's why the west-wing door was open. He came back inside when he heard me shouting in my father's study, and he forgot to lock it back up in all the commotion."

Trave failed to suppress the look of disgust that sprang involuntarily to his face in response to this further revelation of Silas's depravity. But it was soon replaced by a look of puzzlement. "Why did Sasha support him, though?" he asked. "That's what I don't understand."

"Perhaps he paid her."

"No, it's more than that. There are things about this case that I just can't fathom. Like what she was doing at Marjean Church on the day I went there. And why she ran away. I suppose I'll never know. Not unless she decides to tell me, and that doesn't seem very likely."

"Why? Don't you know where she is?"

"No. She's still alive, because she writes letters to her mother from somewhere in France, but there's never a return address. And I can't trace her, because she's done nothing wrong. Not like Mary Rocard or whatever *she* calls herself now."

A cloud passed across Stephen's face, and the trembling of his hand became far more noticeable than before. This was really why he was here, Trave realised with a start. For news of Mary. Surely he couldn't still love her. Not after what she'd done to him. It defied all logic.

"Have you heard anything?" Stephen asked in a low voice.

"Not a whisper. Nothing since the first flurry of information came through from Laroche, the policeman in Marjean, at the end of last month. He found out that she went to a place near the Swiss border after her parents were killed back in 1944 and that it was the brother of the priest at Marjean who took her in. It turns out he was a rich man who made a fortune after the war in some kind of speculation. And his only child was our friend, Paul Martin. The two of them grew up together, and I expect they're still together now. Where I don't know. But I'm pretty sure they've got enough money to stay out of sight for a long time."

"How long?"

"I don't know. Maybe the landlord of the inn at Marjean knows something about them, but he's not saying. I think he was the one who tipped them off that I was coming back to England. But there are no other leads. They've disappeared off the face of the earth. And if I had to guess, I'd say it'll stay that way."

Trave had not anticipated the effect that his final words would have on Stephen. The young man's face seemed to collapse in on itself, and he began to cry in great shuddering gasps that visibly shook his thin, undernourished body from top to bottom.

Trave didn't know what to do. He felt the normal English embarrassment in the presence of another person's strong emotion, but he held himself still, resisting the temptation to get up and walk away.

Slowly Stephen pulled himself together. "She broke my heart," he said, and the words didn't seem melodramatic. Just a statement of fact. "I loved her like she was the sun and the moon and the stars. And all she was doing was playing with me. Setting me up to die on the end of a rope. I gave her everything I had and it meant nothing to her. Nothing at all."

"But she changed her mind. She confessed to the crime in order to save you at the end. She didn't need to do that. It was because she hated herself for what she'd done to you. She told me that," said Trave, desperately seeking some consolation to offer his companion.

"Maybe. But it was also vanity. You know it was," insisted Stephen. "A final gesture to show that she had the power of life and death in her hands. I hate her, and yet I love her too. It tears me apart every minute of the day."

"We're human beings. We don't stop loving people just because they're gone," said Trave, thinking of his own lost son.

"No. But the trouble is I don't know what to hold onto anymore. Everyone I ever cared about turned out to be someone I never knew. It's a hall of mirrors I'm living in. Sometimes I wish old Murdoch had had his way and this was all over. It'd certainly be a lot easier."

Trave leant over and gripped Stephen's hand, lifting him from his chair.

"Come with me," he said. "There's something I need to show you."

He walked quickly to his car, propelling Stephen along beside him. And then he drove fast, not needing to slow down to read the road signs. He knew exactly where he was going, even though he'd only been to the place twice in his life before.

Fifteen minutes later, he pulled over onto a muddy grass verge on the side of a narrow country road. It was nothing more than that. There were beech woods growing on either side over carpets of dead leaves left over from the fall, and a bunch of white chrysanthemums was tied to a tree trunk a little farther down the road. Vanessa had already been here, Trave realised. She knew the exact spot even better than he did.

"This is where my son died," he said to Stephen once they had both got out of the car. "It was about this time of day. He came round the corner, lost control of his motorbike, and hit that tree over there. And then he died. I don't know how quickly. The doctors couldn't say. And I don't know where he was going or why he was driving too fast. All I know is that he never came back.

"There was certainly no reason for his dying. None at all. It just turned out that way. And there's no reason for what happened to you, Stephen. Except you lived. You didn't die on the end of a rope. And now you've got to make something of your life, do you hear me? Precisely because there isn't any meaning, because there might not be any God, it makes everything in this world all the more precious. And that's why you have to live, Stephen. Not for me, not for anyone else. But for you. Do you understand me? Live. Nothing less will do."

And Stephen did understand. He smiled, and his face was suddenly lit up by the beauty of who he really was. And for a moment, looking at him, Trave thought he saw his son again. For a moment it was as if Joe had never died.